The daughter of a town marshal, **Linda Lael Miller** is a *New York Times* bestselling author of more than one hundred historical and contemporary novels. Linda's books have hit #1 on the *New York Times* bestseller list seven times. Raised in Northport, Washington, she now lives in Spokane, Washington.

New York Times bestselling author **Maisey Yates** lives in rural Oregon with her three children and her husband, whose chiseled jaw and arresting features continue to make her swoon. She feels the epic trek she takes several times a day from her office to her coffee maker is a true example of her pioneer spirit.

#1 *New York Times* Bestselling Author

LINDA LAEL MILLER

AT HOME IN STONE CREEK

HARLEQUIN®
BESTSELLING
AUTHOR
COLLECTION

Recycling programs
for this product may
not exist in your area.

ISBN-13: 978-1-335-20994-8

At Home in Stone Creek
First published in 2009. This edition published in 2021.
Copyright © 2009 by Linda Lael Miller

Rancher's Wild Secret
First published in 2019. This edition published in 2021.
Copyright © 2019 by Maisey Yates

This edition published by arrangement with Harlequin Books S.A.

For questions and comments about the quality of this book,
please contact us at CustomerService@Harlequin.com.

Harlequin Enterprises ULC
22 Adelaide St. West, 40th Floor
Toronto, Ontario M5H 4E3, Canada
www.Harlequin.com

Printed in U.S.A.

CONTENTS

Also by Linda Lael Miller

HQN

Painted Pony Creek

Country Strong

The Carsons of Mustang Creek

A Snow Country Christmas
Forever a Hero
Always a Cowboy
Once a Rancher

The Brides of Bliss County

The Marriage Season
The Marriage Charm
The Marriage Pact
Christmas in Mustang Creek

The Parable series

Big Sky Secrets
Big Sky Wedding
Big Sky Summer
Big Sky River
Big Sky Mountain
Big Sky Country

McKettricks of Texas

An Outlaw's Christmas
A Lawman's Christmas
McKettricks of Texas: Austin
McKettricks of Texas: Garrett
McKettricks of Texas: Tate

Visit her Author Profile page on Harlequin.com,
or lindalaelmiller.com, for more titles!

AT HOME IN STONE CREEK

Linda Lael Miller

For Karen Beaty, with love.

Chapter 1

Ashley O'Ballivan dropped the last string of Christmas lights into a plastic storage container, resisting an uncharacteristic urge to kick the thing into the corner of the attic instead of stacking it with the others. For her, the holidays had been anything *but* merry and bright; in fact, the whole year had basically sucked. But for her brother, Brad, and sister Olivia, it qualified as a personal best—both of them were happily married. Even her workaholic twin, Melissa, had had a date for New Year's Eve.

Ashley, on the other hand, had spent the night alone, sipping nonalcoholic wine in front of the portable TV set in her study, waiting for the ball to drop in Times Square.

How lame was that?

It was worse than lame—it was *pathetic*.

She wasn't even thirty yet, and she was well on her way to old age.

With a sigh, Ashley turned from the dusty hodge-podge surrounding her—she went all out, at the Mountain View Bed and Breakfast, for every red-letter day on the calendar—and headed for the attic stairs. As she reached the bottom, stepping into the corridor just off the kitchen, a familiar car horn sounded from the driveway in front of the detached garage. It could only be Olivia's ancient Suburban.

Ashley had mixed feelings as she hoisted the ladder-steep steps back up into the ceiling. She loved her older sister dearly and was delighted that Olivia had found true love with Tanner Quinn, but since their mother's funeral a few months before, there had been a strain between them.

Neither Brad nor Olivia nor Melissa had shed a single tear for Delia O'Ballivan—not during the church service or the graveside ceremony or the wake. Okay, so there wasn't a greeting card category for the kind of mother Delia had been—she'd deserted the family long ago, and gradually destroyed herself through a long series of tragically bad choices. For all that, she'd still been the woman who had given birth to them all.

Didn't that count for something?

A rap sounded at the back door, as distinctive as the car horn, and Olivia's glowing, pregnancy-rounded face filled one of the frost-trimmed panes in the window.

Oddly self-conscious in her jeans and T-shirt and an ancient flannel shirt from the back of her closet, Ashley mouthed, "It's not locked."

Beaming, Olivia opened the door and waddled across the threshold. She was due to deliver her and Tanner's first child in a matter of days, if not hours, and from the looks of her, Ashley surmised she was carrying either quadruplets or a Sumo wrestler.

"You know you don't have to knock," Ashley said, keeping her distance.

Olivia smiled, a bit wistfully it seemed to Ashley, and opened their grandfather Big John's old barn coat to reveal a small white cat with one blue eye and one green one.

"Oh, no you don't," Ashley bristled.

Olivia, a veterinarian as well as Stone Creek, Arizona's one and only real-deal animal communicator, bent awkwardly to set the kitten on Ashley's immaculate kitchen floor, where it meowed pitifully and turned in a little circle, pursuing its fluffy tail. Every stray dog, cat or bird in the county seemed to find its way to Olivia eventually, like immigrants gravitating toward the Statue of Liberty.

Two years ago, at Christmas, she'd even been approached by a reindeer named Rodney.

"Meet Mrs. Wiggins," Olivia chimed, undaunted. Her china-blue eyes danced beneath the dark, sleek fringe of her bangs, but there was a wary look in them that bothered Ashley...even shamed her a little. The two of them had always been close. Did Olivia think Ashley was jealous of her new life with Tanner and his precocious fourteen-year-old daughter, Sophie?

"I suppose she's already told you her life story," Ashley said, nodding toward the cat, scrubbing her hands down the thighs of her jeans once and then heading for the sink to wash up before filling the electric kettle. At least *that* hadn't changed—they always had tea together, whenever Olivia dropped by—which was less and less often these days.

After all, unlike Ashley, Olivia had a life.

Olivia crooked up a corner of her mouth and began struggling out of the old plaid woolen coat, flecked, as always, with bits of straw. Some things never changed— even with Tanner's money, Olivia still dressed like what she was, a country veterinarian.

"Not much to tell," Livie answered with a slight lift of one shoulder, as nonchalantly as if telepathic exchanges with all manner of finned, feathered and furred creatures were commonplace. "She's only four-teen weeks old, so she hasn't had time to build up much of an autobiography."

"I do not want a cat," Ashley informed her sister.

Olivia hauled back a chair at the table and collapsed into it. She was wearing gum boots, as usual, and they looked none too clean. "You only *think* you don't want Mrs. Wiggins," she said. "She needs you and, whether you know it or not, you need her."

Ashley turned back to the kettle, trying to ignore the ball of cuteness chasing its tail in the middle of the kitchen floor. She was irritated, but worried, too. She looked back at Olivia over one stiff shoulder. "Should you be out and about, as pregnant as you are?"

Olivia smiled, serene as a Botticelli Madonna. "Preg-nancy isn't a matter of degrees, Ash," she said. "One either is or isn't."

"You're pale," Ashley fretted. She'd lost so many loved ones—both parents, her beloved granddad, Big John. If anything happened to any of her siblings, what-ever their differences, she wouldn't be able to bear it.

"Just brew the tea," Olivia said quietly. "I'm per-fectly all right."

While Ashley didn't have her sister's gift for talking to animals, she *was* intuitive, and her nerves felt all twitchy, a clear sign that something unexpected was about to happen. She plugged in the kettle and joined Olivia at the table. "Is anything wrong?"

"Funny you should ask," Olivia answered, and though the soft smile still rested on her lips, her eyes were solemn. "I came here to ask *you* the same question. Even though I already know the answer."

As much as she hated the uneasiness that had sprung up between herself and her sisters and brother, Ashley tended to bounce away from any mention of the subject like a pinball in a lively game. She sprang right up out of her chair and crossed to the antique breakfront to fetch two delicate china cups from behind the glass doors, full of strange urgency.

"Ash," Olivia said patiently

Ashley kept her back to her sister and lowered her head. "I've just been a little blue lately, Liv," she admitted softly. "That's all."

She would never get to know her mother.

The holidays had been a downer.

Not a single guest had checked into her Victorian bed-and-breakfast since before Thanksgiving, which meant she was two payments behind on the private mortgage Brad had given her to buy the place several years before. It wasn't that her brother had been pressing her for the money—he'd offered her the deed, free and clear, the day the deal was closed, but she'd insisted on repaying him every cent.

On top of all that, she hadn't heard a word from Jack McCall since his last visit, six months ago. He'd suddenly packed his bags and left one sultry summer night, while she was sleeping off their most recent bout of lovemaking, without so much as a goodbye.

Would it have killed him to wake her up and explain? Or just leave a damn note? Maybe pick up a phone?

"It's because of Mom," Olivia said. "You're grieving for the woman she never was, and that's okay, Ashley. But it might help if you talked to one of us about how you feel."

Weary rage surged through Ashley. She spun around to face Olivia, causing her sneakers to make a squeaking sound against the freshly waxed floor, remembered that her sister was about to have a baby, and sucked all her frustration and fury back in on one ragged breath.

"Let's not go there, Livie," she said.

The kitten scrabbled at one leg of Ashley's jeans and, without thinking, she bent to scoop the tiny creature up into her arms. Minute, silky ears twitched under her chin, and Mrs. Wiggins purred as though powered by batteries, snuggling against her neck.

Olivia smiled again, still wistful. "You're pretty angry with us, aren't you?" she asked gently. "Brad and Melissa and me, I mean."

"No," Ashley lied, wanting to put the kitten down but unable to do so. Somehow, nearly weightless as that cat was, it made her feel anchored instead of set adrift.

"Come on," Olivia challenged quietly. "If I weren't nine and a half months along, you'd be in my face right now."

Ashley bit down hard on her lower lip and said nothing.

"Things can't change if we don't talk," Olivia persisted.

Ashley swallowed painfully. Anything she said

would probably come out sounding like self-pity, and Ashley was too proud to feel sorry for herself, but she also knew her sister. Olivia wasn't about to let her off the hook, squirm though she might. "It's just that nothing seems to be working," she confessed, blinking back tears. "The business. Jack. That damn computer you insisted I needed."

The kettle boiled, emitting a shrill whistle and clouds of steam.

Still cradling the kitten under her chin, Ashley unplugged the cord with a wrenching motion of her free hand.

"Sit down," Olivia said, rising laboriously from her chair. "I'll make the tea."

"No, you won't!"

"I'm pregnant, Ashley," Olivia replied, "not incapacitated."

Ashley skulked back to the table, sat down, the tea forgotten. The kitten inched down her flannel work shirt to her lap and made a graceful leap to the floor.

"Talk to me," Olivia prodded, trundling toward the counter.

Ashley's vision seemed to narrow to a pinpoint, and when it widened again, she swayed in her chair, suddenly dizzy. If her blond hair hadn't been pulled back into its customary French braid, she'd have shoved her hands through it. "It must be an awful thing," she murmured, "to die the way Mom did."

Cups rattled against saucers at the periphery of Ashley's awareness. Olivia returned to the table but stood beside Ashley instead of sitting down again. Rested a hand on her shoulder. "Delia wasn't in her right mind, Ashley. She didn't suffer."

"No one cared," Ashley reflected, in a miserable whisper. "She died and no one even *cared*."

Olivia didn't sigh, but she might as well have. "You were little when Delia left," she said, after a long time. "You don't remember how it was."

"I remember praying every night that she'd come home," Ashley said.

Olivia bent—not easy to do with her huge belly— and rested her forehead on Ashley's crown, tightened her grip on her shoulder. "We all wanted her to come home, at least at first," she recalled softly. "But the reality is, she didn't—not even when Dad got killed in that lightning storm. After a while, we stopped needing her."

"Maybe *you* did," Ashley sniffled. "Now she's gone forever. I'm never going to know what she was really like."

Olivia straightened, very slowly. "She was—"

"Don't say it," Ashley warned.

"She drank," Olivia insisted, stepping back. The invisible barrier dropped between them again, a nearly audible shift in the atmosphere. "She took drugs. Her brain was pickled. If you want to remember her differently, that's your prerogative. But don't expect me to rewrite history."

Ashley's cheeks were wet, and she swiped at them with the back of one hand, probably leaving streaks in the coating of attic dust prickling on her skin. "Fair enough," she said stiffly.

Olivia crossed the room again, jangled things around at the counter for a few moments, and returned with a pot of steeping tea and two cups and saucers.

"This is getting to me," she told Ashley. "It's as if the earth has cracked open and we're standing on opposite sides of a deep chasm. It's bothering Brad and Melissa,

too. We're *family,* Ashley. Can't we just agree to dis-
agree as far as Mom is concerned and go on from there?"

"I'll try," Ashley said, though she had to win an inner
skirmish first. A long one.

Olivia reached across the table, closed her hand
around Ashley's. "Why didn't you tell me you were having trouble getting the computer up and running?" she
asked. Ashley was profoundly grateful for the change
of subject, even if it did nettle her a little at the same
time. She hated the stupid contraption, hated anything
electronic. She'd followed the instructions to the letter,
and the thing *still* wouldn't work.

When she didn't say anything, Olivia went on. "Sophie and Carly are cyberwhizzes—they'd be glad to
build you a website for the B&B and show you how to
zip around the Internet like a pro."

Brad and his wife, the former Meg McKettrick, had
adopted Carly, Meg's half sister, soon after their marriage. The teenager doted on their son, three-year-old
Mac, and had befriended Sophie from the beginning.

"That would be…nice," Ashley said doubtfully. The
truth was, she was an old-fashioned type, as Victorian, in some ways, as her house. She didn't carry a
cell phone, and her landline had a rotary dial. "But you
know me and technology."

"I also know you're not stupid," Olivia responded,
pouring tea for Ashley, then for herself. Their spoons
made a cheerful tinkling sound, like fairy bells, as they
stirred in organic sugar from the chunky ceramic bowl
in the center of the table.

The kitten jumped back into Ashley's lap then, star-
tling her, making her laugh. How long had it been since
she'd laughed?

Too long, judging by the expression on Olivia's face.

"You're really all right?" Ashley asked, watching her sister closely.

"I'm better than 'all right,'" Olivia assured her. "I'm married to the man of my dreams. I have Sophie, a barn full of horses out at Starcross Ranch, and a thriving veterinary practice." A slight frown creased her forehead. "Speaking of men…?"

"Let's not," Ashley said.

"You still haven't heard from Jack?"

"No. And that's fine with me."

"I don't think it *is* fine with you, Ashley. He's Tanner's friend. I could ask him to call Jack and—"

"No!"

Olivia sighed. "Yeah," she said. "You're right. That would be interfering, and Tanner probably wouldn't go along with it anyhow."

Ashley stroked the kitten even as she tried not to bond with it. She was zero-for-zero on that score. "Jack and I had a fling," she said. "It's obviously over. End of story."

Olivia arched one perfect eyebrow. "Maybe you need a vacation," she mused aloud. "A new man in your life. You could go on one of those singles' cruises—"

Ashley gave a scoffing chuckle—it felt good to engage in girl talk with her sister again. "Sure," she retorted. "I'd meet guys twice my age, with gold chains around their necks and bad toupees. Or worse."

"What could be worse?" Olivia joked, grinning over the gold rim of her teacup.

"Spray-on hair," Ashley said decisively.

Olivia laughed.

"Besides," Ashley went on, "I don't want to be out of town when you have the baby."

Olivia nodded, turned thoughtful again. "You should get out more, though."

"And do what?" Ashley challenged. "Play bingo in the church basement on Mondays, Wednesdays and Fridays? Join the Powder Puff bowling league? In case it's escaped your notice, O pregnant one, Stone Creek isn't exactly a social whirlwind."

Olivia sighed again, in temporary defeat, and glanced at her watch. "I'm supposed to meet Tanner at the clinic in twenty minutes—just a routine checkup, so don't panic. Meet us for lunch afterward?"

The kitten climbed Ashley's shirt, its claws catching in the fabric, nestled under her neck again. "I have some errands to run," she said, with a shake of her head. "You're going to stick me with this cat, aren't you, Olivia?"

Olivia smiled, stood, and carried her cup and saucer to the sink. "Give Mrs. Wiggins a chance," she said. "If she doesn't win your heart by this time next week, I'll try to find her another home." She took Big John's ratty coat from the row of pegs next to the back door and shoved her arms into the sleeves, reclaimed her purse from the end of the counter, where she'd set it on the way in. "Shall I ask Sophie and Carly to come by after school and have a look at your computer?"

Ashley enjoyed the girls, and it would be nice to bake a batch of cookies for someone. Besides, she was tired of being confronted by the dark monitor, tower and printer every time she went into the study. "I guess," she answered.

"Done deal," Olivia confirmed brightly, and then she was out the door, gone.

Ashley held the kitten in front of her face. "You're not staying," she said.

"Meow," Mrs. Wiggins replied.

"Oh, all right," Ashley relented. "But I'd better not find any snags in my new chintz slipcovers!"

The helicopter swung abruptly sideways in a dizzying arch, setting Jack McCall's fever-ravaged brain spinning. He hoped the pilot hadn't seen him grip the edges of his seat, bracing for a crash.

His friend's voice sounded tinny, coming through the earphones. "You belong in a hospital," he said. "Not some backwater bed-and-breakfast."

All Jack really knew about the toxin raging through his system was that it wasn't contagious—the CDC had ordered him into quarantine until that much had been determined—but there was still no diagnosis and no remedy except a lot of rest and quiet. "I don't like hospitals," he responded, hoping he sounded like his normal self. "They're full of sick people."

Vince Griffin chuckled at that, but it was a dry sound, rough at the edges. "What's in Stone Creek, Arizona?" he asked. "Besides a whole lot of nothin'?"

Ashley O'Ballivan was in Stone Creek, and she was a whole lot of somethin', but Jack had neither the strength nor the inclination to explain. Given the way he'd ducked out on her six months before, after taking an emergency call on his cell phone, he didn't expect a welcome, knew he didn't deserve one. But Ashley, being Ashley, would take him in, whatever her misgivings, same as she would a wounded dog or a bird with a broken wing.

He had to get to Ashley—he'd be all right then.

He closed his eyes, letting the fever swallow him.

There was no telling how much time had passed when he surfaced again, became aware of the chopper blades slowing overhead. The magic flying machine bobbed on its own updraft, sending the broth he'd sipped from a thermos scalding its way up into the back of his throat.

Dimly, he saw the ancient ambulance waiting on the airfield outside Stone Creek; it seemed that twilight had descended, but he couldn't be sure. Since the toxin had taken him down, he hadn't been able to trust his perceptions.

Day turned into night.

Up turned into down.

The doctors had ruled out a brain tumor, but he still felt as though something was eating his brain.

"Here we are," Vince said.

"Is it dark or am I going blind?"

Vince tossed him a worried look. "It's dark," he said.

Jack sighed with relief. His clothes—the usual black jeans and black turtleneck sweater—felt clammy against his flesh. His teeth began to chatter as two figures unloaded a gurney from the back of the ambulance and waited for the blades to stop so they could approach.

"Great," Vince remarked, unsnapping his seat belt. "Those two look like volunteers, not real EMTs. The CDC parked you at Walter Reed, and that wasn't good enough for you because—?"

Jack didn't answer. He had nothing against the famous military hospital, but he wasn't associated with the U.S. government, not officially at least. He couldn't see taking up a bed some wounded soldier might need, and, anyhow, he'd be a sitting duck in a regular facility.

The chopper bounced sickeningly on its runners, and Vince, with a shake of his head, pushed open his door and jumped to the ground, head down.

Jack waited, wondering if he'd be able to stand on his own. After fumbling unsuccessfully with the buckle on his seat belt, he decided not.

When it was safe, the EMTs came forward, following Vince, who opened Jack's door.

Jack hauled off his headphones and tossed them aside.

His old friend Tanner Quinn stepped around Vince, his trademark grin not quite reaching his eyes.

"You look like hell warmed over," he told Jack cheerfully.

"Since when are you an EMT?" Jack retorted.

Tanner reached in, wedged a shoulder under Jack's right arm, and hauled him out of the chopper. His knees immediately buckled, and Vince stepped up, supporting him on the other side.

"In a place like Stone Creek," Tanner replied, "everybody helps out."

"Right," Jack said, stumbling between the two men keeping him on his feet. They reached the wheeled gurney—Jack had thought they never would, since it seemed to recede into the void with every awkward step—and he found himself on his back.

Tanner and the second man strapped him down, a process that brought back a few bad memories.

"Is there even a hospital in this hellhole of a place?" Vince asked irritably, from somewhere in the cold night.

"There's a pretty good clinic over in Indian Rock," Tanner answered easily, "and it isn't far to Flagstaff." He paused to help his buddy hoist Jack and the gurney into the back of the ambulance. "You're in good hands, Jack. My wife is the best veterinarian in the state."

Jack laughed raggedly at that.

Vince muttered a curse.

Tanner climbed into the back beside Jack, perched on some kind of fold-down seat. The other man shut the doors.

"I'm not contagious," Jack said to Tanner.

"So I hear," Tanner said, as his partner climbed into the driver's seat and started the engine. "You in any pain?"

"No," Jack struggled to quip, "but I might puke on those Roy Rogers boots of yours."

"You don't miss much, even strapped to a gurney." Tanner chuckled, hoisted one foot high enough for Jack to squint at it and hauled up the leg of his jeans to show off the fancy stitching on the boot shaft. "My brother-in-law gave them to me," he said. "Brad used to wear them onstage, back when he was breaking hearts out there on the concert circuit. Swigged iced tea out of a whiskey bottle all through every performance, so everybody would think he was a badass."

Jack looked up at his closest and most trusted friend and wished he'd listened to Vince. Ever since he'd come down with the illness, a week after snatching a five-year-old girl back from her noncustodial parent—a small-time drug runner with dangerous aspirations and a lousy attitude—he hadn't been able to think about anyone or anything but Ashley. When he *could* think.

Now, in one of the first clearheaded moments he'd experienced since checking himself out of the hospital the day before, he realized he might be making a major mistake—not by facing Ashley; he owed her that much and a lot more. No, he could be putting her in danger, and putting Tanner and his daughter and his pregnant veterinarian wife in danger, as well.

"I shouldn't have come here," he said, keeping his voice low.

Tanner shook his head, his jaw clamped down hard, as though irritated by Jack's statement. Since he'd gotten married, settled down and sold off his multinational construction company to play at being an Arizona rancher, Tanner had softened around the edges a little, but Jack knew his friend was still one tough SOB.

"This is where you belong," Tanner insisted. Another grin quirked one corner of his mouth. "If you'd had sense enough to know that six months ago, old buddy, when you bailed on Ashley without so much as a fare-thee-well, you wouldn't be in this mess."

Ashley. The name had run through his mind a million times in those six months, but hearing somebody say it out loud was like having a fist close around his insides and squeeze hard.

Jack couldn't speak.

Tanner didn't press for further conversation.

The ambulance bumped over country roads, finally hit smooth blacktop.

"Here we are," Tanner said. "Ashley's place."

"I knew something was going to happen," Ashley told Mrs. Wiggins, peeling the kitten off the living room curtains as she peered out at the ambulance stopped in the street. "I *knew* it."

Not bothering to find her coat, Ashley opened the door and stepped out onto the porch. Tanner got out on the passenger side and gave her a casual wave as he went around back.

Ashley's heart pounded. She stood frozen for a long moment, not by the cold, but by a strange, eager sense of dread. Then she bolted down the steps, careful not to slip, and hurried along the walk, through the gate.

"What...?" she began, but the rest of the question died in her throat.

Tanner had opened the back of the ambulance, but then he just stood there, looking at her with an odd expression on his face.

"Brace yourself," he said.

Jeff Baxter, part of a rotating group of volunteers, like Tanner, left the driver's seat and came to stand a short but eloquent distance away. He looked like a man trying to brace himself for an imminent explosion.

Impatient, Ashley wedged herself between the two men, peered inside.

Jack McCall sat upright on the gurney, grinning stupidly. His black hair, military-short the last time she'd seen him, was longer now, and sleekly shaggy. His eyes blazed with fever.

"Whose shirt is that?" he asked, frowning.

Still taken aback, Ashley didn't register the question right away. Several awkward moments had passed by the time she glanced down to see what she was wearing.

"Yours," she answered, finally.

Jack looked relieved. "Good," he said.

Ashley, beside herself with surprise until that very instant, landed back in her own skin with a jolt. "What are you doing here?" she demanded.

Jack scooted toward her, almost pitched out of the ambulance onto his face before Tanner and Jeff moved in to grab him by the arms.

"Checking in," he said, once he'd tried—and failed—to shrug them off. "You're still in the bed-and-breakfast business, aren't you?"

You're still in the bed-and-breakfast business, aren't you?

Damn, the man had nerve.

"You belong in a hospital," she said evenly. "Not a bed-and-breakfast."

"I'm willing to pay double," Jack offered. His face, always strong, took on a vulnerable expression. "I need a place to lay low for a while, Ash. Are you game?"

She thought quickly. The last thing in the world she wanted was Jack McCall under her roof again, but she couldn't afford to turn down a paying guest. She'd have to dip into her savings soon if she did, and not just to pay Brad.

The bills were piling up.

"Triple the usual rate," she said.

Jack squinted, probably not understanding at first, then gave a raspy chuckle. "Okay," he agreed. "Triple it is. Even though it *is* the off-season."

Jeff and Tanner half dragged, half carried him toward the house.

Ashley hesitated on the snowy sidewalk.

First the cat.

Now Jack.

Evidently, it was her day to be dumped on.

Chapter 2

"What *happened* to him?" Ashley whispered to Tanner, in the hallway outside the second-best room in the house, a small suite at the opposite end of the corridor from her own quarters. Jeff and Tanner had already put the patient to bed, fully dressed except for his boots, and Jeff had gone downstairs to make a call on his cell phone.

Jack, meanwhile, had sunk into an instant and all-consuming sleep—or into a coma. It was a crapshoot, guessing which.

Tanner looked grim; didn't seem to notice that Mrs. Wiggins was busily climbing his right pant leg, her infinitesimal claws snagging the denim as she scaled his knee and started up his thigh with a deliberation that would have been funny under any other circumstances.

"All I know is," Tanner replied, "I got a call from

Jack this afternoon, just as Livie and I were leaving the clinic after her checkup. He said he was a little under the weather and wanted to know if I'd meet him at the airstrip and bring him here." He paused, cupped the kitten in one hand, raised the little creature to nose level, and peered quizzically into its mismatched eyes before lowering it gently to the floor. Straightening from a crouch, he added, "I offered to put him up at our place, but he insisted on coming to yours."

"You might have called me," Ashley fretted, still keeping her voice down. "Given me some warning, at least."

"Check your voice mail," Tanner countered, sounding mildly exasperated. "I left at least four messages."

"I was out," Ashley said, defensive, "buying kitty litter and kibble. Because *your wife* decided I needed a cat."

Tanner grinned at the mention of Olivia, and something eased in him, gentling the expression in his eyes. "If you'd carry a cell phone, like any normal human being, you'd have been up to speed, situationwise." He paused, with a mischievous twinkle. "You might even have had time to bake a welcome-back-Jack cake."

"As if," Ashley breathed, but as rattled as she was over having Jack McCall land in the middle of her life like the flaming chunks of a latter-day Hindenburg, there was something else she needed to know. "What did the doctor say? About Olivia, I mean?"

Tanner sighed. "She's a couple of weeks overdue—Dr. Pentland wants to induce labor tomorrow morning."

Worry made Ashley peevish. "And you're just telling me this now?"

"As I said," Tanner replied, "get a cell phone."

Before Ashley could come up with a reply, the front door banged open downstairs, and a youthful female voice called her name, sounding alarmed.

Ashley went to the upstairs railing, leaned a little, and saw Tanner's daughter, Sophie, standing in the living room, her face upturned and so pale that her freckles stood out, even from that distance. Sixteen-year-old Carly, blond and blue-eyed like her sister, Meg, appeared beside her.

"There's an ambulance outside," Sophie said. "What's happening?"

Tanner started down the stairs. "Everything's all right," he told the frightened girl.

Carly glanced from Tanner to Ashley, descending behind him. "We meant to get here sooner, to set up your computer," Carly said, "but Mr. Gilvine kept the whole Drama Club after school to rehearse the second act of the new play."

"How come there's an ambulance outside," Sophie persisted, gazing up at her father's face, "if nobody's sick?"

"I didn't say nobody was sick," Tanner told her quietly, setting his hands on her shoulders. "Jack's upstairs, resting."

Sophie's panic rose a notch. "Uncle Jack is sick? What's wrong with him?"

That's what I'd like to know, Ashley thought.

"From the symptoms, I'd guess it's some kind of toxin."

Sophie tried to go around Tanner, clearly intending to race up the stairs. "I want to see him!"

Tanner stopped her. "Not now, sweetie," he said, his tone at once gruff and gentle. "He's asleep."

"Do you still want us to set up your computer?" Carly asked Ashley.

Ashley summoned up a smile and shook her head. "Another time," she said. "You must be tired, after a whole day of school and then play practice on top of that. How about some supper?"

"Mr. Gilvine ordered pizza for the whole cast," Carly answered, touching her flat stomach and puffing out her cheeks to indicate that she was stuffed. "I already called home, and Brad said he'd come in from the ranch and get us as soon as we had your system up and running."

"It can wait," Ashley reiterated, glancing at Tanner.

"I'll drop you off on the way home," he told Carly, one hand still resting on Sophie's shoulder. "My truck's parked at the fire station. Jeff can give us a lift over there."

Having lost her mother when she was very young, Sophie had insecurities Ashley could well identify with. The girl adored Olivia, and looked forward to the birth of a brother or sister. Tanner probably wanted to break the news about Livie's induction later, with just the three of them present.

"Call me," Ashley ordered, her throat thick with concern for her sister and the child, as Tanner steered the girls toward the front door.

Tanner merely arched an eyebrow at that.

Jeff stepped out of the study, just tucking away his cell phone. "I'm in big trouble with Lucy," he said. "Forgot to let her know I'd be late. She made a soufflé and it fell."

"Uh-oh," Tanner commiserated.

"We get to ride in an ambulance?" Sophie asked, cheered.

"Awesome," Carly said.

And then they were gone.

Ashley raised her eyes to the ceiling. Recalled that Jack McCall was up there, sprawled on one of her guest beds, buried under half a dozen quilts. Just how sick was he? Would he want to eat, and if so, what?

After some internal debate, she decided on home-made chicken soup.

That was the cure for everything, wasn't it?

Everything, that is, except a broken heart.

Jack McCall awakened to find something furry standing on his face.

Fortunately, he was too weak to flail, or he'd have sent what his brain finally registered as a kitten flying before he realized he wasn't back in a South American jail, fighting off rats willing to settle for part of his hide when the rations ran low.

The animal stared directly into his face with one blue eye and one green one, purring as though it had a motor inside its hairy little chest.

He blinked, decided the thing was probably some kind of mutant.

"Another victim of renegade genetics," he said.

"Meooooow," the cat replied, perhaps indignant.

The door across the room opened, and Ashley elbowed her way in, carrying a loaded tray. Whatever was on it smelled like heaven distilled to its essence, or was that the scent of her skin and that amazing hair of hers?

"Mrs. Wiggins," she said, "get down."

"Mrs.?" Jack replied, trying to raise himself on his pillows and failing. This was a fortunate thing for the cat, who was trying to nest in his hair by then. "Isn't she a little young to be married?"

"Yuk-yuk," Ashley said, with an edge.

Jack sighed inwardly. All was not forgiven, then, he concluded.

Mrs. Wiggins climbed down over his right cheek and curled up on his chest. He could have sworn he felt some kind of warm energy flowing through the kitten, as though it were a conduit between the world around him and another, better one.

Crap. He was really losing it.

"Are you hungry?" Ashley asked, as though he were any ordinary guest.

A gnawing in the pit of Jack's stomach told him he was—for the first time since he'd come down with the mysterious plague. "Yeah," he ground out, further weakened by the sight of Ashley. Even in jeans and the flannel shirt he'd left behind, with her light hair springing from its normally tidy braid, she looked like a goddess. "I think I am."

She approached the bed—cautiously, it seemed to Jack, and little wonder, after some of the acrobatics they'd managed in the one down the hall before he left—and set the tray down on the nightstand.

"Can you feed yourself?" she asked, keeping her distance. Her tone was formal, almost prim.

Jack gave an inelegant snort at that, then realized, to his mortification, that he probably couldn't. Earlier, he'd made it to the adjoining bathroom and back, but the effort had exhausted him. "Yes," he fibbed.

She tilted her head to one side, skeptical. A smile flittered around her mouth, but didn't come in for a landing. "Your eyes widen a little when you lie," she commented.

He sure hoped certain members of various drug and gunrunning cartels didn't know that. "Oh," he said.

Ashley dragged a fussy-looking chair over and sat down. With a little sigh, she took a spoon off the tray and plunged it into a bright-blue crockery bowl. "Open up," she told him.

Jack resisted briefly, pressing his lips together— he still had *some* pride, after all—but his stomach betrayed him with a long and perfectly audible rumble. He opened his mouth.

The fragrant substance turned out to be chicken soup, with wild rice and chopped celery and a few other things he couldn't identify. It was so good that, if he'd been able to, he'd have grabbed the bowl with both hands and downed the stuff in a few gulps.

"Slow down," Ashley said. Her eyes had softened a little, but her body remained rigid. "There's plenty more soup simmering on the stove."

Like the kitten, the soup seemed to possess some sort of quantum-level healing power. Jack felt faint tendrils of strength stirring inside him, like the tender roots of a plant splitting through a seed husk, groping tentatively toward the sun.

Once he'd finished the soup, sleep began to pull him downward again, toward oblivion. There was something different about the feeling this time; rather than an urge to struggle against it, as before, it was more an impulse to give himself up to the darkness, settle into it like a waiting embrace.

Something soft brushed his cheek. Ashley's fingertips? Or the mutant kitten?

"Jack," Ashley said.

With an effort, he opened his eyes.

Tears glimmered along Ashley's lashes. "Are you going to die?" she asked.

Jack considered his answer for a few moments; not easy, with his brain short-circuiting. According to the doctors at Walter Reed, his prognosis wasn't the best. They'd admitted that they'd never seen the toxin before, and their plan was to ship him off to some secret government research facility for further study.

Which was one of the reasons he'd bolted, conned a series of friends into springing him and then relaying him cross-country in various planes and helicopters.

He found Ashley's hand, squeezed it with his own. "Not if I can help it," he murmured, just before sleep sucked him under again.

Their brief conversation echoed in Ashley's head, over and over, as she sat there watching Jack sleep until the room was so dark she couldn't see anything but the faintest outline of him, etched against the sheets.

Are you going to die?

Not if I can help it.

Ashley overcame the need to switch on the bedside lamp, send golden light spilling over the features she knew so well—the hazel eyes, the well-defined cheekbones, the strong, obstinate jaw—but just barely. Leaving the tray behind, she rose out of the chair and made her way slowly toward the door, afraid of stepping on Mrs. Wiggins, frolicking at her feet like a little ghost.

Reaching the hallway, Ashley closed the door softly behind her, bent to scoop the kitten up in one hand, and let the tears come. Silent sobs rocked her, making her shoulders shake, and Mrs. Wiggins snuggled in close under her chin, as if to offer comfort.

Was Jack truly in danger of dying?

She sniffled, straightened her spine. Surely Tanner wouldn't have agreed to bring him to the bed-and-breakfast—to her—if he was at death's door.

On the other hand, she reasoned, dashing at her cheek with the back of one hand, trying to rally her scattered emotions, Jack was bone-stubborn. He always got his way.

So maybe Tanner was simply honoring Jack's last wish.

Holding tightly to the banister, Ashley started down the stairs.

Jack hadn't wanted to *live* in Stone Creek. Why would he choose to *die* there?

The phone began to ring, a persistent trilling, and Ashley, thinking of Olivia, dashed to the small desk where guests registered—not that *that* had been an issue lately—and snatched up the receiver.

"Hello?" When had she gotten out of the habit of answering with a businesslike, "Mountain View Bed and Breakfast"?

"I hear you've got an unexpected boarder," Brad said, his tone measured.

Ashley was unaccountably glad to hear her big brother's voice, considering that they hadn't had much to say to each other since their mother's funeral. "Yes," she assented.

"According to Carly, he was sick enough to arrive in an ambulance."

Ashley nodded, remembered that Brad couldn't see her, and repeated, "Yes. I'm not sure he should be here—Brad, he's in a really bad way. I'm not a nurse and I'm—" She paused, swallowed. "I'm scared."

"I can be there in fifteen minutes, Ash."

Fresh tears scalded Ashley's eyes, made them feel raw. "That would be good," she said.

"Put on a pot of coffee, little sister," Brad told her. "I'm on my way."

True to his word, Brad was standing in her kitchen before the coffee finished perking. He looked more like a rancher than a famous country singer and sometime movie star, in his faded jeans, battered boots, chambray shirt and denim jacket.

Ashley couldn't remember the last time she'd hugged her brother, but now she went to him, and he wrapped her in his arms, kissed the top of her head.

"Olivia…" she began, but her voice fell away.

"I know," Brad said hoarsely. "They're inducing labor in the morning. Livie will be fine, honey, and so will the baby."

Ashley tilted her head back, looked up into Brad's face. His dark-blond hair was rumpled, and his beard was growing in, bristly. "How's the family?"

He rested his hands on her shoulders, held her at a little distance. "You wouldn't have to ask if you ever stopped by Stone Creek Ranch," he answered. "Mac misses you, and Meg and I do, too."

The minute Brad had known she needed him, he'd been in his truck, headed for town. And now that he was there, her anger over their mother's funeral didn't seem so important.

She tried to speak, but her throat had tightened again, and she couldn't get a single word past it.

One corner of Brad's famous mouth crooked up.

"Where's Lover Boy?" he asked. "Lucky thing for him that he's laid up—otherwise I'd punch his lights out for what he did to you."

The phrase *Lover Boy* made Ashley flinch. "That's over," she said.

Brad let his hands fall to his sides, his eyes serious now. "Right," he replied. "Which room?"

Ashley told him, and he left the kitchen, the inside door swinging behind him long after he'd passed through it.

She kept herself busy by taking mugs down from the cupboard, filling Mrs. Wiggins's dish with kibble the size of barley grains, switching on the radio and then switching it off again.

The kitten crunched away at the kibble, then climbed onto its newly purchased bed in the corner near the fireplace, turned in circles for a few moments, kneaded the fabric, and dropped like the proverbial rock.

After several minutes had passed, Ashley heard Brad's boot heels on the staircase, and poured coffee for her brother; she was drinking herbal tea.

As if there were a hope in hell she'd sleep a wink that night by avoiding caffeine.

Brad reached for his mug, took a thoughtful sip.

"Well?" Ashley prompted.

"I'm not a doctor, Ash," he said. "All I can tell you for sure is, he's breathing."

"*That's* helpful," Ashley said.

He chuckled, and the sound, though rueful, consoled her a little. He turned one of the chairs around backward, and straddled it, setting his mug on the table.

"Why do men like to sit like that?" Ashley wondered aloud.

He grinned. "You've been alone too long," he answered.

Ashley blushed, brought her tea to the table and sat down. "What am I going to do?" she asked.

Brad inclined his head toward the ceiling. "About McCall? That's up to you, sis. If you want him out of here, I can have him airlifted to Flagstaff within a couple hours."

This was no idle boast. Even though he'd retired from the country-music scene several years before, at least as far as concert tours went, Brad still wrote and recorded songs, and he could have stacked his royalty checks like so much cordwood. On top of that, Meg was a McKettrick, a multimillionaire in her own right. One phone call from either one of them, and a sleek jet would be landing outside of town in no time at all, fully equipped and staffed with doctors and nurses.

Ashley bit her lower lip. God knew why, but Jack wanted to stay at her place, and he'd gone through a lot to get there. As impractical as it was, given his condition, she didn't think she could turn him out.

Brad must have read her face. He reached out, took her hand. "You still love the bastard," he said. "Don't you?"

"I don't know," she answered miserably. She'd definitely loved the man she'd known before, but this was a new Jack, a different Jack. The *real* one, she supposed. It shook her to realize she'd given her heart to an illusion.

"It's okay, Ashley."

She shook her head, started to cry again. "Nothing is okay," she argued.

"We can make it that way," Brad offered quietly. "All we have to do is talk."

She dried her eyes on the sleeve of Jack's old shirt.

It seemed ironic, given all the things hanging in her closet, that she'd chosen to wear that particular garment when she'd gotten dressed that morning. Had some part of her known, somehow, that Jack was coming home?

Brad was waiting for an answer, and he wouldn't break eye contact until he got one.

Ashley swallowed hard. "Our mother died," she said, cornered. "Our *mother*. And you and Olivia and Melissa all seemed—relieved."

A muscle in Brad's jaw tightened, relaxed again. He sighed and shoved a hand through his hair. "I guess I *was* relieved," he admitted. "They said she didn't suffer, but I always wondered—" He paused, cleared his throat. "I wondered if she was in there somewhere, hurting, with no way to ask for help."

Ashley's heart gave one hard beat, then settled into its normal pace again. "You didn't hate her?" she asked, stunned.

"She was my mother," Brad said. "Of course I didn't hate her."

"Things might have been so different "

"Ashley," Brad broke in, "things *weren't* different. That's the point. Delia's gone, for good this time. You've got to let go."

"What if I can't?" Ashley whispered.

"You don't have a choice, Button."

Button. Their grandfather had called both her and Melissa by that nickname; like most twins, they were used to sharing things. "Do you miss Big John as much as I do?" she asked.

"Yes," Brad answered, without hesitation, his voice still gruff. He looked down at his coffee mug for a second or so, then raised his gaze to meet Ashley's again.

"Same thing," he said. "He's gone. And letting go is something I have to do about three times a day."

Ashley got up, suddenly unable to sit still. She brought the coffee carafe to the table and refilled Brad's cup. She spoke very quietly. "But it was a one-time thing, letting go of Mom?"

"Yeah," Brad said. "And it happened a long, long time ago. I remember it distinctly—it was the night my high school basketball team took the state championship. I was sure she'd be in the bleachers, clapping and cheering like everybody else. She wasn't, of course, and that was when I got it through my head that she wasn't coming back—ever."

Ashley's heart ached. Brad was her big brother; he'd always been strong. Why hadn't she realized that he'd been hurt, too?

"Big John *stayed,* Ashley," he went on, while she sat there gulping. "He stuck around, through good times and bad. Even after he'd buried his only son, he kept on keeping on. Mom caught the afternoon bus out of town and couldn't be bothered to call or even send a postcard. I did my mourning long before she died."

Ashley could only nod.

Brad was quiet for a while, pondering, taking the occasional sip from his coffee mug. Then he spoke again. "Here's the thing," he said. "When the chips were down, I basically did the same thing as Mom—got on a bus and left Big John to take care of the ranch and raise the three of you all by himself—so I'm in no position to judge anybody else. Bottom line, Ash? People are what they are, and they do what they do, and you have to decide either to accept that or walk away without looking back."

Ashley managed a wobbly smile. Sniffled once. "I'm sorry I'm late on the mortgage payments," she said.

Brad rolled his eyes. "Like I'm worried," he replied, his body making the subtle shifts that meant he'd be leaving soon. With one arm, he gestured to indicate the B&B. "Why won't you just let me sign the place over to you?"

"Would you do that," Ashley challenged reasonably, "if our situations were reversed?"

He flushed slightly, got to his feet. "No," he admitted, "but—"

"But what?"

Brad grinned sheepishly, and his powerful shoulders shifted slightly under his shirt.

"But you're a man?" Ashley finished for him, when he didn't speak. "Is that what you were going to say?"

"Well, yeah," Brad said.

"You'll have the mortgage payments as soon as I get a chance to run Jack's credit card," she told her brother, rising to walk him to the back door. Color suffused her cheeks. "Thanks for coming into town," she added. "I feel like a fool for panicking."

In the midst of pulling on his jacket, Brad paused. "I'm a big brother," he said, somewhat gruffly. "It's what we do."

"Are you and Meg going to the hospital tomorrow, when Livie…?"

Brad tugged lightly at her braid, the way he'd always done. "We'll be hanging out by the telephone," he said. "Livie swears it's a normal procedure, and she doesn't want everyone fussing 'as if it were a heart transplant,' as she put it."

Ashley bit down on her lower lip and nodded. She already had a nephew—Mac—and two nieces, Carly and

Sophie, although technically Carly, Meg's half sister, whom her dying father had asked her to raise, wasn't really a niece. Tomorrow, another little one would join the family. Instead of being a nervous wreck, she ought to be celebrating.

She wasn't, she decided, so different from Sophie. Having effectively lost Delia when she was so young, she'd turned to Olivia as a substitute mother, as had Melissa. Had their devotion been a burden to their sister, only a few years older than they were, and grappling with her own sense of loss?

She stood on tiptoe and kissed Brad's cheek. "Thanks," she said again. "Call if you hear anything."

Brad gave her braid another tug, turned and left the house.

Ashley felt profoundly alone.

Jack had nearly flung himself at the singing cowboy standing at the foot of his bed, before recognizing him as Ashley's famous brother, Brad. Even though the room had been dark, the other man must have seen him tense.

"I know you're awake, McCall," he'd said.

Jack had yawned. "O'Ballivan?"

"Live and in person," came the not-so-friendly reply.

"And you're sneaking around my room because…?"

O'Ballivan had chuckled at that. Hooked his thumbs through his belt loops. "Because Ashley's worried about you. And what worries my baby sister worries *me,* James Bond."

Ashley was worried about him? Something like elation flooded Jack. "Not for the same reasons, I suspect," he said.

Mr. Country Music had gripped the high, spooled

rail at the foot of the bed and leaned forward a little to make his point. "Damned if I can figure out why you'd come back here, especially in the shape you're in, after what happened last summer, except to take up where you left off." He paused, gripped the rail hard enough that his knuckles showed white even in the gloom. "You hurt her again, McCall, and you have my solemn word—I'm gonna turn right around and hurt *you*. Are we clear on that?"

Jack had smiled, not because he was amused, but because he liked knowing Ashley had folks to look after her when he wasn't around—and when he was. "Oh, yeah," Jack had replied. "We're clear."

Obviously a man of few words, O'Ballivan had simply nodded, turned and walked out of the room.

Remembering, Jack raised himself as high on the pillows as he could, strained to reach the lamp switch. The efforts, simple as they were, made him break out in a cold sweat, but at the same time, he felt his strength returning.

He looked around the room, noting the flowered wallpaper, the pale rose carpeting, the intricate woodwork on the mantelpiece. Two girly chairs flanked the cold fireplace, and fat flakes of January snow drifted past the two sets of bay windows, both sporting seats beneath, covered by cheery cushions.

It was a far cry from Walter Reed, he thought.

An even further cry from the jungle hut where he'd hidden out for nearly three months, awaiting his chance to grab little Rachel Stockard, hustle her out of the country by boat and then a seaplane, and return her to her frantic mother.

He'd been well paid for the job, but it was the memory of the mother-daughter reunion, after he'd surrendered the child to a pair of FBI agents and a Customs official in Atlanta, that made his throat catch more than two weeks after the fact.

Through an observation window, he'd watched as Rachel scrambled out of the man's arms and raced toward her waiting mother. Tears pouring down her face, Ardith Stockard had dropped to her knees, arms outspread, and gathered the little girl close. The two of them had clung to each other, both trembling.

And then Ardith had raised her eyes, seen Jack through the glass, and mouthed the words, "Thank you."

He'd nodded, exhausted and already sick.

Closing his eyes, Jack went back over the journey to South America, the long game of waiting and watching, finally finding the small, isolated country estate where Rachel had been taken after she was kidnapped from her maternal grandparents' home in Phoenix, almost a year before.

Even after locating the child, he hadn't been able to make a move for more than a week—not until her father and his retinue of thugs had loaded a convoy of jeeps with drugs and firepower one day, and roared off down the jungle road, probably headed for a rendezvous with a boat moored off some hidden beach.

Jack had soon ascertained that only the middle-aged cook—and he had reason not to expect opposition from her—and one guard stood between him and Rachel. He'd waited until dark, risking the return of the jeep convoy, then climbed to the terrace outside the child's room.

"Did you come to take me home to my mommy?" Rachel had shrilled, her eyes wide with hope, when he stepped in off the terrace, a finger to his lips.

Her voice carried, and the guard burst in from the hallway, shouting in Spanish.

There had been a brief struggle—Jack had felt something prick him in the side as the goon went down—but, hearing the sound of approaching vehicles in the distance, he hadn't taken the time to wonder.

He'd grabbed Rachel up under one arm and climbed over the terrace and back down the crumbling rock wall of the house, with its many foot-and handholds, to the ground, running for the trees.

It was only after the reunion in Atlanta that Jack had suddenly collapsed, dizzy with fever.

The next thing he remembered was waking up in a hospital room, hooked up to half a dozen machines and surrounded by grim-faced Feds waiting to ask questions.

Chapter 3

Ashley did not expect to sleep at all that night; she had too many things on her mind, between the imminent birth of Olivia's baby, lingering issues with her mother and siblings, and Jack McCall landing in the middle of her formerly well-ordered days like the meteor that allegedly finished off the dinosaurs.

Therefore, sunlight glowing pink-orange through her eyelids and the loud jangle of her bedside telephone came as a surprise.

She groped for the receiver, nearly throwing a disgruntled Mrs. Wiggins to the floor, and rasped out a hoarse, "Hullo?"

Olivia's distinctive laugh sounded weary, but it bubbled into Ashley's ear and then settled, warm as summer honey, into every tuck and fold of her heart. "Did I wake you up?"

"Yes," Ashley admitted, her heart beating faster as she raised herself onto one elbow and pushed her bangs back out of her face. "Livie? Did you—is everything all right—what—?"

"You're an aunt again," Olivia said, choking up again. "Twice over."

Ashley blinked. Swallowed hard. "Twice over? Livie, you had *twins?*"

"Both boys," Olivia answered, in a proud whisper. "And before you ask, they're fine, Ash. So am I." There was a pause, then a giggle. "I'm not too sure about Tanner, though. He's only been through this once before, and Sophie didn't bring along a sidekick when she came into the world."

Ashley's eyes burned, and her throat went thick with joy. "Oh, Livie," she murmured. "This is wonderful! Have you told Melissa and Brad?"

"I was hoping you'd do that for me," Olivia answered. "I've been working hard since five this morning, and I could use a nap before visiting hours roll around."

First instinct: Throw on whatever clothes came to hand, jump in the car and head straight for the hospital, visiting hours be damned. Ashley wanted a look at her twin nephews, wanted to see for herself that Olivia really was okay.

In the next instant, she remembered Jack.

She couldn't leave a sick guest alone, which meant she'd have to rustle up someone to keep an eye on him before she could visit Olivia and the babies.

"You're in Flagstaff, right?" she asked, sitting up now.

"Good heavens, no," Olivia replied, with another laugh. "We didn't make it that far—I went into labor at three-thirty this morning. I'm at the clinic over in Indian Rock—thanks to the McKettricks, they're equipped with incubators and just about everything else a new baby could possibly need."

"Indian Rock?" Ashley echoed, still a little groggy. Forty miles from Stone Creek, Meg's hometown was barely closer than Flagstaff, and lay in the opposite direction.

"I'll explain later, Ash," Olivia said. "Right now, I'm beat. You'll call Brad and Melissa?"

"Right away," Ashley promised. Happiness for her sister and brother-in-law welled up into her throat, a peculiar combination of pain and pleasure. "Just one more thing—have you named the babies?"

"Not yet. We'll probably call one John Mitchell, for Big John and Dad, and the other Sam. Even though Tanner and I knew we were having two babies—our secret—we need to give it some thought."

Practically every generation of the O'Ballivan family boasted at least one Sam, all the way back to the founder of Stone Creek Ranch. For all her delight over the twins' birth, Ashley felt a little pang. She'd always planned to name her own son Sam.

Not that she was in any danger of having children.

"C-Congratulations, Livie. Hug Tanner for me, too."

"Consider it done," Olivia said.

Goodbyes were said, and Ashley had to try three times before she managed to hang up the receiver.

After drawing a few deep breaths and wiping away *mostly* happy tears, Ashley regained her composure, remembered that she'd promised to pass the news along to the rest of her family.

Brad answered the telephone out at the ranch, sounding wide-awake. The sun couldn't have been up for long, but by then, he'd probably fed all the dogs, horses and cattle on the place and started breakfast for Meg, Carly, Mac and himself. "That's great," he said, once Ashley had assured him that both Olivia and the babies were doing well. "But what are they doing in Indian Rock?"

"Olivia said she'd explain later," Ashley answered.

The next call she placed was to her own twin, Melissa, who lived on the other side of town. A lawyer and an absolute genius with money, Melissa owned the spacious two-family home, renting out one side and thereby making the mortgage payment without touching her salary.

A man answered, and the voice wasn't familiar.

A little alarmed—reruns of *City Confidential* and *Forensic Files* were Ashley's secret addiction—she sat up a little straighter and asked, "Is this 555-2293?"

"I think so," he said. "Melissa?"

Melissa came on the line, sounding breathless. "Olivia?"

"Your *other* sister," Ashley said. "Livie asked me to call you. The babies were born this morning—"

"Babies?" Melissa interrupted. "Plural?"

"Twins," Ashley answered.

"Nobody said anything about twins!" Being something of a control freak, Melissa didn't like surprises—even good ones.

Ashley smiled. "They do run in the family, you know," she reminded her sister. "And apparently Tanner and Olivia wanted to surprise us. She says all is well, and she's going to catch some sleep before visiting hours."

"Boys? Girls? One of each?" Melissa asked, rapid-fire.

"Both boys," Ashley said. "No for-sure names yet. And who is that man who just answered your phone?"

"Later," Melissa said, lowering her voice.

Ashley's imagination spiked again. "Just tell me you're all right," she said. "That some stranger isn't forcing you to pretend—"

"Oh, for Pete's sake," Melissa broke in, sounding almost snappish. She'd been worried about Olivia, too, Ashley reasoned, calming down a little, but still unsettled. "I'm not bound with duct tape and being held captive in a closet. You're watching too much crime-TV again."

"Say the code word," Ashley said, just to be absolutely sure Melissa was safe.

"You are so paranoid," Melissa griped. Ashley could just see her, pushing back her hair, which fell to her shoulders in dark, gleaming spirals, picture her eyes flashing with irritation.

"Say it, and I'll leave you alone."

Melissa sighed. "Buttercup," she said.

Ashley smiled. After a rash of child abductions when they were small, Big John had helped them choose the secret word and instructed them never to reveal it to anyone outside the family. Ashley never had, and she was sure Melissa hadn't, either.

They'd liked the idea of speaking in code—their version of the twin-language phenomenon, Ashley supposed. Between the ages of three and seven, they'd driven everyone crazy, chattering away in a dialect made up of otherwise ordinary words and phrases.

If Melissa had said, "I plan to spend the afternoon sewing," for instance, Ashley would have called out the National Guard. Ashley's signal, considerably less autobiographical, was, "I saw three crows sitting on the mailbox this morning."

"Are you satisfied?" Melissa asked.

"Are you PMS-ing?" Ashley countered.

"I wish," Melissa said.

Before Ashley could ask what she'd meant by that, Melissa hung up.

"She's PMS-ing," Ashley told Mrs. Wiggins, who was curling around her ankles and mewing, probably ready for her kitty kibble.

Hastily, Ashley took a shower, donned trim black woolen slacks and an ice-blue silk blouse, brushed and braided her hair, and went out into the hallway.

Jack's door was closed—she was sure she'd left it open a crack the night before, in case he called out— so she rapped lightly with her knuckles.

"In," he responded.

Ashley rolled her eyes and opened the door to peek inside the room. Jack was sitting on the edge of the bed, his back very straight. He needed a shave, and his eyes were clear when he turned his head to look at her.

"You're better," she said, surprised.

He gave a slanted grin. "Sorry to disappoint you."

Ashley felt her temper surge, but she wasn't about to give Jack McCall the satisfaction of getting under her skin. Not today, when she'd just learned that she had twin nephews. "Are you hungry?"

"Yeah," he said. "Bacon and eggs would be good."

Ashley raised one eyebrow. He'd barely managed chicken soup the night before, and now he wanted a trucker's breakfast? "You'll make yourself sick," she told him, hiking her chin up a notch.

"I'm already sick," he pointed out. "And I still want bacon and eggs."

"Well," Ashley said, "there aren't any. I usually have grapefruit or granola."

"You serve paying guests *health food?*"

Ashley sucked in a breath, let it out slowly. She wasn't about to admit, not to Jack McCall, at least, that she hadn't had a guest, paying or otherwise, in way too long. "Some people," she told him carefully, "care about good nutrition."

"And some people want bacon and eggs."

She sighed. "Oh, for heaven's sake."

"It's the least you can do," Jack wheedled, "since I'm paying triple for this room and the breakfast that's supposed to come with the bed."

"All right," she said. "But I'll have to go to the store, and that means *you'll* have to wait."

"Fine by me," Jack replied lightly, extending his feet and wriggling his toes, his expression curious, as though he wasn't sure they still worked. "I'll be right here." The wicked grin flashed again. "Get a move on, will you? I need to get my strength back."

Ashley shut the door hard, drew another deep breath in the hallway, and started downstairs, careful not to trip over the gamboling Mrs. Wiggins.

Reaching the kitchen, she poured kibble for the kitten, cleaned and refilled the tiny water bowl, and gathered her coat, purse and car keys.

"I'll be back in a few minutes," she told the cat.

The temperature had dropped below freezing during the night, and the roads were sheeted in ice. Ashley's trip to the supermarket took nearly forty-five minutes, the store was jammed, and by the time she got home, she was in a skillet-banging mood. She was an innkeeper, not a nurse. Why hadn't she insisted that Tanner and Jeff take Jack to one of the hospitals in Flagstaff?

She built a fire on the kitchen hearth, hoping to cheer herself up a little—and take the chill out of her bones—then started a pot of coffee brewing. Next, she laid four strips of bacon in the seasoned cast-iron frying pan that had been Big John's, tossed a couple of slices of bread into the toaster slots, and took a carton of eggs out of her canvas grocery bag.

She knew how Jack liked his eggs—over easy—just as she knew he took his coffee black and strong. It galled her plenty that she remembered those details—and a lot more.

Cooking angrily—so much for her motto that every recipe ought to be laced with love—Ashley nearly jumped out of her skin when she heard his voice behind her.

"Nice fire," he said. "Very cozy."

She whirled, openmouthed, and there he was, standing in the kitchen doorway, but leaning heavily on the jamb.

"What are you doing out of bed?" she asked, once the adrenaline rush had subsided.

Slowly, he made his way to the table, dragged back a chair and dropped into the seat. "I couldn't take that wallpaper for another second," he teased. "Too damn many roses and ribbons."

Knowing that wallpaper was a stupid thing to be sensitive about, and sensitive just the same, Ashley opened a cupboard, took down a mug and filled it, even though the coffeemaker was still chortling through the brewing process. Set the mug down in front of him with a thump.

"Surely you're not *that* touchy about your décor," Jack said.

"Shut up," Ashley told him.

His eyes twinkled. "Do you talk to all your guests that way?"

As so often happened around Jack, Ashley spoke without thinking first. "Only the ones who sneaked out of my bed in the middle of the night and disappeared for six months without a word."

Jack frowned. "Have there been a lot of those?"

Jack McCall was the first—and only—man Ashley had ever slept with, but she'd be damned if she'd tell him so. After all, she realized, he hadn't just broken her heart once—he'd done it *twice*. She'd been shy in high school, but the day she and Jack met, in her freshman year of college at the University of Arizona, her world had undergone a seismic shift.

They talked about getting married after Ashley finished school, had even looked at engagement rings. Jack had been a senior, and after graduation, he'd enlisted in the Navy. After a few letters and phone calls, he'd simply dropped out of her life.

She'd gotten her BA in liberal arts.

Melissa had gone on to law school, Ashley had returned to Stone Creek, bought the B&B with Brad's help and tried to convince herself that she was happy.

Then, just before Christmas, two years earlier, Jack had returned. She'd been a first-class fool to get involved with him a second time, to believe it would last. He came and went, called often when he was away, showed up again and made soul-wrenching love to her just when she'd made up her mind to end the affair.

"I haven't been hibernating, you know," she said

stiffly, turning the bacon, pushing down the lever on the toaster and sliding his perfectly cooked eggs off the burner. "I date."

Right. Melissa had fixed her up twice, with guys she knew from law school, and she'd gone out to dinner once, with Melvin Royce, whose father owned the Stone Creek Funeral Home. Melvin had spent the whole evening telling her that death was a beautiful thing—not to mention lucrative—cremation was the way to go, and corpses weren't at all scary, once you got used to them.

She hadn't gone out with anyone since.

Oh, yes, she was a regular party girl. If she didn't watch out, she'd end up as tabloid fodder.

Not. The tabloids were Brad's territory, and he was welcome to them, as far as she was concerned.

"I'm sorry, Ashley," Jack said quietly, when they'd both been silent for a long time. She couldn't help noticing that his hand shook slightly as he took a sip of his coffee and set the mug down again.

"For what?"

"For everything." He thrust splayed fingers through his hair, and his jaw tightened briefly, under the blue-black stubble of his beard.

"Everything? That covers a lot of ground," Ashley said, sliding his breakfast onto a plate and setting it down in front of him with an annoyed flourish.

Jack sighed. "Leaving you. It was a dumb thing to do. But maybe coming back is even dumber."

The remark stung Ashley, made her cheeks burn, and she turned away quickly, hoping Jack hadn't noticed. "You arrived in an ambulance," she said. "Feel free to leave in one."

"Will you sit down and talk to me? Please?"

Ashley faced him, lest she be thought a coward.

Mrs. Wiggins, the little traitor, started up Jack's right pant leg and settled in his lap for a snooze. He picked up his fork, broke the yolk on one of his eggs, but his eyes were fastened on Ashley.

"What happened to you?" Ashley asked, without planning to speak at all. There it was again, the Jack Phenomenon. She wasn't normally an impulsive person.

Jack didn't look away, but several long moments passed before he answered. "The theory is," he said, "that a guy I tangled with on a job injected me with something."

Ashley's heart stopped, started again. She joined Jack at the table, but only because she was afraid her knees wouldn't support her if she remained standing. "A job? What kind of job?"

"You know I'm in security," Jack hedged, avoiding her eyes now, concentrating on his breakfast. He ate slowly, deliberately.

"Security," Ashley repeated. All she really knew about Jack was that he traveled, made a lot of money and was often in danger. These were not things he'd actually told her—she'd gleaned them from telephone conversations she'd overheard, stories Sophie and Olivia had told her, comments Tanner had made.

"I've got to leave again, Ashley," Jack said. "But this time, I want you to know why."

She *wanted* Jack to leave. So why did she feel as though a trapdoor had just opened under her chair, and she was about to fall down the rabbit hole? "Okay—why?" she asked, in somebody else's voice.

"Because I've got enemies. Most of them are in prison—or dead—but one has a red-hot grudge against me, a score to settle, and I don't want you or anybody else in Stone Creek to get hurt. I should have thought things through before I came here, but the truth is, all I could focus on was being where you are."

The words made her ache. Ashley longed to take Jack's hand, but she wouldn't let herself do it. "What kind of grudge?"

"I stole his daughter."

Ashley's mouth dropped open. She closed it again.

Jack gave a mirthless little smile. "Her name is Rachel. She's seven years old. Her mother went through a rebellious period that just happened to coincide with a semester in a university in Venezuela. She fell in with a bad crowd, got involved with a fellow exchange student— an American named Chad Lombard, who was running drugs between classes. Her parents ran a background check on Lombard, didn't like the results and flew down from Phoenix to take their daughter home. Ardith was pregnant—the folks wanted her to give the baby up and she refused. She was nineteen, sure she was in love with Lombard, waited for him to come and get her, put a wedding band on her finger. He didn't. Eventually, she finished school, married well, had two more kids. The new husband wanted to adopt Rachel, and that meant Lombard had to sign off, so the family lawyers tracked him down and presented him with the papers and the offer of a hefty check. He went ballistic, said he wanted to raise Rachel himself, and generously offered to take Ardith back, too, if she'd leave the other two kids behind and divorce the man she'd married. Naturally, she didn't want to go that route. Things were quiet for a while, and then one day Rachel disappeared from her backyard. Lombard called that night to say Phoenix P.D. was wasting its time looking for Rachel, since he had the child and they were already out of the country."

Although Ashley had never been a mother herself, it was all too easy to understand how frantic Ardith and the family must have been.

"And they hired you to find Rachel and bring her home?"

"Yes," Jack answered, after another long delay. The long speech had clearly taken a lot out of him, but the amazed admiration she felt must have been visible in her eyes, because he added, "But don't get the idea that I'm some kind of hero. I was paid a quarter of a million dollars for bringing Rachel back home safely, and I didn't hesitate to accept the money."

"I didn't see any of this in the newspapers," Ashley mused.

"You wouldn't have," Jack replied. He'd finished half of his breakfast, and although he had a little more color than before, he was still too pale. "It was vital to keep the story out of the press. Rachel's life might have depended on it, and mine definitely did."

"Weren't you scared?"

"Hell," Jack answered, "I was terrified."

"You should lie down," she said softly.

"I don't think I can make it back up those stairs," Jack said, and Ashley could see that it pained him to admit this.

"You're just trying to avoid the wallpaper," she joked, though she was dangerously close to tears. Carefully, she helped him to his feet. "There's a bed in my sewing room. You can rest there until you feel stronger."

His face contorted, but he still managed a grin. "You're strong for a woman," he said.

"I was raised on a ranch," Ashley reminded him, ducking under his right shoulder and supporting him as she steered him across the kitchen to her sewing room. "I used to help load hay bales in our field during harvest, among other things."

Jack glanced down at her face, and she thought she saw a glimmer of respect in his eyes. "*You* bucked bales?"

"Sure did." They'd reached the sewing room door, and Ashley reached out to push it open. "Did you?"

"Are you kidding?" Jack's chuckle was ragged. "My dad is a dentist. I was raised in the suburbs—not a hay bale for miles."

Like the account of little Rachel's rescue, this was news to Ashley. She knew nothing about Jack's background, wondered how she could have fallen so hard for a man who'd never mentioned his family, let alone introduced her to them. In fact, she'd assumed he didn't *have* a family.

"Exactly what *is* your job title, anyway?"

He looked at her long and hard, wavering just a few feet from the narrow bed. "Mercenary," he said.

Ashley took that in, but it didn't really register, even after the Rachel story. "Is that what it says on your tax return, under *Occupation?*"

"No," he answered.

They reached the bed, and she helped him get settled. Since he was on top of the blankets, she covered him with a faded quilt that had been passed down through the O'Ballivan clan since the days when Maddie and Sam ran the ranch.

"You do file taxes, don't you?" Ashley was a very careful and practical person.

Jack smiled without opening his eyes. "Yeah," he said. "What I do is unconventional, but it isn't illegal."

Ashley stepped back, torn between bolting from the room and lying down beside Jack, enfolding him in her arms. "Is there anything I can get you?"

"My gear," he said, his eyes still closed. "Tanner brought it in. Leather satchel, under the bed upstairs."

Ashley gave a little nod, even though he wouldn't see it. What kind of *gear* did a mercenary carry? Guns? Knives?

She gave a little shudder and left the door slightly ajar.

Upstairs, she found the leather bag under Jack's bed. The temptation to open it was nearly overwhelming, but she resisted. Yes, she was curious—*beyond* curious—but she wasn't a snoop. She didn't go through guests' luggage any more than she read the postcards they gave her to send for them.

When she got back to the sewing room, Jack was sleeping. Mrs. Wiggins curled up protectively on his chest.

Ashley set the bag down quietly and slipped out. Busied herself with routine housekeeping chores, too soon finished.

She was relieved when Tanner showed up at the kitchen door, looking worn out but blissfully happy.

"I came to babysit Jack while you go and see Olivia and the boys," he said, stepping past her and helping himself to a cup of lukewarm coffee. "How's he doing?"

Ashley watched as her brother-in-law stuck the mug

into the microwave and pushed the appropriate buttons. "Not bad—for a mercenary."

Tanner paused, and his gaze swung in Ashley's direction. "He told you?"

"Yes. I need some answers, Tanner, and Jack is too sick to give them."

The new father turned away from the counter, the microwave whirring behind him, leaned back and folded his arms, watching Ashley, probably weighing the pros and cons of spilling what he knew—which was plenty, unless she missed her guess.

"He's talking about leaving," Ashley prodded, when Tanner didn't say anything right away. "I'm used to that, but I think I deserve to know what's going on."

Tanner gave a long sigh. "I'd trust Jack with my life—I trusted him with *Sophie's*, when she ran away from boarding school right after we moved here, but the truth is, I don't know a hell of a lot more about him than you do."

"He's your best friend."

"And he plays his cards close to the vest. When it comes to security, he's the best there is." Tanner paused, thrust a hand through his already mussed hair. "I can tell you this much, Ashley—if he said he loved you, he meant it, whatever happened afterward. He's never been married, doesn't have kids, his dad is a dentist, his mother is a librarian, and he has three younger brothers, all of whom are much more conventional than Jack. He likes beer, but I've never seen him drunk. That's the whole shebang, I'm afraid."

"Someone injected him with something," Ashley said in a low voice. "That's why he's sick."

"Good God," Tanner said.

A silence fell.

"And he's leaving as soon as he's strong enough," Ashley said. "Because some drug dealer named Chad Lombard has a grudge against him, and he's afraid of putting all of us in danger."

Tanner thought long and hard. "Maybe that's for the best," he finally replied. Ashley knew Tanner wasn't afraid for himself, but he had to think about Olivia and Sophie and his infant sons. "I hate it, though. Turning my back on a friend who needs my help."

Ashley felt the same way, though Jack wasn't exactly a friend. In fact, she wasn't sure how to describe their relationship—if they had one at all. "This is Stone Creek," she heard herself say. "We have a long tradition of standing shoulder to shoulder and taking trouble as it comes."

Tanner's smile was tired, but warm. "Go," he said. "Tuckered out as she is, Olivia is dying to show off those babies. I'll look after Jack until you get home."

Ashley hesitated, then got her coat and purse and car keys again, and left for the clinic in Indian Rock.

Chapter 4

Olivia was sitting up in bed, beaming, a baby tucked in the crook of each arm, when Ashley hurried into her room. There were flowers everywhere—Brad and Meg had already been there and gone, having brought Carly and Sophie to see the boys before school.

"Come and say hello to John and Sam," Olivia said gently.

Ashley, clutching a bouquet of pink and yellow carnations, hastily purchased at a convenience store, moved closer. She felt stricken with wonder and an immediate and all-encompassing love for the tiny red-faced infants snoozing in their swaddling blankets.

"Oh, Livie," she whispered, "they're beautiful."

"I agree," Olivia said proudly. "Do you want to hold them?"

Ashley swallowed, then reached out for the bundle

on the right. She sat down slowly in the chair closest to Olivia's bed.

"That's John," Olivia explained, her voice soft with adoring exhaustion.

"How can you tell?" Ashley asked, without lifting her eyes from the baby's face. He seemed to glow with some internal light, as though he were trailing traces of heaven, the place he'd so recently left.

Livie chuckled. "The twins aren't identical, Ashley," she said. "John is a little smaller than Sam, and he has my mouth. Sam looks like Tanner."

Ashley didn't respond; she was too smitten with young John Mitchell Quinn. By the time she swapped one baby for the other, she could tell the difference between them.

A nurse came and collected the babies, put them back in their incubators. Although they were healthy, like most twins they were underweight. They'd be staying at the clinic for a few days after Olivia went home.

Olivia napped, woke up, napped again.

"I'm so glad you're here," she said once.

Ashley, who had been rising from her chair to leave, sat down again. Remembered the carnations and got up to put them in a water-glass vase.

"How did you wind up in Indian Rock instead of Flagstaff?" Ashley asked, when Olivia didn't immediately drift off.

Olivia smiled. "I was on a call," she said. "Sick horse. Tanner wanted me to call in another vet, but this was a special case, and Sophie was spending the night at Brad and Meg's, so he came with me. We planned to go on to Flagstaff for the induction when I was finished, but the babies had other ideas. I went into labor in the barn, and Tanner brought me here."

Ashley shook her head, unable to hold back a grin. Her sister, nine and a half months pregnant by her own admission, had gone out on a call in the middle of the night. It was just like her. "How's the horse?"

"Fine, of course," Olivia said, still smiling. "I'm the best vet in the county, you know."

Ashley found a place for the carnations—they looked pitiful among all the dozens and dozens of roses, yellow from Brad and Meg, white from Tanner, and more arriving at regular intervals from friends and coworkers. "I know," she agreed.

Olivia reached for her hand, squeezed. "Friends again?"

"We were never *not* friends, Livie."

Olivia shook her head. Like all O'Ballivans, she was stubborn. "We were always *sisters*," she said. "But sisters aren't necessarily friends. Let's not let the mom-thing come between us again, okay?"

Ashley blinked away tears. "Okay," she said.

Just then, Melissa streaked into the room, half-hidden behind a giant potted plant with two blue plastic storks sticking out of it. She was dressed for work, in a tailored brown leather jacket, beige turtleneck and tweed trousers.

Setting the plant down on the floor, when she couldn't find any other surface, Melissa hurried over to Olivia and kissed her noisily on the forehead.

"Hi, Twin-Unit," she said to Ashley.

"Hi." Ashley smiled, glanced toward the doorway in case the mystery man had come along for the ride. Alas, there was no sign of him.

Melissa looked around for the babies. Frowned. She did everything fast, with an economy of motion; she'd come to see her nephews and was impatient at the delay. "Where are they?"

"In the nursery," Olivia answered, smiling. "How many cups of coffee have you had this morning?"

Melissa made a comical face. "Not nearly enough," she said. "I'm due in court in an hour, and where's the nursery?"

"Down the hall, to the right," Olivia told her. A worried crease appeared in her otherwise smooth forehead. "The roads are icy. Promise me you won't speed all the way back to Stone Creek after you leave here."

"Scout's honor," Melissa said, raising one hand. But she couldn't help glancing at her watch. "Yikes. Down the hall, to the right. Gotta go."

With that, she dashed out.

Ashley followed, double-stepping to catch up.

"Who was the man who answered your phone this morning?" she asked.

Melissa didn't look at her. "Nobody important," she said.

"You spent the night with him, and he's 'nobody important'?"

They'd reached the nursery window, and since Sam and John were the only babies there, spotting them was no problem.

"Could we not discuss this now?" Melissa asked, pressing both palms to the glass separating them from their nephews. "Why are they in incubators? Is something wrong?"

"It's just a precaution," Ashley answered gently. "They're a little small."

"Aren't babies *supposed* to be small?" Melissa's eyes were tender as she studied the new additions to the family. When she turned to face Ashley, though, her expression turned bleak.

"He's my boss," she said.

Ashley took a breath before responding. "The one who divorced his latest trophy wife about fifteen minutes ago?"

Melissa stiffened. "I knew you'd react that way. Honestly, Ash, sometimes you are such a prig. The marriage was over years ago—they were just going through the motions. And if you think I had anything to do with the breakup—well, you ought to know better."

Ashley closed her eyes briefly. She *did* know better. Her twin was an honorable person; nobody knew that better than she did. "I wasn't implying that you're a home-wrecker, Melissa. It's just that you're not over Daniel yet. You need time."

Daniel Guthrie, the last man in Melissa's life, owned and operated a fashionably rustic dude ranch between Stone Creek and Flagstaff. An attractive widower with two young sons, Dan was looking for a wife, someone to settle down with, and he'd never made a secret of it. Melissa, who freely admitted that she *could* love Dan and his children if she half tried, wanted a career—after all, she'd worked hard to earn her law degree.

It was a classic lose-lose situation.

"I didn't have sex with Alex," Melissa whispered, though Ashley hadn't asked. "We were just *talking.*"

"I believe you," Ashley said, putting up both hands in a gesture of peace. "But Stone Creek is a small town. If some bozo's car was parked in your driveway all night, word is bound to get back to Dan."

"Dan has no claim on me," Melissa snapped. "*He's* the one who said we needed a time-out." She sucked in a furious breath. "And Alex Ewing is *not* a bozo. He's up for the prosecutor's job in Phoenix, and he wants me to go with him if he gets it."

Ashley blinked. "You would move to—to Phoenix?"

Melissa widened her eyes. "Phoenix isn't Mars, Ashley," she pointed out. "It's less than two hours from here. And just because you're content to quietly fade away in Stone Creek, quilting and baking cookies for visiting strangers, that doesn't mean *I* am."

"But—this is home."

Melissa looked at her watch again, shook her head. "Yeah," she said. "That's the problem."

With that, she walked off, leaving Ashley staring after her.

I am not *"content to quietly fade away in Stone Creek,"* she thought.

But wasn't that exactly what she was doing?

Making beds, cooking for guests, putting up decorations for various holidays only to take them down again? And, yes, quilting. That was her passion, her artistic outlet. Nothing wrong with that.

But Melissa's remarks *had* brought up the question Ashley usually avoided.

When was her *life* supposed to start?

Jack woke with a violent start, expecting darkness and nibbling rats.

Instead, he found himself in a small, pretty room with pale green walls. An old-fashioned sewing machine, the treadle kind usually seen only in antiques malls and elderly ladies' houses stood near the door. The quilt covering him smelled faintly of some herb—probably lavender—and memories.

Ashley.

He was at her place.

Relief flooded him—and then he heard the sound. Distant—a heavy step—definitely *not* Ashley's.

Leaning over the side of the bed, which must have been built for a child, it was so short and so narrow, Jack found his gear, fumbled to open the bag, extracted his trusty Glock, that marvel of German engineering. Checked to make sure the clip was in—and full.

The mattress squeaked a little as he got to his feet, listening not just with his ears, but with every cell, with all the dormant senses he'd learned to tap into, if not to name.

There it was again—that thump. Closer now. Definitely masculine.

Jack glanced back over one shoulder, saw that the kitten was still on the bed, watching him with curious, mismatched eyes.

"Shhh," he told the animal.

"Meooow," it responded.

The sound came a third time, nearer now. Just on the other side of the kitchen doorway, by Jack's calculations.

Think, he told himself. He knew he was reacting out of all proportion to the situation, but he couldn't help it. He'd had a lot of practice at staying alive, and his survival instincts were in overdrive.

Chad Lombard couldn't have tracked him to Stone Creek; there hadn't been time. But Jack was living and breathing because he lived by his gut as well as his mind. The small hairs on his nape stood up like wire.

Using one foot, the Glock clasped in both hands, he eased the sewing room door open by a few more inches.

Waited.

And damn near shot the best friend he'd ever had when Tanner Quinn strolled into the kitchen.

"Christ," Jack said, lowering the gun. With his long outgoing breath, every muscle in his body seemed to go slack.

Tanner's face was hard. "That was my line," he said.

Jack sagged against the doorframe, his eyes tightly shut. He forced himself to open them again. "What the hell are you doing here?"

"Playing nursemaid to you," Tanner answered, crossing the room in a few strides and expertly removing the Glock dangling from Jack's right hand. "Guess I should have stuck with my day job."

Jack opened his eyes, sick with relief, sick with whatever that goon in South America had shot into his veins. "Which is what?" he asked, in an attempt to lighten the mood.

Tanner set the gun on top of the refrigerator and pulled Jack by the arm. Squired him to a chair at the kitchen table.

"Raising three kids and being a husband to the best woman in the world," he answered. "And if it's all the same to you, I'd like to stick around long enough to see my grandchildren."

Jack braced an elbow on the tabletop, covered his face with one hand. "I'm sorry," he said.

Tanner hauled back a chair of his own, making plenty of noise in the process, and sat down across from Jack, ignoring the apology. "What's going on, McCall?" he demanded. "And don't give me any of your bull crap cloak-and-dagger answers, either."

"I need to get out of here," Jack said, meeting his friend's gaze. "Now. Today. Before somebody gets hurt."

Tanner flung a scathing glance toward the Glock, gleaming on top of the brushed-steel refrigerator. "Seems to me, *you're* the main threat to public safety around here. Dammit, you could have shot Ashley—or Sophie or Carly—"

"I said I was sorry."

"Oh, well, that changes everything."

Jack sighed. And then he told Tanner the same story he'd told Ashley earlier. Most of it was even true.

"You call this living, Jack?" Tanner asked, when he was finished. "When are you going to stop playing Indiana Jones and settle down?"

"Spoken like a man in love with a pregnant veterinarian," Jack said.

At last, Tanner broke down and grinned. "She's not pregnant anymore. Olivia and I are now the proud parents of twin boys."

"As of when?" Jack asked, delighted and just a shade envious. He'd never thought much about kids until he'd gotten to know Sophie, after Tanner's first wife, Katherine, was killed, and then Rachel, the bravest seven-year-old in Creation.

"As of this morning," Tanner answered.

"Wow," Jack said, with a shake of his head. "It would *really* have sucked if I'd shot you."

"Yeah," Tanner agreed, going grim again.

"All the more reason for me to hit the road."

"And go where?"

"Dammit, I don't know. Just away. I shouldn't have

come here in the first place—I was out of my mind with fever—"

"You were out of your mind, all right," Tanner argued. "But I think it has more to do with Ashley than the toxin. There's a pattern here, old buddy. You always leave—and you always come back. That ought to tell you something."

"It tells me that I'm a jerk."

"You won't get any argument there," Tanner said, without hesitation.

"I can't keep doing this. Every time I've left that woman, I've meant to stay gone. But Ashley haunts me, Tanner. She's in the air I breathe and the water I drink—"

"It's called *love,* you idiot," Tanner informed him.

"Love," Jack scoffed. "This isn't the Lifetime channel, old buddy. And it's not as if I'm doing Ashley some big, fat favor by loving her. My kind of romance could get her *killed.*"

Tanner's mouth crooked up at one corner. "You watch the *Lifetime channel?*"

"Shut up," Jack bit out.

Tanner laughed. "You are so screwed," he said.

"Maybe," Jack snapped. "But you're not being much help here, in case you haven't noticed."

"It's time to stop running," Tanner said decisively. "Take a stand."

"Suppose Lombard shows up? He'd like nothing better than to take out everybody I care about."

Tanner's expression turned serious again, and both his eyebrows went up. "What about your dad, the dentist, and your mom, the librarian, and your three brothers, who probably have the misfortune to look just like you?"

Something tightened inside Jack, a wrenching grab, cold as steel. "Why do you think I haven't seen them since I got out of high school?" he shot back. "Nobody knows I *have* a family, and I want it to stay that way."

Tanner leaned forward a little. "Which means your name isn't Jack McCall," he said. "Who the hell are you, anyway?"

"Dammit, you *know* who I am. We've been through a lot together."

"Do I? Jack is probably your real first name, but I'll bet it doesn't say *McCall* on your birth certificate."

"My birth certificate conveniently disappeared into cyberspace a long time ago," Jack said. "And if you think I'm going to tell you my last name, so you can tap into a search engine and get the goods on me, you're a bigger sucker than I ever guessed."

Tanner frowned. He loved puzzles, and he was exceptionally good at figuring them out. "Wait a second. You and Ashley dated in college, and she knew you as Jack McCall. Did you change your name in high school?"

"Let this go, Tanner," Jack answered tightly. He had to give his friend something, or he'd never get off his back—that much was clear. And while they were sitting there planning his segment on *Biography,* Chad Lombard was looking for him. By that scumbag's watch, it was payback time. "I was one of those difficult types in high school—my folks, with some help from a judge, sent me to one of those military schools where they try to scare kids into behaving like human beings. One of the teachers was a former SEAL. Long story short, the Navy tapped me for their version of Special Forces and put me through college. I never went home, after that, and the name change was their idea, not mine."

Tanner let out a long, low whistle. "Hot damn," he muttered. "Your folks must be frantic, wondering what happened to you."

"They think I'm dead," Jack said, stunned at how much he was giving up. That toxin must be digesting his brain. "There's a grave and a headstone; they put flowers on it once in a while. As far as they're concerned, I was blown to unidentifiable smithereens in Iraq."

Tanner glared at him. "How could you put them through that?"

"Ask the Navy," Jack said.

Outside, snow crunched under tires as Ashley pulled into the driveway.

"End of conversation," Jack told Tanner.

"That's what *you* think," Tanner replied, pushing back his chair to stand.

"I'll be out of here as soon as I can arrange it," Jack warned quietly.

Tanner skewered him with a look that might have meant "Good riddance," though Jack couldn't be sure.

The back door opened, and Ashley blew in on a freezing wind. Hurrying to Tanner, she threw her arms around his waist and beamed up at him.

"The babies are *beautiful!*" she cried, her eyes glistening with happy tears. "Congratulations, Tanner."

Tanner hugged her, kissed the top of her head. "Thanks," he said gruffly. Then, with one more scathing glance at Jack, he put on his coat and left, though not before his gaze strayed to the Glock on top of the refrigerator.

Fortunately, Ashley was too busy taking off her own coat to notice.

Jack made a mental note to retrieve the weapon before she saw it.

"You're up," she told him cheerfully. "Feeling better?"

He'd never left her willingly, but this time, the prospect nearly doubled him over. He sat up a little straighter. "I love you, Ashley," he said.

She'd been in the process of brewing coffee; at his words, she stopped, stiffened, stared at him. "What did you say?"

"I love you. Always have, always will."

She sagged against the counter, all the joy gone from her eyes. "You have a strange way of showing it, Jack McCall," she said, after a very long time.

"I can't stay, Ash," he said hoarsely, wishing he could take her into his arms, make love to her just once more. But he'd done enough damage as it was. "And this time, I won't be back. I promise."

"Is that supposed to make me feel better?"

"It would if you knew what it might mean if I stayed."

"What would it mean, Jack? If you stayed, that is."

"I told you about Lombard. He's the vindictive type, and if he ever finds out about you—"

"Suppose he does," Ashley reasoned calmly, "and you're not here to protect me. What then?"

Jack closed his eyes. "Don't say that."

"Stone Creek isn't a bad place to raise a family," she forged on, with a dignity that broke Jack's heart into two bleeding chunks. "We could be happy here, Jack. Together."

He got to his feet. "Are you saying you love me?"

"Always have," she answered, "always will."

"It wouldn't work," Jack said, wishing he hadn't been such a hooligan back in his teens. None of this would be happening if he hadn't ended up in military school and shown a distinct talent for covert action. He'd probably be a dentist in the Midwest, with a wife and kids and a dog, and his parents and his brothers would be dropping by for Sunday afternoon barbecues instead of visiting an empty grave.

"Wouldn't it?" Ashley challenged. "Make love to me, Jack. And then tell me it wouldn't work."

The temptation burned in his veins and hardened his groin until it hurt. "Ashley, don't."

She began to unbutton her blue silk blouse.

"Ashley."

"What's the matter, Jack? Are you chicken?"

"Ashley, *stop* it." It wasn't a command, it was a plea. "I'm not who you think I am. My name isn't Jack McCall, and I—"

Her blouse was open. Her lush breasts pushed against the lacy pink fabric of her bra. He could see the dark outline of her nipples.

"I don't care what your name is," she said. "I love you. You love me. Whoever you are, take me to bed, unless you want to have me on the kitchen floor."

He couldn't resist her any more than he'd been able to resist coming back every time he left. She was an addiction.

He held out his hand, and she came to him.

Somehow, they managed to get up the stairs, along the hallway, into her bedroom.

He didn't remember undressing her, or undressing himself.

It was as though their clothes had burned away in the heat.

Even a few minutes before, Jack wouldn't have believed he had the strength for sex, but the drive was deep, elemental, as much a part of him as Ashley herself.

There was no foreplay—their need for each other was too great.

The two of them fell sideways onto her bed, kissing as frantically as half-drowned swimmers trying to breathe, their arms and legs entwined.

He took her in one hard stroke, and found her ready for him.

She came instantly, shouting his name, clawing at his back with her fingernails. He drove in deep again, and she began the climb toward another pinnacle, writhing beneath him, flinging her hips up to meet his.

"Jack," she sobbed, *"Jack!"*

He fought to keep control, wondered feverishly if he'd die from the exertion. Oh, but what a way to go.

"Jack—"

"For God's sake, Ashley, lie still—"

Of course she didn't. She went wild beneath him.

Jack gave a ragged shout and spilled himself into her. He felt her clenching around him as she erupted in an orgasm of her own, with a long, continuous cry of exultant surrender.

Afterward, they lay still for a long time, spent, gasping for breath.

Jack felt himself hardening within her, thickening.

"Say it, Jack," she said. "Say you're going to leave me. I dare you."

He couldn't; he searched for the words, but they were nowhere to be found.

So he kissed her instead.

Ashley awakened alone, at dusk, naked and soft-boned in her bed.

The aftershocks of Jack's lovemaking still thrummed

in her depths, even as panic surged within her. Damn, he'd done it again—he'd driven her out of her mind with pleasure and then left her.

She scrambled out of bed, pulled on her ratty chenille robe, and hurried downstairs.

"Jack?" She felt like a fool, calling his name when she knew he was already gone, but the cry was out of her mouth before she could stop it.

"In here," he called back.

Ashley's heart fluttered, and so did the pit of her stomach.

She followed the echo of his voice as far as the study doorway, found him sitting at her computer. The monitor threw blue shadows over the planes of his face.

"Hope you don't mind," he said. "My laptop came down with a case of jungle rot, so I trashed it somewhere in the mountains of Venezuela, and I haven't had a chance to get another one."

Ashley groped her way into the room, like someone who'd forgotten how to walk, and landed in the first available chair, a wingback she'd reupholstered herself, in pink, green and white chintz. "Make yourself at home," she said, and then blushed because the words could be taken so many ways.

His fingers flew over the keyboard, with no pause when he looked her way. "Thanks," he said.

"You've made a remarkable recovery, it seems to me," Ashley observed.

"The restorative powers of good sex," Jack said, "are legendary."

He was legendary. It had been hours since they'd made love, but Ashley still felt a deliciously orgasmic twinge every few moments.

"Answering email?" she asked, to keep the conversation going.

Jack shook his head. "I don't get email," he said. "After I booted this thing up and ran all the setups, I did a search. Noticed you didn't have a website. You can't run a business without some kind of presence on the Internet these days, Ashley—not unless you want to go broke."

"You're building a *Web site?*"

"I'm setting up a few prototypes. You can have a look later, see if you like any of them."

"You're a man of many talents, Jack McCall."

He grinned. He'd showered and shaved since leaving her bed, she noticed. And he was wearing fresh clothes—blue jeans and a white T-shirt. "I began to suspect you thought that while you were digging your heels into the small of my back and howling like a she-wolf calling down the moon."

Ashley laughed, but her cheeks burned. She *had* acted like a hussy, abandoning herself to Jack, body and soul, and she didn't regret a moment of it. "Pretty cocky, aren't you?" she said.

Jack swiveled the chair around. "Come here," he said gruffly.

Her heart did a little jig, and her breath caught. "Why?"

"Because I want you," he replied simply.

She stood up, crossed to him, allowed him to set her astraddle on his lap. Moaned as he opened her bathrobe, baring her breasts.

Jack nibbled at one of her nipples, then the other. "Ummm," he murmured, shifting in the chair. He continued to arouse delicious feelings in her breasts with his lips and tongue.

Her eyes widened when she realized he'd opened his jeans. He drew his knees a little farther apart, and she gave a crooning gasp when she felt him between her legs, hot and hard, prodding.

Just as he entered her, he leaned forward again, took her right nipple into his mouth, tongued it and then began to suckle.

Ashley choked out an ecstatic sob and threw back her head, her hair falling loose down her back. "Oh, God," she whimpered. "Oh, God, not yet—"

But her body seized, caught in a maelstrom of pleasure, spasmed wildly, and seized again. Taken over, possessed, she rode him relentlessly, recklessly, her very soul ablaze with a light that blinded her from the inside.

Jack waited until she'd gone still, the effort at restraint visible in his features, and when he let himself go, the motions of his body were slow and graceful. Ashley watched his face, spellbound, until he'd stopped moving.

He sighed, his eyes closed.

And then they flew open.

"You *are* on the pill, aren't you?" he asked.

She had been, before he left. After he was gone, there had been no reason to practice birth control.

Ashley shook her head.

"What?" Jack choked out.

Ashley closed her robe, moved to rise off his lap.

But he grasped her hips and held her firmly in place. "Ashley?" he rasped.

"No, Jack," she said evenly. "I'm not on the pill."

He swore under his breath.

"Don't worry," she told him, hiding her hurt. "I'm not going to trap you."

He was going hard inside her again—angry hard.

His eyes smoldering, his hands still holding her by the hips, he began to raise and lower her, raise and lower her, along the growing length of his shaft.

She buckled with the first orgasm, bit back a cry of response.

Jack settled back in the chair, watching her face, already driving her toward another, stronger climax.

And then another, and still another.

When his own release came, much later, he didn't utter a sound.

Chapter 5

In some ways, that last bout of lovemaking had been the most satisfying, but it left Ashley feeling peevish, just the same. When it was over, and she'd solidified her sex-weakened knees by an act of sheer will, she tugged her bathrobe closed and cinched the belt with a decisive motion.

"Good night," she told Jack, her chin high, her face hot.

"'Night," he replied. Having already refastened his jeans, he turned casually back to the computer monitor. To look at him, nobody would have guessed they'd been having soul-bending sex only a few minutes before.

"I'll need a credit card," Ashley said.

Jack slanted a look at her. "I beg your pardon?" he drawled.

Ashley's blush deepened to crimson. "Not for the sex," she said primly. "For the room."

Jack's attention was fixed on the monitor again. "My wallet's in the bag with my other gear. Help yourself."

As she stormed out, she thought she heard him chuckle. Fury zinged through her, like a charge.

Since she was no snoop, she snatched up the leather bag, resting on the sewing room floor, and marched right back to the study. Set it down on the desk with a hard thump, two inches from Jack's elbow.

He sighed, flipped the brass catch on the bag, and rummaged inside until he found his wallet. Extracted a credit card.

"Here you go, Madam," he said, holding it between two fingers.

Ashley snatched the card, unwilling to pursue the word *Madam.* "How long will you be staying?"

The question hung between them for several moments.

"Better put me down for two weeks," Jack finally said. "The food's good here, and the sex is even better."

Ashley glanced at the card. It was platinum, so it probably had a high limit, and the expiration date was three years in the future. The name, however, was wrong.

"'Mark Ramsey'?" she read aloud.

"Oops. Sorry." Jack took the card back.

"Is that your real name?"

"Of course not." Frowning with concentration, Jack thumbed through a stack of cards, more than most people carried, certainly.

"What *is* your name, then?" *Since I just had about fourteen orgasms straddling your lap, I think I have a right to know.*

"Jack McCall," he said sweetly, handing her a gold card. "Try this one."

"What name did you use when you rescued Rachel?"

"Not this one, believe me. But if a man calls here or, worse yet, comes to the door, asking for Neal Mercer, you've never heard of me."

Ashley's palms were sweaty. She sank disconsolately into the same chair she'd occupied earlier, before the lap dance. "Just how many aliases do you have, anyway?"

Jack was focused on the keyboard again. "Maybe a dozen. Are you going to run that card or not?"

Ashley leaned a little, peered at the screen. A picture of her house, in full summer regalia, filled it. Trees leafed out. Flowers blooming. Lawn greener than green and neatly mowed. She could almost smell sprinkler-dampened grass.

"Where did you get that?" she asked.

"The picture?" Jack didn't look at her. "Downloaded it from the Chamber of Commerce website. I'm setting you up to take credit cards next—the usual?"

She sighed. "Yes."

"Why the sigh?" He was watching her now.

"I have so much to learn about computers," Ashley said, after biting her lip. That was only part of what was bothering her, of course. She loved this man, and he claimed to love her in return, and she didn't even know who he was.

How crazy was that?

"It's not so hard," he told her, switching to another page on the screen, one filled with credit card logos. "I'll show you how."

"What's your name?"

He chuckled. "Rumpelstiltskin?"

"Hilarious. Do you even *remember* who you really are?"

He turned in the swivel chair, gazing directly into

her eyes. "Jack McKenzie," he said solemnly. "As if it mattered."

"Why wouldn't it matter?" Ashley asked in a whisper.

"Because Jacob 'Jack' McKenzie is dead. Buried at Arlington, with full military honors."

She stared at him, confounded.

"Get some sleep, Ashley," Jack said, and now he sounded weary.

She was too proud to ask if he planned on sharing her bed—wasn't even sure she wanted him there. Yes, she loved him, with her whole being, there was no escaping that. But they might as well have lived in separate universes; she wasn't an international spy. She was a small-town girl, the operator of a modest B&B. Intrigue wasn't in her repertoire.

Slowly, she rose from the chair. She walked into the darkened living room, flipped on a lamp and proceeded to the check-in desk. There, she ran Jack's credit card.

It went through just fine.

She returned the card to him. "There'll be a slip to sign," she said flatly, "but that can wait until morning."

Jack merely nodded.

Ashley left the study again, scooped up a mewing Mrs. Wiggins as she passed and climbed the stairs.

Jack waited until he'd heard Ashley's bedroom door close in the distance, then set up yet another email account, and brought up the message page. Typed in his mother's email address at the library.

Hi, Mom, he typed. *Just a note to say I'm not really dead...*

Delete.

He clicked to the search engine, entered the URL of the website for his dad's dental office.

There was Dr. McKenzie, in a white coat, looking like a man you'd trust your teeth to without hesitation. The old man was broad in the shoulders, with a full head of silver hair and a confident smile—Jack supposed he'd look a lot like his dad someday, if he managed to live long enough.

The average web surfer probably wouldn't have noticed the pain in Doc's eyes, but Jack did. He looked deep.

"I'm sorry, Dad," he murmured.

His cell phone, buried in the depths of his gear bag, played the opening notes of "Folsom Prison Blues."

Startled, Jack scrabbled through T-shirts and underwear until he found the cell. He didn't answer it, but squinted at the caller ID instead. It read, "Blocked."

A chill trickled down Jack's spine as he waited to see if the caller would leave a voice mail. This particular phone, a throwaway, was registered to Neal Mercer, and only a few people had the number.

Ardith.

Rachel.

An FBI agent or two.

Chad Lombard? There was no way he could have it, unless Rachel or Ardith had told him. Under duress.

A cold sweat broke out between Jack's aching shoulder blades.

A little envelope flashed on the phone screen.

After sucking in a breath, Jack accessed his voice mail.

"Jack? It's Ardith." She sounded scared. She'd changed her name, changed Rachel's, bought a condo on a shady street in a city far from Phoenix and started a new life, hoping to stay under Lombard's radar.

Jack waited for her to go on.

"I think he knows where we are," she said, at long last. "Rachel—I mean, Charlotte—is sure she saw him drive by the playground this afternoon—oh, God, I hope you get this—" Another pause, then Ardith recited a number. "Call me."

Jack shuddered as he hit the call back button. Cell calls were notoriously easy to listen in on, if you had the right equipment and the skill, and given the clandestine nature of his life's work, Lombard surely did. If Rachel *had* seen her father drive past the playground, and not just someone who resembled him, the bastard was already closing in for the kill.

"H-hello?" Ardith answered.

"It's Jack. This has to be quick, Ardith. You need to get *Charlotte* and leave. Right now."

"And go where?" Ardith asked, her voice shaking. "For all I know, he's waiting right outside my door!"

"I'll send an escort. Just be ready, okay?"

"But where— ?"

"You'll know when you get here. My people will use the password we agreed on. Don't go with them unless they do."

"Okay," Ardith said, near tears now.

They hung up without goodbyes.

Jack immediately contacted Vince Griffin, using Ashley's landline, and gave the order, along with the password.

"Call me after you pick them up," he finished.

"Will do," Vince responded. "I take it she and the kid are right where we left them?"

"Yes," Jack said. It was beyond unlikely that Ashley's phone was bugged, but Vince's could be. He had to take the chance, hope to God nobody was listening in, that his longtime friend and employee wouldn't be followed. "Be careful."

"Always," Vince said cheerfully, and hung up.

Jack heard a sound behind him, regretted that the Glock was hidden behind a pile of quilts in the sewing room.

Ashley stood, pale-faced, in the study doorway. "They're coming here? Rachel and her mother?"

"Yes," Jack said, letting out his breath. *You could have shot Ashley,* he heard Tanner say. A chill burned through him. "They won't be here long—just until I can find them a safe place to start over."

"They can stay as long as they need to," Ashley said, but she looked terrified. "There's no safer place than Stone Creek."

It wouldn't be a safe place for long if Lombard tracked his ex-girlfriend and his daughter to the small Arizona town, but Jack didn't point that out. There was no need to say it aloud.

Jack shut down the computer and retired to the sewing room.

Knowing she wouldn't sleep, Ashley showered, put on blue jeans and an old T-shirt, and returned to the kitchen, where she methodically assembled the ingredients for the most complicated recipe in her collection— her great-grandmother's rum-pecan cake.

The fourth batch was cooling when dawn broke, and Ashley was sitting at the table, a cup of coffee untouched in front of her.

Jack stepped out of the sewing room, a shaving kit under one arm. His smile was wan, and a little guilty.

"Smells like Christmas in here," he said, very quietly. "Did you sleep?"

Ashley shook her head, vaguely aware that she was covered in cake flour, the fallout of frenzied baking. "Did you?"

"No," Jack said, and she knew by the hollow look in his eyes that he was telling the truth. "Ashley, I'm sorry—"

"Please," Ashley interrupted, "stop saying that."

She couldn't help comparing that morning to the one before, when she'd virtually seduced Jack right there in the kitchen. Was it only yesterday that she'd visited Olivia and the babies at the clinic in Indian Rock, had that disturbing conversation with Melissa outside the nursery? Dear God, it seemed as though a hundred years had passed since then.

The wall phone rang.

Jack tensed.

Ashley got up to answer. "It's only Melissa," she said. She always knew when Melissa was calling.

"I'm picking up twin-vibes," her sister announced. "What's going on?"

"Nothing," Ashley said, glancing at the clock on the fireplace mantel. "It's only six in the morning, Melissa. What are you doing up so early?"

"I told you, I've got vibes," Melissa answered, sounding impatient.

Jack left the kitchen.

"Nothing's wrong," Ashley said, winding the telephone cord around her finger.

"You're lying," Melissa insisted flatly. "Do I have to come over there?"

Ashley smiled at the prospect. "Only if you want a

home-cooked breakfast. Blueberry pancakes? Cherry crepes?"

"You," Melissa accused, "are deliberately torturing me. Your own sister. You *know* I'm on a diet."

"You're five foot three and you weigh 110 pounds. If you're on a diet, I'm having you committed." Remembering that their mother had died in the psychiatric ward of a Flagstaff hospital, Ashley instantly regretted her choice of words. This was a subject she wanted to avoid, at least until she regained her emotional equilibrium. Melissa, like Brad and Olivia, had had a no-love-lost relationship with Delia.

"Cherry crepes," Melissa mused. "Ashley O'Ballivan, you are an evil woman." A pause. "Furthermore, you have some nerve, grilling me about Alex Ewing, when Jack McCall is back."

Ashley frowned. "How did you know that?"

"Your neighbor, Mrs. Pollack, works part-time in my office, remember? She told me he arrived in an ambulance, day before yesterday. Is there a reason you didn't mention this?"

"Yes, Counselor," Ashley answered, "there is. Because I didn't want you to know."

"Why not?" Melissa sounded almost hurt.

"Because I knew I'd look like an idiot when he left again."

"Not to be too lawyerly, or anything, but why invite me to breakfast if you were trying to hide a man over there?"

Ashley laughed, but it was forced, and Melissa probably picked up on that, though mercifully, she didn't comment. "Because I'm overstocked on cherry crepes and I need the freezer space?" she offered.

"You were supposed to say something like, 'Because you're my twin sister and I love you.'"

"That, too," Ashley responded.

"I'll be over before work," Melissa said. "You're really okay?"

No, Ashley thought. *I'm in love with a stranger, someone wants to kill him, and my bed-and-breakfast is about to become a stop on a modern underground railroad.*

"I will be," she said aloud.

"Damn right you will," Melissa replied, and hung up without a goodbye. Of course, there hadn't been a "hello," either.

Classic Melissa.

The upstairs shower had been running through most of her conversation with Melissa—Ashley had heard the water rushing through the old house's many pipes. Now all was silent.

Thinking Jack would probably be downstairs soon, wanting breakfast, Ashley fed Mrs. Wiggins and then took a plastic container filled with the results of her *last* cooking binge from the freezer.

A month ago she'd made five dozen crepes, complete with cherry sauce from scratch, when one of her college friends had called to say she'd just found out her husband was having an affair.

Before that, it had been a double-fudge brownie marathon—beginning the night of her mother's funeral. She'd donated the brownies to the residents of the nursing home three blocks over, since, in her own way, she was just as calorie-conscious as Melissa.

Baking therapy was one thing. Scarfing down the results was quite another.

Half an hour passed, and Jack didn't reappear.

Ashley waited.

A full hour had passed, and still no sign of him.

Resigned, she went upstairs. Knocked softly at his bedroom door.

No answer.

Her imagination kicked in. The man had *aliases,* for heaven's sake. He'd abducted a drug dealer's seven-year-old daughter from a stronghold in some Latin American jungle.

Maybe he'd sneaked out the front door.

Maybe he was lying in there, dead.

"Jack?"

Nothing.

She opened the door, her heart in her throat, and stuck her head inside the room.

He wasn't in the bed.

She raised her voice a little. "Jack?"

She heard the buzzing sound then, identified it as an electric shaver, and was just about to back out of the room and close the door behind her, as quietly as possible, when his bathroom door opened.

His hair was damp from the shower, and he was wearing a towel, loincloth style, and nothing else. He grinned as he shut off the shaver.

"I'm not here for sex," Ashley said, and then could have kicked herself.

Jack laughed. "Too bad," he said. "Nothing like a quickie to get the day off to a good start. So to speak."

A quickie indeed. Ashley gave him a look, meant to hide the fact that she found the idea more than appealing. "Breakfast will be ready soon," she said coolly. "And Melissa is joining us, so try to behave yourself."

He stepped out of the bathroom.

Her gaze immediately dropped to the towel. Shot back to his face.

He was grinning. "But we're alone *now,* aren't we?"

"I'm still not on birth control, remember?" Ashley's voice shook.

"*That* horse is pretty much out of the barn," Jack drawled. He was walking toward her.

She didn't move.

He took her hand, pulled her to him, pushed the door shut.

Kissed her breathless.

Unsnapped her jeans, slid a hand inside her panties. All without breaking the kiss.

Ashley moaned into his mouth, wet where he caressed her.

He maneuvered her to the bed, laid her down.

Ashley was already trying to squirm out of her jeans. When it came to Jack McCall—McKenzie—*whoever*—she was downright easy.

Jack finally ended the kiss, proceeded to rid her of her shoes, of the binding denim, and then her practical cotton underpants.

She whimpered in anticipation when he knelt between her legs, parted her thighs, kissed her—*there*.

A shudder of violent need moved through her.

"Slow and easy," he murmured, between nibbles and flicks of his tongue.

Slow and easy? She was on fire.

She shook her head from side to side. "Hard," she pleaded. "Hard and fast, Jack. *Please...*"

He went down on her in earnest then, and after a few

glorious minutes, she shattered completely, peaking and then peaking again.

Jack soothed her as she descended, stroking her thighs and murmuring to her until she sank into satisfaction.

She'd expected him to mount her, but he didn't.

Instead, he dressed her again, nipping her once through the moist crotch of her panties before tucking her legs into her jeans, sliding them up her legs, tugging them past her bottom. He even slipped her feet into her shoes and tied the laces.

"What about—the quickie?" she asked, burning again because he'd teased her with that little scrape of his teeth. Because as spectacular as her orgasm had been, it had left her wanting—*needing*—more.

"I guess that will have to wait," Jack said, sitting down beside her on the bed and easing her upright next to him. "Didn't you say your sister would be here for breakfast at any moment?"

She looked down at the towel—either it had miraculously stayed in place or he'd wrapped it around his waist again when she wasn't looking—and saw the sizable bulge of his erection. "You've got a hard-on," she said matter-of-factly.

Jack chuckled. "Ya think?"

Melissa's voice sounded from downstairs. "Ash? I'm here!"

Ashley bolted to her feet, blushing. "Coming!" she called back.

"You can say that again," Jack teased.

Smoothing her hair with both hands, tugging at her T-shirt, Ashley hurried out of the room.

"I'll be right down!" she shouted, from the top of the stairs.

Melissa's reply was inaudible.

Ashley dashed into her bathroom and splashed her face with cold water, then checked herself out in the full-length mirror on the back of the door.

She looked, she decided ruefully, like a woman who'd just had a screaming climax—and needed more.

Quickly, she applied powder to her face, but the tell-tale glow was still there.

Damn.

There was nothing to do but go downstairs, where her all-too-perceptive twin was waiting for cherry crepes. If she didn't appear soon, Melissa would come looking for her.

"You were having sex," Melissa said two minutes later, when Ashley forced herself to step into the kitchen.

"No, I wasn't," Ashley replied, with an indignant little sniff.

"Liar."

Ashley crossed the room, turned the oven on to pre-heat, and got very busy taking the frozen crepes out of their plastic container, transferring them to a baking dish. All the while, she was careful not to let Melissa catch her eye.

"Olivia and the twins are coming home today," Melissa said lightly, but something in her voice warned that she wasn't going to let the sex issue drop.

"I thought the babies had to stay until they were bigger," Ashley replied, still avoiding Melissa's gaze.

"Tanner hired special nurses and had two state-of-the-art incubators brought from Flagstaff," Melissa explained.

Once the crepes were in the oven, Ashley had no choice but to turn around and look at Melissa.

"You *were* having sex," Melissa repeated.

Ashley flung her hands out from her sides. "*Okay. Yes,* I was having sex!" She sighed. "Sort of."

"What do you mean, *sort of?* How do you 'sort of' have sex?"

"Never mind," Ashley snapped. "Isn't it enough that I admitted it? Do you want details?"

"Yes, actually," Melissa answered mischievously, "but I'm obviously not going to get them."

Jack pushed open the inside door and stepped into the kitchen.

"Yet," Melissa added, in a whisper.

Ashley rolled her eyes.

"Hello, Jack," Melissa said.

"Melissa," Jack replied.

Like Brad and Olivia, Melissa wasn't in the Jack McCall fan club. They'd all turned in their membership cards the last time he ditched Ashley.

"Just passing through?" Melissa asked sweetly.

"Like the wind," Jack answered. "Your brother already threatened me, so maybe we can skip that part."

Ashley raised her eyebrows. Brad had *threatened* Jack?

"As long as somebody got the point across," Melissa chimed.

"Oh, believe me, I get it."

"Will you both stop bickering, please?" Ashley asked.

Melissa sneezed. Looked around. "Is there a *cat* in this house?"

Jack grinned. "I could find the little mutant, if you'd like to pet it."

Melissa sneezed again. "I'm—*allergic!* Ashley, you *know* I'm all—all—*atchoo!*"

Ashley had completely forgotten about Mrs. Wiggins, and about her sister's famous allergies. Olivia insisted it was all in Melissa's head, since she'd been tested and the results had been negative.

"I'm sorry, I—"

Another sneeze.

"Bless you," Jack said generously.

Melissa grabbed up her coat and purse and ran for the back door. Slammed it behind her.

"Well," Jack commented, "that went well."

"Shut up," Ashley said.

Jack let out a magnanimous sigh and spread his hands.

Ashley went to the cupboard, got out two plates, set them on the table with rather more force than necessary. "You," she said, "are complicating my life."

"Are you talking to me or the cat?" Jack asked, all innocence.

"You," Ashley replied tersely. "I'm not getting rid of the cat."

"But you *are* getting rid of me? After that orgasm?"

"Shut up."

Jack chuckled, pressed his lips together, and pretended to zip them closed.

Ashley served the crepes. They both ate.

All without a single word passing between them.

After breakfast, Jack retreated to the study, and Ashley cleaned up the kitchen. Melissa called just as she was closing the dishwasher door.

"It wasn't the cat," Melissa said, first thing.

"Duh," Ashley responded.

"I mean, I thought it was, but I'm probably catching cold or something—"

"Either that, or you're allergic to Jack."

"He's bad news, Ash," Melissa said.

"I guess I could take up with Dan," Ashley said mildly. "I hear he's looking for a domestic type."

"Don't you dare!"

Ashley smiled, even though tears suddenly scalded her eyes. She was destined to love one man—Jack McCall—for the rest of her life, maybe for the rest of eternity.

And Melissa was right.

He was the worst possible news.

Chapter 6

"I'm going out to Tanner and Olivia's after work today," Melissa said. "Gotta see my nephews in their natural habitat. Want to ride along?"

By the time Melissa left her office, even if she knocked off at five o'clock—a rare thing for her—it would be dark out. Ardith and Rachel would surely arrive that night, and Ashley wanted to be on hand to welcome the pair and help them settle in.

She'd already decided to put the secret guests in the room directly across from Jack's; it had twin beds and a private bathroom. Jack would surely want to be in close proximity to them in case of trouble, and the feeling was undoubtedly mutual.

"I didn't sleep very well last night," she confessed. "By the time you leave work, I'll probably be snoring."

"Whatever you say," Melissa said gently. "Be careful, Ash. When the sex is good, it's easy to get carried away."

"Sounds like you're speaking from experience," Ashley replied. "Have you seen Dan lately?"

Melissa sighed. "We're not speaking," she said, with a sadness she usually kept hidden. "The last time we did, he told me we should both start seeing other people." A sniffle. "I heard he's going out with some waitress from the Roadhouse, over in Indian Rock."

"Is that why you're considering leaving Stone Creek? Because Dan is dating someone else?"

Melissa began to cry. There was no sob, no sniffle, no sound at all, but Ashley knew her sister was in tears. That was the twin bond, at least as they experienced it.

"Why do I have to choose?" Melissa asked plaintively. "Why can't I have Dan *and* my career? Ash, I worked so hard to get through law school—even with Brad footing the bills, it was *really* tough."

Ashley hadn't been over this ground with Melissa, not in any depth, anyway, because they'd been semi-estranged since the day of their mother's funeral. "Is that what Dan wants, Melissa? For you to give up your law practice?"

"He has two young sons, Ash. The ranch is *miles* from anywhere. In the winter, they get snowed in—Dan homeschools Michael and Ray from the first blizzard, sometimes until Easter, because the ranch road is usually impassible. Unless I wanted to travel by dogsled, I couldn't possibly commute. I'd go bonkers." Melissa pulled in a long, quivery breath. "I might even pull a 'Mom,' Ashley. If I got desperate enough. Get on a bus one fine afternoon and never come back."

"I can't see you doing that, Melissa."

"Well, *I* can. I love Dan. I love the boys—way too much to do to them what Delia did to us."

"Mel—"

"Here's how much I love them. I'd rather Dan married that waitress than someone who was always looking for an escape route—like me."

"Have you and Dan talked about this, Melissa? *Really* talked about it?"

"Sort of," Melissa admitted wearily. "His stock response was, 'Mel, we can work this out.' Which means I stay home and cook and clean and sew slipcovers, while he's out on the trail, squiring around a bunch of executive greenhorns trying to find their inner cowboys."

"How do you *know* that's what it means? Did Dan actually say so, Melissa, or is this just your take on the situation?"

"'*Just*' my 'take' on the situation?" Melissa countered, sounding offended. "I'm not some naive Martha Stewart clone like—like—"

"Like me?"

"I didn't say that!"

"You didn't have to, Counselor." *A Martha Stewart clone?* Was that how other people saw her? Because she enjoyed cooking, decorating, quilting? Because she'd never had the kind of world-conquering ambition Brad and Melissa shared?

"Ashley, I truly didn't mean—"

Ashley had always been the family peacemaker, and that hadn't changed. "I know you didn't mean to hurt my feelings, Melissa," she said gently. *Oh, but you did.* "And maybe it *is* time I had a little excitement in my life."

With Jack around, excitement was pretty much a sure thing.

Out-of-the-stratosphere sex and a drug dealer bent on revenge.

Who could ask for more?

There was a smile in Melissa's voice, along with a tremulous note of relief. "Kiss the babies for me, if you see them before I do," she said.

Ashley hadn't decided whether or not she'd make the drive out to Starcross Ranch that day. It wasn't so far, but the roads were probably slick. Although she had snow tires, her car was a subcompact, and it didn't have four-wheel drive.

"I'll do that," she answered, and the call was over.

Jack, she soon discovered, was in the study, working on potential websites for the bed-and-breakfast. He was remarkably cool, calm and collected, considering the circumstances, but Ashley couldn't help noticing that his nondescript cell phone was within easy reach.

She went upstairs, cast one yearning look toward her bed. Climbing into it wasn't an option—she might have another wakeful night if she went to sleep at that hour of the day.

Using her bedside phone, she placed a call to Olivia.

Her sister answered on the second ring. "Dr. O'Ballivan," she said, all business. Olivia had taken Tanner's name when they married, but she still used her own professionally.

Olivia was managing marriage, motherhood and a career, at least so far. Why couldn't Melissa do the same thing?

"You sound very businesslike, for someone who just

went through childbirth twice in the space of ten minutes," Ashley said.

Olivia laughed. "That's modern medicine for you. Have twins one day, go home the next. Tanner hired nurses to look after the babies round the clock until I've rested up, so I'm a lady of leisure these days."

"How are they?"

"Growing like corn in August," Olivia replied.

"Good," Ashley said. "Are you up for a visitor? Please say so if you're not—I promise I'll understand."

"I'd *love* to have a visitor," Olivia said. "Tanner's out feeding the range cattle, Sophie's at school, and of course the day nurse is busy doting on the two new men in the house. Ginger isn't in the mood for chitchat, so I'm at loose ends."

Ashley couldn't help smiling. Ginger, an aging golden retriever, was Olivia's constant companion, and the two of them usually had a lot to say to each other. "I'll be out as soon as I've showered and dressed," she said. "Do you need anything from town?"

"Nope. Loaded up on groceries over the weekend," Olivia answered. "The roads have been plowed and sanded, but be careful anyway. There's another snowstorm rolling in tonight."

Ashley promised to drive carefully and said goodbye.

She tried to be philosophical about the approaching storm, but for her, once Christmas had come and gone, snow lost its charm. Unlike her siblings, she didn't ski.

The shower perked her up a little—she used her special ginseng-and-rice soap, and the scent was heavenly. After drying off with the kind of soft, thick towel one would expect a "Martha Stewart clone" to have on hand, she dressed in a long black woolen skirt, a lavender sweater with raglan sleeves, and high black boots.

She brushed her hair out and skillfully redid her braid.

Frowned at her image in the steamy mirror.

Maybe she ought to change her hair. Get one of those saucy, layered cuts, with a few shimmery highlights thrown in for good measure. Drive to one of the malls in Flagstaff and have a makeover at a department-store cosmetics counter.

Jazz herself up a little.

The trouble was, she'd never aspired to jazziness.

Her natural color, a coppery-blond, suited her just fine, and so did the style. The braid was tidy, feminine, and practical, considering the life she led.

On the other hand, she'd been wearing that same French braid since college. Spiral curls, like Melissa's, might look sexy on her.

Did she *want* to be sexier?

Look how much trouble she'd gotten herself into with the same old hairdo and minimal makeup.

Quickly, she applied lip gloss and a light coat of mascara and headed downstairs. Pausing in the study doorway, she allowed herself the pleasure of watching Jack for a few moments before saying, "I'm going out to Olivia and Tanner's. Want to come along?"

Jack turned in the swivel chair. "Maybe some other time," he said. "I think I'd better stick around, in case Vince shows up with Ardith and Rachel sooner than expected."

Ashley didn't know who Vince was, though she had caught the name when she accidentally-on-purpose overheard Jack's phone conversation with Ardith the night before.

"Did he call?" She wanted to ask Jack if he was feeling ill again, but something stopped her. "Vince, I mean?"

Jack nodded. "They're on their way."

"No trouble?"

His gaze was direct. "Depends on how you define *trouble*," he replied. "Ardith has a husband and two other children besides Rachel. She's had to leave them behind—at least for the time being."

Ashley's heart pinched. She knew what it was to await the return of a missing mother. "Aren't the police doing anything?"

"They were willing to send a patrol car by Ardith's place every once in a while. Under civil law, unless Lombard actually attacks or kills her or Rachel, there isn't much the police can do."

"That's insane!"

"It's the law."

"The husband and the other children—aren't they in danger, too?" Wouldn't the whole family be better off together, Ashley wondered, even if they had to establish new identifies? At least they'd have each other.

"The more people involved," Jack told her grimly, "the harder it is to hide. For now, they're safer apart."

"A man like Lombard—wouldn't he go after the rest of the family, if only to force Ardith out into the open?"

"He might do anything," Jack admitted. "From what I've seen, though, Lombard is fixated on getting Rachel back and not much else. Ardith is in his way, and he won't hesitate to take her out to get what he wants."

Ashley hugged herself. Even inside, wearing warm

clothes, she felt chilled. "But *why* is he so obsessed? He wasn't around when Rachel was born—he couldn't have bonded with her the way a father normally would."

"Why does he run drugs?" Jack countered. "Why does he kill people? We're not dealing with a rational person here, Ashley. If I had to hazard a guess at his motive, I'd say it's pure ego. Lombard is a sociopath, if not worse. He sees Rachel as an object, something that *belongs* to him." He paused, and she saw pain in his eyes. "Do me a favor?" he asked hoarsely.

"What?"

"Don't come back here tonight. Stay with Tanner and Olivia. Or with Brad and his wife."

Ashley swallowed. "You think Lombard's coming— Here?" She'd known Jack thought exactly that, on some level, but it seemed so incredible that she had to ask.

"Let's just say I'd rather not take a chance."

"But you *will* be taking a chance, with your own life."

"That's one hell of a lot better than taking a chance with yours. Once I figure out what to do with Ardith and Rachel, make sure they're someplace Lombard will never find them, I'm going to draw that crazy son-of-a-bitch as far from Stone Creek as I can."

"This isn't going to end, is it? Not unless—"

"Not unless," Jack said, rising from the chair, approaching her, "I kill him, or he kills me."

"My God," Ashley groaned, putting a hand to her mouth.

Jack gripped her shoulders firmly, but with a gentleness that reminded her of their lovemaking. "I'll never be able to forgive myself if you get caught in the cross fire, Ashley. If you meant it when you said you loved me, then do what I ask. Take the cat, leave this house, and don't come back until I give the all clear."

"I *did* mean it, but—"

He brushed her chin with the pad of his thumb. "I understand that you come from sturdy pioneer stock and all that, Ashley. I know the O'Ballivans have always held their own against all comers, faced down any trouble that came their way. But Chad Lombard is no ordinary bad guy. He's the devil's first cousin. You don't want to know the things he's done—you wouldn't be able to get them out of your head."

Ashley stared into Jack's eyes, so deathly afraid for him that it didn't occur to her to be afraid for herself. "When you went looking for Rachel in South America," she said, her mouth so dry that she almost couldn't get the words out, "that wasn't your first run-in with Lombard, was it?"

"No," he said, after a long, long time.

"What hap—?"

"You don't want to know. I sure as hell wish *I* didn't." He slid his hands down her upper arms, squeezed her elbows. "Go, Ashley. Do this for me, and I'll never ask you for another thing."

"That's what I'm afraid of," she told him.

He leaned in, kissed her forehead. Took a deep breath, seeming to draw in the scent of her and hold it as long as possible. "Go," he repeated.

She agonized in silence for a long moment, then nodded in reluctant agreement. She'd wanted to meet Ardith and Rachel, but maybe it would be better—for them as well as for her—if that never happened.

"You'll call when you get to your sister's place?" Jack asked.

"Yes," Ashley said.

She turned away from Jack slowly, went back upstairs, packed a small suitcase.

She didn't say goodbye to Jack; there was something too final about that. Instead, she collected Mrs. Wiggins and set out for Starcross Ranch, though when she arrived at Tanner and Olivia's large, recently renovated house, she left her suitcase and the kitten in the car.

The last thing the Quinns needed, with new babies and incubators and three shifts of nurses already in residence, was a relative looking for a place to hide out. After the visit, she would drive on to Meg and Brad's, ask to spend the night in their guesthouse.

Although she knew she'd be welcome, Brad would want to know what was going on. After all, she had a perfectly good place of her own.

Lying wouldn't do any good—her brother knew Jack was there, knew their history, at least as a couple.

She would have to tell Brad the truth—but how much of it?

Jack hadn't asked her to keep any secrets. Given the situation, though, he might have thought that went without saying.

Tanner stepped out onto the porch as she came up the walk. He smiled, but his eyes were filled with unasked questions.

Ashley dredged up a tattered smile from somewhere inside, pasted it to her mouth. "Hello, Tanner," she said.

"Jack called," he told her.

Ashley stopped in the middle of the walk. A special system of wires kept the concrete clear of ice and snow, and she could feel the heat of it, even through the soles of her boots.

"Oh," she said.

He passed her on the walk without another word. Went to her car, reached in for the suitcase and the kitten.

"I was going to spend the night over at Brad and Meg's," she said, pausing on the porch steps.

"You're staying here," Tanner said. "It's not as though we don't have room, and I promise, the dogs won't eat your cat."

"But—the babies—Olivia—the last thing you need is—"

Beside her now, Tanner tried for a smile of his own and fell short. "Brad and Meg will be over later, with the kids. Melissa's stopping by when she's through at work. Time for a family meeting, kiddo, and you're the guest of honor."

Curiously, Ashley felt both deflated and uplifted by this news. "If it's about giving up Jack, you can all forget it," she said firmly.

Tanner didn't respond to that. Somehow, even with a protesting cat in one hand and a suitcase handle in the other, he managed to open the front door. "Olivia's in the kitchen," he told her. "I'll put your things in the guestroom. Cat included."

In that house, the "guestroom" was actually a suite, with a luxurious bath, a flat-screen TV above the working fireplace, and its own kitchenette.

Ginger rose from her cushy bed, tail wagging, when Ashley stepped into the main kitchen. Ashley bent to greet the sweet old dog.

Dressed in jeans and an old flannel shirt, Olivia sat in the antique rocking chair in front of the bay windows, a receiving blanket draped discreetly over her chest, nursing one of the babies. Seeing Ashley, she smiled, but her eyes were troubled.

Ashley went to her sister, bent to kiss the top of her head.

"Tell me what's going on, Ashley," Olivia said. "Tanner gave me a few details after he talked to Jack on the phone earlier, but he was pretty cryptic."

Ashley pulled one of the high-backed wooden chairs over from the table and sat down, facing Olivia. Their knees didn't quite touch.

Tanner came into the room, went to the coffeepot and filled a cup for Ashley. "You look like you could use a shot of whiskey," he commented. "But now that Sophie's a teenager, always having friends over, we decided to remove all temptation. This will have to do."

"Thanks," Ashley said, smiling a little and taking the cup.

Olivia was rocking the chair a little faster, her gaze fixed on Ashley. "Talk to us," she ordered.

Ashley sighed. When Brad and Meg and Melissa arrived, she'd have to repeat the whole incredible story— what little she knew of it, anyway—but it was clear that Olivia would brook no delay. So Ashley told her sister and brother-in-law what she knew about Rachel's rescue, and Chad Lombard's determination to, one, get his daughter back and, two, take revenge on Jack for stealing her away.

Tanner didn't look surprised; he probably knew more than she did, since he and Jack were close friends. Ashley didn't risk as much as a glance in Olivia's direction. She hated worrying her sister, especially now.

"Jack sent someone to bring Ardith and Rachel to Stone Creek," she finished. "And he wanted me out of the house in case Lombard managed to follow them somehow."

"It was certainly generous of Jack," Olivia said, with a bite in her tone, "to bring all this trouble straight to *your* door."

Tanner glanced at Olivia, grimaced slightly. "He was sick, Liv," he told her. "Out of his head with fever."

Olivia sighed.

"I'm in love with Jack," Ashley said bravely. "You might as well know."

Olivia and Tanner exchanged looks.

"What a surprise," Tanner said, one corner of his mouth tilting up briefly.

"You do realize," Olivia said seriously, her gaze boring into Ashley's face, "that this situation is hopeless? Even if Jack manages to get the woman and her little girl to safety, this Lombard character will always be a threat."

Tanner pulled up a chair beside Olivia and took her hand. "Liv," he said, "Jack is the best at what he does. He won't let anything happen to Ashley."

Tears filled Olivia's expressive eyes, then spilled down her cheeks. Ginger gave a little whimper and lumbered over to lay her muzzle on her mistress's knee. Rolled her brown eyes upward.

"I will *not* calm down," Olivia told the dog. "This is serious!"

This time, Tanner and Ashley looked at each other.

"I agree with Ginger," Tanner told his wife quietly. "You need to stay calm. We all do." By now, he was used to Olivia's telepathic conversations with animals. Ashley couldn't remember a time when her big sister didn't communicate with four-legged creatures of all species.

"How can I, when my sister is in mortal danger?" Olivia snapped, watching Ashley. "All because of *your* friend."

"Jack *is* my friend," Tanner responded, his voice still even. "And that's why I'm going to do whatever I can to help him."

Olivia turned her head quickly, stared at her husband. *"What?"*

"I can't just turn my back on him, Liv," Tanner said. "Not even for you."

"What about Sophie? What about John and Sam? They need their father, and *I* need my husband!"

Tanner started to speak, then stopped himself. Ashley saw a small muscle bunch in his jaw, go slack.

Ginger whimpered again, still gazing up at Olivia in adoring sorrow, her dog eyes liquid.

"That's easy for *you* to say," Olivia told the dog.

"This is why I didn't want to stay here," Ashley told Tanner sadly. "I've been in this house for five minutes, and I'm already causing trouble."

"You didn't do anything wrong," Olivia said, her voice and expression softening, her eyes still shining with tears. "Before Big John died, when Brad was away from home, busy with his career, I promised our grandfather I'd look after you and Melissa, and I intend to keep my word, Ashley."

"I'm not a little girl anymore," Ashley reminded her sister.

Olivia didn't answer. She was intent on tucking either John or Sam against her shoulder, patting his tiny back. The receiving blanket still covered her. When the burp came, Olivia smiled proudly.

Tanner stood up, gently took his son and carried him out of the kitchen.

Olivia straightened her clothing and laid the blanket aside. Gave Ginger a few reassuring strokes on the head before sending the animal back to her bed nearby.

"You are going to be the most amazing mother," Ashley said.

"Don't try to change the subject," Olivia warned. She was smiling, but her eyes remained moist and fierce with determination to protect her little sister. "So, you really are in love with Jack McCall?"

"Afraid so," Ashley replied. "And I think it's forever."

"Is he planning to stay this time?" Olivia's tone was kind, if wary.

Ashley raised her shoulders slightly, lowered them again. "He paid for two weeks at the B&B," she said.

Olivia's eyes narrowed, then widened. "Two weeks? That's all?"

"It's something," Ashley said, feeling like a candidate for some reality show about women trying to get over the wrong man. She made a lame attempt at a joke. "If we decide to make this permanent, I won't be charging him for bed and board."

Olivia didn't laugh, or even smile. "What if he leaves?"

"I think there's a good chance that he will," Ashley admitted. Then, without thinking, she rested one hand against her lower belly.

Olivia read the gesture with unerring accuracy. "Ashley—are you *pregnant?*"

"It's too early to know, doctor," Ashley said. "Unless there's a second-day test out there that I haven't heard about."

"*Unprotected sex?* Ashley, what are you *thinking?*"

"For once, I'm not. And it's kind of a relief."

"What if there's a baby? Jack might not be around to help you raise it."

"I'd manage, Olivia, as other women do, and *have* since cave days, if not longer."

"A child needs a father," Olivia said.

"Spoken like a very lucky woman with a husband who adores her," Ashley answered, without a shred of malice.

Tanner returned before Olivia could answer, took her by both hands, and gently hoisted her to her feet. "Time for your nap, Mama Bear," he told her.

Olivia didn't resist, but she did pin Ashley with a big-sister look and say, "We're not finished with this conversation."

Ashley simply spread her hands.

Shade by shade, shadow by shadow, night finally came.

Ashley had called from Olivia's place, as promised. They hadn't exchanged more than a few words, and those had been stiff and stilted.

It was no great wonder to Jack that Ashley was projecting a chill: She'd been banished from her own house by a man who had no damn business being there at all.

He was getting antsy.

He'd heard nothing about Ardith and Rachel since his first terse conversation with Vince Griffin, right after the pickup. On the bright side, the toxin seemed to be in abeyance, though he still broke out in cold sweats at irregular intervals, and spates of weakness invariably followed in their wake.

To keep from going crazy, or maybe to make sure he did, Jack logged on to his father's website again. Clicked to the Associates page.

There were his brothers, Dean and Jim. The last time Jack had seen them, they'd been in junior high, wannabe Romeos with braces and acne. Now, they looked like infomercial hosts.

He smiled.

A blurb at the bottom of the page showed a snapshot of Bryce, the youngest. In a wild break with McKenzie tradition, he was studying to be an optometrist.

There was no mention of Jack himself, of course. But his mother wasn't on the site, either, and that bothered him.

His dad had always been a big believer in family values.

What a disappointment I must have been, Jack thought, frowning as he left the website and ran another search. There might be a recent picture of his mom on the library's site. After all, she'd been the director when he'd left for military school.

The director's face beamed from the main page, and it wasn't his mother's.

Frowning, Jack ran another search, using her name.

That was when he found the obituary, dated three years ago, a week after her fifty-third birthday.

The picture was old, a close-up taken on a long-ago family vacation.

The headshot showed her beaming smile, the bright eyes behind the lenses of her glasses. Jack's own eyes burned so badly that he had to blink a few times before he could read beyond her name, Marlene Estes McKenzie.

She'd died at home, according to the writer of the obit, surrounded by family and friends. In lieu of flowers, her husband and sons requested that donations be made to a well-known foundation dedicated to fighting breast cancer.

Breast cancer.

Jack breathed deeply until his emotions were at least somewhat under control, then, against his better judgment, he reached for Ashley's phone, dialed the familiar number.

"Dr. McKenzie's residence," a woman's voice chimed.

Jack couldn't speak for a moment.

"Hello?" the woman asked pleasantly. "Is anyone there? Hello?"

He finally found his voice. "My name is—Mark Ramsey. Is the doctor around?"

"I'm so sorry," came the answer. "My husband is out of town at a convention, but either of his sons would be happy to see you if this is an emergency."

"It isn't," Jack said. Then, with muttered thanks, he quietly hung up.

He got out of the chair, walked to the window, looked out at the street. A blue pickup truck drove past. The house opposite Ashley's blurred.

All this time, Jack had imagined his mother visiting his grave at Arlington. Squaring her shoulders, sniffling a little, mourning her firstborn's "heroic" death in Iraq. Instead, she'd been lying in a grave of her own.

He rubbed his eyes with a thumb and forefinger.

How long had his dad waited, after his first wife's death, to remarry?

What kind of person was the new Mrs. McKenzie? Did Dean and Jim and Bryce like her?

Jack ached to call Ashley, needed to hear her voice.

But what would he say? *Hi, I just found out my mother died three years ago?* He wasn't sure he'd be able to get through the sentence without breaking down.

He moved away from the window. No sense making a target of himself.

The night grew darker, colder and lonelier.

And still Jack didn't turn on a light. Nor did he head for the kitchen to raid Ashley's refrigerator, even though he hadn't eaten since breakfast.

He'd done a lot of waiting in his life. He'd waited for precisely the right moment to rescue children and diplomats and wealthy businessmen held for ransom. He'd waited to be rescued himself once, with nearly every bone in his body broken.

Waiting was harder now.

In his mind, he heard the voice of a young soldier. "You'll be all right now, sir. We're United States Marines."

Jack's throat tightened further.

And then the throwaway cell phone rang.

Sweat broke out on Jack's upper lip. He'd spoken to Vince over Ashley's phone. He'd warned Ardith not to use the cell number again, in case it was being monitored.

It was unlikely that the FBI would be calling him up to chat. They had their own ways of getting in touch.

Holding his breath, he pressed the Talk button, but didn't speak.

"I'll find you," Chad Lombard said.

"Why don't I make it easy for you?" Jack answered lightly.

"Like, how?" Lombard asked, a smirk in his voice.

"We agree on a time and place to meet. One way or another, this thing will be over."

Lombard laughed. "I must be crazy. I kind of like that idea. It has a high-noon sort of appeal. But how do I know you'll come alone, and not with a swarm of FBI and DEA agents?"

"How do I know *you'll* come alone?" Jack countered.

"I guess we'll just have to trust each other."

"Yeah, right. When and where, hotshot?"

"I'll be in touch about that," Lombard said lightly. "Oh, and by the way, I've already killed you, for all intents and purposes. The poison ought to be in your bone marrow by now, eating up your red blood cells. Still, I'd like to be around to see you shut down, Robocop."

Jack's stomach clenched, but his voice came out sounding even and in charge.

"I'll be waiting to hear from you," he said, and hung up.

Chapter 7

Oh, and by the way, I've already killed you, for all intents and purposes. The poison ought to be in your bone marrow by now, eating up your red blood cells.

Lombard's words pulsed somewhere in the back of Jack's mind, like a distant drumbeat. The man was a skilled liar- -and that was one of his more admirable traits, but this time, instinct said he was telling the truth.

Jack had never been afraid of death, and he still wasn't. But he was *very* afraid of leaving Ashley exposed to dangers she couldn't possibly imagine, even after all he'd told her. Tanner and her brother would *try* to protect her, and they were both men to be reckoned with, but were they in the same league with Lombard and his henchmen?

One-on-one, Lombard was no match for either of them.

The trouble was, Lombard never *went* one-on-one; he was too big a coward for that.

Coupled with the news of his mother's passing, *three years ago,* the knowledge that some concoction of jungle-plant extracts and nasty chemicals was already devouring his bone marrow left Jack reeling a little.

Suck it up, McCall, he thought. *One crisis at a time.*

It was after midnight when a local cab pulled up in front of Ashley's house.

Jack watched nervously from the study window as Vince got out of the front passenger seat, tucking his wallet into the back pocket of his chinos as he did so, and then opened the rear door, curbside.

Rachel scrambled out to the sidewalk, standing with her small hands on her hips like some miniature queen surveying her kingdom. She was soon followed by a much less confident Ardith, hunched over in a black trench coat and hooded scarf.

The cab drove away, and Vince steered Ardith and Rachel up the front walk.

Jack was quick to open the door; Rachel flashed past him, clad in jeans and a blue coat that looked like it might have been rescued from a thrift store, with Ardith slinking along behind.

"A *cab?*" Jack bit out, the minute he and Vince came face-to-face on the unlighted porch.

"Hide in plain sight," Vince said casually.

Jack let it pass for the moment, mainly because Rachel was tugging at the back of his shirt in a rapidly escalating effort to get his attention.

"My name is Charlotte now," she announced, "but you can still call me Rachel if you want to."

Jack grinned. He wanted to hoist the child into his arms, but didn't. After the conversation with Lombard, ·ouldn't quite shake the vision of his bones going hollow, caving in on themselves at the slightest exertion. He would need all his strength to deal with the inevitable.

Get over it, he told himself. If he lived long enough, he would check into a hospital, find out whether or not he was a candidate for a marrow transplant. In the meantime, there were other priorities, like keeping Rachel and Ashley and Ardith alive from one moment to the next.

"Are you hungry?" Jack asked, thinking of Ashley's freezer full of cherry crepes and other delicacies. God, what would it be like to live like a normal man—marry Ashley, live in this house, this Norman Rockwell town, for good?

"Just tired," Ardith said. Even trembling inside the bulky raincoat, she looked stick-thin, at least fifteen pounds lighter than the last time he'd seen her. And Ardith hadn't had all that much weight to spare in the first place.

"Yes!" Rachel blurted, the word toppling over the top of her mother's answer. "I'm *starved.*"

"I wouldn't mind something to gnaw on myself," Vince said, his gaze slightly narrowed as he studied his boss, there in the dimness of Ashley's entryway.

"We rode in a helicopter!" Rachel sang out, on the way to the kitchen.

Jack stopped at the base of the stairs, conscious of Ardith's exhaustion. She seemed to exude it through every pore. The unseen energy of despair vibrated around her, pervaded Jack's personal space.

"You two go on to the kitchen," Jack told Vince and the little girl, indicating the direction with a motion of one hand. "Help yourselves to whatever you find though he kept his tone even, the glance he gave the pilot said, *We'll talk about the cab later.*

Jack did not regard himself as a hard man to work for—sure, his standards were high, but he paid top wages, provided health insurance and a generous retirement plan for his few but carefully chosen employees. On the other hand, he didn't tolerate carelessness of any kind, and Vince knew that.

Vince grimaced slightly, keenly aware of Jack's meaning, and shepherded Rachel toward the kitchen.

"Don't burn too many lights," Jack added, "and stay away from the windows."

Vince stiffened at the predictability of the order, but he didn't turn around to give Jack a ration of crap, the way he might have done in less dire circumstances.

Jack shifted his gaze to Ardith, but she'd turned her face away. He put a hand to the small of her back and ushered her up the stairs.

"Are you all right?" he asked quietly.

"I'm scared to death," Ardith replied, still without looking at him.

Even through the raincoat and whatever she was wearing underneath, Jack could feel the knobbiness of her spine against the palm of his hand.

"When is this going to be over, Jack?" she blurted, when they'd reached the top. She was staring at him now, her eyes huge and black with sorrow and fear. "When can I go back to my husband and my children?"

"When it's safe," Jack said, but he was thinking, *When Chad Lombard is on a slab.*

"When it's safe!" Ardith echoed. "You know as well as I do that 'when it's safe' might be *never!*"

She was right about that; unless he took Lombard

out, once and for all, she and Rachel would probably have to keep running.

"You can't think that way," Jack pointed out. "You'll drive yourself crazy if you do." He guided her toward the room across from his, the one Ashley had set aside for Ardith and Rachel.

Although he'd been the one to send Ashley away, he wished for a brief and fervent moment that she had stayed. Being a woman, she'd know how to calm and comfort Ardith in ways that would probably never enter his testosterone-saturated brain.

And he needed to tell *somebody* that his mother had died. He couldn't confide in Vince—they didn't have that kind of relationship. Ardith had enough problems of her own, and Rachel was a little kid.

Jack opened the door of the small but still spacious suite, with its flowery bedspreads, lace curtains and bead-fringed lamps. He'd closed the shutters earlier, and laid the makings of a fire on the hearth.

Taking a match from the box on the mantel, he lit the wadded newspaper and dry kindling, watched with primitive satisfaction as the blaze caught.

Ardith looked around, finally shrugged out of the raincoat.

"I want to call Charles," she said, clearly expecting a refusal. "I haven't talked to my husband since—"

"If you want to put him and the other kids in Lombard's crosshairs, Ardith," Jack said evenly, giving her a sidelong glance as he straightened, then stood there, soaking in the warmth of the fire, "you go right ahead."

She was boney as hell, beneath a sweat suit that must have been two sizes too big for her, and her once-beautiful face looked gaunt, her cheekbones protruding, her skin gray and slack. She'd aged a decade since gathering her small daughter close in that airport.

Ardith glanced toward the open door of the suite, then turned her gaze back to Jack's face. "I have two other children besides Rachel," she said slowly.

Jack added wood to the fire, now that it was crackling, and replaced the screen. Turned to Ardith with his arms folded across his chest.

"Meaning what?" he asked, afraid he already knew what she was about to say.

She sagged, limp-kneed, onto the side of one of the twin beds, her head down. "Meaning," she replied, after biting down so hard on her lower lip that Jack half expected to see blood, "that Chad is wearing me down."

Jack went to the door, peered out into the hall, found it empty. In the distance, he could hear Vince and Rachel in the kitchen. Pans were clattering, and the small countertop TV was on.

He shut the door softly. "Don't even tell me you're thinking of turning Rachel over to Lombard," he said.

A tear slithered down one of Ardith's pale cheeks, and she didn't move to wipe it away. Maybe she wasn't even aware that she was crying. Her eyes blazed, searing into Jack. "Are you judging me, Mr. McCall? May I remind you that you work for me?"

"May I remind you," Jack retorted calmly, "that Lombard is an international drug runner? That he tortures and kills people on a regular basis—for fun?"

Ardith dragged in a breath so deep it made her entire body quiver. "I wish I'd never gotten involved with him."

"Get in line," Jack said. "I'm sure your parents would agree, along with your present husband. The fact is, you *did* 'get involved,' in a big way, and now you've got a seven-year-old daughter who deserves all the courage and strength you can muster up."

"I'm running on empty, Jack. I can't keep this up much longer."

"Where does that leave Rachel?"

Misery throbbed in her eyes. "With you?" she asked, in a small voice. "She'd be safe, I know she would, and—"

"And you could go back home and pretend none of this ever happened? That you never met Lombard and gave birth to his child—*your* child?"

"You make me sound horrible!"

Jack thrust out a sigh. "Look, I know this is hard. It's *worse* than hard. But you can't bail on that little girl, Ardith. Deep down, you don't even want to. You've got to tough this out, for Rachel's sake and your own."

"What if I can't?" Ardith whispered.

"You can, Ardith, because you don't have a choice."

"Couldn't the FBI or the DEA help? Find her another family—?"

"Christ," Jack said. "You can't be serious."

Ardith fell onto her side on the bed, her knees drawn up to her chest in a fetal position, and sobbed, deeply and with a wretchedness that tore at the fabric of his soul. It was one of the worst sounds Jack had ever heard.

"You're exhausted," he said. "You'll feel different when you've had something to eat and a good night's sleep. We'll come up with some kind of solution, Ardith. I promise."

Footsteps sounded on the stairs, then in the hallway, and Rachel burst in. "Mommy, we found beef stew in the fridge and—" she stopped, registering the sight her mother made, lying there on the bed. Worry contorted the child's face, made her shoulders go rigid. "Why are you crying?"

Stepping behind Rachel so she couldn't see him, Jack glared a warning at Ardith.

Ardith stopped wailing, sat up, sniffled and dashed at her cheeks with the backs of both hands. "I was just missing your daddy and the other kids," she said. She straightened her spine, snatched tissues from a decorative box on the table between the beds, and blew her nose.

"I miss them, too," Rachel said. "And Grambie and Gramps, too."

Ardith nodded, set the tissue aside. "I know, sweetheart," she said. Somehow, she summoned up a smile, misty and faltering, but a smile nonetheless. "Did someone mention beef stew? I could use something like that."

Rachel's attention had shifted to the cheery fireplace. "We get our own *fireplace?*" she enthused.

Jack thought back to the five days he and Rachel had spent navigating that South American jungle after he'd nabbed her from Lombard's remote estate. They'd dealt with mosquitoes, snakes, chattering monkeys with a penchant for throwing things at them, and long, dark nights with little to cover them but the stars and the weighted, humid air.

Rachel hadn't complained once. When they were traveling, she got to ride on Jack's back or shoulders, and she enjoyed it wholeheartedly. She'd chattered incessantly, every waking moment, about all the things she'd have to tell her mommy, her stepfather, and her little brother and sister when they were together again.

"Your own fireplace," Jack confirmed, his voice husky.

He and Ardith exchanged glances, and then they all went downstairs, to the kitchen, for some of Ashley's beef stew.

Ashley waited until she was sure Olivia and Tanner were sound asleep, then crept out of the guest suite. The night nurse sat in front of the television set in the den, sound asleep.

Behind Ashley, Mrs. Wiggins mewed.

Ashley turned, a finger to her lips, hoisted the kitten up for a nuzzle, then carried the little creature back into the suite, set her down, and carefully closed the door.

Her eyes burned as the kitten meowed at being left behind.

Reaching the darkened and empty kitchen, Ashley let out her breath, going over the plan she'd spent several hours rehearsing in her head.

She would disable the alarm, then reset it before closing the door behind her. Drive slowly out to the main road, waiting until she reached the mailboxes before turning her headlights on.

Ginger, snoozing on her dog bed in the corner, lifted her golden head, gave Ashley a slow, curious once-over.

Ashley put a finger to her lips, just as she'd done earlier, with the kitten.

A voice bloomed in her mind.

Don't go, it said.

Ashley blinked. Stared at the dog. Shook her head.

No. She had *not* received a telepathic message from Olivia's dog. She was still keyed up from the family meeting, and worried about Jack, and her imagination was running away with her, that was all.

I'll tell, the silent, internal voice warned. *All I have to do is bark.*

"Hush," Ashley said, fumbling in her purse for her car keys. "I'm not hearing this. It's all in my head."

"It's snowing."

Unnerved, Ashley tried to ignore Ginger, who had now risen on all four paws, as though prepared to carry out a threat she couldn't possibly have made.

Ashley went to the nearest window, the one over the sink, and peered through it, squinting.

Snowflakes the size of golf balls swirled past the glass.

Ashley glanced back at Ginger in amazement. "Well, it *is* January," she rationalized.

"You can't drive in this blizzard."

"Stop it," Ashley said, though she couldn't have said whether she was talking to the golden retriever or to herself. Or both.

The dog simply stood there, ready to bark.

Nonsense, Ashley thought. *Olivia hears animals.* You don't.

Still, either her imagination or the dog had a point. Her small hybrid car wouldn't make it out of the driveway in weather like that. The yard was probably under a foot of snow, and visibility would be zero, if not worse.

She had to think.

As quietly as possible, she drew back a chair at the big kitchen table and sat down.

Ginger relaxed a little, but she was still watchful.

Just sitting at that table caused Ashley to flash back to the family meeting earlier that evening. Meg and Brad, Melissa, Olivia and Tanner—even Sophie and Carly and little Mac, had all been there.

As the eldest of the four O'Ballivan siblings, Brad had been the main spokesperson.

"Ashley," he'd said, "you're not going home until McCall is gone. And Tanner and I plan to make sure he is, first thing in the morning."

She'd gaped at her brother, understanding his reasoning but stung to fury just the same. Looking around, she'd seen the same grim determination in Tanner's face, Olivia's, even Melissa's.

Outraged, she'd reminded them all that she was an adult and would come and go as she pleased, thank you very much.

Only Sophie and Carly had seemed even remotely sympathetic, but neither of them had spoken up on her behalf.

"You can't hold me prisoner here," Ashley had protested, her heart thumping, adrenaline burning through her veins like acid.

"Oh, yeah," Brad had answered, his tone and expression utterly implacable. "We can."

She'd decided right then that she'd get out —yes, their intentions were good, but it was the principle of the thing—but she'd also kept her head. She'd pretended to agree.

She'd helped make supper.

She'd loaded the dishwasher afterward.

She'd even rocked one of the babies—John, she thought—to sleep after Olivia had nursed him.

The evening had seemed endless.

Finally, Meg and Brad had left, taking Mac and Carly with them. Sophie, having finished her homework, had given Ashley a hug before retiring to her room for the night.

Ashley had yawned a lot and vanished into her own lush quarters.

She'd taken a hot bath, put on her pajamas and one of Olivia's robes, watched a little television—some mindless reality show.

And she'd waited, listening to the old-new house settle around her, Mrs. Wiggins curled up on her lap, as though trying to hold her new mistress in her chair with that tiny, weightless body of hers.

Once she was sure the coast was clear, Ashley had quietly dressed, never thinking to check the weather. Such was her state of distraction.

Now, here she sat, alone in her sister's kitchen at one-thirty in the morning, engaged in a standoff with a talking dog.

"I can take the Suburban," she whispered to Ginger. "It will go anywhere."

"What's so important?" Ginger seemed to ask.

Ashley shook her head again, rubbed her temples with the fingertips of both hands. "Jack," she said, keeping her voice down because, one, she didn't want to be overheard and stopped from leaving and, two, she was talking to a *dog,* for pity's sake. "*Jack* is so important. He's sick. And something is wrong. I can feel it."

"You could ask Tanner to go into town and help him out."

Ashley blinked. Was this really happening? If the conversation *was* only in her mind, why did the other side of it just pop up without her framing the words first?

"I can't do that," she said. "Olivia and the babies might need him."

Resolved, she rose from her chair, crossed to the

wooden rack where Olivia kept various keys, and helped herself to the set that would unlock and start the venerable old Suburban.

She jingled the key ring at Ginger.

"Go ahead," she said. "Bark."

Ginger gave a huge sigh. *"I'll give you a five minute head start,"* came the reply, *"then I'm raising the roof."*

"Fair enough," Ashley agreed, scrambling into Big John's old woolen coat, the one Olivia wore when she was working, hoping it would give her courage. "Thanks."

"I was in love once," Ginger said, sounding wistful.

Ashley moved to the alarm-control panel next to the back door. Racked her brain for the code, which Olivia had given to her in case of emergency, finally remembered it.

Grabbed her coat and dashed over the threshold.

The cold slammed into her like something solid and heavy, with sharp teeth.

Her car was under a mound of snow, the Suburban a larger mound beside it. Perhaps because of the emotions stirred by the family meeting, Tanner had forgotten to park the rigs in the spacious garage with his truck, the way he normally would have on a winter's night.

Hastily, she climbed onto the running board and wiped off the windshield with one arm, grateful for the heavy, straw-scented weight of her grandfather's old coat, even though it nearly swallowed her. Then she opened the door of the Suburban, got in and rammed the key into the ignition.

The engine sputtered once, then again, and finally roared to life.

Ashley threw it into Reverse, backed into the turn-around, spun her wheels for several minutes in the deep snow.

Swearing under her breath, she slammed the steering wheel with one fist, missed it, and hit the horn instead.

"Do. Not. Panic," she told herself out loud.

Just how many minutes had passed, she wondered frantically. Had Ginger already started barking? Had anyone heard the Suburban's horn when she hit it by accident?

She drew a deep breath, thrust it out in a whoosh.

No, she decided.

Lights would be coming on in the house if the dog were raising a ruckus. The howling wind had probably covered the bleat of the horn.

She shifted the Suburban into the lowest gear, tried again to get the old wreck moving. It finally tore free of the snowbank, the wheels grabbing.

As she turned the vehicle around and zoomed down the driveway, she heard the alarm system go off in the house, even over the wind and the noise of the engine.

Crap. She'd either forgotten to reset the system, or done it incorrectly.

Looking in the rearview mirror would have been useless, since the back window was coated with snow and frost, so Ashley sped up and raced toward the main road, praying she wouldn't hit a patch of ice and spin off into the ditch.

I'm sorry, she told Tanner and Olivia, the babies and Sophie and the night nurse, the alarm shrieking like a convention of angry banshees behind her. *I'm so sorry.*

Her kitchen was completely dark.

Shivering from the cold and from the harrowing ride

into town, Ashley shut the door behind her, dropped her key into the pocket of Big John's coat and reached for the light switch.

"Don't move," a stranger's voice commanded. A *male* stranger's voice.

Flipping the switch was a reflex; light spilled from the fluorescent panels in the ceiling, revealing a man she'd never seen before— or had she?—seated at her table, holding a gun on her.

"Who are you?" she asked, amazed to discover that she could speak, she was so completely terrified.

The man stood, the gun still trained squarely on her central body mass. "The pertinent question here, lady, is who are *you?*"

A strange boldness surged through Ashley, fear borne high on a flood of pure, indignant rage. "I am Ashley O'Ballivan," she said evenly, "and this is my house."

"Oh," the man said.

Just then, the inside door swung open and Jack was there, brandishing a gun of his own.

What was this? Ashley wondered wildly. Tombstone?

"Lay it down, Vince," Jack said, his voice stone-cold.

Vince complied, though not with any particular grace. The gun made an ominous thump on the table-top. "Chill, man," he said. "You told me to stand watch and that's all I was doing."

Ashley's gaze swung back to Jack. She was furious and relieved, and a host of other things, too, all at once.

"I do not allow firearms in my house," she said.

Vince chuckled.

Jack told him to get lost, shoving his own pistol into the front of his pants. The move was too expert, too deft, and the gun itself looked military.

Vince ambled out of the room, shaking his head once as he passed Jack.

"What are you doing here?" Jack asked, as though *she* were the intruder.

"Do I have to say it?" Ashley countered, flinging her purse aside, fighting her way out of Big John's coat, which suddenly felt like a straightjacket. *"I live here, Jack."*

"I thought we agreed that you wouldn't come back until I gave you a heads-up," Jack said, keeping his distance.

Considering Ashley's mood, that was a wise decision on his part, even if he *was* armed and almost certainly dangerous.

"I changed my mind," she replied, tight-lipped, her arms folded stubbornly across her chest. "And who is that—that *person,* anyway?"

"Vince works for me," Jack said.

Another car crunched into the driveway. A door slammed.

Jack swore, untucking his shirt so the fabric covered the gun in the waistband of his jeans.

Tanner slammed through the back door.

"Well," Jack observed mildly, "the gang's all here."

"Not yet," Tanner snapped. "Brad's on his way. What the *hell* is going on, Ashley? You set off the alarm, the dog is probably *still* barking her brains out, and the babies are permanently traumatized—not to mention Sophie and Olivia!"

"I'm sorry," Ashley said.

A cell phone rang, somewhere on Tanner's person.

He pulled the device from his coat pocket, after fumbling a lot, squinted at the caller ID and took the call. "She's at her place," he said, probably to Olivia. A crimson flush climbed his neck, pulsed in his jaw. And his anger was nothing compared to what Brad's would be. "No, don't worry—I think things are under control…"

Ashley closed her eyes.

Brakes squealed outside.

Tanner's voice seemed to recede, and then the call ended.

Brad nearly tore down the door in his hurry to get inside.

Jack looked around, his expression drawn but pleasant.

"Cherry crepes, anyone?" he asked mildly.

Chapter 8

"I know a place the woman and the little girl will be safe," Brad said wearily, once the excitement had died down and Ashley, her brother, Jack and Tanner were calmly seated around her kitchen table, eating the middle-of-the-night breakfast she'd prepared to keep from going out of her mind with anxiety.

Vince, the man with the gun, was conspicuously absent, while Ardith and Rachel slept on upstairs. Remarkably, the uproar hadn't awakened them, probably because they were so worn-out.

Jack shifted in his chair, pushed back his plate. For a man who believed so strongly in bacon and eggs, he hadn't eaten much. "Where?" he asked.

"Nashville," Brad replied. Then he threw out the name of one of the biggest stars in country music. "She's a friend," he added, as casually as if just *anybody* could wake up a famous woman in the middle of the night and ask her to shelter a pair of strangers for an indefinite length of time. "And she's got more high-tech security than the president. Bodyguards, the whole works."

"She'd do that?" Jack asked, grimly impressed.

Brad raised one shoulder in a semblance of a shrug. "I'd do it for her, and she knows that," he said easily. "We go way back."

"Sounds good to me," Tanner put in, relaxing a little. Everyone, naturally, was showing the strain.

"Me, too," Jack admitted, and though he didn't sigh, Ashley sensed the depths of his relief. "How do we get them there?"

"Very carefully," Brad said. "I'll take care of it."

Jack seemed to weigh his response for a long time before giving it. "There's a woman's life at stake here," he said. "And a little girl's future."

"I got that," Brad answered. His gaze slid to Ashley, then moved back to Jack's face, hardening again. "Of course, I want something in return."

Ashley held her breath.

Jack maintained eye contact with Brad. "What?"

"You, gone," Brad said. "For good."

"Now, *wait just one minute*—" Ashley sputtered.

"He's right," Jack said. "Lombard wants me, Ashley, not you. And I intend to keep it that way."

"So when do we make the move?" Tanner asked.

"Now," Brad responded evenly, a muscle bunching in his jawline. He could surely feel Ashley's glare boring into him. "I can have a jet at the airstrip within an hour or two, and I think we need to get them out of here before sunrise."

"Can't you let Rachel and her mother rest, just for

this one night?" Ashley demanded. "They must be absolutely exhausted by all this—"

"It has to be tonight," Brad insisted.

Jack nodded, sighed as he got to his feet. "Make the calls," he told Brad. "I'll get them out of bed."

Things were moving too fast. Ashley gripped the table edge, swaying with a sudden sensation of teetering on the brink of some bottomless abyss. "Wait," she said.

She might as well have been invisible, inaudible. A ghost haunting her own house, for all the attention anyone paid her.

Brad was already reaching for his cell phone. "When I get back from Nashville," he said, watching Jack, "I expect you to be history."

Jack nodded, avoiding Ashley's desperate gaze. "It's a deal," he said, and left the room.

Ashley immediately sprang out of her chair, without the faintest idea of what she would do next.

Tanner took a gentle hold on her wrist and eased her back down onto the cushioned seat.

Brad placed a call to his friend. Apologized for waking her up. Exchanged a few pleasantries—yes, Meg was fine and Mac was growing like a weed, and sure there would be other kids. Give him time.

Ashley listened in helpless sorrow as he went on to explain the Ardith-Rachel situation and ask for help.

The singer agreed immediately.

Brad called for a private jet. He might as well have been ordering a pizza, he was so casual about it. Only with a pizza, he would at least have had to give a credit card number.

When Brad said, "jump," the response was invariably, "How high?"

Because she'd always known him as her big brother, the broad scope of his power always came as a surprise to her.

Things accelerated after the phone calls.

Resigned, Ashley got to work preparing food for the trip, so Ardith and Rachel wouldn't starve, though the jet probably offered catered meals.

Her guests stumbled sleepily into the kitchen just as she was finishing, herded there by Jack, their clothes rumpled and hastily donned, their eyes glazed with confusion, weariness and fear.

The little girl favored Ashley with a wan, blinking smile. "Have you been taking care of Jack?" she asked.

Ashley's heart turned over. "I've been trying," she said truthfully, studiously ignoring Brad, Tanner and Jack himself.

Vince had wandered in behind them. "Want me to go along for the ride?" he asked, meeting no one's eyes.

"No," Jack said tersely. "You're done here."

"For good?" Vince asked.

"For now," Jack replied.

Vince turned to Brad. "Catch a ride to the airstrip with you?"

Jack gave the man a quick glance, his eyes ever so slightly narrowed. "I'll take you there myself," he said, adding a brisk, "Later."

"You stopped trusting me, boss?" Vince asked, with an odd grin.

"Maybe," Jack said.

Some of the color drained from Vince's face. "Am I fired?"

"Don't push it," Jack answered.

In the end, it was decided that Tanner would drive

Vince back to his helicopter once Brad, Ardith and Rachel were aboard the jet, ready for takeoff. Later, Tanner would see that Jack boarded a commercial airliner in Flagstaff, bound for Somewhere Else.

Holding back tears, Ashley handed her brother the food she'd packed, tucked into a basket with a cheery red-and-white-checkered napkin for a cover.

Something softened in Brad's eyes as he accepted the offering, but he didn't say anything.

And neither did Ashley.

A gulf had opened between Ashley and the big brother she had always loved and admired, far wider than the one created by their mother's death. Even knowing he was doing what he thought was right—what probably *was* right—Ashley felt steamrolled, and she resented it.

Soon, Brad was gone, along with Ardith and Rachel.

Approximately an hour later, Tanner and the chastened Vince left, too.

Jack and Ashley sat on opposite sides of the kitchen table, unable to look at each other.

After a long, long time, Jack said, "My mother died three years ago. And I didn't have a clue."

Startled, Ashley sat up straighter in her chair. "I'm sorry," she said.

"Breast cancer," Jack explained gruffly, his eyes moist.

"Oh, Jack. That's terrible."

He nodded. Sighed heavily.

"I guess this is our last night together," Ashley said, at some length.

"I guess so," Jack agreed miserably.

Purpose flowed through Ashley. "Then let's make it count," she said. She locked the back door. She flipped off the lights. And then she took Jack's hand, there in the darkness, and led him upstairs to her bed.

Every moment, every gesture, was precious, and very nearly sacred.

Jack undressed Ashley the way an archeologist might uncover a fragile treasure, with a cherishing tenderness that stirred not only her body, but her soul. Head back, she surrendered her naked breasts to him, reveled in the sensations wrought by his lips and tongue.

A low, crooning sound escaped her, and she found just enough control to open his shirt, her fingers fumbling with the buttons. She needed to feel his flesh, bare and hard, yet warm against her palms and splayed fingers.

They kissed, long and deep, with a sweet urgency all the better for the smallest delay.

In time, Jack eased her onto the bed, sideways, and spread her legs to nuzzle and then suckle her until she was gasping with need and exaltation.

She whispered his name, a ragged sound, and tears burned in her eyes. How would she live without him, without this? How colorless her days would be, when he was gone, and how empty her nights. He'd taught her body to crave these singular pleasures, to need them as much as she needed air and water and the light of the sun.

But, no, she thought sorrowfully. She mustn't spoil what was probably their last night together by leaving the moment, journeying into a lonely and uncertain future. It was *now* that mattered, and only now. Jack's hands on her inner thighs, Jack's mouth on the very center of her femininity.

Dear God, it felt so good, the way he was loving her, almost too good to be borne.

The first climax came softly, seizing her, making her buckle and moan in release.

"Don't stop," she pleaded, entangling her fingers in his hair.

She hoped he would *never* cut his hair short again.

He chuckled against her moist, straining flesh, nipped at her ever so lightly with his teeth and brought her to another orgasm, this one sharp and brief, a sudden and wild flexing deep within her. "Oh, I'm a long way from finished," he assured her gruffly, before falling to her again.

Ashley could never have said afterward how many times she rose and fell on the hot tide of primitive satisfaction, flailing and writhing and crying out with each new abandoning of her ordinary self.

When he finally took her, she gloried in the heat and length and hardness of him, in the pulsing and the renewed wanting. Her body became greedier than before, demanding, reaching, shuddering. And Jack drove deep, eventually losing control, but only after a long, delicious period of restraint.

They made love time and again that night, holding each other in silence while they recovered between bouts of fevered passion.

"I'll come back if I can," Jack told her, at one point, barely able to breathe, he was so spent. "Give me a year before you fall in love with somebody else, okay?"

A year. It seemed like an eternity to Ashley, she was so aware of every passing moment, every tick of the celestial clock. At the same time, though, she knew it was safe to promise. She'd wait a lifetime, a dozen lifetimes, because for her, there *was* no man but Jack.

She nodded, dampening his bare shoulder with her tears, and finally slept.

* * *

Jack eased himself out of Ashley's arms, and her bed, around eight o'clock the next morning. It was one of those heartrendingly beautiful winter days, with sunlight glaring on pristine snow. Everything seemed to be draped in purity.

He dressed in his own room, gathered the few belongings he'd brought with him, and tucked them into his bag.

Given his druthers, he would have sat quietly in a chair, watching Ashley sleep, memorizing every line and curve of her, so he could hold her image in his mind and his heart until he died.

But Jack was the sort of man who rarely got his druthers.

He had things to do.

First, he'd meet with Chad Lombard.

If he survived that—and it was a crapshoot, whether he or Lombard or neither of them would walk away—he'd check himself into a hospital.

Feeling more alone than he ever had—and given some of the things he'd been through that was saying a lot—Jack gravitated to the computer in Ashley's study. He called up his dad's website, clicked to the Contact Us link, wrote an email he never intended to send.

Hello, Dad. I'm alive, but not for long, probably...

He went on to explain why he'd never come home from military school, why he'd let everyone in his family believe he was dead. He apologized for any pain they must have suffered because of his actions, and resisted the temptation to lay any of the blame on the Navy.

The mission had been a tough one, with a high price, but no one had held a gun to his head. He'd made the decision himself and, in most ways, he had never regretted it.

He went on to say that he hoped his mother hadn't had to endure too much pain, and asked for forgiveness. In sketchy terms, he described the toxin that was probably killing him.

In closing, he wrote, *You should know that I met a woman. If things were different, I'd love to settle down with her right here in this little Western town, raise a flock of kids with her. But some things aren't meant to be, and it's beginning to look as if this is one of them.*

No matter how it may seem, I love you, Dad.

I'm sorry.

Jack.

He was about to hit the Delete button—writing the piece had been a catharsis—when two things happened at once. His cell phone rang, and somebody knocked hard at the front door.

Simultaneously, Jack answered the call and admitted Tanner Quinn to the house he'd soon be leaving, probably forever.

No more cherry crepes.

No more mutant cat.

No more Ashley.

"Mercer?" Lombard asked affably, "is that you?"

Jack shifted to the Neal Mercer persona, because Lombard knew him by that name, gestured for Tanner to come inside, but be quiet about it.

Ashley was still sleeping, and Jack didn't want to wake her. Leaving was going to be hard enough, without a face-to-face goodbye.

On the other hand, didn't he owe her that much?

"What?" he asked Lombard.

"I've decided on a place for the showdown," Lombard said. "Tombstone, Arizona. Fitting, don't you think?"

"You're a regular John Wayne," Jack told him.

Tanner raised his eyebrows in silent question. Jack shook his head, pointed to his gear bag, waiting just inside the door.

Tanner picked up the bag, carried it out to his truck. The exhaust spewed white steam into the cold, bright air.

Leavin' on a jet plane… Jack thought.

"Tomorrow," Lombard went on. "High noon."

"High *drama*, you mean," Jack scoffed.

"Be there," Lombard ordered, dead serious now, and hung up.

Jack sighed and clicked the phone shut.

Glanced up at the ceiling.

Tanner returned from the luggage run, waiting with his big rancher's hands stuffed into the pockets of his sheepskin coat.

"Give me a minute," Jack said.

Tanner nodded, his eyes full of sympathy.

Jack turned from that. Sympathy wasn't going to help him now.

He had to be strong. Stronger than he'd ever been.

Upstairs, he entered Ashley's room, sat down on the edge of the bed, and watched her for a few luxurious moments, moments he knew he would cherish until he died, whether that was in a day, or several decades.

Ashley opened her eyes, blinked. Said his name.

For a lot of years, Jack had claimed he didn't have a heart. For all his money, love was something he simply couldn't afford.

Now he knew he'd lied—to himself and everyone else.

He had a heart, all right, and it was breaking.

"I love you," he said. "Always have, always will."

She sat up, threw her arms around his neck, clung to him for a few seconds. "I love you, too," she murmured, trembling against him. Then she drew back, looked deep into his eyes. "Thanks," she said.

"For—?" Jack ground out the word.

"The time we had. For not leaving without saying goodbye."

He nodded, not trusting himself to speak just then.

"If you can come back—"

Jack drew out of her embrace, stood. In the cold light of day, returning to Stone Creek, to Ashley, seemed unlikely, a golden dream he'd used to get through the night.

He nodded again. Swallowed hard.

And then he left.

He was boarding a plane in Flagstaff, nearly two hours later, before he remembered that he hadn't closed the email he'd drafted on Ashley's computer, spilling his guts to his father.

Ashley wasn't exactly a techno-whiz, he thought, with a sad smile, but if she stumbled upon the message somehow, she'd know most of his secrets.

She might even send the thing, on some do-gooder impulse, though Jack doubted that. In any case, she'd know about the damage the toxin was doing to his bone marrow and be privy to his deepest regrets as far as his family was concerned.

She'd know he'd loved her, too. Wanted to spend his life with her.

That shining dream could still come true, he supposed,

but a lot of chips would have to fall first, and land in just the right places. The odds, he knew, were against him.

Nothing new there.

He took his seat on the small commuter plane, fastened his seat belt, and shut off his cell phone.

Tanner had been right there when he'd bought his ticket—he'd chosen Phoenix, said he'd probably head for South America from there, and gone through all the proper steps, checking his gear bag and filling out a form declaring that there was a firearm inside, properly secured.

What he *didn't* tell his friend was that he planned to charter a flight to Tombstone as soon as he reached Phoenix and have it out with Chad Lombard, once and for all.

Takeoff was briefly delayed, due to some mechanical issue.

During the wait, Jack switched his phone on again, placed a short call that drew an alarmed stare from the woman sitting next to him and smiled as he put the cell away.

"Air marshal," he explained, in an affable undertone.

The woman didn't look reassured. In fact, she moved to an empty seat three rows forward. A word to the flight attendants about the man in 7-B and he'd be off the plane, tangled in a snarl with a pack of TSA agents until three weeks after forever.

For some reason, she didn't report him. Maybe she didn't watch the news a lot, or fly much.

Jack settled back, closed his eyes, and tried not to think about Ashley and the baby they might have conceived together, the future they might have shared.

That proved impossible, of course, like the old game of trying not to think about a pink elephant.

The plane lifted off, bucked through some turbulence and streaked toward his destiny—and Chad Lombard's.

Carly McKettrick O'Ballivan watched her aunt with concern, while Meg, who was both Carly's sister *and* her adoptive mother—how weird was that?—puttered around the big kitchen, trying to distract Ashley.

Meg was expecting a baby, and the news might have cheered Ashley up, but Carly and her mother-sister had agreed on the way into town to wait until Brad-dad was back from wherever he'd gone.

Unable to bear Ashley's pale face and sorrowful eyes any longer, Carly excused herself and wandered toward the study. She'd set up the computer, she decided. Use this strange morning constructively.

School was closed on account of megasnow, but nothing stopped members of the McKettrick clan when they wanted to get somewhere. Meg had told Carly they were going to town, fired up her new Land Rover right after breakfast, acting all mysterious and sad, buckled a squirmy Mac into his car seat, and off they'd gone.

Carly, a sucker for adventure, had enjoyed the ride into town, over roads buried under a foot of snow. Once, Meg had even taken an overland route, causing Mac to giggle and Carly to shout, "Yee-haw!"

Even the plows weren't out yet—that's how deep the stuff was.

To Carly's surprise, someone had beaten her to the computer gig. The monitor was dark, but the machine was on, whirring quietly away in the otherwise silent room.

She sat down in the swivel chair, touched the mouse.

An email message popped up on the monitor screen.

Since Brad and Meg were big on personal privacy, Carly didn't actually read the email, but she couldn't help noticing that it was signed, "Love, Jack."

She barely knew Jack McCall, but she'd liked him. Which was more than could be said for Brad and Meg.

They clearly thought the man was bad news.

Carly bit her lower lip. If Jack had gone to all the trouble of writing that long email, she reasoned, her heart thumping a little, surely he'd intended to send it.

With so much going on—Carly had no idea what any of it actually was, except that it had obviously done a real number on Ashley, so it must be pretty heavy stuff—he'd probably just forgotten.

Carly took a deep breath, moved the cursor, and hit Send.

"Carly!" Meg called, clearly approaching.

Carly closed the message panel. "What?"

Meg appeared in the doorway of the study. "School's open after all," she said. "I just heard it on the kitchen radio."

Carly sighed. "Awesome," she said, meaning exactly the opposite.

Meg chuckled. "Get a move on, kiddo," she ordered.

"Are there snowshoes around here someplace?" Carly countered. "Maybe a dogsled and a team, so I can *mush* to school?"

"Hugely funny," Meg said, grinning. Like all the other grown-ups, she looked tired. "I'd drive you to school in the Land Rover, but I don't think I should leave Ashley just yet."

Carly agreed, with the teenage reluctance that was

surely expected of her, and resigned herself to the loss of that greatest of all occasions, a snow day.

Trudging toward the high school minutes later, she wondered briefly if she should have left that email in the outbox, maybe told Meg or Ashley about it.

But her friends were converging up ahead, laughing and hurling snowballs at each other, and she hurried to join them.

Ashley both hoped for and dreaded a call from Jack, but none came.

Not while Meg was there, and not when she left.

A ranch hand from Starcross brought Mrs. Wiggins back home, and Ashley was glad and grateful, but still wrung out. She felt dazed, disjointed, as though she were truly beside herself.

She slept.

She cooked.

She slept some more, and then cooked some more.

At four o'clock that afternoon, Brad showed up.

"He's gone," she said, meaning Jack, meeting her taciturn-looking brother at the back door. "Are you happy now?"

"You know I'm not," Brad said, moving past her to enter the house when she would have blocked his way. He helped himself to coffee and, out of spite, Ashley didn't tell him it was decaf. If he expected a buzz from the stuff, something to jump-start the remainder of his day, he was in for a disappointment.

"Are Ardith and Rachel safe?" she asked.

"Yes," Brad answered, leaning back against the counter to sip his no-octane coffee and study her. "You all right?"

"Oh, I'm just fabulous, thank you."

"Ashley, give it up, will you? You know Jack couldn't stay."

"I also know the decision was mine to make, Brad—not yours."

Her brother gave a heavy sigh. She could see how drained he was, but she wouldn't allow herself to feel sorry for him. Much. "You'll get over this," he told her, after a long time.

"Gee, thanks," she said, wiping furiously at her already-clean counters, keeping as far from Brad as she could. "That makes it all better."

"Meg's going to have a baby," Brad said, out of the blue, a few uncomfortable moments later. "In the spring."

Ashley froze.

Olivia had twins.

Now Meg and Brad were adding to their family, something she should have been glad about, considering that Meg had suffered a devastating miscarriage a year after Mac was born and there had been some question as to whether or not she could have more children.

"Congratulations," Ashley said stiffly, unable to look at him.

"You'll get your chance, Ash. The right man will come along and—"

"The right man *came* along, Brad," Ashley snapped, "and now he's gone."

But at least, this time, Jack had said goodbye.

This time, he hadn't wanted to go.

Small consolations, but something.

Brad set his mug aside, crossed to Ashley, took her

shoulders in his hands. "I'd have done anything," he said hoarsely, "to make this situation turn out differently."

Ashley believed him, but it didn't ease her pain.

She let herself cry, and Brad pulled her close and held her, big brother-style, his chin propped on top of her head.

"O'Ballivan tough," he reminded her. It was their version of something Meg's family, the McKettricks, said to each other when things got rocky.

"O'Ballivan tough," she agreed.

But her voice quavered when she said it.

She felt anything *but* tough.

She'd go on, just the same, because she had no other choice.

Jack arrived in Earp-country at eleven forty-five that morning and, after paying the pilot of the two-seat Cessna he'd chartered in Phoenix, climbed into a waiting taxi. Fortunately, Tombstone wasn't a big town, so he wouldn't be late for his meeting with Chad Lombard.

Anyway, he was used to cutting it close.

There were a lot of tourists around, as Jack had feared. He'd hoped the local police would be notified, find some low-key way to clear the streets before the shootout took place.

Some of them might be Lombard's men.

And some of them might be Feds.

Because of the innocent bystanders and because both the DEA and the FBI had valid business of their own with Lombard, Jack had taken a chance and tipped them off while waiting for the commuter jet to take off from Flagstaff.

He stashed his gear bag behind a toilet in a gas station restroom, tucked his Glock into his pants, covered it with his shirt and stepped out onto the windy street.

If he hadn't been in imminent danger of being picked off by Lombard or one of the creeps who worked for the bastard, he might have found the whole thing pretty funny.

He even amused himself by wishing he'd bought a round black hat and a gunslinger's coat, so he'd look the part.

Wyatt Earp, on the way to the OK Corral.

He was strolling down a wooden sidewalk, pretending to take in the famous sights, when the cell phone rang in the pocket of his jean jacket.

"Yo," he answered.

"You called in the Feds!" Lombard snarled.

"Yeah," Jack answered. "You're outnumbered, bucko."

"I'm going to take you out last," Lombard said. "Just so you can watch all these mommies and daddies and little kiddies in cowboy hats bite the freaking dust!"

Jack's blood ran cold. He'd known this was a very real possibility, of course—that was the main reason he'd called in reinforcements—but he'd hoped, against all reason, that even Lombard wouldn't sink that low.

After all, the man had a daughter of his own.

"Where are you?" Jack asked, with a calmness he sure as hell didn't feel. Worse yet, the weakness was rising inside him again, threatening to drop him to the ground.

Lombard laughed then, an eerie, brittle sound. "Look up," he said.

Jack lifted his eyes.

Lombard stood on a balcony overlooking the main street, opposite Jack. And he was wearing an Earp hat and a long coat, holding a rifle in one hand.

"Gun!" Jack yelled. "Everybody out of the street!"

The crowd panicked and scattered every which way, bumping into each other, screaming. Scrambling to shield children and old ladies and little dogs wearing neckerchiefs.

Lombard raised the rifle as Jack drew the Glock.

But neither of them got a chance to fire.

Another shot ripped through the shining January day, struck Lombard, and sent him toppling, in what seemed like slow motion, over the balcony railing, which gave way picturesquely behind him, like a bit from an old movie.

People shrieked in rising terror, as vulnerable to any gunmen Lombard might have brought along as backup as a bunch of ducks in a pond.

Feds rushed into the street, hustling the tourists into restaurants and hotel lobbies and souvenir shops, crowd control at its finest, if a little late.

Government firepower seemed to come out of the woodwork.

Somebody was taking pictures—Jack was aware of a series of flashes at the periphery of his vision.

He walked slowly toward the spot where Chad Lombard lay, either dead or dying, oblivious to the pandemonium he would have enjoyed so much.

Lombard stared blindly up at the blue, blue sky, a crimson patch spreading over the front of his collarless white shirt. Damned if he hadn't pinned a star-shaped badge to his coat, just to complete the outfit.

The Feds closed in, the sniper who had taken Lombard out surely among them. A hand came to rest on Jack's shoulder.

More pictures were snapped.

"Thanks, McCall," a voice said, through a buzzing haze.

He didn't look up at the agent, the longtime acquaintance he'd called from the plane in Flagstaff. Taking the cell phone out of his pocket, he turned it slowly in one hand, still studying Lombard.

Lombard didn't look like a killer, a drug runner. Jack could see traces of Rachel in the man's altar-boy features.

"We had trouble spotting him until he climbed out onto that balcony," Special Agent Fletcher said. "By our best guess, he stole the gunslinger getup from one of those old-time picture places— "

"Why didn't you clear the streets earlier?" Jack demanded.

"Because we got here about five seconds before you did," Fletcher answered. "Are you all right, McCall?"

Jack nodded, then shook his head.

Fletcher helped Jack to his feet. "Which is it?" he rasped. "Yes or no?"

Jack swayed.

His vision shrank to a pinpoint, then disappeared entirely.

"I guess it's no," he answered, just before he lost consciousness.

Chapter 9

The first sound Jack recognized was a steady *beep-beep-beep*. He was in a hospital bed, then, God knew where. Probably going about the business of dying.

"Jack?"

He struggled to open his eyes. Saw his father looming over him, a pretty woman standing wearily at the old man's side. If it hadn't been for her, Jack would have thought he was hallucinating.

Dr. William "Bill" McKenzie smiled, switched on the requisite lamp on the wall above Jack's head.

The spill of light made him wince.

"I see you've still got all your hair," Jack said, very slowly and in a dry-throated rasp. "Either that, or that's one fine rug perched on top of your head."

Bill laughed, though his eyes glistened with tears. Maybe they were goodbye tears. "You always were a smart-ass," he said. "This is my real hair. And speaking of hair, yours is too long. You look like a hippie."

People still used the word *hippie?*

Obviously, his dad's generation did. For all he knew, Bill McKenzie had been a hippie, once upon a time. There was so much they didn't know about each other.

"How did you find me?" Jack asked. The things he felt were too deep to leap right into—there had to be a transition here, a gradual shift.

"It wasn't too hard to track you down. You were all over the Internet, the TV and the newspapers after that incident in Tombstone. You were treated in Phoenix, and then some congressman's aide got in touch with me—soon as you were strong enough, I had you brought home, where you belong."

Home, Jack thought. *To die?*

Jack's gaze slid to the woman, who looked uncomfortable. *My stepmother,* he thought, and felt a fresh pang of loss because his mom should have been standing there beside his dad, not this stranger.

"Abigail," Bill explained hoarsely. "My wife."

"If you'll excuse me," Abigail said, after a nod of greeting, and headed for the nearest exit.

Bill sighed, trailed her with his eyes.

Jack glimpsed tenderness in those eyes, and peace. "How long have I been here?" he asked, after a long time.

"Just a few days," Bill answered. He cleared his throat, looking for a moment as though he might make a run for the corridor, just as Abigail had done. "You're in serious condition, Jack. Not out of the woods by any means."

"Yeah," Jack said, trying to accept what was probably inevitable. "I know. And you're here to say goodbye?"

The old man's jaw clamped down hard, the way it

used to when he was about to give one of his sons hell for some infraction and then ground him for a decade. "I'm *here*," he said, almost in a growl, "because you're my son, and I thought you were dead."

"Like Mom."

Bill's eyes, hazel like Jack's own, flashed. "We'll talk about your mother another time," he said. "Right now, boy, you're in one hell of a fix, and that's going to be enough to handle without going into all the *other* issues."

"It's a bone marrow thing," Jack recalled, but he was thinking about Ashley. She wasn't much for media, but even she had probably seen him on the news. "Something to do with a toxin manufactured especially for me."

"You need a marrow donor," Bill told him bluntly. "It's your only chance, and, frankly, it will be touch and go. I've already been tested, and so have your brothers. Bryce is the only match."

A chance, however small, was more than Jack had expected to get. He must have been mulling a lot of things over on an unconscious level while he was submerged in oblivion, though, because there was a sense of clarity behind the fog enveloping his brain.

"Bryce," he said. "The baby."

"He wouldn't appreciate being called that," Bill replied, with a moist smile. His big hand rested on Jack's, squeezed his fingers together. "Your brother will be ready when you are."

Jack imagined Ashley, the way she'd looked and smelled and felt, warm and naked beneath him. He saw her baking things, playing with the kitten, parking herself in front of the computer, her brow furrowed slightly with confusion and that singular determination of hers.

If he got through this thing, he could go back to her.

Swap his old life for a new one, straight across, and never look back.

But suppose some buddy of Lombard's decided to step up and take care of unfinished business?

No, he decided, discouraged to the core of his being. There were too many unknown factors; he couldn't start things up with Ashley again, even if he got lucky and survived the ordeal he was facing, until he was sure she'd be in no danger.

"So when is this transplant supposed to go down?" he asked his dad.

"Yesterday wouldn't have been too soon," Bill replied. "They were only waiting for you to stabilize a little."

"I'd like to see my brothers," Jack said, but even as he spoke, the darkness was already sucking him back under, into the dreamless place churning like an ocean beneath the surface of his everyday mind. "If they're speaking to me, that is."

Bill dashed at his wet eyes with the back of one large hand. "They're speaking to you, all right," he replied. "But if you pull through, you can expect all three of them to read you the riot act for disappearing the way you did."

If you pull through.

Jack sighed. "Fair enough," he said.

Reaching deep into her mind and heart in the days after Jack's leaving, Ashley had found a new strength. She'd absorbed the media blitz, with Jack and Chad Lombard playing their starring roles, with a stoicism that surprised even her. After the first wave, she'd stopped watching, stopped reading.

Enough was enough.

Every sound bite, every news clip, every article brought an overwhelming sense of sorrow and relief, in equal measures.

Two days after the Tombstone Showdown, as the reporters had dubbed it, a pair of FBI agents had turned up at Ashley's door.

They'd been long on questions and short on answers.

All they'd really been willing to divulge was that she was in no danger from Chad Lombard's organization; some of its members had been taken into federal custody in Arizona. The rest had scattered to the four winds.

And Jack was alive.

That gave her at least a measure of relief.

It was the questions that fed her sorrow, innocuous and routine though they were. Something about the tone of them, a certain sad resignation—there were no details forthcoming, either in the media or from the visiting agents, but she sensed that Jack was still in trouble.

Had Jack McCall told her anything about his association with any particular government agencies and if so, what? the agents wanted to know.

Had he left anything behind when he went away?

If Mr. McCall agreed, would she wish to visit him in a location that would be disclosed at a later time?

No, Jack hadn't told her anything, beyond the things the FBI already knew, and no, he hadn't left anything behind. Yes, she wanted to see him and she'd appreciate it if they'd disclose the mysterious location.

They refused, though politely, and left, promising to contact her later.

After that, she'd heard nothing more.

Since then, Ashley had been seized by a strange and fierce desperation, a need to do *something,* but she had no idea where Jack was, or what kind of condition he was in. She only knew that he'd collapsed in Tombstone—there had been pictures in the newspapers and on the web.

Both Brad and Tanner had "their people" beating the bushes for any scrap of information, but either they'd really come up with nothing, as they claimed, or they simply didn't want Jack McCall found. Ever.

Melissa was searching, too; even though she wasn't any fonder of Jack than Brad and Olivia were, she and Ashley had the twin link. Melissa knew, better than any of the others, exactly what her sister was going through.

The results of that investigation? So far, zip.

After a week, Jack disappeared from the news, displaced by accounts of piracy at sea, the president's latest budget proposal, and the like.

By the first of February, Ashley was very good at pretending she didn't care where Jack McCall was, what he was doing, whether or not he would —or could— come back.

She'd decided to Get on with Her Life.

Carly and Sophie had spent hours with her, after school, when they weren't rehearsing their parts in the drama club's upcoming play, fleshing out one of the websites Jack had created, showing her how to surf the Net, how to run searches, how to access and reply to email.

In fact, they'd both managed to earn special credit at school for undertaking the task.

Slowly, Ashley had begun to understand the mysteries of navigating cyberspace.

She quickly became proficient at web surfing, and especially at monitoring her modest but attractive website, already bringing in more business than she knew what to do with.

The B&B was booked solid for Valentine's Day weekend, and the profit margin on her "Hearts, Champagne and Roses" campaign looked healthy indeed.

With two weeks to go before the holiday arrived, she was already baking and freezing tarts, some for her guests to enjoy, and some for the annual dance at the Moose Lodge. This year, the herd was raising money to resurface the community swimming pool.

She'd agreed to serve punch and help provide refreshments, not out of magnanimity, but because she baked for the dance every year. And, okay, partly because she knew everybody in town was talking about her latest romantic disaster—this one had gone national, with CNN coverage and an article in *People,* not that she'd been specifically mentioned—and she wanted to show them all that she wasn't moping. No, sir, not her.

She was O'Ballivan tough.

If she still cried herself to sleep once in a while, well, nobody needed to know that. Nobody except Mrs. Wiggins, her small, furry companion, always ready to comfort her with a cuddle.

As outlined in the piece in *People,* Ardith and Rachel were back home, in a suburb of Phoenix, happily reunited with the rest of the family.

Yes, Ashley thought, sitting there at her computer long after she should have taken a bubble bath and gone to bed, day by day, moment by moment, she was getting over Jack.

Really and truly.

Or not.

Glancing out the window, she saw Melissa's car, a red glow under the streetlight, swinging into her driveway.

"Good," Ashley said to Mrs. Wiggins, who was perched on her right shoulder like a parrot. "I could use a little distraction."

Melissa was just coming through the back door when Ashley reached the kitchen. Her hair was flecked with snow and her grin was wide. Looking askance at Mrs. Wiggins, now nestling into her basket in front of the fireplace, Ashley's twin gave a single nose twitch and carefully kept her distance.

"It happened!" she crowed, hauling off her red tailored coat. "Alex got the prosecutor's job, and I'm going to be one of his assistants! I start the first of March and I've already got a line on a condo in Scottsdale —"

"Wonderful," Ashley said.

Melissa narrowed her beautiful eyes in mock suspicion. "Well, *that* was an enthusiastic response," she replied, draping the coat over the back of one of the chairs at the table.

Ashley's smile felt wobbly on her mouth, and a touch too determined. "If this is what you want, then I'm happy for you. I'm going to miss you a lot, that's all. Except for when you were in law school, we've never really been apart."

Melissa approached, laid a winter-chilled hand on each of Ashley's shoulders. "I'll only be two hours away," she said. "You'll visit me a lot, and of course I'll come back to Stone Creek as often as I can."

"No, you won't," Ashley said, turning away to start some tea brewing, so she wouldn't have to struggle to keep that stupid, slippery smile in place any longer. "You'll be too busy with your caseload, and you know it."

"I need to get away," Melissa said, so sadly that Ashley immediately turned to face her again, no longer concerned about hiding her own misgivings.

"Because?" Ashley prompted.

Melissa rarely looked vulnerable—a good lawyer appeared confident at all times, she often said—but she did then. That sheen in her eyes—was she crying?

"Because," Melissa said, after pushing back her spirally mane of hair with one hand, "things are heating up between Dan and the waitress. Her name is Holly and according to one of the receptionists at the office, they've been in Kruller's Jewelry Store three times in the last week, looking at rings."

Ashley sighed, wiped her hands on her patchwork apron, her own creation, made up of quilt scraps. "Sit down, Melissa," she said.

To her amazement, Melissa sat.

Of the two of them, Melissa had always been the leader, the one who decided things and gave impromptu motivational speeches.

Forgetting the tea preparations, Ashley took the chair closest to her sister's. "That's why you're leaving Stone Creek?" she asked quietly. "Because Dan and this Holly person might get married?"

"'Might,' nothing," Melissa huffed, but her usually straight shoulders sagged a little beneath her very professional white blouse. "As hot and heavy as things were between Dan and me, he never said a *word* about looking at engagement rings. If he's shopping for diamonds, he's *serious* about this woman."

"And?"

Melissa flushed a vibrant pink, with touches of crimson. "And I *might* still be *just a little* in love with him," she admitted.

"You can't have it all, Melissa," Ashley reminded her sister gently. "No one does. You made a choice and now you either have to change it or accept things as they are and move on."

Melissa blinked. "That's easy for *you* to say!"

"Is it?" Ashley asked.

"What am I saying?" Melissa immediately blurted out. "Ash, I'm sorry—I know the whole Jack thing has been—"

"We're not talking about Jack," Ashley said, a mite stiffly. "We're talking about Dan—and you. He's probably marrying this woman on the rebound—if the rumors about the rings are even true in the first place—because he really cared about you. And he might be making the mistake of a lifetime."

"That's *his* problem," Melissa snapped.

"Don't be a bitch," Ashley replied. "You didn't want him, or the life he offered, remember? What did you expect, Melissa? That Dan would wait around until you retire from your seat on the Supreme Court someday, and write your memoirs?"

"Whose side are you on, anyway?" Melissa asked peevishly.

"Yours," Ashley said, and she meant it. "Just talk to Dan before you take the job in Phoenix, Melissa. Please?"

"*He's* the one who broke it off!"

"Don't you want to be sure things can't be patched up?"

"Have you been paying attention? It's *too late,* Ashley."

"Maybe it is, maybe it isn't," Ashley said, getting up to resume the tea making. "You'll never know if you don't talk things over with Dan while there's still time."

"What am I supposed to do?" Melissa demanded, losing a little steam now. "Drive out there to the back of beyond, knock on his door, and ask him if he'd like to live in a city and be Mr. Melissa O'Ballivan? I can tell you right now what the answer would be—and besides, what if I interrupted—well—*something*—?"

"Like what? Chandelier-swinging sex? Dan has kids, Melissa—he and Holly Hot-Biscuits probably don't go at it in the living room on a regular basis."

Melissa sputtered out a laugh, wholly against her will. *"Holly Hot-Biscuits?"* she crowed. "Ashley O'Ballivan, could it be that you actually have a *racy* side?"

"You'd be surprised," Ashley said, recalling, with a well-hidden pang, some of the sex she and Jack had had. A chandelier would have been superfluous.

"Maybe I wouldn't," Melissa teased. At least she'd cheered up a little. Perhaps that could be counted as progress. "You miss Jack a lot, don't you?"

"When I let myself," Ashley admitted, though guardedly, concentrating on scooping tea leaves into a china pot. "The other night, I dreamed he was—he was standing at the foot of my bed. I could see through him, because he was—dead."

Melissa softened, in that quicksilver way she had. Tough one minute, tender the next—that was Melissa O'Ballivan. "Jack can't be dead," she reasoned, looking as though she wanted to get up from her chair, cross the room, and wrap Ashley in a sisterly embrace, but wisely refraining.

Ashley wasn't accepting hugs these days—from anybody.

She felt too bruised, inside and out.

"Why not?" she asked reasonably, over the sound of the water she ran to fill the kettle.

"Because someone would have told Tanner," Melissa said, very gently. "Come to Scottsdale with me, Ash. Right now, this weekend. Help me decide on the right condo. It would be good for you to get away, change your perspective, soak up some of that delicious sunshine—"

The idea had a certain appeal—she was sick of snow, for one thing—but there was the B&B to think about. She had guests coming for Valentine's Day, after all, and lots of preparations to make. She'd even rented out her private quarters, planning to sleep on the couch in her study.

"Maybe after the holiday," she said. Except that she'd have skiers then, with any luck at all—she'd been pitching that on her new blog, on the website. And after that, it would be time to think about Easter.

"Can you handle Valentine's Day, Ash?" Melissa asked, with genuine concern. "You're still pretty raw."

"And you're not?" Ashley challenged, but gently. "Yes, I can 'handle' it, because I have to." She brought two cups to the table, along with milk and sugar cubes. "What is it with us, Melissa? Brad got it right with Meg, and Olivia with Tanner. Why can't we?"

"I think we're romantically challenged," Melissa decided.

"Or stubborn and proud," Ashley pointed out archly. Her meaning was clear: *Melissa* was stubborn and proud. *She* would have crawled over broken glass for Jack McCall, if it meant they could be together.

Not that she particularly wanted anyone else to know that.

All of which probably made her a candidate for an episode of *Dr. Phil,* during Unhealthy Emotional Dependency week. She would serve as the bad example. *This could happen to you.*

"Don't knock pride," Melissa said cheerfully. "And some people call stubbornness 'persistence.'"

"*Some* people can put a spin on anything," Ashley countered. "Are you going to clear things up with Dan before you leave, or not?"

"Not," Melissa said brightly.

"Chicken."

"You got it. If that man looks me in the eye and says he's in love with Holly Hot-Biscuits, I'll die of mortification on the spot."

"No, you won't. You're too strong. And at least you'd know where you stand." *I'd give anything for another chance with Jack.*

"I *know* where I stand," Melissa answered, pouring tea for Ashley and then for herself, and then warming her hands around the cup instead of drinking the brew. "Up the creek without a paddle."

"That's a mixed metaphor," Ashley couldn't help pointing out.

"Whatever," Melissa said.

And that, for the time being, was the end of the discussion.

A week after the transplant, the jury was still out on whether the procedure had been successful or not, but by pulling certain strings Jack had been reluctantly released from the hospital, partly on the strength of his well-respected father's promise to make sure he was looked after and did not overexert himself. He went home to Oak Park, Illinois, his old hometown, and let Abigail and the old man install him in his boyhood bedroom in the big brick Federal on Shady Lane.

Not that there were any leaves on the trees to provide shade.

Abigail, though shy around him, had taken pains to get his room ready for occupancy—she'd put fresh sheets on the bed, dusted, aired the place out.

The obnoxious rock-star posters, a reminder of his checkered youth, were still on the walls. The antiquated computer, which he'd built himself from scavenged components, remained on his desk, in front of the windows. Hockey sticks and baseball bats occupied every corner.

The sight of it all swamped Jack, made him miss his mother more acutely than ever.

And that was nothing compared to the way he missed Ashley.

Bryce, soon to be an optometrist, appeared in the doorway. He was in his mid-twenties, but he looked younger to Jack.

"You're going to make it, Jack," Bryce said, and he spoke in a man's voice, not a boy's.

So many things had changed.

So many hadn't.

"Thanks to you, maybe I will."

"No maybe about it," Bryce argued.

There was a brief, awkward pause. "What do you think of Abigail?" Jack asked, pulling back the chair at his desk and sitting down. He still tired too easily.

Bryce closed the door, took a seat on the edge of Jack's

bed. Loosely interlaced his fingers and let his hands dangle between his blue-jeaned knees. "She's been good for Dad. He was a real wreck after Mom died."

"I guess that must have been a hard time," Jack ventured, turning his head to look out over the street lined with skeleton trees, waiting for spring.

"It was pretty bad," Bryce admitted. "Did Dad tell you the government is having your headstone removed from the cemetery at Arlington, and the empty box dug up?"

"Guess they need the space," Jack said, as an infinite sadness washed over him. Once, he'd been a hotshot. Now he was sick of guns and violence and war.

"Yeah," Bryce agreed quietly. "Who's the woman?"

Jack tensed. "What woman?"

"The one you mentioned in the email you sent to Dad's office."

Jack closed his eyes briefly, longing for Ashley. Wondering if she'd finally mastered the fine art of computing well enough to check out the Sent Messages folder.

"I'm getting engaged on Valentine's Day," Bryce said, to fill the gap left by Jack's studied silence. "Her name is Kathy. We went to college together."

"Congratulations," Jack managed.

"I wanted to be like you, you know," Bryce went on. "Raise hell. Get sent away to military school. Maybe even bite the sand in Iraq."

Jack managed a tilt at one corner of his mouth, enough to pass for a grin—he hoped. "Thank God you changed your mind," he said. "Mom and Dad—after I disappeared—how were they?"

"Devastated," Bryce answered.

Jack shoved a hand through his hair. Sighed. What had he expected? That they'd go merrily on, as if nothing had happened? *Oh, well, Jack's gone, but we still have three sons left, don't we, and they're all going to graduate school.*

"I need to see Mom's grave," he said.

"I'll take you there," Bryce responded immediately. "After my last class, of course."

Jack smiled. "Of course."

Bryce rose, made that leaving sound by huffing out his breath. "Be nice to Abigail, okay?" he said. "Dad loves her a lot, and she's really trying to fit in without usurping Mom's place."

"I haven't been nice?"

"You've been...reserved."

"Staying alive has been taking up all my time," Jack answered. "Again, thanks to you, I've got a fighting chance. I'll never forget what you did, Bryce. No two ways about it, donating marrow hurts."

Bryce cleared his throat, reached for the doorknob, but didn't quite turn it. "It could take time," he said, letting Jack's comment pass. "All of us being a family again, I mean. But don't give up on us, okay? Don't just take off or something, because I can't even tell you how hard that would be for Dad. He's already lost so much."

"I'm not going anywhere," Jack promised. "I might need that grave at Arlington after all, you know. Maybe they shouldn't be too quick to lay the new resident to rest."

Bryce flushed. "Who's the woman?" he asked again.

Jack met his brother's gaze. "Her name is Ashley O'Ballivan. She runs a bed-and-breakfast in Stone Creek, Arizona. Do me a favor, little brother. Don't get any ideas about calling her up and telling her where I am."

"Why don't *you* call her?"

"Because I still don't know if I'm going to live or die."

Bryce finally turned the knob, opened the door to go. "Maybe she'd like to hear from you, either way. Spend whatever time you have left—"

"And maybe she'd like to get on with her life," Jack broke in brusquely.

After Bryce was gone, Jack booted up the ancient computer—or tried to, anyhow. The cheapest pay-as-you-go cell phone on the market probably had more power.

Giving up on surfing the web, catching up on all he'd missed since Tombstone, he tried to interest himself in the pile of high school yearbooks stacked on a shelf in his closet.

What a hotheaded little jerk he'd been, he thought. A throwback, especially in comparison to his brothers.

He revisited his junior year, flipping pages until he found Molly Henshaw, the love of his adolescent life. Although he hadn't been a praying man, Jack had begged God to let him marry Molly someday.

Looking at her class picture, he remembered that she'd had acne, which she tried to cover with stuff closer to orange than flesh tone. Big hair, too. And a come-hither look in her raccoonlike eyes. Even in the photograph, he could see the clumps of mascara coating her lashes.

Must have been the come hither, he decided.

And thank God for unanswered prayers.

Having come to that conclusion, Jack decided to go downstairs, where Abigail was undoubtedly flitting around the kitchen. Time to make a start at getting to know his father's new wife, though their acquaintance might be a short one if his body rejected Bryce's marrow.

For his dad's sake, because there were so many things he couldn't make up for, he had to give it a shot.

Ironically, he knew it was what his mother would have wanted.

Later, he'd log on to his dad's computer, in the den. See if Ashley's website was up and running.

With luck, there would be a picture of her, smiling like the welcoming hostess she was, dressed in something flowered, with her hair pulled back into that prim French braid he always wanted to undo.

For now, that would have to be enough.

Abigail was in the kitchen, the room where Jack had had so many conversations with his mother. Feminine and modestly pretty, Abigail wore a flowered apron, her hair was pinned up in a loose chignon at her nape, and her hands were white with flour.

She smiled shyly at Jack. "Your father likes peach pie above all things," she confided.

"I'm pretty fond of it myself," Jack answered, grinning. "You're a baker, Abigail?"

His stepmother shrugged. She couldn't have been more different, physically anyway, from his mom. She'd been tall and full-figured, always lamenting humorously that she should have lived in the 1890s, when women with bosoms and hips were appreciated. Abigail was petite and trim; she probably gardened, maybe knitted and crocheted.

His mother had loved to play golf and sail, and to Jack's recollection, she'd never baked a pie or worn an apron in her life.

"A baker and a few other things, too," Abigail said, with a quirky little smile playing briefly on her mouth. "I retired from real estate a year before Bill and I met. Sold my company for a chunk of cash and decided to spend the rest of my life doing what I love…baking, planting flowers, sewing. Oh, and fussing over my husband."

Jack swiped a slice of peach from the bowl waiting to be poured into the pie pan, and she didn't slap his hand. "Married before?" he asked casually. "Any kids?"

Abigail shook her head, and a few tendrils of her graying auburn hair escaped the chignon. "I was too busy with my career," she said, without a hint of regret. "Besides, I always promised myself I'd wait for the right man, no matter how long it took. Turned out to be Bill McKenzie."

He'd underestimated Abigail, that much was clear. She was an independent woman, living the life she chose to live, not someone looking for an easy life married to a prosperous dentist. In fact, Abigail probably had a lot more money than his dad did, and that was saying something.

"He's happy, Abigail. Thank you for that." Jack reached for a second slice, and this time, she did swat his hand, smiling and shaking her head.

She took a cereal bowl from the cupboard, scooped in a generous portion of fruit with a soup spoon, and handed him the works.

Jack decided he knew all he needed to know about Abigail—she loved his father, and that was as good as it got. Leaning in a little, he kissed her cheek.

"Welcome aboard, Abigail," he said hoarsely.

She smiled. "Thanks," she replied, and went back to building the pie.

Chapter 10

"Ms. O'Ballivan? My name is Bryce McKenzie and I—"

Ashley shifted the telephone receiver from her left ear to her right, hunching one shoulder to hold it in place, busy rolling out pie dough on the butcher's block next to the counter. "I'm sorry, Mr. McKenzie," she said, distracted, "but we're all booked up for Valentine's Day—"

The man replied with an oddly familiar chuckle. Something about the timbre of it struck a chord somewhere deep in Ashley's core. "Excuse me?" he said.

"The bed-and-breakfast—I guess I just assumed you were calling because of the publicity my website's been getting—"

Again, that sense of familiarity flittered, in the pit of Ashley's stomach now.

"I'm Jack McKenzie's brother," Bryce explained.

McKenzie. The name finally registered in Ashley's befuddled memory, the one Jack had admitted leaving behind so long ago. "Oh," she said, stretching the phone cord taut so she could collapse into a kitchen chair. *"Oh."*

"I probably shouldn't be calling you like this, but—well—"

"Is Jack all right?"

Bryce McKenzie sighed. "Yes and no," he said carefully.

Ashley put a floury hand to her heart, smearing her T-shirt with white finger marks. "Tell me about the 'no' part, Mr. McKenzie," she said.

"Bryce," he corrected. And then, after clearing his throat, he explained that Jack had needed a bone marrow transplant. The patient was up and around, and he was taking antirejection drugs, but he didn't seem to be recovering—or regressing—and his family was worried.

They'd had a family meeting, Bryce concluded, one Jack hadn't been privy to, and decided as a unit that seeing Ashley again might be the boost he needed to get better.

Ashley listened with her eyes closed and her heart hammering.

"Where is he now?" she asked, very quietly, when Bryce had finished.

"We live in Chicago, so he's here," he answered. "There's plenty of room at my dad's place, if you wanted to stay there. I mean, if you even want to come in the first place, that is."

Ashley's heart thrummed. Valentine's Day was a

week away and she had to be there to greet her guests, make them comfortable—didn't she? This was her chance to take the business to a whole new level, make some progress, stay caught up on her payments to Brad and fortify her faltering savings.

And none of that was as important as seeing Jack again.

"I think," she said shakily, "that if Jack wanted to see me, he would have called himself."

"He wants to make sure he's going to live through this first," Bryce answered candidly. Then, after sucking in an audible breath, he added, "Will you come? It could make all the difference in his recovery—or, at least, that's what we're hoping."

Ashley looked around her kitchen, cluttered now with the accoutrements of serious cooking. The freezer was full, the house was ready for the onslaught of lovers planning a romantic getaway.

How could she leave now?

How could she *stay?*

"I'll be there as soon as I can book a flight," she heard herself say.

"One of us will pick you up at O'Hare," Bryce said, his voice light with relief. "Just call back with your flight number and arrival time."

Ashley wrote down the cell numbers he gave her and promised to get in touch with him as soon as she had the necessary information.

"This is crazy," she told Mrs. Wiggins, as soon as she'd hung up.

"Meooow," Mrs. Wiggins replied, curling against Ashley's ankle.

Having made the decision, Ashley was full of sudden energy. She made airline reservations for the next day, flying out of Flagstaff, connecting in Phoenix, and then going on to Chicago. When that was done, she called Bryce back.

"You're sure Jack wants to see me?" she asked, having second thoughts.

"I'm sure," Bryce said, with a smile in his voice.

The next call was to Melissa, at her office, and Ashley was almost panicking by then. The moment Melissa greeted her with a curious "Hello"—Ashley never called her at work—the whole thing spilled out.

Ashley held her breath, after the spate of words, awaiting Melissa's response.

"I see," Melissa said cautiously.

"I might be back before Valentine's Day," Ashley blurted, anxious to assuage her sister's misgivings about Jack, "but I can't be absolutely sure, and I need you to cover for me if necessary."

"I don't know beans about running a bed-and-breakfast," Melissa said gamely, "much less *cooking*. But I'll be there, Ash. Get your bags packed."

Tears burned Ashley's eyes. She could always count on Melissa, on any member of her family, to come through in a pinch. Why had she doubted that, even for a moment? "Thanks, Melissa."

"You'll have to send the cat to Olivia's place," Melissa warned, though her tone was good-natured. "You know how my allergies flare up when I'm around anything with fur."

"I know," Ashley said sweetly, "that you're a hypochondriac. But I love you anyway."

"Gee, thanks," Melissa replied. "No cat," she clarified firmly. "The deal's off if Olivia won't take him."

"Her," Ashley said, smiling. "How many male cats do you know with the name 'Mrs. Wiggins'?"

"I don't know *any* cats, whatever the gender," Melissa answered, "and I don't want to, either."

Ashley grinned to herself. "I'm sure Olivia will cat-sit," she conceded. "One more thing. Could you serve punch at the Valentine's Day dance? I promised and I did all this baking and I'm not sure I'll be back in time—"

"Oh, for Pete's sake," Melissa said. "*Yes,* if it comes to that, but you'd better do your darndest to be home before the first guests arrive. I mean well, but we're taking a risk here. I'm not the least bit domestic, remember, and I could put you out of business without half trying."

Ashley laughed, sniffled once. "I promise I'll do my O'Ballivan best," she said. "Have you seen Dan yet?"

"No," Melissa said, "and don't mention his name again, if you don't mind."

After the call ended, Ashley wrestled her one and only suitcase down from the attic—she rarely traveled—and set it on her bed, open.

Mrs. Wiggins immediately climbed into it, as though determined to make the journey with her mistress.

"Not this time," Ashley said, gently removing the furball.

The next dilemma was, what did a person pack for a trip to Chicago in the middle of winter?

She decided on her trademark broomstick skirts, lightweight tunic sweaters, and some jeans, for good measure.

When she called Starcross Ranch, hoping to speak to Olivia, Tanner answered instead. Ashley asked if Mrs. Wiggins could bunk in for a few days.

"Sure," Tanner said, as Ashley had known he would. But he also wanted an explanation. "Where are you off to, in such a hurry?"

Tanner was Jack's friend, and he'd surely been as worried about him as Ashley had. Although it was possible that the two men had been in touch, her instincts told her they hadn't.

Ashley drew a deep breath, let it out slowly, and hoped she was doing the right thing by telling Tanner. And by jetting off to Chicago when Jack hadn't asked her to come.

"Jack's in Chicago," she said. "He's had a bone marrow transplant—something to do with the toxin—and his family is worried about him. He's not getting worse, but he's not getting better, either."

Tanner murmured an exclamation. "I see," he said. "Jack didn't call you himself?"

"No," Ashley admitted, her shoulders sagging a little.

Tanner considered that, must have decided against giving an opinion, one way or the other. "You'll keep me in the loop?" he asked presently.

"Yes," Ashley said.

"I'll be there to get the cat sometime this afternoon. Do you want a ride to the airport?"

"I've got that covered," Ashley replied. "Thanks, Tanner. I really appreciate this."

"We're family," Tanner pointed out. "Brad could probably charter a jet—"

"I don't need a jet," Ashley interrupted, though gently. "And I'm not really ready to discuss any of this with Brad. Not just yet, anyhow."

"Is there a plan?" Tanner asked. "And if so, what is it?"

Ashley smiled, even though her eyes were burning again. "No plan," she said. "I'm not even sure Jack wants me there. But I have to see him, Tanner."

"Of course you do," Tanner agreed, sounding both relieved and resigned. "Brad is going to wonder where you've gone, though. He keeps pretty close tabs on his three little sisters, you know. But don't worry about that—I'll handle him."

She heard Olivia's voice in the background, asking what was going on.

"Let me talk to her," Ashley said, and told the whole story all over again.

"I don't like it that you're going alone," Olivia told her, a minute or so later. "I've got the babies to look after, and I think Sophie is coming down with a cold, but maybe Melissa could go along—"

"Melissa is going to house-sit," Ashley said. "And she'll have her hands full holding down the fort, especially if I'm not back before Valentine's Day. I'll be *fine*, Livie."

"You're sure? What if Jack—?"

"What if he doesn't want to see me? I'll handle it, Liv. I'm a big girl now, remember?"

Olivia's laugh was warm, and a little teary. "Godspeed, little sister," she said. "And call us when you get there."

"I will," Ashley said, thinking how lucky she was.

The next few hours passed in a haze of activity—there were project lists to make for Melissa, and dozens of other details, too.

As promised, Tanner showed up late that afternoon to collect a mewing Mrs. Wiggins in the small pet carrier Olivia had sent along.

"Tell Jack I said hello," Tanner said, as he was leaving.

Ashley nodded, and her brother-in-law planted a light kiss on the top of her head.

"Take care," he told her. And then he was gone.

Melissa showed up when she got off work, and she and Ashley went over the lists—which guests to put where, how to reheat the food she'd prepared ahead of time, frozen and carefully labeled, how to take reservations and run credit cards, and a myriad of other things.

Melissa looked overwhelmed, but in true O'Ballivan spirit, she vowed to do her best.

Knowing she wouldn't sleep if she stayed in Stone Creek that night, Ashley loaded her suitcase into the car and set out for Flagstaff, intending to check into a hotel near the airport and have a room-service supper.

Her flight was leaving at six-thirty the next morning.

Along the way, though, she pulled off onto the snowy road leading to the cemetery where her mother was buried, parked near Delia's grave, and waded toward the headstone.

There were no heartfelt words, no tears.

Ashley simply felt a need to be there, in that quiet place. Somehow, a sense of closure had stolen into her heart when she wasn't looking. She could let go now, move on.

The weather was bitterly cold, though, and she soon got back in her car and made her steady, careful way toward Flagstaff.

She would always love the mother she'd longed to have, she reflected, but it was time to go forward, appreciate the *living* people she loved, those who loved her in return: Brad and Meg, Olivia and Tanner, Melissa and little Mac and Carly and sweet Sophie and the babies.

And Jack.

She didn't obsess over what might happen when she arrived in Chicago. For once in her life, she was taking a risk, going for what she wanted.

And she wanted Jack McCall—McKenzie—whoever he was.

Once she'd arrived in Flagstaff, she chose a hotel and checked in, ordered a bowl of cream of broccoli soup, ate it, and soaked in a warm bath until the chill seeped out of her bones. Most of it, anyway.

A part of her would remain frozen until she'd seen Jack for herself.

"You did *what?*" Jack demanded, after supper that night, when he and Bryce wound up the evening sitting in chairs in front of the fireplace. It had been a hectic thing, supper, with brothers and their wives, nieces and nephews, and even a few neighbors there to share in the meal celebrating Jack's return from the dead.

"I called Ashley O'Ballivan," Bryce repeated, with no more regret than he'd shown the first time. "She'll be here late tomorrow afternoon. I'm picking her up at O'Hare."

Jack sat back, absorbing the news. A part of him soared, anticipating Ashley's arrival. Another part wanted to find a place to hide out until she was gone again.

"You've got a lot of nerve, little brother," he finally said, with no inflection in his voice at all. "Especially considering that I told you I'm not ready to see her."

"Until you're sure you won't die," Bryce confirmed confidently. "Jack, *all* of us are terminal. Maybe you won't be around long. Maybe you'll live to be a hundred. But in the meantime, you need to see *this woman,* even if it's only to say goodbye."

Saying goodbye to Ashley the last time had been one of the hardest things Jack had ever had to do. Saying goodbye to her again, especially for eternity, might be more than he could bear.

His conscience niggled at him. What about what *Ashley* had to bear?

Jack closed his eyes. "I'll get you for this," he told his brother.

Bryce chuckled. "You'll have to get well first," he replied.

"You think you can take me?" Jack challenged, grinning now, both infuriated and relieved.

"I'm not a little kid anymore," Bryce pointed out. "I might be able to take you—even with all your para-military skills."

Jack opened his eyes, looked at his younger brother with new respect. "Maybe you could," he said.

Bryce stood, stretched and yawned mightily. "Better get back to my apartment," he said. "Busy day tomorrow."

Ashley, Jack thought, full of conflicting emotions he couldn't begin to identify. What was he so afraid of? Not commitment, certainly—at least as far as Ashley was concerned.

"After this," he told his departing brother, "mind your own business."

"Not a chance," Bryce said lightly.

And then he was gone.

The first signs of an approaching blizzard hit Chicago five minutes after Ashley's plane landed at O'Hare, and the landing had been so bumpy that her knuckles were white from gripping the armrests—letting go of them was a slow and deliberate process.

She was such a homebody, completely unsuited to an adventurer like Jack. If she'd had a brain in her head, she decided, gnawing at her lower lip, she would have turned right around and flown back to Arizona where she belonged, blizzard or no blizzard.

She waited impatiently while all the passengers in the rows ahead of hers gathered their coats and carry-ons and meandered up the aisle at the pace of spilled peanut butter.

They had all the time in the world, probably.

Ashley knew she might not.

She hurried up the Jetway when her turn finally came, having returned the flight attendant's farewell smile with a fleeting one of her own.

Finding her way along a maze of moving walkways took more time, and she was almost breathless when she finally stepped out of the secure area, scanning the waiting sea of strange faces. Bryce had promised to hold up a sign with her name on it, so they could recognize each other, but even standing on tiptoe, she didn't see one.

"Ashley?"

She froze, turned to see Jack standing at her elbow. A strangled cry, part sob and part something else entirely, escaped her.

He looked so thin, so pale. His eyes were, as Big John used to say, like two burned holes in a blanket.

"Hey," he said huskily.

Ashley swallowed, still unable to move. "Hey," she responded.

He grinned, resembling his old self a little more, and crooked his arm, and she took it.

"You're glad to see me?" she asked, afraid of the answer. His grin, after all, could have been a reflex.

"If I'd been given a choice," he replied, "I would have asked you not to come. But, yeah, I'm glad to see you."

"Good," Ashley said uncertainly, aware of the strangeness between them. And the ever-present electrical charge.

"My interfering brother is waiting over in baggage claim," he said. "Let's go find him, before this storm gets any worse and we get stuck in rush-hour traffic. It's a long drive out to Oak Park."

Ashley nodded, overjoyed to be there and, at the same time, wishing she'd stayed home.

Once she'd met Bryce McKenzie—he was taller than his brother, though not so broad in the shoulders—and collected her solitary, out-of-style suitcase, the three of them headed for the parking garage, Bryce carrying the bag.

Fortunately, Bryce drove a big SUV with four-wheel drive, and he didn't seem a bit worried about the weather. Ashley sat in the front passenger seat, while Jack climbed painfully into the back.

The snow was coming down so hard and so fast by then, and the traffic was so intense, that Ashley wondered if they would reach Oak Park alive.

They did, eventually, and all the McKenzies were waiting in the entryway of the large brick house when they pulled into the circular driveway out front.

Introductions were made—Jack's father and stepmother, his brothers and their wives, Bryce's fiancée, Kathy—and most of their names went out of Ashley's head as soon as she'd heard them.

She could think of nothing—and no one—but Jack.

Jack, who'd sat silent in the backseat of his brother's SUV all the way from the airport. Bryce, bless his heart, had tried hard to keep the conversation going, asking Ashley if her flight had been okay, inquiring about Stone Creek and what it was like there.

Ashley, as uncomfortable in her own way as Jack was in his, had given sparse answers.

She shouldn't have come.

Just as she'd feared, Jack didn't want her there.

The McKenzies welcomed her heartily, though, and Mrs. McKenzie—Abigail—served a meat-loaf supper so delicious that Ashley made a mental note to ask for the recipe.

Jack, seated next to her, though probably not by his own choosing, ate sparingly, as she did, and said almost nothing.

"You must be tired," Jack's father said to her, when the meal was over and Ashley automatically got up to help clear the table. The older man's gaze shifted to his eldest son. "Jack, why don't you show Ashley to her room so she can rest?"

Jack nodded, gestured for Ashley to precede him, and followed her out of the dining room.

The base of the broad, curving staircase was just ahead.

Ashley couldn't help noticing how slowly Jack moved. He was probably exhausted. "You don't have to—"

"Ashley," he interrupted blandly, "I can still climb stairs."

She lowered her gaze, then forced herself to look at him again. "I'm sorry, Jack—I—I shouldn't have come, but—"

He drew the knuckles of his right hand lightly down the side of her cheek. "Don't be sorry," he said. "I guess—well—it's hard on my pride, your seeing me like this."

Ashley was honestly puzzled. Sure, he'd lost weight, and his color wasn't great, but he was still *Jack*. "Like what?"

Jack spread his arms, looked down at himself, met her eyes again. She saw misery and sorrow in his expression. "I might be dying, Ashley," he said. "I wanted you to remember me the way I was before."

Ashley stiffened. "You are *not* going to die, Jack McCall. I won't tolerate it."

He gave a slanted grin. "Is that so?" he replied. "What do you intend to do to prevent it, O'Ballivan?"

"Take a pregnancy test," Ashley said, without planning to at all.

Jack's eyes widened. "You think you're—?"

"Pregnant?" Ashley finished for him, lowering her voice lest the conversation carry into the nearby dining room.

"Yeah," Jack said, somewhat pointedly.

"I might be," Ashley said. This was yet another thing she hadn't allowed herself to think about—until now. "I'm late. *Very* late."

He took her elbow, squired her up the stairs with more energy than he'd shown since she'd come face-to-face with him at O'Hare. "Is that unusual?"

"Yes," Ashley whispered, *"it's unusual."*

He smiled, and a light spread into his eyes that hadn't been there before. "You're not just saying this, are you? Trying to give me a reason to live or something like that?"

"If you can't come up with a reason to live, Jack McCall," Ashley said, waving one arm toward the distant dining room, where his family had gathered, "you're in even sorrier shape than I thought."

He frowned. "Jack *McKenzie,*" he said, clearly thinking of something else. "I'm going by my real name now."

"Well, bully for you," Ashley said.

"'Bully for me'?" He laughed. "God, Ashley, you should have been born during the Roosevelt administration—the *Teddy* Roosevelt administration. Nobody says 'Bully for you' anymore."

Ashley folded her arms. "*I* do," she said.

His eyes danced—it was nice to know she was so entertaining—then went serious again. "Why are you here?"

She bristled. "You *know* why."

"No," Jack said, sounding honestly mystified. "I thought we agreed that I'd come back to Stone Creek after this was all over, and we'd stay apart until then."

Ashley's throat constricted as she considered the magnitude of what Jack was facing. "And *I* thought we agreed that we love each other. Whether you live or die, I want to be here."

Pain contorted his face. "Ashley—"

"I'm not going anywhere until I know what's going to happen to you," Ashley broke in. "When will you know whether the transplant worked or not?"

The change in him was downright mercurial; Jack's eyes twinkled again, and his features relaxed. He made a show of checking his watch. "I'm expecting an email from God at any minute," he teased.

"That isn't funny!"

"Not much is, these days." He took her upper arms in his hands. "Ashley, as soon as this blizzard lets up, I want you to get on an airplane and go back to Stone Creek."

"Well, here's a news flash for you: just because you *want* something doesn't mean you're going to get it."

He grinned, shook his head. "Strange that I never noticed how stubborn you can be."

"Get used to it."

He crossed the hall, opened a door.

She peeked inside, saw a comfortable-looking room with an antique four-poster bed, a matching dresser and chest of drawers, and several overstuffed chairs.

"I won't sleep," she warned.

"Neither will I," Jack responded.

Ashley turned, faced him squarely. Spoke from her heart. "Don't die, Jack," she said. "Please—whatever happens between us—don't just give up and die."

He leaned in, kissed her lightly on the mouth. "I'll do my best not to," he said. Then he turned and started back toward the stairs.

"Aren't you going to bed?" Ashley asked, feeling lonely and very far from home.

"Later," he said, winking at her. "Right now, I'm going to call drugstores until I find one that delivers during snowstorms."

Ashley's heart caught; alarm reverberated through her like the echo of a giant brass gong. "Are you running low on one of your medications?"

"No," Jack answered. "I'm going to ask them to send over one of those sticks."

"Sticks?" Ashley frowned, confused.

"The kind a woman pees on," he explained. "Plus sign if she's pregnant, minus if she's not."

"That can wait," Ashley protested. "Have you looked out a window lately?"

"I've got to know," Jack said.

"You're insane."

"Maybe. Good night, Ashley."

She swallowed. "Good night," she said. Stepping inside the guestroom, she closed the door, leaned her forehead against it, and breathed deeply and slowly until she was sure she wouldn't cry.

Her handbag and suitcase had already been brought upstairs. Sinking down onto the side of the bed, Ashley rummaged through her purse until she found the cell phone she'd bought on a wave of technological confidence, after she'd finally mastered her computer.

She dialed her own number at the bed-and-breakfast, and Melissa answered on the first ring.

"Ashley?" The twin-vibe strikes again.

"Hi, Melissa. I'm here—in Chicago, I mean—and I'm—I'm fine."

"You don't *sound* fine," Melissa argued. "How's Jack?"

"He looks terrible, and I don't think he's very happy that I'm here."

"Oh, Ash—I'm sorry. Was the bastard rude to you?"

Ashley smiled, in spite of everything. "He's not a bastard, Melissa," she said, "and no, he hasn't been rude."

"Then—?"

"I think he's given up," Ashley admitted miserably. "It's as if he's decided to die and get it over with. And he doesn't want me around to see it happen."

"Look, maybe you should just come home—"

"I can't. We're socked in by the perfect storm. I've

never seen so much snow—even in Stone Creek." She paused. "And I wouldn't leave anyway. How's everything there?"

"It's fine. I've had to turn away at least five people who wanted to book rooms for Valentine's Day weekend." Melissa still sounded worried. "You do realize that you might be there a while? Do you have enough money, Ash?"

"No," Ashley said, embarrassed. "Not for a long haul."

"I can help you out if you need some," Melissa offered. "Brad, too."

Ashley gulped down her O'Ballivan pride, and it wasn't easy to swallow. "I'll let you know," she said, with what dignity she had left. "Do me a favor, will you? Call Tanner and Olivia and let them know I got here okay?"

"Sure," Melissa said.

They said their goodbyes soon after that, and hung up.

As tired as she was, Ashley knew she wouldn't sleep.

She took a bath, brushed her teeth and put on her pajamas.

She watched a newscast on the guestroom TV, waited until the very end for the weather report.

More snow on the way. O'Hare was shut down, and the police were asking everyone to stay off the roads except in the most dire emergencies.

At quarter after ten, a knock sounded on Ashley's door.

"It's me," Jack called, in a loud whisper. "Can I come in?"

Before Ashley could answer, one way or the other,

the door opened and he stepped inside, carrying a white bag in one hand.

"Nothing stops the post office or pharmacy delivery drivers," he said, holding out the bag.

The pregnancy test, of course.

Ashley's hand trembled as she reached out to accept it. "Come back later," she said, moving toward her bathroom door.

Jack sat down on the side of her bed. "I'll wait," he said.

Chapter 11

Huddled in the McKenzies' guest bathroom, Ashley stared down at the plastic stick in mingled horror and delight.

A plus sign.

She was pregnant.

Ashley made some rapid calculations in her head; normally, if she hadn't been under stress, it would have been a no-brainer to figure out that the baby was due sometime in September. Because she was frazzled, it took longer.

"Well?" Jack called from the other side of the door. As a precaution, Ashley had turned the lock; otherwise, he might have stormed in on her, he was so anxious to learn the results.

Ashley swallowed painfully. She was bursting with the news, but if she told Jack now, she would, in effect, be trapping him. He'd feel honor-bound to marry her, whether he really wanted to or not.

And suppose he died?

That, of course, would be awful either way.

But maybe knowing about the baby would somehow heal Jack, inspire him to try harder to recover. To believe he could.

The knob jiggled. "Ashley?"

"I'm all right."

"Okay," Jack replied, "but are you *pregnant?*"

"It's inconclusive," Ashley said, too earnestly and too cheerfully.

"I read the package. You get either a plus or a minus," Jack retorted, not at all cheerful, but very earnest. "Which is it, Ashley?"

Ashley closed her eyes for a moment, offered up a silent prayer for wisdom, for strength, for courage. She simply wasn't a very good liar; Jack would see through her if she tried to deceive him. And, anyway, deception seemed wrong, however good her intentions might be. The child was as much Jack's as her own, and he had a right to know he was going to be a father.

"It's—it's a plus."

"Open the door," Jack said. Was that jubilation she heard in his voice, or irritation? Joy—or dread?

Ashley pushed the lock button in the center of the knob, and stepped back quickly to avoid being run down by a man on a mission. She was still holding the white plastic stick in one hand.

Jack took it from her, examined the little panel at one end, giving nothing away by his expression. His shoulders were tense, though, and his breathing was fast and shallow.

"My God," he said finally. "Ashley, *we made a baby.*"

"You and me," Ashley agreed, sniffling a little.

Jack raised his eyes to hers. She thought she saw a quickening there, something akin to delight, but he looked worried, too. "You weren't going to tell me?" he asked. "I wouldn't exactly describe a plus sign as 'inconclusive.'"

"I didn't know how you'd react," Ashley said. She *still* couldn't read him—was he glad or sad?

"How I'd react?" he echoed. "Ashley, this is the best thing that's ever happened to me, besides you."

Ashley stared at him, stricken to silence, stricken by joy and surprise and a wild, nearly uncontainable hope.

"You do *want* this baby, don't you?" Jack asked.

"Of course I do," Ashley blurted. "I wasn't sure *you* did, that's all."

Jack looked down at the stick again, shaking his head and grinning.

"I peed on that, you know," Ashley pointed out, reaching for the test stick, intending to throw it away.

Jack held it out of her reach. "We're keeping this. You can glue it into the kid's baby book or something."

"Jack, it's not sanitary," Ashley pointed out. Why was she talking about trivial things, when so much hung in the balance?

"Neither are wet diapers," Jack reasoned calmly. "Sanitation is all well and good, but a kid needs good old-fashioned germs, too, so he—or she—can build up all the necessary antibodies."

"You don't have to marry me if you don't want to," Ashley said, too quickly, and then wished she could bite off her tongue.

"Sure, I do," Jack said. "Call me old-fashioned, but I think a kid ought to have two legal parents."

"Sure, you *have* to marry me, or sure, you *want* to?" Ashley asked.

"Oh, I want to, all right," Jack told her, his voice hoarse, his eyes glistening. "The question is, do you want to spend the rest of your life with me? You could be a widow in six months, or even sooner. A widow with a baby to raise."

"Not if you fight to live, Jack," Ashley said.

He looked away, evidently staring into some grim scenario only he could see. "There's plenty of money," he said, as though speaking to someone else. "If nothing else, I made a good living doing what I did. You would never want for anything, and neither would our baby."

"I don't care about money," Ashley countered honestly, and a little angrily, too. *I care about you, and this baby, and our life together. Our long,* long *life together.* "I love you, remember?"

He set the test stick carefully aside, on the counter by the sink, and pulled Ashley out into the main part of the small suite. "I can't propose to you in a bathroom," he said.

Ashley laughed and cried.

Awkwardly, Jack dropped to one knee, still holding her hand. "I love you, Ashley O'Ballivan. Will you marry me?"

"Yes," she said.

He gave an exuberant shout, got to his feet again and pulled her into his arms, practically drowning her in a deep, hungry kiss.

The guestroom door popped open.

"Oops," Dr. McKenzie the elder said, blushing.

Jack and Ashley broke apart, Jack laughing, Ashley embarrassed and happy and not a little dazed.

Bill looked even more chagrined than before. "I heard a yell and I thought—"

"Everything's okay, Dad," Jack said, with gruff affection. "It's better than okay. I just asked Ashley to marry me, and she said yes."

"I see," Bill said, smiling, and quietly closed the door.

A jubilant "Yes!" sounded from the hallway. Ashley pictured her future father-in-law punching the air with one fist, a heartening thought.

"I still might die," Jack reminded her.

"Welcome to the human race," Ashley replied. "From the moment any of us arrive here, we're on our way out again."

"I'd like to make love to you right now," Jack said.

"Not here," Ashley answered. "I couldn't—not in your dad's house."

Jack nodded slowly. "You're as old-fashioned as I am," he said. "As soon as this storm lets up, though, we're out of here."

They sat down, side by side, on the bed where both of them wanted to make love, and neither intended to give in to desire.

Not just yet, anyway.

"How soon can we get married?" Jack asked, taking her hand, stroking the backs of her knuckles with the pad of his thumb.

Ashley's heart, full to bursting, shoved its way up into her throat and lodged there. "Wait a second," she protested, when she finally gathered the breath to speak. The aftershocks of Jack's kiss were still banging around inside her. "There are things we have to decide first."

"Like?"

"Like where we're going to live," Ashley said, nervous now. She liked Chicago, what little she'd seen of the place, that is, but Stone Creek would always be home.

"Wherever you want," Jack told her quietly. "And I know that's the old hometown. Just remember that your family isn't exactly wild about me."

"They'll get over it," Ashley told him, with confidence. "Once they know you're going to stick around this time."

"Just *try* shaking me off your trail, lady," Jack teased. He leaned toward her, kissed her again, this time lightly, and in a way that shook her soul.

"Does that mean you won't go back to whatever it is you do for a living?" Ashley ventured.

"It means I'm going to shovel snow and carry out the trash and love you, Ashley. For as long as we both shall live."

Tears of joy stung her eyes. "That probably won't be enough to keep you busy," she fretted. "You're used to action—"

"I'm sick of action. At least, the kind that involves covert security operations. Vince can run the company, along with a few other people I trust. I can manage it from the computer in your study."

"I thought you didn't trust Vince anymore," Ashley said.

"I got a little peeved with him," Jack admitted, "but he's sound. He'd have been long gone if he wasn't."

"You wouldn't be taking off all of the sudden—on some important job that required your expertise?"

"I'm good at what I do, Ashley," Jack said. "But I'm

not so good that I can't delegate. Maybe I'll hang out with Tanner sometimes, though, riding the range and all that cowboy-type stuff."

"Do you know how to ride a horse?"

Jack chuckled. "It can't be that much different from riding a camel." He grinned. "And I'd be a whole lot closer to the ground."

That last statement sobered both of them.

Jack might not be just closer to the ground, he might wind up *under* it.

"I'm going to make it, Ashley," he assured her.

She dropped her forehead against his shoulder, wrapped her arms around him, let herself cling for a few moments. "You'd better," she said. "You'd just better."

Three days later, the storm had finally moved on, leaving a crystalline world behind, trees etched with ice, blankets of white covering every roof.

A private jet, courtesy of Brad, skimmed down onto the tarmac at a private airfield on the fringes of the Windy City, and Jack and Ashley turned to say temporary farewells to Jack's entire family, gathered there to see them off.

The whole clan would be traveling to Stone Creek for the wedding, which would take place in two weeks. Valentine's Day would have been perfect, but with so many guests already booked to stay at the bed-and-breakfast, it was impossible, and neither Jack nor Ashley wanted to wait until the next one rolled around.

Bill McKenzie pumped his eldest son's hand, the hem of his expensive black overcoat flapping in a brisk breeze, then drew him into a bear hug.

"Better get yourselves onto that plane and out of this

wind," Bill said, at last, his voice choked. He bent to kiss Ashley's cheek. "I always wanted a daughter," he added, in a whisper.

Jack nodded, then shook hands with each of his brothers. Every handshake turned into a hug. Lastly, he embraced Abigail, his stepmother.

Ashley looked away, grappling with emotions of her own, watched as the metal stairs swung down out of the side of the jet with an electronic hum. The pilot stood in the doorway, grinning, and she recognized Vince Griffin—the man who'd held a gun on her in her own kitchen, the night Ardith and Rachel arrived.

"Better roll, boss," he called to Jack. "There's more weather headed this way, and I'd like to stay ahead of it."

Jack took Ashley's arm, steered her gently up the steps, into the sumptuous cabin of the jet. There were eight seats, each set of two facing the other across a narrow fold-down table.

"Aren't you going to ask what I'm doing here?" Vince asked Jack, blustering with manly bravado and boyishly earnest at the same time.

"No," Jack answered. "It's obvious that you wangled the job so you could be the one to take us home to Stone Creek."

Home to Stone Creek. That sounded so good to Ashley, especially coming from Jack.

Vince laughed. "I'm trying to get back in your good graces, boss," he said, flipping a switch to retract the stairs, then shutting and securing the cabin door. "Is it working?"

"Maybe," Jack said.

"I hate it when you say 'maybe,'" Vince replied.

"Just fly this thing," Jack told him mildly, with mischief in his eyes. "I want to stay ahead of the weather as much as you do."

Vince nodded, retreated into the cockpit, and shut the door behind him.

Solicitously, Jack helped Ashley out of her coat, sat her down in one of the sumptuous leather seats and swiveled it to buckle her seat belt for her.

A thrill of anticipation went through her.

Not yet, she told herself.

Jack must have been reading her mind. "As soon as we get home," he vowed, leaning over her, bracing himself on the armrests of her seat, "we're going to do it like we've never done it before."

That remark inspired another hot shiver. "Are we, now?" she said, her voice deliberately sultry.

Jack thrust himself away from her, since the plane was already taxiing down the runway, took his own seat across from hers and fastened his belt for takeoff.

Four and a half hours later, they landed outside Stone Creek.

Brad and Meg were waiting to greet them, along with Olivia and Tanner, Carly and Sophie, and Melissa.

"*Thank God* you're back," Melissa said, close to Ashley's ear, after hugging her. "I thought I was going to have to *cook*."

Brad stood squarely in front of Jack, Ashley noticed, out of the corner of her eye, his arms folded and his face stern.

Jack did the same thing, gazing straight into Brad's eyes.

"Uh-oh," Melissa breathed. "Testosterone overload."

Neither man moved. Or spoke.

Olivia finally nudged Brad hard in the ribs. "Behave yourself, big brother," she said. "Jack will be part of the family soon, and that means the two of you have to get along."

It didn't mean any such thing, of course, but to Ashley's profound relief, Brad softened visibly at Olivia's words. Then, after some hesitation, he put out a hand.

Jack took it.

After the shake, Brad said, "That doesn't mean you can mistreat my kid sister, hotshot."

"Wouldn't think of it," Jack said. "I love her." He curved an arm around Ashley, pulled her close against his side, looked down into her upturned face. "Always have, always will."

Two weeks later
Stone Creek Presbyterian Church

"It's tacky," Olivia protested to Melissa, zipping herself into her bridesmaid's dress with some difficulty, since she was still a little on the pudgy side from having the twins. "Coming to a wedding with a U-Haul hitched to the back of your car!"

Melissa rolled her eyes. "I have to be in Phoenix bright and early Monday morning to start my new job," she said, yet again. The three sisters had been over the topic many times. Most of Melissa's belongings had already been moved to the fancy condo in Scottsdale; the rented trailer contained the last of them.

Initially, flushed with the success of helping Ashley steer the bed-and-breakfast through the Valentine's Day rush, Melissa had seemed to be wavering a little on the subject of moving away. After all, she liked her job at the small, local firm where she'd worked since graduating from law school, but then Dan Guthrie had suddenly eloped with Holly the Waitress. Now nothing would move Melissa to stay.

She was determined to shake the dust of Stone Creek off her feet and start a whole new life—elsewhere.

Ashley turned her back to her sisters and her mind to her wedding, smoothing the beaded skirt of her ivory-silk gown in front of the grainy full-length mirror affixed to the back of the pastor's office door. She and Melissa had scoured every bridal shop within a two-hundred-mile radius to find it, while Olivia searched the Internet, and the dress was perfect.

Not so the bridesmaids' outfits, Ashley reflected, happily rueful. They were bright yellow taffeta, with square necklines, puffy sleeves, big bows at the back, and way too many ruffles.

What was I thinking? Ashley asked herself, stifling a giggle.

The answer, of course, was that she *hadn't* been thinking. She'd fallen wholly, completely and irrevocably in love with Jack McKenzie, dazed in the daytime, *crazed* at night, when they made love until they were both sweaty and breathless and gasping for air.

The yellow dresses must have seemed like a good idea at the time, she supposed. Olivia and Melissa had surely argued against that particular choice—but Ashley honestly had no memory of it.

"We're going to look like giant parakeets in the pictures," Olivia complained now, but her eyes were warm and moist as she came to stand behind Ashley in front of the mirror. "You look so beautiful."

Ashley turned, and she and Olivia embraced. "I'll

make it up to you," Ashley said. "Having to wear those awful dresses, I mean."

Melissa looked down at her billowing skirts and shuddered. "I don't see how," she said doubtfully.

A little silence fell.

Olivia straightened Ashley's veil.

"I wish Mom and Dad and Big John could be here," Ashley admitted softly.

"I know," Olivia replied, kissing her cheek.

The church organist launched into a prelude to "Here Comes the Bride."

"Showtime," Melissa said, giving Ashley a quick squeeze. "Be happy."

Ashley nodded, blinking. She couldn't cry now. It would make her mascara run.

A rap sounded at the office door, and Brad entered at Olivia's "Come in," looking beyond handsome in his tuxedo. "Ready to be given away?" he asked solemnly, his gaze resting on Ashley in surprised bemusement, as though she'd just changed from a little girl to a woman before his very eyes. A grin crooked up a corner of his mouth. "We can always duck out the back door and make a run for it if you've changed your mind."

Ashley smiled, shook her head. Walked over to her brother.

Brad kissed her forehead, then lowered the front of the veil. "Jack McKenzie is one lucky man," he said gravely, but a genuine smile danced in his eyes. "Gonna be okay?"

Ashley took his arm. "Gonna be okay," she confirmed.

"We're supposed to go down the aisle first," Melissa said, grabbing Olivia's hand and dragging her past Brad and Ashley, through the open doorway, and into the corridor that opened at both ends of the small church.

"Is he out there?" Ashley whispered to Brad, suddenly nervous, as he escorted her over the threshold between one life and another.

"Jack?" Brad pretended not to remember. "I'm pretty sure I spotted him up front, with Tanner beside him. Guess it could have been the pastor, though." He paused for dramatic effect. "Oh, yeah. The pastor's wearing robes. The man I saw was in a tuxedo, tugging at his collar every couple of seconds."

"Stop it," Ashley said, but she was smiling. "I'm nervous enough without you giving me a hard time, big brother."

They joined Melissa and Olivia at the back of the church.

Over their heads, and through a shifting haze of veil, extreme anticipation, and almost overwhelming joy, Ashley saw Jack standing up front, his back straight, his head high with pride.

In just two weeks, he'd come a long way toward a full recovery, filling out, his color returning. He claimed it was the restorative power of good sex.

Ashley blushed, remembering some of that sex, and looking forward to a lot more of it.

The organist struck the keys with renewed vigor.

"There's our cue," Brad whispered to Ashley, bending his head slightly so she could hear.

"Go!" Melissa said to Olivia, giving her a little push.

Olivia moved slowly up the aisle, between pews jammed with McKenzies, O'Ballivans, McKettricks, and assorted friends.

Just before starting up the aisle herself, Melissa

turned, found Ashley's hand under the bouquet of snow-white peonies Brad had had flown in from God-knew-where and squeezed it hard.

"Go," Brad told Melissa, with a chuckle.

She made a face at him and started resolutely up the aisle.

Once she and Olivia were both in front of the altar, opposite Jack and Tanner, the organist pounded the keys with even more vigor than before. Ashley *floated* toward the altar, gripping Brad's strong arm, her gaze fixed on Jack.

The guests rose to their feet, beaming at Ashley.

Jack smiled, encouraged her with a wink.

And then she was at his side.

She heard the minister ask, "Who giveth this woman in marriage?"

Heard Brad answer, "Her family and I."

Ashley's eyes began to smart again, and she wondered if anyone had ever died of an overdose of happiness.

Brad retreated, and after that, Ashley was only peripherally aware of her surroundings. Her entire focus was on Jack.

Somehow, she got through the vows.

She and Jack exchanged rings.

And then the minister pronounced them man and wife.

Jack raised the front of Ashley's veil to kiss her, and his eyes widened a little, in obvious appreciation, when he saw that she'd forsworn her usual French braid for a shoulder-length style that stood out around her face.

She'd spent the morning at Cora's Curl and Twirl over in Indian Rock, Cora herself doing the honors, snipping and blow-drying and phoofing endlessly.

The wedding kiss was chaste, at least in appearance. Up close and personal, it was nearly orgasmic.

"Ladies and gentlemen," the minister said triumphantly, raising his voice to be heard at the back of the church, "may I present Mr. and Mrs. Jack McKenzie!"

Cheers erupted.

The organ thundered.

Jack and Ashley hurried down the aisle, emerging into the sunlight, and were showered with birdseed and good wishes.

The reception, held at the bed-and-breakfast, was everything a bride could hope for. Even the weather cooperated; the snow had melted, the sun was out, the sky cloudless and heartbreakingly blue.

"I ordered a sunny day just for you," Jack whispered to her, as he helped her out of the limo in front of the house.

For the next two hours, the place was crammed to the walls with wedding guests. Pictures were taken, punch and cake were served. So many congratulatory hugs, kisses and handshakes came their way that Ashley began to wish the thing would *end* already.

She and Jack would spend their wedding night right there at home, although they were leaving on their honeymoon the next day.

The sky was beginning to darken toward twilight when the guests began to leave, one by one, couple by couple, and then in groups.

Bill and Abigail McKenzie and their large extended family would occupy all the guestrooms at the bed-and-breakfast, so they lingered, somewhat at loose ends until Brad diplomatically invited them out to Stone Creek Ranch, where the party would continue.

Goodbyes were said.

Except for the caterers, already cleaning up, Melissa was the last to leave.

"I may never forgive you for this wretched dress," she told Ashley, tearing up.

"Maybe you'll get back at me one of these days," Ashley answered softly, as Jack moved away to give the twins room to say their farewells. Melissa planned to drive to Scottsdale that same night. "You'll be the bride, and I'll be the one who has to look like a giant parakeet."

Melissa huffed out a breath, shook her head. "I think you're safe from that horrid fate," she said wistfully. "I plan to throw myself into my career. Before you know it, I'll be a Supreme Court Justice, just as you said." She gave a wobbly little smile that didn't quite stick. "At least my memoirs will probably be interesting."

Ashley kissed her sister's cheek. "Take care," she said.

Melissa chuckled. "As soon as I swap this dress for a pair of jeans and a sweatshirt, and the heels for sneakers, I'll be golden."

With that, Melissa headed for the downstairs powder room, where she'd stashed her getaway clothes.

When she emerged, she was dressed for the road, and the ruffly yellow gown was wadded into a bundle under her right arm.

"Will you still love me if I toss this thing into the first Dumpster I see?" she quipped, as she and Ashley stood at the front door.

"I'll still love you," Ashley said, "no matter what."

Melissa gave a brave sniffle. "See you around, Mrs. McKenzie," she said.

And then she opened the front door, dashed across

the porch and down the front steps, and along the walk. She got into her little red sports car, which looked too small to pull a trailer, tossed the offending bridesmaid's dress onto the passenger seat and waved.

Jack was standing right behind Ashley when she turned from closing the door, and he kissed her briefly on the mouth. "She's an O'Ballivan," he said. "She'll be all right."

Ashley nodded. Swallowed.

"The caterers will be out of here in a few minutes," Jack told her, with a twinkle. "I promised to overtip if they'd just kick it up a notch. Wouldn't you like to get out of that dress, beautiful as it is?"

She stood on tiptoe, kissed the cleft in her husband's chin. "I might need some help," she told him sweetly. "It has about a million buttons down the back."

Jack chuckled. "I'm just the man for the job," he said.

Mrs. Wiggins came, twitchy-tailed, out of the study, where she'd probably been hiding from the hubbub of the reception, batted playfully at the lace trim on the hem of Ashley's wedding gown.

"No you don't," she told the kitten, hoisting the little creature up so they were nose to nose, she and Mrs. Wiggins. "This dress is going to be an heirloom. Someday, another bride will wear it."

"Our daughter," Jack said, musing. "If she's as beautiful as her mother, every little boy under the age of five ought to be warned."

Ashley smiled, still holding Mrs. Wiggins. "Get rid of the caterers," she said, and headed for the stairs.

Barely a minute later, she was inside the room that had been hers alone, until today—not that she and Jack hadn't shared it every night since they got back from Chicago.

The last wintry light glowed at the windows, turning the antique lace curtains to gold. White rose petals covered the bed, and someone had laid a fire on the hearth, too.

Their suitcases stood just outside the closet door, packed and ready to go. Tomorrow at this time, she and Jack would be in Hawaii, soaking up a month of sunshine.

Ashley's heart quickened. She put a hand to her throat briefly, feeling strangely like a virgin, untouched, eager to be deflowered, and a little nervous at the prospect.

The room looked the same, and yet different, now that she and Jack were married.

Married. Not so long ago, she'd pretty much given up on marriage—and then Jack "McCall" had arrived by ambulance, looking for a place to heal.

So much had happened since then, some of it terrifying, most of it better than good.

Mrs. Wiggins leaped up onto a slipper chair near the fireplace and curled up for a long winter's snooze.

Carefully, Ashley removed the tiara that held her veil in place and set the mound of gossamer netting aside. She stood in front of the bureau mirror and fluffed out her hair with the fingers of both hands.

Her cheeks glowed, and so did her eyes.

The door opened softly, and Jack came into the room, no tuxedo jacket in evidence, unfastening his cuff links as he walked toward Ashley. Setting the cuff links aside on the dresser top, he took her into his arms, buried his hands in her hair, and kissed her thoroughly.

Ashley's knees melted, just as they always did.

Eventually, Jack tore his mouth from hers, turned her around, and began unfastening the buttons at the back of her dress. In the process, he bent to nibble at her skin as he bared it, leaving tiny trails of fire along her shoulder blades, her spine and finally the small of her back.

The dress fell in a pool at her feet, leaving her in her petticoat, bra, panty hose and high heels.

She shivered, not with fear or cold, but with eagerness. She wanted to give herself to Jack—as his wife.

But he left her, untucking his white dress shirt as he went. Crouched in front of the fireplace to light a blaze on the hearth.

Another blaze already burned inside Ashley.

Jack straightened, unfastened his cummerbund with a grin of relief, and tossed it aside. Started removing his shirt.

His eyes smoldered as he took Ashley in, slowly, his gaze traveling from her head to her feet and then back up again.

As if hypnotized, she unhooked her bra, let her breasts spill into Jack's full view. His eyes went wide as her nipples hardened, eager for his lips and tongue.

It seemed to take forever, this shedding of clothes, garment by garment, but finally they were both naked, and the fire snapped merrily in the grate, and Jack eased Ashley down onto the bed.

Because of her pregnancy—news they had yet to share with the rest of the family, because it was too new and too precious—his lovemaking was poignantly gentle.

He parted her legs, bent her knees, ran his hands from there to her ankles.

Ashley murmured, knowing what he was going to do, needing it, needing him.

He nuzzled her, parted the curls at the juncture of her thighs, and his sigh of contented anticipation reverberated through her entire system.

She tangled her fingers in his hair, held him close.

He chuckled against her flesh, and she moaned.

And then he took her full in his mouth, now nibbling, now suckling, and Ashley arched her back and cried out in surrender.

"Not so fast," Jack murmured, between teasing flicks of his tongue. "Let it happen slowly, Mrs. McKenzie."

"I—I don't think I—can wait—"

Jack turned his head, dragged his lips along the length of her inner thigh, nipped at her lightly as he crossed to the other side. "You can wait," he told her.

"*Please,* Jack," she half sobbed.

He slid his hands under her bare bottom, lifted her high, and partook of her with lusty appreciation.

She exploded almost instantaneously, her body flexing powerfully, once, twice, a third time.

And then she fell, sighing, back to the bed.

He was kissing her lower belly, where their baby was growing, warm and safe and sheltered.

"I love you, Jack," Ashley said, weak with the force of her releases.

He turned her to lie full length on the bed, poised himself over her, took her in a slow, even stroke.

"Always have," she added, trying to catch her breath and failing. "Always will."

Epilogue

Jack McKenzie stood next to his daughter's crib, gazing down at her in wonder. Katie—named for his grandmother—was nearly three months old now, and she looked more like Ashley every day. Although the baby was too young to understand Christmas, they'd hung up a stocking for her, just the same.

The door of his and Ashley's bedroom opened quietly behind him.

"The doctor is on the phone," she said quietly.

Jack turned, took her in, marveled anew, the way he did every time he saw his wife, that it was possible to go to sleep at night loving a woman so much, and wake up loving her even more.

"Okay," he said.

She approached, held out the cell phone he'd left downstairs when he brought Katie up to bed. They'd been putting the finishing touches on the Christmas tree by the front windows, he and Ashley, and the place was decorated to the hilt, though there would be no paying guests over the holidays.

Busy with a new baby, not to mention a husband, Ashley had decided to take at least a year off from running the bed-and-breakfast. She still cooked like a French chef, which was probably why he'd gained ten pounds since they'd gotten married, and she was practically an expert on the computer.

So far, she didn't seem to miss running a business.

She'd been baking all day, since half the family would be there for a special Christmas Eve supper, after the early services at the church.

They'd stayed home, waiting for the call.

He took the cell phone, cleared his throat, said hello.

Ashley moved close to him, leaned against his side, somehow supporting him at the same time. Her head rested, fragrant, against his shoulder.

He kissed her crown, drew in the scent of her hair.

"This is Dr. Schaefer," a man said, as if Jack needed to be told. He and Ashley had been bracing themselves for this call ever since Jack's last visit to the clinic up in Flagstaff, a few days before, where they'd run the latest series of tests.

"Yes," Jack said, his voice raspy. Wrapping one arm around Ashley's waist. He felt fine, but that didn't mean he was out of danger.

And there was so very much at stake.

"All the results are normal, Mr. McKenzie," he heard Dr. Schaefer say, as though chanting the words through an underwater tunnel. "I think we can safely assume the marrow transplant was a complete success, and so were the antirejection medications."

Jack closed his eyes. "Normal," he repeated, for Ashley's benefit as well as his own.

She squeezed him hard.

"Thanks, Doctor," he said.

A smile warmed the other man's voice. "Have a Merry Christmas," the doctor said. "Not that you need to be told."

"You, too," Jack said. "And thanks again."

He closed the phone, tucked it into the pocket of his shirt, turned to take Ashley into his arms.

"Guess what, Mrs. McKenzie," he said. "We have a future together. You and me and Katie. A long one, I expect."

She beamed up at him, her eyes wet.

Downstairs, the doorbell chimed.

Ashley squeezed Jack's hand once, crossed to the crib, and tucked Katie's blanket in around her.

"I suppose they'll let themselves in," Jack said, watching her with the same grateful amazement he always felt.

Ashley smiled, and came back to his side, and they went down the stairs together, hand in hand.

Brad and Meg, with Carly and Mac and the new baby, Eva, stood in the entryway, smiling, snow dusting the shoulders of their coats and gleaming in their hair.

Olivia and Tanner arrived only moments later, with the twins, who were walking now, and Sophie.

"Where's Melissa?" Olivia asked, looking around.

"She'll be here soon," Ashley said. "She called about an hour ago—there was a lot of traffic leaving Scottsdale."

Ashley looked up at Jack, and they silently agreed to wait until everyone had arrived before sharing the good news about his test results.

The men spent the next few minutes carrying brightly wrapped packages in from the trucks parked out front, while the women and smaller children headed for the kitchen, where a savory supper was warming in the ovens.

Ashley and Meg and Olivia carried plates and silverware into the dining room, while Carly and Sophie kept the smaller children entertained.

A horn tooted outside, in the snowy driveway, and then Melissa hurried through the back door.

"It's cold out there!" she cried, spreading her arms for the rush of small children, wanting hugs. "And I think I saw Santa Claus just as I was pulling into town."

Soon, they were all gathered in the dining room, the grand tree in the parlor in full view through the double doors.

"I have news," Melissa said, just as Jack was about to offer a toast.

Everyone waited.

"I'm coming back to Stone Creek," Melissa told them all. "I'm about to become the new county prosecutor!"

The family cheered, and when some of the noise subsided, Ashley and Jack rose from their chairs, each with an arm around the other.

"The test results?" Olivia asked, in a whisper. Then, reading Jack's and Ashley's expressions, a joyous smile broke over her face. "They were good?"

"Better than good," Ashley answered.

Supper was almost cold by the time the cheering was over, but nobody noticed.

It was Christmas Eve, after all.

And they were together, at home in Stone Creek.

* * * * *

RANCHER'S WILD SECRET

Maisey Yates

Chapter 1

The launch party for Maxfield Vineyards' brand-new select label was going off without a hitch, and Emerson Maxfield was bored.

Not the right feeling for the brand ambassador of Maxfield Vineyards, but definitely the feeling she was battling now.

She imagined many people in attendance would pin the look of disinterest on her face on the fact that her fiancé wasn't present.

She looked down at her hand, currently wrapped around a glass of blush wine, her fourth finger glittering with the large, pear-shaped diamond that she was wearing.

She wasn't bored because Donovan wasn't here.

Frankly, *Donovan* was starting to bore her, and that reality caused her no small amount of concern.

But what else could she do?

Her father had arranged the relationship, the engagement, two years earlier, and she had agreed. She'd been sure that things would progress, that she and Donovan could make it work because on paper they *should* work.

But their relationship wasn't…changing.

They worked and lived in different states and they didn't have enough heat between them to light a campfire.

All things considered, the party was much less boring than her engagement.

But all of it—the party and the engagement—was linked. Linked to the fact that her father's empire was the most important thing in his world.

And Emerson was a part of that empire.

In fairness, she cared about her father. And she cared about his empire, deeply. The winery was her life's work. Helping build it, grow it, was something she excelled at.

She had managed to get Maxfield wines into Hollywood awards' baskets. She'd gotten them recommended on prominent websites by former talk show hosts.

She had made their vineyard label something *better* than local.

Maxfield Vineyards was the leading reason parts of Oregon were beginning to be known as the new Napa.

And her work, and her siblings' work, was the reason Maxfield Vineyards had grown as much as it had.

She should be feeling triumphant about this party.

But instead she felt nothing but malaise.

The same malaise that had infected so much of what she had done recently.

This used to be enough.

Standing in the middle of a beautiful party, wearing

a dress that had been hand tailored to conform perfectly to her body—it used to be a thrill. Wearing lipstick like this—the perfect shade of red to go with her scarlet dress—it used to make her feel…

Important.

Like she mattered.

Like everything was put together and polished. Like she was a success. Whatever her mother thought.

Maybe Emerson's problem was the impending wedding.

Because the closer that got, the more doubts she had.

If she could possibly dedicate herself to her job *so much* that she would marry the son of one of the world's most premier advertising executives.

That she would go along with what her father asked, even in this.

But Emerson loved her father. And she loved the winery.

And as for romantic love…

Well, she'd never been in love. It was a hypothetical. But all these other loves were not. And as far as sex and passion went…

She hadn't slept with Donovan yet. But she'd been with two other men. One boyfriend in college, one out of college. And it just hadn't been anything worth upending her life over.

She and Donovan shared goals and values. Surely they could mesh those things together and create a life.

Why not marry for the sake of the vineyard? To make her father happy?

Why not?

Emerson sighed and surveyed the room.

Everything was beautiful. Of course it was. The

party was set in her family's gorgeous mountaintop tasting room, the view of the vineyards stretching out below, illuminated by the full moon.

Emerson walked out onto the balcony. There were a few people out there, on the far end, but they didn't approach her. Keeping people at a distance was one of her gifts. With one smile she could attract everyone in the room if she chose. But she could also affect a blank face that invited no conversation at all.

She looked out over the vineyards and sighed yet again.

"What are you doing out here?"

A smile tugged at the corner of Emerson's mouth. Because of course, she could keep everyone but her baby sister Cricket from speaking to her when she didn't want to be spoken to. Cricket basically did what she wanted.

"I just needed some fresh air. What are *you* doing here? Weren't you carded at the door?"

"I'm twenty-one, thank you," Cricket sniffed, looking…well, not twenty-one, at least not to Emerson.

Emerson smirked. "Oh. How could I forget?"

Truly, she *couldn't* forget, as she had thrown an absolutely spectacular party for Cricket, which had made Cricket look wide-eyed and uncomfortable, particularly in the fitted dress Emerson had chosen for her. Cricket did not enjoy being the center of attention.

Emerson *did* like it. But only on her terms.

Cricket looked mildly incensed in the moonlight. "I didn't come out here to be teased."

"I'm sorry," Emerson responded, sincere because she didn't want to hurt her sister. She only wanted to mildly goad her, because Cricket was incredibly goadable.

Emerson looked out across the vast expanse of fields and frowned when she saw a figure moving among the vines.

It was a man. She could tell even from the balcony that he had a lean, rangy body, and the long strides of a man who was quite tall.

"Who's that?" she asked.

"I don't know," Cricket said, peering down below. "Should I get Dad?"

"No," Emerson said. "I can go down."

She knew exactly who was supposed to be at the party, and who wasn't.

And if this man was one of the Coopers from Cowboy Wines, then she would have reason to feel concerned that he was down there sniffing around to get trade secrets.

Not that their top rival had ever stooped to that kind of espionage before, but she didn't trust anyone. Not really.

Wine-making was a competitive industry, and it was only becoming more so.

Emerson's sister Wren always became livid at the mere mention of the Cooper name, and was constantly muttering about all manner of dirty tricks they would employ to get ahead. So really, anything was possible.

"I'll just run down and check it out."

"You're going to go down and investigate by yourself?"

"I'm fine." Emerson waved a hand. "I have a cell phone, and the place is heavily populated right now. I don't think I'm going to have any issues."

"Emerson…"

Emerson slipped back inside, and out a side door,

moving quickly down the stairs, not listening to her sister at all. She didn't know why, but she felt compelled to see who the man was for herself.

Maybe because his arrival was the first truly interesting thing to happen all evening. She went in the direction where she'd last seen the figure, stepping out of the golden pool of light spilling from the party and into the grapevines. The moonlight illuminated her steps, though it was pale and left her hands looking waxen.

She rounded one row of grapevines into the next, then stopped, frozen.

She had known he was tall, even from a distance. But he was…very tall. And broad.

Broad shoulders, broad chest. He was wearing a cowboy hat, which seemed ridiculous at night, because it wasn't keeping the sun off him. He had on a tight black T-shirt and a pair of jeans.

And he was not a Cooper.

She had never seen the man before in her life. He saw her and stopped walking. He lifted his head up, and the moonlight caught his features. His face was sculpted, beautiful. So much so that it immobilized her. That square jaw was visible in even this dim light.

"I… Have you lost your way?" she asked. "The party is that way. Though… I'm fairly certain you're not on the guest list."

"I wasn't invited to any party," he said, his voice rough and raspy, made for sin.

Made for sin?

She didn't know where such a thought had come from.

Except, it was easy to imagine that voice saying all kinds of sinful things, and she couldn't credit why.

"Then… Forgive me, but what are you doing here?"

"I work here," he said. "I'm the new ranch hand."

Damn if she wasn't Little Red Riding Hood delivered right to the Big Bad Wolf.

Except, she wasn't wearing a scarlet cloak. It was a scarlet dress that clung to her generous curves like wrapping paper around a tempting present.

Her dark hair was lined silver by the moonbeams and tumbling around naked shoulders.

He could picture her in his bed, just like that. Naked and rumpled in the sheets, that hair spread everywhere.

It was a shame he wasn't here for pleasure.

He was here for revenge.

And if he had guessed correctly based on what he knew about the Maxfield family, this was Emerson Maxfield. Who often had her beautiful face splashed across magazine covers for food and wine features, and who had become something of an It Girl for clothing brands as well. She was gorgeous, recognizable… and engaged.

But none of that would have deterred him, if he really wanted her.

What the hell did he care if a man had put a ring on a woman's finger? In his opinion, if an engaged or married woman was looking elsewhere, then the man who'd put the ring on her finger should've done a better job of keeping her satisfied.

If Holden could seduce a woman, then the bastard he seduced her away from deserved it.

Indiscretion didn't cause him any concern.

But there were a whole lot of women and a whole

lot of ways for him to get laid, and he wasn't about to sully himself inside a Maxfield.

No matter how gorgeous.

"I didn't realize my father had hired someone new," she said.

It was funny, given what he knew about her family, the way that she talked like a little private school princess. But he knew she'd gone to elite schools on the East Coast, coming back home to Oregon for summer vacations, at least when her family wasn't jet-setting off somewhere else.

They were the wealthiest family in Logan County, with a wine label that competed on the world stage.

Her father, James Maxfield, was a world-class visionary, a world-class winemaker…and a world-class bastard.

Holden had few morals, but there were some scruples he held dear. At the very top of that list was that when he was with a woman, there was no coercion involved. And he would never leave one hopeless, blackmailed and depressed. No.

But James Maxfield had no such moral code.

And, sadly for James, when it came to dealing out justice to men who had harmed someone Holden cared about very much, he didn't have a limit on how far he was willing to go. He wondered what Emerson would think if she knew what her father had done to a woman who was barely her age.

What he'd done to Holden's younger sister.

But then, Emerson probably wouldn't care at all.

He couldn't see how she would *not* know the way her father behaved, given that the whole family seemed to run the enterprise together.

He had a feeling the Maxfield children looked the other way, as did James's wife. All of them ignoring his bad behavior so they could continue to have access to his bank account.

"I just got here today," he said. "Staying in one of the cabins on the property."

There was staff lodging, which he had found quaint as hell.

Holden had worked his way up from nothing, though his success in real estate development was not anywhere near as splashed over the media as the Maxfield's success was. Which, in the end, was what allowed him to engage in this revenge mission, this quest to destroy the life and reputation of James Maxfield.

And the really wonderful thing was, James wouldn't even see it coming.

Because he wouldn't believe a man of such low status could possibly bring him down. He would overlook Holden. Because James would believe that Holden was nothing more than a hired hand, a lackey.

James would have no idea that Holden was a man with a massive spread of land in the eastern part of the state, in Jackson Creek.

Because James Maxfield thought of no one but himself. He didn't think anyone was as smart as he was, didn't think anyone was anywhere near as important.

And that pride would be his downfall in the end.

Holden would make sure of it.

"Oh," she said. She met his eyes and bit her lip.

The little vixen was flirting with him.

"Aren't you meant to be in there hosting the party?"

She lifted a shoulder. "I guess so." She didn't seem at

all surprised that he recognized who she was. But then, he imagined Emerson was used to being recognized.

"People will probably be noticing that you're gone."

"I suppose they might be," she said. She wrinkled her nose. "Between you and me, I'm getting a little tired of these things."

"Parties with free food and drinks? How could you get tired of that?"

She lifted one elegant shoulder. "I suppose when the drinks are always free, you lose track of why they're special."

"I wouldn't know anything about that."

He'd worked for every damn thing he had.

"Oh. Of course. Sorry. That's an incredibly privileged thing to say."

"Well, if you're who I think you are, you're incredibly privileged. Why wouldn't you feel that way?"

"Just because it's true in my life doesn't mean it's not a tacky thing to say."

"Well, I can think of several tacky things to say right back that might make you feel a little bit better."

She laughed. "Try me."

"If you're not careful, Little Red, wandering through the wilderness like this, a Big Bad Wolf might gobble you up."

It was an incredibly obvious and overtly sexual thing to say. And the little princess, with her engagement ring glittering on her left hand, should have drawn up in full umbrage.

But she didn't. Instead, her body seemed to melt slightly, and she looked away. "Was that supposed to be tacky?"

"It was," he said.

"I guess it didn't feel that way to me."

"You should head back to that party," he said.

"Why? Am I in danger out here?"

"Depends on what you consider danger."

There was nothing wrong—he told himself—with building a rapport with her. In fact, it would be a damned useful thing in many ways.

"Possibly talking to strange men in vineyards."

"Depends on whether or not you consider me strange."

"I don't know you well enough to have that figured out yet." A crackle of interest moved over his skin, and he didn't know what the hell was wrong with him that the first time he'd felt anything remotely like interest in a hell of a long time was happening now.

With Emerson Maxfield.

But she was the one who took a step back. She was the one whose eyes widened in fear, and he had to wonder if his hatred for the blood that ran through her veins was as evident to her as it was to him.

"I have to go," she said. "I'm… The party."

"Yes, ma'am," he said.

He took a step toward her, almost without thinking.

And then she retreated, as quickly as she could on those impractical stiletto heels.

"You better run, Little Red," he said under his breath.

And then he rocked back on his heels, surveying the grapevines and the house up on the hill. "The Big Bad Wolf is going to gobble all of this up."

Chapter 2

"Emerson," her dad said. "I have a job for you."

Emerson was tired and feeling off balance after last night. She had done something that was so out of character she still couldn't figure out what she'd been thinking.

She had left the party, left her post. She had chased after a strange man out in the grapevines. And then...

He had reminded her of a wolf. She'd gone to a wolf sanctuary once when she was in high school, and she'd been mesmerized by the powerful pack alpha. So beautiful. So much leashed strength.

She'd been afraid. But utterly fascinated all at once. Unable to look away...

He worked on the property.

And that should have been a red light to her all the way down. An absolute *stop, don't go any further*. If the diamond on her finger couldn't serve as that warning, then his status as an employee should have.

But she had felt drawn to him. And then he'd taken a step toward her. And it was like suddenly the correct instincts had woken up inside of her and she had run away.

But she didn't know why it had taken that long for her to run. What was wrong with her?

"A job," she said blankly, in response to her father.

"I've been watching the profits of Grassroots Winery down in town," he said. "They're really building a name for themselves as a destination. Not just a brand that people drink when they're out, but a place people want to visit. We've proved this is an incredibly successful location for weddings and other large events. The party you threw last night was superb."

Emerson basked in the praise. But only for a moment. Because if there was praise, then a request couldn't be far behind.

"One of the things they're offering is rides through the vineyard on horseback. They're also doing sort of a rustic partnership with the neighboring dude ranch, which sounds more like the bastion of Cowboy Wines. Nothing I want to get involved with. We don't want to lower the value of our brand by associating with anything down-market. But horse rides through the vineyards, picnics, things like that—I think those could be profitable."

Emerson had met the owner of Grassroots Winery, Lindy Dodge, on a couple of occasions, and she liked the other woman quite a lot. Emerson had a moment of compunction about stepping on what had clearly been Lindy's idea, but then dismissed it.

It wasn't uncommon at all for similar companies to

try comparable ventures. They often borrowed from each other, and given the number of wineries beginning to crop up in the area, it was inevitable there would be crossover.

Plus, to the best of her ability Emerson tried not to look at the others as competition. They were creating a robust wine trail that was a draw in and of itself.

Tourists could visit several wineries when they came to Logan County, traveling from Copper Ridge through Gold Valley and up into the surrounding mountains. That the area was a destination for wine enthusiasts was good for everyone.

The only vineyard that Maxfield Vineyards really viewed as competition was Cowboy Wines. Which Emerson thought was funny in a way, since their brand could not be more disparate from Maxfield's if they tried.

And she suspected they *did* try.

She also suspected there was something darker at the root of the rivalry, but if so, James never said.

And neither had Wren, the middle sister. Wren's role in the company often saw her clashing with Creed Cooper, who worked in the same capacity for his family winery, and Wren hated him with every fiber of her being. Loudly and often.

"So what is the new venture exactly?" Emerson asked.

"I just told you. Trail rides and picnics, but we need a way to make it feel like a Maxfield endeavor. And that, I give over to you."

"That sounds like it would be more Wren's thing." Wren was responsible for events at the winery, while Emerson dealt more globally with brand representation.

"I think ultimately this will be about the way you influence people. I want you to find the best routes, the prime views for the trips, take some photos, put it up on your social media. Use the appropriate pound signs."

"It's a… It's a hashtag."

"I'm not interested in learning what it is, Emerson. That's why I have you."

"Okay. I can do that."

She did have a massive online reach, and she could see how she might position some photos, which would garner media interest, and possibly generate a story in *Sip and Savor* magazine. And really, it would benefit the entire area. The more that Maxfield Vineyards—with its vast reach in the world of wine—brought people into the area, the more the other vineyards benefited too.

"That sounds good to me," she said.

"That's why I hired a manager for the ranching portion of the facility. I need him to oversee some new construction, because if we're going to have guests in the stables, everything needs to be updated. I need for him to oversee the acquisition of a few horses. Plus, the rides, etc."

"Oh," she said. "This…person. This man you hired. He's…tall?"

James shrugged. "I don't know. I didn't consider his height. Did you?"

"No," she said, her face flaming. She felt like a child with her hand caught in the cookie jar. "I just… I think I saw him last night. Down in the vineyard. I left the party to check and see what was happening." Total honesty with her father came as second nature to her.

She tried to be good. She tried to be the daughter he had raised her to be, always.

"You left the party?"

"Everything was well in hand. I left Cricket in charge."

That might be a stretch. But while she was as honest with her father as possible, she tended to leave out some things like...her feelings. And this would be one of those times.

"I met him briefly, then I went back to the house. That's all. He told me he worked on the property."

"You have to be careful," her father said. "You don't want any photographs taken of you alone with a man who's not Donovan. You don't need anything to compromise your engagement."

Sometimes she wondered if her father realized they didn't live in the Victorian era.

"Nothing is going to compromise my engagement to Donovan."

"I'm glad you're certain about it."

She was, in spite of her occasional doubts. Her father might not understand that times had changed, but she did. She felt certain Donovan was carrying on with other women in the absence of a physical relationship with her. Why would she assume anything else? He was a man, after all.

She knew why her father was so invested in her marriage to Donovan. As part of his planned retirement, her father was giving ownership stakes in the winery to each of his daughters' husbands.

He felt Donovan would be an asset to the winery, and Emerson agreed. But she wasn't sure how that fit into a marriage.

Clearly, Donovan didn't much care about how that fit into a marriage either.

And she doubted he would be able to muster up any jealousy over her behavior.

"Image," her father said, bringing her back to the moment. "It isn't what you do that matters, Emerson, it's what the world *thinks* you're doing."

There was something about the way her father said it, so smooth and cold, that made her feel chilled. It shouldn't chill her, because she agreed that image was important in their business.

Still, it *did* chill her.

Emerson shifted. "Right. Well, no worries there. Image is my expertise."

"It's all about the brand," he said.

"I tell you that," she said.

"And you've done it well."

"Thank you," she said, nearly flushed with pleasure. Compliments from James Maxfield were rare, and she clung to them when she got them.

"You should head down to the stables. He'll be waiting for you."

And if that made her stomach tighten, she ignored the sensation. She had a job to do. And that job had nothing to do with how tall the new ranch manager was.

She was as pretty in the ridiculously trendy outfit she was wearing now as she'd been in that red dress.

She was wearing high-cut black pants that went up past her belly button, loose fitted through the leg, with a cuff around the ankle, paired with a matching black top that was cropped to just beneath her breasts and showed a wedge of stomach. Her dark hair was in a high bun, and she was wearing the same red lipstick she'd had on the night before, along with round sunglasses that covered her eyes.

He wished he could see her eyes. And as she approached, she pushed the glasses up to the top of her head.

He hadn't been prepared for how beautiful she was.

He thought he'd seen her beauty in the moonlight, thought he'd seen it in photographs, but they didn't do her justice. He'd been convinced that the blue of her eyes was accomplished with some kind of a filter. But it was clear to him now, out in the bright sun with the green mountains surrounding them, and her eyes reflecting that particular blue from the center of the sky, that if anything, her eyes had been downplayed in those photographs.

"Good morning," she said.

"Good morning to you too. I take it you spoke with your father?"

It took all of his self-control for that word to come out smoothly.

"Yes," she said. "I did."

"And what do you think of his proposition?"

In Holden's opinion, it was a good one. And when he was through ruining James and sinking his brand, Holden might well buy the entire property and continue making wine himself. He was good at selling things, making money. He could make more money here.

"It's good. I think a few well-placed selfies will drum up interest."

"You're probably right. Though, I can't say I'm real up on selfies."

That was a lie. His younger sister was a pretty powerful influencer. A model, who had met James Maxfield at one of the parties that had brought their type together. He was angry at himself for the part his own money had played in all of this.

Because Soraya had been innocent. A sweet girl from a small town who had been catapulted into a lifestyle she hadn't been prepared to handle.

Holden could relate well enough.

He certainly hadn't known how to handle money in the beginning.

But he'd been helping his family dig out of the hole they'd found themselves in. The first thing he'd done was buy his mother a house. Up on a hill, fancy and safe from the men who had used her all throughout Holden's childhood.

And his sweet, younger half sister… She'd tumbled headfirst into fame. She was beautiful, that much had always been apparent, but she had that lean, hungry kind of beauty, honed by years of poverty, her backstory lending even more interest to her sharp cheekbones and unerring sense of style.

She had millions of people following her, waiting to see her next picture. Waiting to see which party she would attend.

And she attended the wrong one when she met James Maxfield.

He'd pounced on her before Holden could say "daddy issues." And James had left her devastated. Holden would never forget having to admit his sister for a psychiatric hold. Soraya's suicide attempt, the miscarriage… The devastation.

It was burned in him.

Along with the reality that his money hadn't protected her. His money had opened her up to this.

Now all that was left was revenge, because he couldn't make it right. He couldn't take her pain away.

But he could take everything away from the Maxfield family.

And that was what he intended to do.

"I don't think we've officially met," she said. She stuck her hand out—the one that didn't have the ring on it. That one angled at her side, the gem sparkling in the sunlight. "I'm Emerson Maxfield."

"Holden Brown," he said, extending his own hand.

If James Maxfield weren't a raging narcissist, Holden might have worried about using his real first name.

But he doubted the older man would ever connect the younger model he'd used for a couple of months and then discarded with Holden. Why would he? James probably barely remembered Soraya's first name, much less any of her family connections. Holden himself wasn't famous. And that was how he liked it. He'd always thought it would be handy to have anonymity. He hadn't imagined it would be for reasons of revenge.

He closed his hand around hers. It was soft, desperately so. The hand of a woman who had never done hard labor in her life, and something in him suddenly felt desperate to make this little princess do some down and dirty work.

Preferably on his body.

He pulled his hand away.

"It's nice to meet you, Holden," she said.

"Nice to meet you too." He bit the pleasantry off at the end, because anything more and he might make a mistake.

"I have some routes in mind for this new venture. Let's go for a ride."

Chapter 3

Let's go for a ride was not sexual.

Not in the context of the ranch. Not to a woman who was so used to being exposed to horses. As she was.

Except, she kept replaying that line over and over in her head. Kept imagining herself saying it to him.

Let's go for a ride.

And then she would imagine herself saying it to him in bed.

She had never, ever felt like this in her entire life.

Her first time had been fine. Painless, which was nice, she supposed, but not exactly exciting.

It had been with her boyfriend at the time, who she'd known very well, and who had been extraordinarily careful and considerate.

Though, he'd cared more about keeping her comfortable than keeping her impassioned. But they had been young. So that seemed fair enough.

Her boyfriend after that had been smooth, urbane and fascinating to her. A world traveler before she had done any traveling of her own. She had enjoyed conversations with him, but she hadn't been consumed by passion or lust or anything like that.

She had just sort of thought she was that way. And she was fine with it. She had a lot of excitement in her life. She wasn't hurting for lack of passion.

But Holden made her feel like she might actually be missing something.

Like there was a part of herself that had been dormant for a very long time.

Right. You've been in the man's presence for...a combined total of forty minutes.

Well, that made an even stronger case for the idea of exploring the thing between them. Because in that combined forty minutes, she had imagined him naked at least six times.

Had thought about closing the distance between them and kissing him on the mouth no less than seven times.

And that was insane.

He was working on the ranch, working for her father. Working for her, in essence, as she was part of the winery and had a stake in the business.

And somehow, that aroused her even more.

A man like her fiancé, Donovan, knew a whole lot about the world.

He knew advertising, and there was a heck of a lot of human psychology involved in that. And it was interesting.

But she had a feeling that a man like Holden could teach her about her own body, and that was more than interesting. It was a strange and intoxicating thought.

Also, totally unrealistic and nothing you're going to act on.

No, she thought as she mounted her horse, and the two of them began riding along a trail that she wanted to investigate as a route for the new venture. She would never give in to this just for the sake of exploring her sensuality. For a whole list of reasons.

So you're just going to marry Donovan and wonder what this could have been like?

Sink into the mediocre sex life that the lack of attraction between you promises. Never know what you're missing.

Well, the thing about fantasies was they were only fantasies.

And the thing about sex with a stranger—per a great many of her friends who'd had sex with strangers—was that the men involved rarely lived up to the fantasy. Because they had no reason to make anything good for a woman they didn't really know.

They were too focused on making it good for themselves. And men always won in those games. Emerson knew her way around her own body, knew how to find release when she needed it. But she'd yet to find a man who could please her in the same way, and when she was intimate with someone, she couldn't ever quite let go... There were just too many things to think about, and her brain was always consumed.

It wouldn't be different with Holden. No matter how hot he was.

And blowing up all her inhibitions over an experience that was bound to be a letdown was something Emerson simply wasn't going to risk.

So there.

She turned her thoughts away from the illicit and forced them onto the beauty around her.

Her family's estate had been her favorite place in the world since she was a child. But of course, when she was younger, that preference had been a hollow kind of favoritism, because she didn't have a wide array of experiences or places to compare it to.

She did now. She'd been all over the world, had stayed in some of the most amazing hotels, had enjoyed food in the most glamorous locales. And while she loved to travel, she couldn't imagine a time when she wouldn't call Maxfield Vineyards home.

From the elegant spirals of the vines around the wooden trellises, all in neat rows spreading over vast acres, to the manicured green lawns, to the farther reaches where it grew wild, the majestic beauty of the wilderness so big and awe-inspiring, making her feel appropriately small and insignificant when the occasion required.

"Can I ask you a question?" His voice was deep and thick, like honey, and it made Emerson feel like she was on the verge of a sugar high.

She'd never felt anything like this before.

This, she supposed, was chemistry. And she couldn't for the life of her figure out why it would suddenly be *this* man who inspired it. She had met so many men who weren't so far outside the sphere of what she should find attractive. She'd met them at parties all around the world. None of those men—including the one her father wanted her to be engaged to—had managed to elicit this kind of response in her.

And yet… Holden did it effortlessly.

"Ask away," she said, resolutely fixing her focus on

the scene around them. Anything to keep from fixating on him.

"Why the hell did you wear *that* knowing we were going out riding?"

She blinked. Then she turned and looked at him. "What's wrong with my outfit?"

"I have never seen anyone get on a horse in something so impractical."

"Oh, come now. Surely you've seen period pieces where the woman is in a giant dress riding sidesaddle."

"Yes," he said. "But you have other options."

"It has to be photographable," she said.

"And you couldn't do some sexy cowgirl thing?"

Considering he was playing the part of sexy cowboy—in his tight black T-shirt and black cowboy hat— she suddenly wished she were playing the part of sexy cowgirl. Maybe with a plaid top knotted just beneath her breasts, some short shorts and cowgirl boots. Maybe, if she were in an outfit like that, she would feel suitably bold enough to ask him for a literal roll in the hay.

You've lost your mind.

"That isn't exactly my aesthetic."

"Your aesthetic is… *I Dream of Jeannie* in Mourning?"

She laughed. "I hadn't thought about it that way. But sure. *I Dream of Jeannie* in Mourning sounds about right. In fact, I think I might go ahead and label the outfit that when I post pics."

"Whatever works," he said.

His comment was funny. And okay, maybe the fact that he'd been clever a couple of times in her presence was bestowing the label of *funny* on him too early. But it made her feel a little bit better about her wayward hormones that he wasn't just beautiful, that he was fascinating as well.

"So today's ride isn't just a scouting mission for you," he said. "If you're worried about your aesthetic."

"No," she said. "I want to start generating interest in this idea. You know, pictures of me on the horse. In fact, hang on a second." She stopped, maneuvering her mount, turning so she was facing Holden, with the brilliant backdrop of the trail and the mountains behind them. Then she flipped her phone front facing and raised it up in the air, tilting it downward and grinning as she hit the button. She looked at the result, frowned, and then did it again. The second one would be fine once she put some filters on it.

"What was that?"

She maneuvered her horse back around in the other direction, stuffed her phone in her pocket and carried on.

"It was me getting a photograph," she said. "One that I can post. 'Something new and exciting is coming to the Maxfield label.'"

"Are you really going to put it like that?"

"Yes. I mean, eventually we'll do official press releases and other forms of media, but the way you use social media advertisements is a little different. I personally am part of that online brand. And my lifestyle—including my clothes—is part of what makes people interested in the vineyard."

"Right," he said.

"People want to be jealous," she said. "If they didn't, they wouldn't spend hours scrolling through photos of other people's lives. Or of houses they'll never be able to live in. Exotic locations they'll never be able to go. A little envy, that bit of aspiration, it drives some people."

"Do you really believe that?"

"Yes. I think the success of my portion of the family empire suggests I know what I'm talking about."

He didn't say anything for a long moment. "You know, I suppose you're right. People choose to indulge in that feeling, but when you really don't have anything, it's not fun to see all that stuff you'll never have. It cuts deep. It creates a hunger, rather than enjoyment. It can drive some people to the edge of destruction."

There was something about the way he said it that sent a ripple of disquiet through her. Because his words didn't sound hypothetical.

"That's never my goal," she said. "And I can't control who consumes the media I put out there. At a certain point, people have to know themselves, don't they?"

"True enough," he said. "But some people don't. And it's worse when there's another person involved who sees weakness in them even when they don't see it themselves. Someone who exploits that weakness. Plenty of sad, hungry girls have been lost along that envious road, when they took the wrong hand desperate for a hand up into satisfaction."

"Well, I'm not selling wild parties," she said. "I'm selling an afternoon ride at a family winery, and a trip here is not that out of reach for most people. That's the thing. There's all this wild aspirational stuff out there online, and the vineyard is just a little more accessible. That's what makes it advertising and not luxury porn."

"I see. Create a desire so big it can never be filled, and then offer a winery as the consolation prize."

"If the rest of our culture supports that, it's hardly my fault."

"Have you ever had to want for anything in your entire life, Emerson?" The question was asked innocuously enough, but the way he asked it, in that dark, rough voice, made it buzz over her skin, crackling like electricity as it moved through her. "Or have you always been given everything you could ever desire?"

"I've wanted things," she said, maybe too quickly. Too defensively.

"What?" he pressed.

She desperately went through the catalog of her life, trying to come up with a moment when she had been denied something that she had wanted in a material sense. And there was only one word that burned in her brain.

You.

Yes, that was what she would say. *I want you, and I can't have you. Because I'm engaged to a man who's not interested in kissing me, much less getting into bed with me. And I'm no more interested in doing that with him.*

But I can't break off the engagement no matter how much I want to because I so desperately need...

"Approval," she said. "That's...that's something I want."

Her stomach twisted, and she kept her eyes fixed ahead, because she didn't know why she had let the word escape out loud. She should have said nothing.

He wasn't interested in hearing about her emotional issues.

"From your father?" he asked.

"No," she said. "I have his approval. My mother, on the other hand..."

"You're famous, successful, beautiful. And you don't have your mother's approval?"

"Yeah, shockingly, my mother's goal for me wasn't to take pictures of myself and put them up on the internet."

"Unless you have a secret stash of pictures, I don't see how your mother could disapprove of these sorts of photographs. Unless, of course, it's your pants. Which I do think are questionable."

"These are *wonderful* pants. And actually deceptively practical. Because they allow me to sit on the horse comfortably. Whatever you might think."

"What doesn't your mother approve of?"

"She wanted me to do something more. Something that was my own. She doesn't want me just running publicity for the family business. But I like it. I enjoy what I do, I enjoy this brand. Representing it is easy for me, because I care about it. I went to school for marketing, close to home. She felt like it was…limiting my potential."

He chuckled. "I'm sorry. Your mother felt like you limited your potential by going to get a degree in marketing and then going on to be an ambassador for a successful brand."

"Yes," she said.

She could still remember the brittle irritation in her mother's voice when she had told her about the engagement to Donovan.

"So you're marrying a man more successful in advertising in the broader world even though you could have done that."

"You're married to a successful man."

"I was never given the opportunities that you were

given. You don't have to hide behind a husband's shadow. You could've done more."

"Yeah, that's about the size of it," she said. "Look, my mother is brilliant. And scrappy. And I respect her. But she's never going to be overly impressed with me. As far as she's concerned, I haven't worked a day in my life for anything, and I took the path of least resistance into this version of success."

"What does she think of your sisters?"

"Well, Wren works for the winery too, but the only thing that annoys my mother more than her daughters taking a free pass is the Cooper family, and since Wren makes it her life's work to go toe-to-toe with them, my mother isn't quite as irritated with everything Wren does. And Cricket... I don't know that anyone knows what Cricket wants."

Poor Cricket was a later addition to the family. Eight years younger than Emerson, and six years younger than Wren. Their parents hadn't planned on having another child, and they especially hadn't planned on one like Cricket, who didn't seem to have inherited the need to please...well, anyone.

Cricket had run wild over the winery, raised more by the staff than by their mother or father.

Sometimes Emerson envied Cricket and the independence she seemed to have found before turning twenty-one, when Emerson couldn't quite capture independence even at twenty-nine.

"Sounds to me like your mother is pretty difficult to please."

"Impossible," she agreed.

But her father wasn't. He was proud of her. She was

doing exactly what he wanted her to do. And she would keep on doing it.

The trail ended in a grassy clearing on the side of the mountain, overlooking the valley below. The wineries rolled on for miles, and the little redbrick town of Gold Valley was all the way at the bottom.

"Yes," she said. "This is perfect." She got down off the horse, snapped another few pictures with herself in them and the view in the background. And then a sudden inspiration took hold, and she whipped around quickly, capturing the blurred outline of Holden, on his horse with his cowboy hat, behind her.

He frowned, dismounting the horse, and she looked into the phone screen, keeping her eyes on him, and took another shot. He was mostly a silhouette, but it was clear that he was a good-looking, well-built man in a cowboy hat.

"Now, *there's* an ad," she said.

"What're you doing?"

He sounded angry. Not amused at all.

"I just thought it would be good to get you in the background. A full-on Western fantasy."

"You said that wasn't the aesthetic."

"It's not mine. Just because a girl doesn't want to wear cutoff shorts doesn't mean she's not interested in looking at a cowboy."

"You can't post that," he said, his voice hard like granite.

She turned to face him. "Why not?"

"Because I don't want to be on your bullshit website."

"It's not a website. It's… Never mind. Are you… You're not, like, fleeing from the law or something, are you?"

"No," he said. "I'm not."

"Then why won't you let me post your picture? It's not like you can really see you."

"I'm not interested in that stuff."

"Well, that stuff is my entire life's work." She turned her focus to the scenery around them and pretended to be interested in taking a few random pictures that were not of him.

"Some website that isn't going to exist in a couple of years is not your life's work. Your life's work might be figuring out how to sell things to people, advertising, marketing. Whatever you want to call it. But the *how* of it is going to change, and it's going to keep on changing. What you've done is figure out how to understand the way people discover things right now. But it will change. And you'll figure that out too. These pictures are not your life's work."

It was an impassioned speech, and one she almost felt certain he'd given before, though she couldn't quite figure out why he would have, or to who.

"That's nice," she said. "But I don't need a pep talk. I wasn't belittling myself. I won't post the pictures. Though, I think they would have caused a lot of excitement."

"I'm not going to be anyone's trail guide. So there's no point using me."

"You're not even *my* trail guide, not really." She turned to face him, and found he was much closer than she had thought. All the breath was sucked from her body. He was so big and broad, imposing.

There was an intensity about him that should repel her, but instead it fascinated her.

The air was warm, and she was a little bit sweaty,

and that made her wonder if *he* was sweaty, and something about that thought made her want to press her face against his chest and smell his skin.

"Have you ever gone without something?"

She didn't know why she'd asked him that, except that maybe it was the only thing keeping her from actually giving in to her fantasy and pressing her face against his body.

"I don't really think that's any of your business."

"Why not? I just downloaded all of my family issues onto you, and I'm not even sure why. Except that you asked. And I don't think anyone else has ever asked. So... It's just you and me out here."

"And your phone. Which is your link to the outside world on a scale that I can barely understand."

Somehow, that rang false.

"I don't have service," she said. "And anyway, my phone is going back in my pocket." She slipped it into the silky pocket of her black pants.

He looked at her, his dark eyes moving over her body, and she knew he was deliberately taking his time examining her curves. Knew that his gaze was deliberately sexual.

And she didn't feel like she could be trusted with that kind of knowledge, because something deep inside her was dancing around the edge of being bold. That one little piece of her that felt repressed, that had felt bored at the party last night...

That one little piece of her wanted this.

"A few things," he said slowly. And his words were deliberate too.

Without thinking, she sucked her lip between her

tceth and bit down on it, then swiped her tongue over the stinging surface to soothe it.

And the intensity in his eyes leaped higher.

She couldn't pretend she didn't know what she'd done. She'd deliberately drawn his focus to her mouth.

Now, she might have done it deliberately, but she didn't know what she wanted out of it.

Well, she did. But she couldn't want *that*. She couldn't. Not when…

Suddenly, he reached out, grabbing her chin between his thumb and forefinger. "I don't know how the boys who run around in your world play, Emerson. But I'm not a man who scrolls through photos and wishes he could touch something. If I want something, I take it. So if I were you… I wouldn't go around teasing."

She stuttered, "I… I… I…" and stumbled backward. She nearly tripped down onto the grass, onto her butt, but he reached out, looping his strong arm around her waist and pulling her upright. The breath whooshed from her lungs, and she found herself pressed hard against his solid body. She put her hand gingerly on his chest. Yeah. He was a little bit sweaty.

And damned if it wasn't sexy.

She racked her brain, trying to come up with something witty to say, something to defuse the situation, but she couldn't think. Her heart was thundering fast, and there was an echoing pulse down in the center of her thighs making it impossible for her to breathe. Impossible for her to think. She felt like she was having an out-of-body experience, or a wild fantasy that was surely happening in her head only, and not in reality.

But his body was hot and hard underneath her hand,

and there was a point at which she really couldn't pretend she wasn't touching an actual man.

Because her fingers burned. Because her body burned. Because everything burned.

And she couldn't think of a single word to say, which wasn't like her, but usually she wasn't affected by men.

They liked her. They liked to flirt and talk with her, and since becoming engaged, they'd only liked it even more. Seeing her as a bit of a challenge, and it didn't cost her anything to play into that a little bit. Because she was never tempted to do anything. Because she was never affected. Because it was only ever a conversation and nothing more.

But this felt like more.

The air was thick with *more*, and she couldn't figure out why him, why now.

His lips curved up into a half smile, and suddenly, in a brief flash, she saw it.

Sure, his sculpted face and body were part of it. But he was...an outlaw.

Everything she wasn't.

He was a man who didn't care at all what anyone thought. It was visible in every part of him. In the laconic grace with which he moved, the easy way he smiled, the slow honeyed timbre of his voice.

Yes.

He was a man without a cell phone.

A man who wasn't tied or tethered to anything. Who didn't have comments to respond to at two in the morning that kept him up at night, as he worried about not doing it fast enough, about doing something to damage the very public image she had cultivated—not just for herself—but for her father's entire industry.

A man who didn't care if he fell short of the expectations of a parent, at least he didn't seem like he would.

Looking at him in all his rough glory, the way that he blended into the terrain, she felt like a smooth shiny shell with nothing but a sad, listless urchin curled up inside, who was nothing like the facade that she presented.

He was the real deal.

He was like that mountain behind him. Strong and firm and steady. Unmovable.

It made her want a taste.

A taste of him.

A taste of freedom.

She found herself moving forward, but he took a step back.

"Come on now, princess," he said, grabbing hold of her left hand and raising it up, so that her ring caught the sunlight. "You don't want to be doing that."

Horror rolled over her and she stepped away.

"I don't... Nothing."

He chuckled. "Something."

"I... My fiancé and I have an understanding," she said. And she made a mental note to actually check with Donovan to see if they did. Because she suspected they might, given that they had never touched each other. And she could hardly imagine that Donovan had been celibate for the past two years.

You have been.

Yeah, she needed to check on the Donovan thing.

"Do you now?"

"Yes," she lied.

"Well, I have an understanding with your father that I'm in his employment. And I would sure hate to take advantage of that."

"I'm a grown woman," she said.

"Yeah, what do you suppose your daddy would think if he found that you were fucking the help?"

Heat washed over her, her scalp prickling.

"I don't keep my father much informed about my sex life," she said.

"The problem is, you and me would be his business. I try to make my sex life no one's business but mine and the lady I'm naked with."

"Me nearly kissing you is not the same as me offering you sex. Your ego betrays you."

"And your blush betrays you, darlin'."

The entire interaction felt fraught and spiky, and Emerson didn't know how to proceed, which was as rare as her feeling at a loss for words. He was right. He worked for her father, and by extension, for the family, for her. But she didn't feel like she had the power here. Didn't feel like she had the control. She was the one with money, with the Maxfield family name, and he was just…a *ranch hand*.

So why did she feel so decidedly at a disadvantage?

"We'd better carry on," she said. "I have things to do."

"Pictures to post."

"But not of you," she said.

He shook his head once. "Not of me."

She got back on her horse, and he did the same. And this time he led the way back down the trail, and she was somewhat relieved. Because she didn't know what she would do if she had to bear the burden of knowing he was watching the back of her the whole way.

She would drive herself crazy thinking about how to

hold her shoulders so that she didn't look like she knew that he was staring at her.

But then, maybe he wouldn't stare at her, and that was the thing. She would wonder either way. And she didn't particularly want to wonder.

And when she got back to her office, she tapped her fingers on the desk next to her phone, and did her very best to stop herself from texting Donovan.

Tap. *Don't.* Tap. *Don't.*

And then suddenly she picked up the phone and started a new message.

Are we exclusive?

There were no dots, no movement. She set the phone down and tried to look away. It pinged a few minutes later.

We are engaged.

That's not an answer.

We don't live in the same city.

She took a breath.

Have you slept with someone else?

She wasn't going to wait around with his back-and-forth nonsense. She wasn't interested in him sparing himself repercussions.

We don't live in the same city. So yes, I have.

And if I did?

Whatever you do before the wedding is your business.

She didn't respond, and his next text came in on the heels of the last.

Did you want to talk on the phone?

No.

K.

And that was it. Because they didn't love each other. She hadn't needed to text him, because nothing was going to happen with her and Holden.

And how do you feel about the fact that Donovan had slept with other people?

She wasn't sure.

Except she didn't feel much of anything.

Except now she had a get-out-of-jail-free card, and that was about the only way she could see it. That wasn't normal, was it? It wasn't normal for him to be okay with the fact that she had asked those questions. That she had made it clear she'd thought about sleeping with someone else.

And it wasn't normal for her to not be jealous when Donovan said he *had* slept with someone else.

But she wasn't jealous.

And his admission didn't dredge any deep feelings up to the surface either.

No, her reaction just underlined the fact that something was missing from their arrangement. Which she had known. Neither of them was under the impression they were in a real relationship. They had allowed themselves to be matched, but before this moment she had been sure feelings would grow in time, but they hadn't, and she and Donovan had ignored that.

But she couldn't…

Her father didn't ask much of her. And he gave her endless support. If she disappointed him…

Well, then she would be a failure all around, wouldn't she?

He's not choosing Wren's husband. He isn't choosing Cricket's.

Well, Wren would likely refuse. Emerson couldn't imagine her strong-headed sister giving in to that. And Cricket… Well, nobody could tame Cricket.

Her father hadn't asked them. He'd asked her. And she'd agreed, because that was who she was. She was the one who could be counted on for anything, and it was too late to stop being who she was now.

Texting Donovan had been insane, leaning in toward Holden had been even more insane. And she didn't have time for any of that behavior. She had a campaign to launch and she was going to do it. Because she knew who she was. She was not the kind of person who kissed men she barely knew, not the kind of person who engaged in physical-only flings, not the kind of person who crossed professional boundaries.

The problem was, Holden made her feel very, very *not* like herself. And that was the most concerning thing of all.

Chapter 4

Emerson was proving to be deeply problematic.

What he should do was go down to the local bar and find himself a woman to pick up. Because God knew he didn't need to be running around getting hard over his enemy's daughter. He had expected to be disgusted by everything the Maxfield family was. And indeed, when he had stood across from James Maxfield in the man's office while interviewing for this position, it had taken every ounce of Holden's willpower not to fly across the desk and strangle the man to death.

The thing was, death would be too easy an out for a man like him. Holden would rather give James the full experience of degradation in life before he consigned him to burning in hell for all eternity. Holden wanted to maximize the punishment.

Hell could wait.

And hell was no less than he deserved.

Holden had finally gotten what he'd come for.

It had come in the form of nondisclosure agreements he'd found in James's office. He'd paid attention to the code on the door when James had let him in for the interview, and all he'd had to do was wait for a time when the man was out and get back in there.

It fascinated Holden that everything was left unguarded, but it wasn't really a mystery.

This was James's office in his family home. Not a corporate environment. He trusted his family, and why wouldn't he? It was clear that Emerson had nothing but good feelings about her father. And Holden suspected everyone else in the household felt the same.

Except the women James had coerced into bed. Employees. All young. All dependent on him for a paycheck. But he'd sent them off with gag orders and payoffs.

And once Holden figured out exactly how to approach this, James would be finished.

But now there was the matter of Emerson.

Holden hadn't expected the attraction that had flared up immediately the first time he'd seen her not to let up.

And she was always…around. The problem with taking on a job as an opportunity to commit corporate espionage, and to find proof either of monetary malfeasance or of the relationship between James and Holden's sister, was that he had to actually *work* during the day.

That ate up a hell of a lot of his time. It also meant he was in close proximity to Emerson.

And speak of the devil, right as he finished mucking out a stall, she walked in wearing skintight tan breeches that molded to every dimple of her body.

"That's a different sort of riding getup," he said.

"I'm not taking selfies today," she said, a teasing gleam in her blue eyes that made his gut tight.

"Just going on a ride?"

"I needed to clear my head," she said.

She looked at him, seeming vaguely edgy.

"What is it?"

But he knew what it was. It was that attraction that he felt every time she was near. She felt it too, and that made it a damn sight worse.

"Nothing. I just… What is it that you normally do? Are you always a ranch hand? I mean, you must specialize in something, or my father wouldn't have hired you to help with the horses."

"I'm good with horses."

Most everything he'd said about himself since coming to the winery was a lie. But this, at least, was true. He had grown up working other people's ranches.

Now he happened to own one of his own, a good-sized spread, but he still did a portion of the labor. He liked working his own land. It was a gift, after so many years of working other people's.

If there was work to be given over to others, he preferred to farm out his office work, not the ranch work.

He'd found an affinity with animals early on, and that had continued. It had given him something to do, given him something to *be*.

He had been nothing but a poor boy from a poor family. He'd been a cowboy from birth. That connection with animals had gotten him his first job at a ranch, and that line of work had gotten him where he was today.

When one of his employers had died, he'd gifted Holden with a large plot of land. It wasn't his ranch, but totally dilapidated fields a few miles from the ranch he now owned.

He hadn't known what the hell to do with land so undeveloped at first, until he'd gone down to the county offices and found it could be divided. From there, he'd started working with a developer.

Building a subdivision had been an interesting project, because a part of him had hated the idea of turning a perfectly good stretch of land into houses. But then, another part of him had enjoyed the fact that new houses meant more people would experience the land he loved and the town he called home.

Making homes for families felt satisfying.

As a kid who had grown up without one at times, he didn't take for granted the effect four walls could have on someone's life.

And that had been a bargain he'd struck with the developer. That a couple of the homes were his to do with as he chose. They'd been gifted to homeless families going on ten years ago now. And each of the children had been given college scholarships, funded by his corporation now that he was more successful.

He'd done the same ever since, with every development he'd created. It wouldn't save the whole world, but it changed the lives of the individuals involved. And he knew well enough what kind of effect that change could have on a person.

He'd experienced it himself.

Cataloging everything good you've done in the past won't erase what you're doing now.

Maybe not. But he didn't much care. Yes, destroying the Maxfield empire would sweep Emerson right up in his revenge, which was another reason he'd thought it might be more convenient to hate everyone connected with James Maxfield.

He'd managed to steer clear of the youngest daughter, Cricket, who always seemed to be flitting in and out of the place, and he'd seen Wren on many occasions, marching around purposefully, but he hadn't quite figured out exactly what her purpose was. Nor did he want to.

But Emerson... Emerson he couldn't seem to stay away from. Or maybe she couldn't stay away from him. At the end of it all, he didn't know if it mattered which it was.

They kept colliding either way.

"You must be very good with horses," she said.

"I don't know about that. But I was here, available to do the job, so your father gave it to me."

She tilted her head to the side, appraising him like he was a confusing piece of modern art. "Are you married?"

"Hell no," he said. "No desire for that kind of nonsense."

"You think love is nonsense?" she pressed.

"You didn't ask me about love. You asked me about marriage."

"Don't they usually go together?"

"Does it for you? Because you nearly kissed me yesterday, and you're wearing another man's ring."

Great. He'd gone and brought that up. Not a good idea, all things considered. Though, it might make her angry, and if he could get her good and angry, that might be for the best.

Maybe then she would stay away.

"I told you, we're not living near each other right now, so we…have an arrangement."

"So you said. But what does that mean?"

"We are not exclusive."

"Then what the hell is the point of being engaged? As I understand it, the only reason to put a ring on a woman's finger is to make her yours. Sure and certain. If you were my woman, I certainly wouldn't let another man touch you."

Her cheeks flushed red. "Well, you certainly have a lot of opinions for someone who doesn't see a point to the institution of marriage."

"Isn't the point *possession*?"

"Women aren't seen as cattle anymore. So no."

"I didn't mean a woman being a possession. The husband and wife possess each other. Isn't that the point?"

She snorted. "I think that often the point is dynasty and connections, don't you?"

"Damn, that's cynical, even for me."

She ignored that. "So, you're good with horses, and you don't believe in marriage," she said. "Anything else?"

"Not a thing."

"If you don't believe in marriage, then what do you believe in?"

"Passion," he said. "For as long as it burns hot. But that's it."

She nodded slowly, and then she turned away from him.

"Aren't you going to ride?"

"I… Not right now. I need to… I need to go think."

And then without another word, Emerson Maxfield ran away from him.

* * *

The cabin was a shit hole. He really wasn't enjoying staying there. He had worked himself out of places like this. Marginal dwellings that had only woodstoves for heat. But this was the situation. Revenge was a dish best served cold, and apparently his ass had to be kind of cold right along with it.

Not that he didn't know how to build a fire. It seemed tonight he'd have to.

He went outside, into the failing light, wearing nothing but his jeans and a pair of boots, and searched around for an ax.

There was no preprepared firewood. That would've been way too convenient, and Holden had the notion that James Maxfield was an asshole in just about every way. It wasn't just Soraya that James didn't care about. It was everyone. Right down to the people who lived and worked on his property. He didn't much care about the convenience of his employees. It was a good reminder. Of why Holden was here.

Though, Emerson seemed to be under the impression that James cared for *her*. An interesting thing. Because when she had spoken about trying to earn the approval of one of her parents, he had been convinced, of course, that she had meant James's.

But apparently, James was proud of his daughter, and supported her.

Maybe James had used up every ounce of his humanity in his parenting. Though, Holden still had questions about that.

And it was also entirely possible that Emerson knew the truth about how her father behaved. And that she was complicit in covering up his actions in order to protect the brand.

Holden didn't know, and he didn't care. He couldn't concern himself with the fate of anyone involved with James Maxfield.

If you drink water from a poison well, whatever happened, happened.

As far as Holden was concerned, each and every grapevine on this property was soaked through with James Maxfield's poison.

He found an ax and swung it up in the air, splitting the log in front of him with ease. That, at least, did something to get his body warmed up, and quell some of the murder in his blood. He chuckled, positioned another log on top of the large stone sitting before him and swung the ax down.

"Well," came the sound of a soft, feminine voice. "I didn't expect to find you out here. Undressed."

He paused, and turned to see Emerson standing there, wearing a belted black coat, her dark hair loose.

She was wearing high heels.

Nothing covered her legs.

It was cold, and she was standing out in the middle of the muddy ground in front of his cabin, and none of it made much sense.

"What the hell are you doing here?" He looked her up and down. "Dressed like that."

"I could ask you the same question. Why didn't you put a shirt on? It's freezing out here."

"Why didn't *you* put pants on?"

She hesitated, but only for a moment, and then her expression went regal, which he was beginning to recognize meant she was digging deep to find all her stubbornness.

"Because I would be burdened by having to take them off again soon. At least, that's what I hope." Only the faint pink color in her cheeks betrayed the fact that she'd embarrassed herself. Otherwise he'd have thought she was nothing more than an ice queen, throwing out the suggestion of a seduction so cold it might give his dick frostbite.

But that wasn't the truth. No, he could see it in that blush. Underneath all that coolness, Emerson was burning.

And damned if he wasn't on fire himself.

But it made no damn sense to him, that this woman, the princess of Maxfield Vineyards, would come all the way out here, dragging her designer heels in the mud, to seduce him.

He looked behind his shoulder at the tiny cabin, then back at her.

"Really," he said.

The color in her cheeks deepened.

Lust and interest fired through him, and damned if he'd do anything to stop it. Dark, tempting images of taking Emerson into that rough cabin and sullying her on the rock-hard mattress… It was satisfying on so many levels, he couldn't even begin to sort through them all.

His enemy's daughter. Naked and begging for him, in a cabin reserved for workers, people James clearly thought so far beneath his own family that he'd not even given a thought to their basic needs.

Knowing Holden could have her in there, in a hundred different ways, fired his blood in a way nothing but rage had for ages.

Damn, he was hungry for her. In this twisted, intense way he had told himself he wasn't going to indulge.

But she was here.

Maybe with nothing on under that coat. Which meant they were both already half undressed, and it begged the question whether or not they should go ahead and get naked the rest of the way.

A look at her hand. He noticed she didn't have her engagement ring on.

"What the hell kind of game are you playing?" he asked.

"You said that whatever happened between you and a woman in bed was between you and that woman. Well, I'm of the same mind. It's nobody's business but ours what happens here." She bit her lip. "I'm going to be really, really honest with you."

There was something about that statement that burned, because if there was one thing he was never going to be with her, it was honest.

"I don't love my fiancé. I haven't slept with him. Why? Because I'm not that interested in sleeping with him. It's the strangest thing. We've been together for a couple of years, but we don't live near each other. And every time we could have, we just didn't. And the fact that we're not even tempted… Well, that tells you something about the chemistry between us. But this…you. I want to do this with you. It's all I can think about, and trust me when I say that's not me. I don't understand it, I didn't ask for it, or want it, but I can't fight it."

"I'm supposed to be flattered that you're deigning to come down from your shining tower because you can't stop thinking about me?"

"I want you," she said, lifting her chin up. "You asked me earlier if there was anything I had ever wanted that I couldn't have. It's you. I shouldn't have you. But I want you. And if my father found out that I was doing this, he would kill us both. Because my engagement to Donovan matters to him."

"You said you had an arrangement," he stated.

"Oh, Donovan wouldn't care. Donovan knows. I mean, in a vague sense. I texted him to make sure I wasn't just making assumptions. And I found out he already has. Been with someone else, I mean. So, it's not a big deal. But my father… He would never want it being made public. Image is everything to him, and my engagement to Donovan is part of the image right now."

And just like that, he sensed that her relationship with her father was a whole lot more complicated than she let on. But her relationship with James wasn't Holden's problem either way. And neither was whether or not Emerson was a good person, or one who covered up her father's transgressions. None of it mattered.

Nothing really mattered right here but the two of them.

The really fascinating thing was, Emerson didn't know who Holden was. And even if she did, she didn't need anything from him. Not monetarily. It had been a long damn time since he'd appealed to a woman in a strictly physical way. Not that women didn't enjoy him physically. But they also enjoyed what he had—a luxury hotel suite, connections, invitations to coveted parties.

He was standing here with none of that, nothing but a very dilapidated cabin that wasn't even his own.

And she wanted him.

And that, he found, was an incredibly compelling aphrodisiac, a turn-on he hadn't even been aware he'd been missing.

Emerson had *no idea* that he was Holden McCall, the wealthiest developer in the state. All she wanted was a roll in the hay, and why the hell not? Sure, he was supposed to hate her and everything she stood for.

But there was something to be said for a hate screw.

"So let me get this straight," he said. "You haven't even kissed me. You don't even know if I want to kiss you. But you were willing to come down here not even knowing what the payoff would be?"

Her face was frozen, its beauty profound even as she stared at him with blank blue eyes, her red lips pressed into a thin line. And he realized, this was not a woman who knew how to endure being questioned.

She was a woman used to getting what she wanted. A woman used to commanding the show, that much was clear. It was obvious that Emerson was accustomed to bulldozing down doors, a characteristic that seemed to stand in sharp contrast to the fact that she also held deep concerns over what her parents thought of her and her decisions.

"That should tell you, then," she said, the words stiff. "It should tell you how strong I think the connection is. If it's not as strong for you, that's fine. You're not the one on the verge of getting married, and you're just a man, after all. So you'll get yours either way. This might be *it* for me before I go to the land of boring, banal monogamous sex."

"So you intend to be fully faithful to this man you're marrying? The one you've never been naked with?"

"What's the point of marriage otherwise? You said that yourself. I believe in monogamy. It's just in my particular style of engagement I feel a little less…intense about it than I otherwise might."

He could take this moment to tell her that her father certainly didn't seem to look at marriage that way. But

that would be stupid. He didn't have enough information yet to come at James, and when he did, he wasn't
going to miss.

"So you just expect that I'll fuck you whether I feel
a connection to you or not. Even if I don't feel like it."

She lifted her chin, her imperiousness seeming to
intensify. "It's my understanding that men always feel
like it."

"Fair enough," he said. "But that's an awfully low
bar, don't you think?"

"I don't…"

"I'll tell you what," he said. "I'm going to give you
a kiss. And if afterward you can walk away, then you
should."

She blinked. "I don't want to."

"See how you feel after the kiss."

He dropped the ax, and it hit the frozen ground with
a dull thump.

He already knew.

He already knew that he was going to have a hard
time getting his hands off her once they'd been on her.
The way that she appealed to him hit a primitive part of
him he couldn't explain. A part of him that was something other than civilized.

She took a step toward him, those ridiculous high
heels somehow skimming over the top of the dirt and
rocks. She was soft and elegant, and he was half dressed
and sweaty from chopping wood, his breath a cloud in
the cold air.

She reached out and put her hand on his chest. And
it took every last ounce of his willpower not to grab
her wrist and pin her palm to him. To hold her against

him, make her feel the way his heart was beginning to rage out of control.

He couldn't remember the last time he'd wanted a woman like this.

And he didn't know if it was the touch of the forbidden adding to the thrill, or if it was the fact that she wanted his body and nothing else. Because he could do nothing for Emerson Maxfield, not Holden Brown, the man he was pretending to be. The man who had to depend on the good graces of his employer and lived in a cabin on the property. There was nothing he could do for her.

Nothing he could do but make her scream his name, over and over again.

And that was all she wanted.

She was a woman set to marry another man. She didn't even want emotions from him.

She wanted nothing. Nothing but his body.

And he couldn't remember the last time that was the case, if ever. Everyone wanted something from him. Everyone wanted a piece of him.

Even his mother and sister, who he cared for dearly, needed him. They needed his money, they needed his support.

They needed him to engage in a battle to destroy the man who had devastated Soraya.

But this woman standing in front of him truly wanted only this elemental thing, this spark of heat between them to become a blaze. And who was he to deny her?

He let her guide it. He let her be the one to make the next move. Here she was, all bold in that coat, with her hand on his chest, and yet there was a hesitancy to her as well. She didn't have a whole lot of experience seducing men, that much was obvious. And damned if he didn't enjoy the moment where she had to steel herself and find the courage to lean in.

There was something so very enjoyable about a woman playing the vixen when it was clear it wasn't her natural role. But she was doing it. For him. All for the desire she felt for him.

What man wouldn't respond to that?

She licked her lips, and then she pressed her mouth to his.

And that was the end of his control.

He wrapped his arm around her waist and pressed her against him, angling his head and consuming her.

Because the fire that erupted between them wasn't something that could be tamed. Wasn't something that could be controlled. Couldn't be tested or tasted. This was not a cocktail to be sipped. He wanted to drink it all down, and her right along with it.

Needed to. There was no other option.

He felt like a dying man making a last gasp for breath in the arms of this woman he should never have touched.

He didn't let his hands roam over her curves, no matter how much he wanted to. He simply held her, licking his way into the kiss, his tongue sliding against hers as he tasted the most luscious forbidden fruit that had ever been placed in front of him.

But it wasn't enough to have a bite. He wanted her juices to run down his chin. And he was going to have just that.

"Want to walk away?" he asked, his voice rough, his body hard.

"No," she breathed.

And then he lifted her up and carried her into the cabin.

Chapter 5

If this moment were to be translated into a headline, it would read: Maxfield Heiress Sacrifices All for an Orgasm.

Assuming, of course, that she would have an orgasm. She'd never had one yet with a man. But if she were going to…it would be with him.

If it were possible, it would be now.

When she had come up to the cabin and seen him standing there chopping wood—of all things—his chest bare, his jeans slung low on his hips, she had known that all good sense and morality were lost. Utterly and completely lost. In a fog of lust that showed no sign of lifting.

There was nothing she could do but give in.

Because she knew, she absolutely *knew*, that whatever this was needed to be explored. That she could not marry Donovan wondering what this thing between herself and Holden was.

Not because she thought there might be something lasting between them—no—she was fairly certain this was one of those moments of insanity that had nothing to do with anything like real life or good sense.

But she needed to know what desire was. Needed to know what sex could be.

For all she knew, this was the key to unlocking it with the man she was going to marry. And that was somewhat important. Maybe Holden was her particular key.

The man who was destined to teach her about her own sexuality.

Whatever the excuse, she was in his arms now, being carried into a modest cabin that was a bit more run-down than she had imagined any building on the property might be.

She had never been in any of the workers' quarters before. She had never had occasion to.

She shivered, with cold or fear she didn't know.

This was like some strange, unexpected, delayed rebellion. Sneaking out of her room in the big house to come and fool around with one of the men who worked for her father. He would be furious if he knew.

And so he would never know.

No one would ever know about this. No one but the two of them.

It would be their dirty secret. And at the moment, she was hoping that it would be very, very dirty. Because she had never had these feelings in her life.

This desire to get naked as quickly as possible. To be as close to someone as possible.

She wanted to get this coat off and rub herself all over his body, and she had never, ever felt that before.

She was a woman who was used to being certain. She knew why she made the decisions she did, and she made them without overthinking.

She was *confident*.

But this was a part of herself she had never been terribly confident in.

Oh, it had nothing to do with her looks. Men liked her curves. She knew that. She didn't have insecurities when it came to her body.

It was what her body was capable of. What it could feel.

That gave her all kinds of insecurity. Enough that in her previous relationships she had decided to make her own pleasure a nonissue. If ever her college boyfriend had noticed that she hadn't climaxed, he had never said. But he had been young enough, inexperienced enough, that he might not have realized.

She was sure, however, that her last ex had realized.

Occasionally he'd asked her if she was all right. And she had gotten very good at soothing his ego.

It's nice to be close.

It was good for me.

And one night, when he had expressed frustration at her tepid response to his kisses, she had simply shrugged and said, *I'm not very sexual.*

And she had believed it. She had believed each and every one of those excuses. And had justified the times when she had faked it, because of course her inability to feel something wasn't his fault.

But just looking at Holden made a pulse pound between her thighs that was more powerful than any sensation she'd felt during intercourse with a man before.

And with his hands on her like they were right now, with her body cradled in his strong arms…

She could barely breathe. She could barely think.

All she felt was a blinding, white-hot shock of need, and she had never experienced anything like it before in her life.

He set her down on the uneven wood floor. It was cold.

"I was going to build a fire," he said. "Wait right here, I'll be back."

And then he went back outside, leaving her standing in the middle of the cabin, alone and not in his arms, which gave her a moment to pause.

Was she really about to do this?

She didn't have any experience with casual sex. She had experience with sex only in the context of a relationship. And she had never, ever felt anything this intense.

It was the intensity that scared her. Not so much the fact that it was physical only, but the fact that it was so incredibly physical.

She didn't know how this might change her.

Because she absolutely felt like she was on the cusp of being changed. And maybe that was dramatic, but she couldn't rid herself of the sensation. This was somehow significant. It would somehow alter the fabric of who she was. She felt brittle and thin, on the verge of being shattered. And she wasn't entirely sure what was going to put her back together.

It was frightening, that thought. But not frightening enough to make her leave.

He returned a moment later, a stack of wood in his arms.

And she watched as he knelt down before the woodstove, his muscles shifting and bunching in his back as he began to work at lighting a fire.

"I didn't realize the cabins were so…rustic."

"They are a bit. Giving you second thoughts?"

"No," she said quickly.

If he changed his mind now, if he sent her away, she would die. She was sure of it.

He was kneeling down half naked, and he looked so damned hot that he chased away the cold.

"It'll take a bit for the fire to warm the place up," he said. "But I can keep you warm in the meantime."

He stood, brushing the dust off his jeans and making his way over to her.

She had meant to—at some point—take stock of the room. To look around and see what furniture it had, get a sense of the layout. But she found it too hard to look away from him. And when he fixed those eyes on her, she was held captive.

Utterly and completely.

His chest was broad, sprinkled with just the right amount of hair, his muscles cut and well-defined. His pants were low, showing those lines that arrow downward, as if pointing toward the most masculine part of him.

She had never been with a man who had a body like this. It was like having only ever eaten store-bought pie, and suddenly being treated to a homemade extravaganza.

"You are… You're beautiful," she said.

He chuckled. "I think that's my line."

"No. It's definitely mine."

One side of his mouth quirked upward into a grin, and even though the man was a stranger to her, suddenly she felt like he might not be.

Because that smile touched her somewhere inside her chest and made her *feel* when she knew it ought not to. Because this should be about just her body. And not in any way about her heart. But it was far too easy to imagine a world where nothing existed beyond this cabin, beyond this man and the intensity in his eyes, the desire etched into every line of his face.

And that body. Hot *damn*, that body.

Yes, it was very easy to imagine she was a different girl who lived in a different world.

Who could slip away to a secluded cabin and find herself swept up in the arms of a rugged cowboy, and it didn't matter whether or not it was *on brand*. Right now, it didn't.

Right now, it didn't.

This was elemental, something deeper than reality. It was fantasy in all of its bright, brilliant glory. Except it was real. Brought to life with stunning visuals, and it didn't matter whether it should be or not.

It was.

It felt suddenly much bigger than her. And because of that, she felt more connected with her body than she ever had before.

Because this wasn't building inside of her, it surrounded her, encompassed her. She could never have contained so much sensation, so much need. And so it became the world around her.

Until she couldn't remember what it was like to draw breath in a space where his scent didn't fill her lungs, where her need didn't dictate the way she stood, the way she moved.

She put her hands on the tie around her waist.

And he watched.

His attention was rapt, his focus unwavering.

The need between her thighs escalated.

She unknotted the belt and then undid the buttons, let her coat fall to her feet.

She was wearing nothing but a red lace bra and panties and her black high heels.

"Oh, Little Red," he growled. "I do like that color on you."

The hunger in his eyes was so intense she could feel it echoing inside of herself. Could feel her own desire answering back.

No man had ever looked at her like this.

They had wanted her, sure. Had desired her.

But they hadn't wanted to consume her, and she had a feeling that her own personal Big Bad Wolf just might.

She expected him to move to her, but instead he moved away, walking over to the bed that sat in the corner of the humble room. He sat on the edge of the mattress, his thighs splayed, his eyes fixed on her.

"I want you to come on over here," he said.

She began to walk toward him, her heels clicking on the floor, and she didn't need to be given detailed instruction, because she somehow knew what he wanted.

It was strange, and it was impossible, that somehow this man she had barely spent any time with felt known to her in a way that men she'd dated for long periods of time never had.

But he did.

And maybe that was something she had overlooked in all of this.

What she wanted to happen between them might be physical, but there was a spiritual element that couldn't be denied. Something that went deeper than just attraction. Something that spoke to a more desperate need.

His body was both deliciously unknown, and somehow right and familiar all at the same time.

And so were his needs.

She crossed the room and draped an arm over his shoulder, lifting her knee to the edge of the mattress, rocking forward so that the center of her pressed against his hardness. "I'm here," she said.

He wrapped his arm around her waist, pushed his fingertips beneath the waistband of her panties and slid his hands down over her ass. Then he squeezed. Hard. And she gasped.

"I'm going to go out on a limb here and guess that part of the attraction you have to all of this is that it's a little bit rough."

She licked her lips, nodded when no words would come.

She hadn't realized that was what she'd wanted, but when he said it, it made sense. When he touched her like this—possessive and commanding—she knew it was what she needed.

"That suits me just fine, princess, because I'm a man who likes it that way. So you have to tell me right now if you can handle it."

"I can handle whatever you give me," she said, her voice coming out with much more certainty than she felt.

Rough.

The word skated over her skin, painted delicious pictures in her mind and made that place between her legs throb with desire.

Rough. Uncivilized. Untamed.

Right then she wanted that, with a desperation that defied explanation.

She wanted to be marked by this. Changed by it. She wanted to have the evidence of it on her skin as well as on her soul.

Because somehow she felt that tonight, in this bed, it might be the only chance she'd have to find out what she was.

What she wanted.

What she desired apart from anything else, apart from family and social expectations. Tonight, this, had nothing to do with what anyone else might expect of her.

This was about her.

And on some level she felt like if she didn't have this, the rest of her life would be a slow descent into the madness of wondering.

"If anything goes too far for you, you just say it, you understand?"

"Yes," she said.

"I want to make you scream," he said. "But I want it to be the good kind."

She had never in her life screamed during sex.

The promise, the heat in his eyes, made her suspect she was about to.

That was when he tightened his grip on her and reversed their positions.

He pinned her down on her back, grabbing both wrists with one hand and stretching her arms up over her head. He had his thighs on either side of her hips, the denim rough against her skin. He was large and hard and glorious above her, his face filled with the kind of intensity that thrilled her down to her core.

She rocked her hips upward, desperate for fulfillment. Desperate to be touched by him.

He denied her.

He held her pinned down and began a leisurely tour of her body with his free hand.

He traced her collarbone, the edge of her bra, down the valley between her breasts and to her belly button. Before tracing the edge of her panties. But he didn't touch her anywhere that she burned for him. And she could feel the need for his touch, as if those parts of her were lit up bright with their demand for him. And still, he wouldn't do it.

"I thought you said this was going to be rough."

"Rough's not fun if you're not good and wet first," he said. And then he leaned in, his lips right next to her ear. "And I'm going to make sure you get really, really wet first."

Just those words alone did the job. An arrow of need pierced her center, and she could feel it, molten liquid there in her thighs. And that was when he captured her mouth with his, kissing her deep and long, cupping her breast with one hand and teasing her nipple with his thumb.

She whimpered, arching her hips upward, frustrated when there was nothing there for her to make contact with.

He touched her slowly, thoroughly, first through the lace of her bra, before pushing the flimsy fabric down and exposing her breasts. He touched her bare, his thumbs calloused as they moved over her body.

And then he replaced them with his mouth.

He sucked deep, and she worked her hips against nothing, desperate for some kind of relief that she couldn't find as he tormented her.

She would have said that her breasts weren't sensitive.

But he was proving otherwise.

He scraped his teeth across her sensitive skin. And then he bit down.

She cried out, her orgasm shocking her, filling her cheeks with embarrassed heat as wave after wave of desire pulsed through her core.

But she didn't feel satisfied, because he still hadn't touched her there.

She felt aching and raw, empty when she needed to be filled.

"There's a good girl," he said, and her internal muscles pulsed again.

He tugged her panties down her thighs, stopping at her ankles before pushing her knees wide, eyeing her hungrily as he did.

Then he leaned in, inhaling her scent, pressing a kiss to the tender skin on her leg. "The better to eat you with," he said, looking her in the eye as he lowered his head and dragged his tongue through her slick folds.

She gasped. This was the first time he had touched her there, and it was so... So impossibly dirty. So impossibly intimate.

Then he was done teasing. Done talking. He grabbed her hips and pulled her forward, his grip bruising as he set his full focus and attention on consuming her.

She dug her heels into the bed, tried to brace herself,

but she couldn't. She had no control over this, over any of it.

He was driving her toward pleasure at his pace, and it was terrifying and exhilarating all at once.

She climaxed again. Impossibly.

It was then she realized he was no longer holding her in place, but she had left her own wrists up above her head, as if she were still pinned there.

She was panting, gasping for breath, when he moved up her body, his lips pressing against hers.

She could taste her own desire there, and it made her shiver.

"Now I want you to turn over," he said.

She didn't even think of disobeying that commanding voice. She did exactly as she was told.

"Up on your knees, princess," he said.

She obeyed, anticipation making the base of her spine tingle as she waited.

She could hear plastic tearing, knew that he must be getting naked. Getting a condom on.

And when he returned to her, he put one hand on her hip, and she felt the head of his arousal pressed against the entrance to her body.

She bit her lip as he pushed forward, filling her.

He was so big, and this was not a position she was used to.

It hurt a bit as he drove his hips forward, a short curse escaping his lips as he sank in to the hilt.

She lowered her head, and he placed his hand between her shoulder blades, drawing it down her spine, then back up. And she wanted to purr like a very contented cat. Then he grabbed hold of both her hips, pulling out slowly, and slamming back home.

She gasped, arching her back as she met him thrust for punishing thrust. She pressed her face down into the mattress as he entered her, over and over again, the only sounds in the room that of skin meeting skin, harsh breaths and the kinds of feral sounds she had never imagined could come from her.

He grabbed hold of her hair, and moved it to one side, and she felt a slight tug, and then with a pull that shocked her with its intensity, he lifted her head as he held her like that, the tug matching his thrust. She gasped, the pain on her scalp somehow adding to the pleasure she felt between her legs.

And he did it over and over again.

Until she was sobbing. Until she was begging for release.

Then he released his hold on her hair, grabbing both her hips again as he raced her to the end, his hold on her bruising, his thrusts pushing her to the point of pain. Then he leaned forward, growling low and biting her neck as he came hard. And she followed him right over the edge into oblivion.

Chapter 6

By the time Emerson went limp in front of him, draped over the mattress like a boneless cat, the fire had begun to warm the space.

Holden was a man who didn't have much in the way of regret in his life—it was impossible when he had been raised with absolutely nothing, and had gotten to a space where he didn't have to worry about his own basic needs, or those of his family. And even now, it was difficult to feel anything but the kind of bone-deep satisfaction that overtook him.

He went into the bathroom and took care of the practicalities, then went back to stoke the fire.

He heard the sound of shifting covers on the bed, and looked over his shoulder to see Emerson lying on her side now, her legs crossed just so, hiding that tempting shadow at the apex of her thighs, her arm draped coquettishly over her breast.

"Enjoying the show?" he asked.

"Yes," she responded, no shame in her voice at all.

"You might return the favor," he said.

She looked down at her own body, as if she only just realized that she was covering a good amount of the tempting bits.

"You're busy," she said. "Making a fire. I would hate to distract."

"You're distracting even as you are."

Maybe even especially as she was, looking timid when he knew how she really was. Wild and uninhibited and the best damn sex he'd ever had in his life.

Hard mattress notwithstanding.

She rolled onto her back then, stretching, raising her arms up above her head, pointing her toes.

He finished with the fire quickly, and returned to the bed.

"I couldn't do it again," she said, her eyes wide.

"Why not?"

"I've never come that many times in a row in my life. Surely it would kill you."

"I'm willing to take the chance," he said.

It surprised him to hear that her response wasn't normal for her. She had seemed more than into it. Though, she had talked about the tepid chemistry between herself and the man she was engaged to.

There was something wrong with that man, because if he couldn't find chemistry with Emerson, Holden doubted he could find it with anyone.

"Well, of course you're willing to take the chance. You're not the one at risk. You only… Once. I already did three times."

"Which means you have the capacity for more," he said. "At least, that's my professional opinion."

"Professional ranch hand opinion? I didn't know that made you an expert on sex."

He chuckled. "I'm an expert on sex because of vast experience in my personal life, not my professional life. Though, I can tell you I've never considered myself a hobbyist when it came to female pleasure. Definitely a professional."

"Well, then I guess I picked a good man to experiment with."

"Is that what this is? An experiment?"

She rolled over so she was halfway on his body, her breast pressed against his chest, her blue eyes suddenly sincere. "I've never had an orgasm with a man before. I have them on my own. But never with… Never with a partner. I've only been with two men. But… They were my boyfriends. So you would think that if it was this easy they would have figured it out. Or I would have figured it out. And I can't for the life of me figure out why we didn't. Myself included."

"Chemistry," he said, brushing her hair back from her face, surprising himself with the tender gesture. But now she was asking him these wide-eyed innocent questions, when she had done things with him only moments ago that were anything but.

"Chemistry," she said. "I thought it might be something like that. Something magical and strange and completely impossible to re-create in a lab setting, sadly."

"We can re-create it right now."

"But what if I can't ever re-create it again? Although,

I suppose now I know that it's possible for me to feel this way, I…"

"I didn't know that I was your one-man sexual revolution."

"Well, I didn't want to put that kind of pressure on you."

"I thrive under pressure."

It was easy to forget, right now, that she was the daughter of his enemy. That he was here to destroy her family. That her engagement and the lack of chemistry between herself and her fiancé would be the least of her worries in the next week.

In fact, maybe he could spare her from the marriage. Because the optics for the family would be pretty damned reduced, probably beyond the point of healing. Her marriage to an ad exec was hardly going to fix that.

And anyway, the man would probably be much less interested in marrying into the Maxfield dynasty when it was reduced to more of a one-horse outfit and they didn't have two coins to rub together.

Holden waited for there to be guilt. But he didn't feel it.

Instead, he felt some kind of indefinable sense of satisfaction. Like in the past few moments he had collected another chess piece that had once belonged to his enemy. And Emerson was so much more than a pawn.

But he didn't know how to play this victory. Not yet.

And anyway, she didn't feel much like a victory or a conquest lying here in bed with him when he was still naked. He felt more than a little bit conquered himself.

"This is terrifying," she whispered. "Because I shouldn't be here. And I shouldn't be with you at all. And I think this is the most relaxed and maybe even the happiest I've ever felt in my life." She looked up at him, and a tear tracked down her cheek, and just like that, the guilt hit him right in the chest. "And I know that it can't go beyond tonight. I know it can't. Because you have your life… And I have mine."

"And there's no chance those two things could ever cross," he said, the words coming out a hell of a lot more hostile than he intended.

"I'm not trying to be snobby or anything," she said. "But there's expectations about the kind of man that I'll end up with. And what he'll bring to the family."

"Princess, I don't know why you're talking about marriage."

"Well, that's another problem in and of itself, isn't it? I'm at that point. Where marriage has to be considered."

"You're at that point? What the hell does that mean? Are we in the 1800s?"

"In a family like mine, it matters. We have to… My father doesn't have sons. His daughters have to marry well, marry men who respect and uphold the winery. His sons-in-law are going to gain a certain amount of ownership of the place, and that means…"

"His sons-in-law are getting ownership of the business?"

"Yes," she said. "I mean, I'll retain my share as well, so don't think it's that kind of draconian nonsense. But when we marry, Donovan is going to get a share of the winery. As large as mine. When Wren marries, it will be the same. Then there's Cricket, and her husband will get a share as well, though not as large. And by the time that's all finished, my father will only have a portion. A very small portion."

"How does that math work? Cricket gets less?"

"Well, so far Cricket doesn't have any interest in running the place, and she never has. So yes."

"No wonder your father is so invested in controlling who you marry."

"It's for my protection as well. It's not like he wants me getting involved with fortune hunters."

"You really are from another world," he said, disdain in his voice, even though he didn't mean it to be there. Because it didn't matter. Because it wasn't true—he had money, he had status. And because he didn't care about her. Or her opinion. He didn't care that she was as shallow as the rest of her family, as her father. It didn't concern him and, in fact, was sort of helpful given the fact that he had taken pretty terrible advantage of her, that he'd lied to her to get her into bed.

"I can tell that you think I'm a snob," she said. "I'm not, I promise. I wouldn't get naked with a man I thought was beneath me."

"Well, that's BS. It's a pretty well-documented fact that people find slumming to be titillating, Emerson."

"Well, I don't. You're different. And yes, I find that sexy. You're forbidden, and maybe I find that sexy too, but it's not about you being less than me, or less than other men that I've been with. Somehow, you're more, and I don't know what to do with that. That's why it hurts. Because I don't know if I will ever feel as contented, ever again, as I do right now lying in this cabin, and this is not supposed to be…"

"It's not supposed to be anything you aspire to. How could it be? When your mother thinks that what you have is beneath you as it is."

She swallowed and looked away. "My life's not mine. It's attached to this thing my father built from scratch.

This legacy that has meant a life that I'm grateful for, whatever you might think. I don't need to have gone without to understand that what I've been given is extraordinary. I do understand that. But it's an incredible responsibility to bear as well, and I have to be…a steward of it. Whether I want to be or not."

And suddenly, he resented it all. Every last bit. The lies that stood between them, the way she saw him, and his perceived lack of power in this moment. He growled, reversing their positions so he was over her.

"None of that matters just now," he said.

She looked up at him, and then she touched his face. "No," she agreed. "I don't suppose it does."

He reached down and found her red lace bra, touching the flimsy fabric and then looking back at her. He took hold of her wrists, like he'd done earlier, and, this time, secured them tightly with the lace.

"Right now, you're here," he said. "And I'm the only thing you need to worry about. You're mine right here, and there's nothing outside this room, off of this bed, do you understand?"

Her breath quickened, her breasts rising and falling with the motion. She nodded slowly.

"Good girl," he said. "You have a lot of responsibilities outside, but when you're here, the only thing you have to worry about is pleasing me."

This burned away the words of the last few minutes, somehow making it all feel okay again, even if it shouldn't. As if securing her wrists now might help him hold on to this moment a little tighter. Before he had to worry about the rest, before he had to deal with the fallout and what it would mean for Emerson.

This thing that she cared about so deeply, this dynasty, which she was willing to marry a man she didn't care about at all to secure.

He would free her from it, and in the end, it might be a blessing.

He looked at the way her wrists were tied, and suddenly he didn't want to free her at all.

What he wanted was to keep her.

He got a condom from his wallet and returned to her, where she lay on the bed, her wrists bound, her thighs spread wide in invitation.

He sheathed himself and gripped her hips, entering her in one smooth stroke. Her climax was instant, and it was hard, squeezing him tight as he pounded into her without mercy.

And he set about proving to her that there was no limit to the number of times she could find her pleasure.

But there was a cost to that game, one that crystallized in his mind after the third time she cried out his name and settled herself against his chest, her wrists still tightly tied.

She was bound to him now.

And she had betrayed a very crucial piece of information.

And the ways it could all come together for him became suddenly clear.

He knew exactly what he was going to do.

Chapter 7

It had been three days since her night in the cabin with Holden. And he was all she could think about. She knew she was being ridiculous. They had another event happening at the winery tonight, and she couldn't afford to be distracted.

There was going to be an engagement party in the large barn, which had been completely and totally made over into an elegant, rustic setting, with vast open windows that made the most of the view, and elegant chandeliers throughout.

Tonight's event wasn't all on her shoulders. Mostly, it was Wren's responsibility, but Emerson was helping, and she had a feeling that in her current state she wasn't helping much.

All she could do was think about Holden. The things

he had done to her body. The things he had taught her about her body.

She felt like an idiot. Spinning fantasies about a man, obsessing about him.

She'd never realized she would be into something like bondage, but he had shown her the absolute freedom there could be in giving up control.

She was so used to controlling everything all the time. And for just a few hours in his bed, he had taken the lead. It was like a burden had been lifted from her.

"Are you there, Emerson? It's me, Wren."

Emerson turned to look at her sister, who was fussing with the guest list in front of her.

"I'm here, and I've been here, helping you obsess over details."

"You're here," Wren said. "But you're not *here*."

Emerson looked down at her left hand and cursed. Because there was supposed to be a ring there. She had taken it off before going to Holden's cabin, but she needed to get it back on before tonight. Before she was circulating in a room full of guests.

Tonight's party was different from a brand-related launch. The event was at the heart of the winery itself, and as the manager of the property, Wren was the person taking the lead. When it came to broader brand representation, it was down to Emerson. But Emerson would still be taking discreet photographs of the event to share on social media, as that helped with the broader awareness of the brand.

Their jobs often crossed, as this was a family operation and not a large corporation. But neither of them minded. And in fact, Emerson considered it a good day when she got to spend extra time with her sister. But less so today when Wren was so apparently frazzled.

"What's wrong with you?" Wren asked, and then her eye fell meaningfully to her left hand. "Did something happen with Donovan?"

"No," Emerson said. "I just forgot to put the ring on."

"That doesn't sound like you. Because you're ever conscious of the fact that a ring like that is a statement."

"I'm well aware of what I'm ever conscious of, *Wren*," she said. "I don't need you to remind me."

"And yet, you forgot something today, so it seems like you need a reminder."

"It's really nothing."

"Except it *is* something. Because if it were nothing, then you wouldn't be acting weird."

"Fine. Don't tell anyone," Emerson said, knowing already that she would regret what she was about to say.

"I like secrets," Wren said, leaning in.

"I had a… I had a one-night stand." Her sister stared at her. Unmoving. "With a man."

Wren huffed a laugh. "Well, I didn't figure you were telling me about the furniture in your bedroom."

"I mean, Donovan and I aren't exclusive, but it didn't feel right to wear his ring while I was…with someone else."

"I had no idea," Wren said, her eyes widening. "I didn't know you were that…"

"Much of a hussy?"

"That *progressive*," she said.

"Well, I'm not. In general. But I was, and am a little thrown off by it. And no one can ever know."

"Solemnly swear."

"You cannot tell Cricket."

"Why would I tell Cricket? She would never be able to look you in the eyes again, and she would absolutely give you away. Not on purpose, mind you."

"No, but it's a secret that she couldn't handle."

"Absolutely."

"Have you met a man that you just…couldn't get out of your head even though he was absolutely unsuitable?"

Wren jolted, her whole body looking like it had been touched by a live wire. "I am very busy with my job."

"Wren."

"Yes. Fine. I do know what it's like to have a sexual obsession with the wrong guy. But I've never…acted on it." The look on her face was so horrified it would have been funny, if Emerson herself hadn't just done the thing that so appalled her sister.

"There's nothing wrong with…being with someone you want, is there? No, I don't really know him, but I knew I wanted him and that seems like a decent reason to sleep with someone, right?"

Wren looked twitchy. "I… Look. Lust and like aren't the same. I get it."

"I like him fine enough," Emerson said. "But we can't ever… *He works for Dad.*"

"Like…in the corporate office?"

"No, like, on the ranch."

"Emersonnnnn."

"What?"

"Are you living out a stable boy fantasy?"

Emerson drew her lip between her teeth and worried it back and forth. "He's not a boy. He's a man. On that you can trust me."

"The question stands."

"Maybe it was sort of that fantasy, I don't know. It was a fantasy, that much I can tell you. But it was supposed to just happen and be done, and I'm obsessing about him instead."

"Who would have ever thought that could happen?" Wren asked in mock surprise.

"In this advanced modern era, I should simply be able to claim my sexuality. Own it! Bring it with me wherever I go. Not…leave it behind in some run-down cabin with the hottest man I've ever seen in my life."

"Those are truly sage words. You should put them on a pretty graphic and post it to your page. Hashtag girl-boss-of-your-own-sexuality. Put your hair up and screw his brains out!"

Emerson shot her sister a deadly glare. "You know I hate that."

"I also know you never put a toe out of line, and yet here you are, confessing an extremely scandalous transgression."

"This secret goes to your grave with you, or I put you in the ground early, do you understand?"

Wren smirked and seemed to stretch a little taller, as if reminding Emerson she'd outgrown her by two inches when she was thirteen. She and Wren definitely looked like sisters—the same dark hair and blue eyes—but Wren wasn't curvy. She was tall and lean, her hair sleek like her build. She'd honed her more athletic figure with Krav Maga, kickboxing and all other manner of relatively violent exercise.

She claimed it was the only reason she hadn't killed Creed Cooper yet.

She also claimed she liked knowing she *could* kill

him if the occasion arose at one of the many different venues where they crossed paths.

Her martial arts skills were yet another reason it was hilarious for Emerson to threaten her sister. She'd be pinned to the ground in one second flat. Though, as the older sibling, she'd done her part to emotionally scar her sister to the point that, when she'd outgrown her, she still believed on some level Emerson could destroy her.

"In all seriousness," Wren said, "it does concern me. I mean, that you're marrying Donovan, and you're clearly more into whoever this other guy is."

"Right. Because I'm going to marry one of the men that work here. That would go over like... What's heavier than a lead balloon?"

"Does it matter?"

"What kind of ridiculous question is that? Of course it matters."

"Dad has never shown the slightest bit of interest in who I'm dating or not dating."

"You're not the oldest. I think... I think he figures he'll get me out of the way first. And it isn't a matter of him showing interest in who I'm dating. He directly told me that Donovan was the sort of man that I should associate with. He set me up with him."

"You're just going to marry who Dad tells you to marry?"

"Would you do differently, Wren? Honestly, I'm asking you."

"I don't think I could marry a man that I wasn't even attracted to."

"If Dad told you a certain man met with his approval, if he pushed you in that direction...you wouldn't try to make it work?"

Wren looked away. "I don't know. I guess I might have to try, but if after two years I still wasn't interested physically…"

"Marriage is a partnership. Our bodies will change. And sex drives and attraction will all change too. We need to have something in common. I mean, it makes way more sense to marry a man I have a whole host of things in common with than it does to marry one who I just want to be naked with."

"I didn't suggest you marry the ranch hand. But perhaps there's some middle ground. A man you like to talk to, and a man you want to sleep with."

"Well, I have yet to find a middle ground that would be suitable for Dad."

Anyway, Emerson didn't think that Holden could be called a middle ground. Not really. He was something so much more than that. Much too much of an extreme to be called something as neutral as middle ground.

"Maybe you should wait until you do."

"Or maybe I should just do what feels best," Emerson said. "I mean, maybe my marriage won't be the best of the best. Maybe I can't have everything. But we are really lucky, you and I. Look at this life." She gestured around the barn. "We have so much. I can make do with whatever I don't have."

Wren looked sad. "I don't know. That seems…tragic to me."

"What about you? You said you wanted a man and you haven't done anything about it."

"That's different."

"So, there's a man you want, and you can't be with him."

"I don't even like him," she said.

Emerson felt bowled over by that statement. Because there was only one man Emerson knew who Wren hated. And the idea that Wren might want him…

Well, no wonder Wren could barely even speak of it. She hated Creed Cooper more than anything else on earth. If the two of them ever touched…well, they would create an explosion of one kind or another, and Emerson didn't know how she hadn't realized that before.

Possibly because she had never before experienced the kind of intense clash she had experienced just a few nights ago with Holden.

"You do understand, then," Emerson said. "That there is a difference between wanting and having. And having for a limited time." She looked down. "Yes, I'm wildly attracted to this guy, and our chemistry is amazing. But it could never be more than that. Though, as someone who has experienced the temporary fun… You know you could."

Wren affected a full-body shudder.

"I really couldn't. I really, really couldn't."

"Suit yourself. But I'm going to go ahead and say that you're not allowed to give me advice anymore, because you live in a big glass house."

"I do not. It's totally different. I'm not marrying someone I shouldn't."

"Well, I'm marrying someone Dad wants me to. I trust Dad. And at the end of the day, I guess that's it. I'm trusting that it's going to be okay because it's what Dad wants me to do, and he's never… He's never steered me wrong. He's never hurt me. All he's ever done is support me."

Her father wanted the best for her. And she knew it.

She was just going to have to trust that in the end, like she trusted him.

"I know," Wren said, putting her arm around Emerson. "At least you have some good memories now."

Emerson smiled. "Really good."

"I don't want details," Wren said, patting Emerson's shoulder.

She flashed back to being tied up in bed with Holden. "I am not giving you details. Those are sacred."

"As long as we're on the same page."

Emerson smiled and went back to the checklist she was supposed to be dealing with. "We are on the same page. Which is currently a checklist. Tonight's party will go off without a hitch."

"Don't jinx it," Wren said, knocking resolutely on one of the wooden tables,

"I'm not going to jinx it. It's one of your parties. So you know it's going to be absolutely perfect."

Chapter 8

The party was going off without a hitch.

Everyone was enjoying themselves, and Emerson was in visual heaven, finding any number of photo opportunities buried in the meticulous decorations that Wren had arranged. With the permission of the couple, she would even share photographs of them, and of the guests. This, at least, served to distract her mildly from the situation with Holden.

Except, there was no *situation*, that was the thing. But it was very difficult for her brain to let go of that truth.

She wanted there to be a situation. But like she had said to Wren earlier, there was really no point in entertaining that idea at all. Marriage was more than just the marriage bed.

And she and Holden might be compatible between

the sheets—they were so compatible it made her pulse with desire even thinking about it—but that didn't mean they would be able to make a *relationship*, much less a *marriage*.

They had nothing in common.

You're assuming. You don't actually know that.

Well, it was true. She didn't know, but she could certainly look at the circumstances of his life and make some assumptions.

A passing waiter caught her eye, and she reached out to take hold of a glass of champagne. That was when a couple of things happened all at once. And because they happened so quickly, the reality took her longer to untangle than it might have otherwise.

The first thing she noticed was a man so stunning he took her breath away as he walked into the room.

The second realization was that she knew that man. Even though he looked so different in the sleekly cut black tux he had on his fit body that the name her brain wanted to apply to him couldn't seem to stick.

The third thing that happened was her heart dropping into her feet.

And she didn't even know why.

Because Holden had just walked in wearing a tux.

It might have taken a moment for her brain to link all those details up, but it had now.

She just couldn't figure out what it meant.

That he looked like this. That he was here.

He took a glass of champagne from a tray, and scanned the room. He looked different. But also the same.

Because while he might be clothed in an extremely refined fashion, there was still a ruggedness about him.

Something wild and untamed, even though, on a surface level, he blended in with the people around them.

No, not blended in.

He could never blend in.

He was actually dressed much nicer than anyone else here.

That suit was clearly custom, and it looked horrendously expensive. As did his shoes. As did…everything about him. And could he really be the same man she had happened upon shirtless cutting wood the other day? The same man who had tied her up in his run-down little cabin? The same man who had done desperate, dirty things to her?

And then his eyes collided with hers.

And he smiled.

It made her shiver. It made her ache.

But even so, it was a stranger's smile. It was not the man she knew, and she couldn't make sense of that certainty, even to herself. He walked across the room, acknowledging no one except for her.

And she froze. Like a deer being stalked by a mountain lion. Her heart was pounding in her ears, the sound louder now than the din of chatter going on around her.

"Just the woman I was looking for," he said.

Why did he sound different? He'd been confident in their every interaction. Had never seemed remotely cowed by her position or her money. And maybe that was the real thing she was seeing now.

Not a different man, but one who looked in his element rather than out of it.

"What are you doing here? And where did you get that suit?"

"Would you believe my fairy godmother visited?" The dark humor twisted his lips into a wry smile.

"No," she said, her heart pounding more viciously in her temple.

"Then would you believe that a few of the mice that live in the cabin made the suit for me?"

"Even less likely to believe that. You don't seem like a friend of mice."

"Honey, I'm not really a friend of anyone. And I'm real sorry for what I'm about to do. But if you cooperate with me, things are going to go a whole lot better."

She looked around. As if someone other than him might have answers. Of course, no one offered any if they did. "What do you mean?"

"You see, I haven't been completely honest with you."

"What?"

She couldn't make any sense of this. She looked around the room to see if they were attracting attention, because surely they must be. Because she felt like what was happening between them was shining bright like a beacon on the hill. But somehow they weren't attracting any attention at all.

"Why don't we go outside. I have a meeting with your father in just a few minutes. Unless…unless you are willing to negotiate with me."

"You have a meeting with my father? Negotiate what?"

The thoughts that rolled through her mind sent her into a panic.

He had obviously filmed what had happened between them. He was going to extort money from her family. He was a con man. No *wonder* he didn't want his picture taken.

All those accusations hovered on the edge of her lips, but she couldn't make them. Not here.

"What do you want?" she asked.

He said nothing. The man was a rock in a suit. No more sophisticated than he'd been in jeans. She'd thought he was different, but he wasn't. This was the real man.

And he was harder, darker than the man she'd imagined he'd been.

Funny how dressing up made that clear.

"What do you want?" she asked again.

She refused to move. She felt like the biggest fool on the planet. How had she trusted this man with her body? He was so clearly not who he said, so clearly...

Of course he hadn't actually wanted her. Of course the only man she wanted was actually just playing a game.

"Revenge," he said. "Nothing more. I'm sorry that you're caught in the middle of it."

"Did you film us?" She looked around, trying to see if people had noticed him yet. They still hadn't. "Did you film us together?"

"No," he said. "I'm not posting anything up on the internet, least of all that."

"Are you going to show my father?"

"No," he said, his lip curling. "This isn't about you, Emerson, whether you believe me or not. It isn't. But what I do next is about you. So I need you to come outside with me."

He turned, without waiting to see if she was with him, and walked back out of the barn. Emerson looked around and then darted after his retreating figure.

When they reached the outdoors, it was dim out, just

like the first night they had met. And when he turned to face her, she had the most ridiculous flashback.

He had been in jeans then. With that cowboy hat. And here he was now in a tux. But it was that moment that brought the reality of the situation into focus.

This man was the same man she had been seduced by. Or had she seduced him? It didn't even make sense anymore.

"Tell me what's going on." She looked him up and down. "You clearly aren't actually a ranch hand."

"Your father *did* hire me. Legitimately. So, I guess in total honesty, I do work for your father, and I am a ranch hand."

"What else are you? Are you paparazzi?"

He looked appalled by that. "I'm not a bottom-feeder that makes his living on the misfortunes of others."

"Then what are you? Why are you here?"

"I came here to destroy the winery."

She drew back. The venom in his voice was so intense she could feel the poison sinking down beneath her skin.

He looked her up and down. "But whether or not I do that is up to you now."

"What the hell are you talking about?"

"Your father. Your father had an affair with my sister."

"Your sister? I don't... My father did not have an affair. My father and mother have been married for...more than thirty years. And your sister would have to be..."

"She's younger than you," Holden said. "Younger than you, and incredibly naive about the ways of the world. And your father took advantage of her. When she got pregnant, he tried to pay her to get an abortion, and when she wouldn't, he left. She miscarried, and she's had nothing but health problems since. She's attempted suicide twice and had to be hospitalized. Your father ruined her. Absolutely ruined her."

"No," Emerson said. "It's a mistake. My father would never do that. He would never hurt…"

"I'm not here to argue semantics with you. You can come with me. I'm about to have a meeting with your father, though he doesn't know why. He'll tell you the whole story."

"What does this have to do with me?"

"It didn't have anything to do with you. Until you came to the cabin the other day. I was happy to leave you alone, but you pursued it, and then… And then you told me something very interesting. About the winery. And who'd own it."

Emerson felt like she might pass out. "The man I marry."

"Exactly." He looked at her, those dark eyes blazing. "So you have two choices, really. Let me have that meeting with your father, and you're welcome to attend, where I'll be explaining to him how I've found stacks of NDAs in his employee files. And it doesn't take a genius to figure out why."

"What?"

"Your father has engaged in many, many affairs with workers here on the property. Once I got ahold of the paperwork in his office, I got in touch with some of the women. Most of them wouldn't talk, but enough did. Coercion. And so much of the money for your vineyard comes through all of your celebrity endorsements. Can you imagine the commercial fallout if your father is found to be yet another man who abuses his power? Manipulates women into bed?"

"I don't believe you."

"It doesn't matter whether you believe me or not, Emerson. What matters is that I know I can make other people believe me. And when this is over, you won't be able to give Maxfield wines away with a car wash."

"I don't understand what that gives you," she said, horror coursing through her veins. She couldn't even entertain the idea of this being true. But the truth of it wasn't the thing, not now. The issue was what he could do.

"Revenge," he said, his voice low and hard.

"Revenge isn't a very lucrative business."

"I don't need the revenge to pay. But... I won't lie to you, I find the idea of revenge and a payout very compelling. The idea of owning a piece of this place instead of simply destroying it. So tell me, how does it work? Your husband getting a stake in the business."

"I get married, and then I just call the lawyers, and they'll do the legal paperwork."

His expression became decisive. "Then you and I are getting married."

"And if I don't?"

"I'll publicize the story. I will make sure to ruin the brand. However, if I marry you, what I'll have is ownership of the brand. And you and I, with our united stakes, will have a hell of a lot of decision-making power."

"But to what end?"

"I want your father to know that I ended up owning part of this. And what I do after that...that will depend on what he's willing to do. But I want to make sure he has to contend with me for as long as I want. Yes,

I could ruin the label. But that would destroy everything that you and your sister have worked so hard for, and I'm not necessarily here to hurt you. But gaining a piece of this... Making sure my sister gets something, making sure your father knows that I'm right there... That has value to me."

"What about Donovan?"

"He's not my problem. But it's your call, Emerson. You can marry Donovan. And inherit the smoldering wreckage that I'll leave behind. Or, you marry me."

"How do I know you're telling the truth?"

"Look up Soraya Jane on your favorite social media site."

"I... Wait. I know who she is. She's... She has millions of followers."

"I know," he said.

"She's your sister."

"Yes."

"And..."

"My name is Holden. Holden McCall. I am not famous on the internet, or really anywhere. But I'm one of the wealthiest developers in the state. With my money, my sister gained some connections, got into modeling. Started traveling."

"She's built an empire online," Emerson said.

"I know," he said. "What she's done is nothing short of incredible. But she's lost herself. Your father devastated her. Destroyed her. And I can't let that stand."

"So I... If I don't marry you...you destroy everything. And the reason for me marrying Donovan doesn't even exist anymore."

"That's the size of it."

"And we have to transfer everything before my father realizes what you're doing."

Emerson had no idea what to do. No idea what to think. Holden could be lying to her about all of this, but if he wasn't, then he was going to destroy the winery, and there was really no way for her to be sure about which one was true until it was too late.

"Well, what do we do, then?"

"I told you, that is up to you."

"Okay. So say we get married. Then what?"

"You were already prepared to marry a man you didn't love, might as well be me."

Except… This was worse than marrying a man she didn't love.

She had trusted Holden with something deep and real. Some part of her that she had never shown to anyone else. She had trusted him enough to let him tie her hands.

To let him inside her body.

And now she had to make a decision about marrying him. On the heels of discovering that she didn't know him at all.

"I'll marry you," she said. "I'll marry you."

Chapter 9

The roar of victory in Holden's blood hadn't quieted, not even by the time they boarded his private plane. They'd left the party and were now taking off from the regional airport, bound for Las Vegas, and he was amused by the fact that they both just so happened to be dressed for a wedding, though they hadn't planned it.

"Twenty-four-hour wedding chapels and no waiting period," he said, lifting a glass of champagne, and then extending his hand and offering it to her.

The plane was small, but nicely appointed, and fairly quiet.

He wasn't extraordinarily attached to a great many of the creature comforts that had come with his wealth. But being able to go where he wanted, when he wanted, and without a plane full of people was certainly his favorite.

"You have your own plane," she said, taking the glass

of champagne and downing it quickly. "You are private-plane rich."

She didn't look impressed so much as pissed.

"Yep," he said.

She shook her head, incredulous. "I... I don't even know what to say to that."

"I didn't ask you to say anything."

"No. You asked me to marry you."

"I believe I *demanded* that you marry me or I'd ruin your family."

"My mistake," she said, her tone acerbic. "How could I be so silly?"

"You may not believe me, but I told you, I didn't intend to involve you in this."

"I just conveniently involved myself?"

"If it helps, I found it an inconvenience at first."

"Why? You felt *guilty*? In the middle of your quest to take down my family and our fortune? Yes, that must've been inconvenient for you."

"I didn't want to drag you into it," he said. "Because I'm not your father. And I sure as hell wasn't going to extract revenge by using you for sex. The sex was separate. I only realized the possibilities when you told me about how your husband would be given an ownership stake in the vineyard."

"Right," she said. "Of course. Because I was an idiot who thought that since you had been inside me, I could maybe have a casual conversation with you."

"I'm sorry, but the information was too good for me to let go. And in the end, your family gets off easier."

"Except that you might do something drastic and destroy the winery with your control of the share."

"I was absolutely going to do that, but now I can own

a piece of it instead. And that benefits me. I also have his daughter, right with me."

"Oh, are you going to hold a gun to my head for dramatics?"

"No gun," he said. "In fact, we're on a private plane, and you're drinking champagne. You're not in any danger from me, and I didn't force you to come with me."

"But you did," she said, her voice thick.

"I offered you two choices."

"I didn't like either of them."

"Welcome to life, princess. You not liking your options isn't the same as you not having any."

She ignored that statement. "This is *not* my life."

"It is now." He appraised her for a long moment, the elegant line of her profile. She was staring out the window, doing her very best not to look at him. "The Big Bad Wolf was always going to try and eat you. You know how the fairy tale goes."

"Say whatever you need to say to make yourself feel better," she said. "You're not a wolf. You're just a dick."

"And your father?"

That seemed to kill her desire to banter with him. "I don't know if I believe you."

"But you believe me just enough to be on a plane with me going to Las Vegas to get married, because if I'm right, if I'm telling the truth…"

"It ruins everything. And I don't think I trust anyone quite so much that I would take that chance. Not even my father. I don't trust you at all, but what choice do I have? Because you're right. I was willing to marry a man that I didn't love to support my family. To support the empire. The dynasty. So why the hell wouldn't I do it now?"

"Oh, but you hate me, don't you?"

"I do," she said. "I really do."

He could sense that there was more she wanted to say, but that she wouldn't. And they were silent for the next hour, until the plane touched down in Nevada.

"Did you want an Elvis impersonator?" he asked, when they arrived on the Strip, at the little white wedding chapel he'd reserved before they landed.

"And me without my phone," she said.

"Did you want to take pictures and post them?"

She narrowed her eyes. "I wanted to beat you over the head with it."

"That doesn't answer my question about Elvis."

"Yeah, that would be good. If we don't have an Elvis impersonator, the entire wedding will be ruined."

"Don't tease me, because I will get the Elvis impersonator."

"Get him," she said, making a broad gesture. "Please. Because otherwise this would be *absurd*."

The edge of hysteria in her voice suggested she felt it was already absurd, but he chose to take what she said as gospel.

And he checked the box on the ridiculous paperwork, requesting Elvis, because she thought he was kidding, and she was going to learn very quickly that he was not a man to be trifled with. Even when it came to things like this.

They waited until their names were called.

And sadly, the only impersonator who was available past ten thirty on a Saturday night seemed to be Elvis from the mid-1970s.

"Do you want me to sing 'Burning Love' or 'Can't

Help Falling in Love' at the end of the ceremony?" he asked in all seriousness.

"Pick your favorite," Emerson replied, her face stony.

And Holden knew she had been certain that this level of farce would extinguish the thing that burned between them. Because she hated him now, and he could see the truth of that in her eyes.

But he was happy to accept her challenge. Happy to stand there exchanging vows with an Elvis impersonator as officiant, and a woman in a feathered leotard as witness, because it didn't change the fact that he wanted her.

Desperately.

That all he could think about was when this was finished, he was going to take her up to a lavish suite and have her fifty different ways.

And she might not think she wanted it, but she would.

She might think that she could burn it all out with her anger, but she couldn't. He knew it.

He knew it because he was consumed by it.

He should feel only rage. Should feel only the need for revenge.

But he didn't.

And she wouldn't either.

"You may kiss the bride," Elvis said.

She looked at him with a warning in her eyes, but that warning quickly became a challenge.

She would learn pretty quickly that he didn't back down from a challenge.

He cupped her chin with his hand, and kissed her, hard and fast, but just that light, quick brush of their mouths left them both breathing hard.

And as soon as they separated, the music began to

play and Elvis started singing about how he just couldn't help falling in love.

Well, Holden could sure as hell help falling in love. But he couldn't keep himself from wanting Emerson. That was a whole different situation.

They signed the paperwork quickly, and as soon as they were in the car that had been waiting for them, he handed her his phone. "Call your lawyer."

"It's almost midnight," she said.

"He'll take a call from you, you know it. We need to get everything set into motion so we have it all signed tomorrow morning."

"*She* will take a call from me," she said pointedly. But then she did as he asked. "Hi, Julia. It's Emerson. I just got married." He could hear a voice saying indiscriminate words on the other end. "Thank you. I need to make sure that I transfer the shares of the company into my husband's name. As soon as possible." She looked over at him. "Where are we staying?"

She recited all of the necessary information back to Julia at his direction, including the information about him, before getting off the phone.

"She'll have everything faxed to us by morning."

"And she won't tip off your father?"

"No," she said. "She's the family lawyer, but she must know… She's going to realize that I eloped. And she's going to realize that I'm trying to bypass my father. That I want my husband to have the ownership shares he—I— is entitled to. She won't allow my father to interfere."

"She's a friend of yours, then."

"We became friends, yes. People who aren't liars make friends."

"I'm wounded."

"I didn't think you could wound granite."

"Why did you comply with what I asked you to do so easily?"

Suddenly, her voice sounded very small and tired. "Because. It makes no sense to come here, to marry you, if I don't follow through with the rest. You'll ruin my family if you don't get what you asked for. I'm giving it to you. Protesting now is like tying my own self to the railroad tracks, and damsel in distress isn't my style." She looked at him, her blue eyes certain. "I made my bed. I'll lie in it."

They pulled up to the front of a glitzy casino hotel that was far from his taste in anything.

But what he did like about Las Vegas was the sexual excess. Those who created the lavish hotel rooms here understood exactly why a man was willing to pay a lot of money for a hotel room. And it involved elaborate showers, roomy bathtubs and beds that could accommodate all manner of athletics.

The decor didn't matter to him at all with those other things taken into consideration.

They got out of the car, and he tipped the valet.

"Your secretary called ahead, Mr. McCall," the man said. "You're all checked in and ready to go straight upstairs. A code has been texted to your phone."

Holden put his arm around her, and the two of them began to walk to an elevator. "I hope you don't think… I… We're going to a hotel room and…" Emerson said.

"Do you think you're going to share a space with me tonight and keep your hands off me?"

They got inside the elevator, and the doors closed. "I hate you," she said, shoving at his chest.

"And you want me," he said. "And that might make you hate me even more, but it doesn't make it not true."

"I want to…"

"Go ahead," he said. "Whatever you want."

"I'm going to tear that tux right off your body," she said, her voice low and feral. "Absolutely destroy it."

"Only if I can return the favor," he said, arousal coursing through him.

"You might not be all that confident when I have the most fragile part of you in my hand."

He didn't know why, but that turned him on. "I'll take my chances."

"I don't understand what this is," she said. "I should be…disgusted by you."

"It's too late. You already got dirty with me, honey. You might as well just embrace it. Because you know how good it is between us. And you wanted me when I was nothing other than a ranch hand. Why wouldn't you want me when you know that I'm a rich man with a vengeful streak a mile wide?"

"You forced me into this."

"I rescued you from that boring bowl of oatmeal you called a fiancé. At least you hate me. You didn't feel anything for him."

Her hackles were up by the time they got to the suite door, and he entered his code. The door opened and revealed the lavish room that had all the amenities he wanted out of such a place.

"This is tacky," she said, throwing her purse down on the couch.

"And?"

"Warm," she said.

She reached behind her body and grabbed hold of her zipper, pulling down the tab and letting her dress fall to the floor.

"I figured you were going to make me work for it."

"Your ego doesn't deserve that. Then you'd get to call it a seduction. I want to fuck you, I can't help myself. But I'm not sure you should be particularly flattered by that. I hate myself for it."

"Feel free to indulge your self-loathing, particularly if at some point it involves you getting that pretty lipstick all over me."

"I'm sure it will. Because I'm here with you. And there's not much I can do about my choices now. We're married. And a stake in the vineyard is close to being transferred into your name. I've already had sex with you. I got myself into this. I might as well have an orgasm."

"We can certainly do better than one orgasm," he said.

She looked good enough to eat, standing there in some very bridal underwear, all white and lacy, and unintentionally perfect for the moment, still wearing the red high heels she'd had on with her dress.

He liked her like this.

But he liked her naked even better.

She walked over to where he stood, grabbed hold of his tie and made good on her promise.

She wrenched the knot loose, then tore at his shirt, sending buttons scattering across the floor. "I hope that was expensive," she said, moving her hand over his bare chest.

"It was," he said. "Very, very expensive. But sadly for you, expensive doesn't mean anything to me. I could buy ten more and not notice the expense."

He could see the moment when realization washed over her. About who had the power. She was so very comfortable with her financial status and she'd had an idea about his, and what that meant, and even though she'd seen the plane, seen him in the tux, the reality of who he'd been all along was just now hitting her.

"And to think," she said, "I was very worried about taking advantage of you that night we were together."

"That says more about you and the way you view people without money than it does about me, sweetheart."

"Not because of that. You work for my father. By extension, for me, since I own part of the winery. And I was afraid that I might be taking advantage of you. But here you were, so willing to blackmail me."

"Absolutely. Life's a bastard, and so am I. That's just the way of things."

"Here I thought she was a bitch. Which I've always found handy, I have to say." She pushed his shirt off his shoulders, and he shed it the rest of the way onto the floor, and then she unhooked his belt, pulling it through the loops.

He grinned. "Did you want to use that?"

"What?"

"You know, you could tie me down if you wanted," he said. "If it would make you feel better. Make you feel like you have some control."

Something flared in her eyes, but he couldn't quite read it. "Why would I want that? That wouldn't give me more control. It would just mean I was doing most of the work." She lifted her wrists up in supplication, her eyes never leaving his. "You can tie my wrists, and I'll still have the control."

He put the tip of the leather through the buckle, and looped it over her wrists, pulling the end tight before he looped it through the buckle again, her wrists held fast together. Then, those blue eyes never leaving his, she sank down onto her knees in front of him.

Chapter 10

She had lost her mind, or something. Her heart was pounding so hard, a mixture of arousal, rage and shame pouring over her.

She should have told him no. She should have told him he was never touching her again. But something about her anger only made her want to play these games with him even more, and she didn't know what that said about her.

But he was challenging her, with everything from his marriage proposal to the Elvis at the chapel. This room itself was a challenge, and then the offer to let her tie him up.

All of it was seeing if he could make her or break her, and she refused to break. Because she was Emerson Maxfield, and she excelled at everything she did. And if this was the way she was going to save her family's dynasty, then she was going to save it on her knees in front of Holden McCall.

"You think I'm just going to give you what you want?" he asked, stroking himself through his pants. She could see the aggressive outline of his arousal beneath the dark fabric, and her internal muscles pulsed.

"Yes," she said. "Because I don't think you're strong enough to resist me."

"You might be right about that," he said. "Because I don't do resisting. I spent too much of my life wanting, and that's not something that I allow. I don't want anymore. I have."

He unhooked the closure on his pants, slid the zipper down slowly and then freed himself.

He wrapped his hand around the base, holding himself steady for her. She arched up on her knees and took him into her mouth, keeping her eyes on his the entire time.

With her hands bound as they were, she allowed him to guide her, her hair wrapped around his fist as he dictated her movements.

It was a game.

She could get out of the restraints if she wanted to. Could leave him standing there, hard and aching. But she was submitting to this fiction that she was trapped, because somehow, given the marriage—which she truly was trapped in—this felt like power.

This choice.

Feeling him begin to tremble as she took him in deep, feeling his power fracture as she licked him, tasted him.

She was the one bound, but he couldn't have walked away from her now if he wanted to, and she knew it.

They both did.

He held all the power outside this room, outside this moment. But she'd claimed her own here, and she was going to relish every second.

She teased him. Tormented him.

"Stand up," he said, the words scraping his throat raw.

She looked up at him, keeping her expression serene. "Are you not enjoying yourself?"

"Stand up," he commanded. "I want you to walk to the bed."

She stood slowly, her hands still held in that position of chosen obedience. Then with her eyes never leaving his, she walked slowly toward the bedroom. She didn't turn away from him until she had to, and even then, she could feel his gaze burning into her. Lighting a fire inside of her.

Whatever this was, it was bigger than them both.

Because he hated her father, and whether or not the reasons that he hated James Maxfield were strictly true or not, the fact was he did.

And she didn't get the impression that he was excited to find himself sexually obsessed with her. But he was.

She actually believed that what he wanted from her in terms of the winery was separate from him wanting her body, because this kind of intensity couldn't be faked.

And most important, it wasn't only on his side.

That had humiliated her at first.

The realization that she had been utterly captivated by this man, even while he was engaged in a charade.

But the fact of the matter was, he was just as enthralled with her.

They were both tangled in it.

Whether they wanted to be or not.

She climbed onto the bed, positioning herself on her back, her arms held straight down in front of her, covering her breasts, covering that space between her thighs. And she held that pose when he walked in.

Hunger lit his gaze and affirmed what she already knew to be true in her heart. He wanted her.

He hated it.

There was something so deliciously wicked about the contrast.

About this control she had over him even now.

A spark flamed inside her stomach.

He doesn't approve of this, or of you. But he can't help himself.

She arched her hips upward unconsciously, seeking some kind of satisfaction.

It was so much more arousing than it had any right to be. This moment of triumph.

Because it was private. Because it was secret.

Emerson lived for appearances.

She had been prepared to marry a man for those appearances.

And yet, this moment with Holden was about nothing more than the desire between two people. That he resented their connection? That only made it all feel stronger, hotter.

He removed his clothes completely as he approached the bed.

She looked down at her own body, realizing she was still wearing her bra and panties, her high heels.

"You like me like this," she whispered.

"I like you any way I can get you," he said, his voice low and filled with gravel.

"You like this, don't you? You had so much commentary on me wanting to slum it with a ranch hand. I think you like something about having a rich girl. Though, now I don't know why."

"Is there any man on earth who doesn't fantasize about corrupting the daughter of his enemy?"

"Did you corrupt me? I must've missed the memo."

"If I haven't yet, honey, then it's going to be a long night." He scooted her up the mattress, and lifted her arms, looping them back over her head, around one of the posts on the bed frame. Her hands parted, the leather from the belt stretching tight over the furniture, holding her fast. "At my mercy," he said.

He took his time with her then.

Took her high heels off her feet slowly, kissing her ankle, her calf, the inside of her thigh. Then he teased the edges of her underwear before pulling them down slowly, kissing her more intimately. He traveled upward, to her breasts, teasing her through the lace before removing the bra and casting it to the floor. And then he stood back, as if admiring his hard work.

"As fun as this is," he said, "I want your hands on me."

She could take her own hands out of the belt, but she refused. Refused to break the fiction that had built between the two of them.

So she waited. Waited as he slowly, painstakingly undid the belt and made a show of releasing her wrists. Her entire body pulsed with need for him. And thankfully, it was Vegas, so there were condoms on the bedside table.

He took care of the necessities, quickly, and then joined her on the bed, pinning her down on the mattress.

She smiled up at him, lifting her hand and tracing

the line of his jaw with her fingertip. "Let's go for a ride," she whispered.

He growled, gripped her hips and held her steady as he entered her in one smooth stroke.

She gasped at the welcome invasion, arching against his body as he tortured them both mercilessly, drove them both higher than she thought she could stand.

And when she looked into his eyes, she saw the man she had been with that first night, not a rich stranger.

Holden.

His last name didn't matter. It didn't matter where he was from. What was real was *this*.

And she knew it, because their desire hadn't changed, even if their circumstances had. If anything, their desire had sharpened, grown in intensity.

And she believed with her whole soul that what they'd shared in his bed had never been about manipulating her.

Because the intensity was beyond them. Beyond sex in a normal sense, so much deeper. So much more terrifying.

She took advantage of her freedom. In every sense of the word.

The freedom of her hands to explore every ridge of muscle on his back, down his spine, to his sculpted ass.

And the freedom of being in this moment. A moment that had nothing to do with anything except need.

This…this benefited no one. In fact, it was a short road off a cliff, but that hadn't stopped either of them.

They couldn't stop.

He lowered his head, growling again as he thrust into her one last time, his entire body shaking with his release.

And she followed him over the edge.

She let out a hoarse cry, digging her fingernails into his skin as she crested that wave of desire over and over again.

She didn't think it would end.

She thought she might die.

She thought she might not mind, if this was heaven, between the sheets with him.

And when her orgasm passed, she knew she was going to have to deal with the fact that he was her husband.

With the reality of what her father would think.

With Holden, her father's enemy, owning a share in the winery.

But those realizations made her head pound and her heart ache.

And she would rather focus on the places where her body burned with pleasure.

Tomorrow would come soon enough, and there would be documents to fax and sign, and they would have to fly back to Oregon.

But that was all for later.

And Emerson had no desire to check her phone. No desire to have any contact with the outside world.

No desire to take a picture to document anything.

Because none of this could be contained in a pithy post. None of it could even be summed up in something half so coherent as words.

The only communication they needed was between their bodies.

Tomorrow would require words. Explanations. Probably recriminations.

But tonight, they had this.

And so Emerson shut the world out, and turned to him.

Chapter 11

By the time he and his new wife were on a plane back to Oregon, Emerson was looking sullen.

"It's possible he'll know what happened by the time we get there," she said.

"But you're confident there's nothing he can do to stop it?"

She looked at him, prickles of irritation radiating off her. A sharp contrast to the willing woman who had been in his bed last night.

"Why do you care? It works out for you either way."

"True. But it doesn't work out particularly well for you."

"And you care about that?"

"I married you."

"Yeah, I still don't really get that. What exactly do you think is going to happen now?"

"We'll have a marriage. Why not?"

"You told me you didn't believe in marriage."

"I also told you I was a ranch hand."

"Have you been married before?" She frowned.

"No. Would it matter if I had?"

"In a practical sense, obviously nothing is a deal breaker, since I'm already married to you, for the winery. So no. But yes. Actually, it does."

"Never been married. No kids."

"Dammit," she said. "It didn't even occur to me that you might have children."

"Well, I don't."

"Thank God."

"Do you want to have some?"

The idea should horrify him. But for some reason, the image of Emerson getting round with his baby didn't horrify him at all. In fact, the side effect of bringing her into his plans pleased him in ways he couldn't quite articulate.

The idea of simply ruining James Maxfield had been risky. Because there was every chance that no matter how hard Holden tried there would be no serious blow-back for the man who had harmed Holden's sister the way that he had.

Wealthy men tended to be tougher targets than young women. Particularly young women who traded on the image of their beauty.

Not that Holden wasn't up to the task of trying to ruin the man.

Holden was powerful in his own right, and he was ruthless with it.

But there was something deeply satisfying about

owning a piece of his enemy's legacy. And not only that, he got James's precious daughter in the bargain.

This felt right.

"I can't believe that you're suggesting we…"

"You wanted children, right?"

"I… Yes."

"So, it's not such an outrageous thought."

"You think we're going to stay married?"

"You didn't sign a prenuptial agreement, Emerson. You leave me, I still get half of your shares of the vineyard."

"You didn't sign one either. I have the impression half of what's yours comes out to an awful lot of money."

"Money is just money. I'll make more. I don't have anything I care about half as much as you care about the vineyard. About the whole label."

"Well, why don't we wait to discuss children until I decide how much I hate you."

"You hate me so much you climbed on me at least five times last night."

"Yes, and in the cold light of day that seems less exciting than it did last night. The chemistry between us doesn't have anything to do with…our marriage."

"It has everything to do with it," he said, his tone far darker and more intense than he'd intended it to be.

"What? You manufactured this chemistry so we could…"

"No. The marriage made sense because of our chemistry. I was hardly going to let you walk away from me and marry another man, Emerson. Let him get his hands on your body when he has had all this time? He's had the last two years and he did nothing? He doesn't deserve you. And your father doesn't get to use you as a pawn."

"My father…"

"He's not a good man. Whether you believe me or not, it's true. But I imagine that when we impart the happy news to him today… You can make that decision for yourself."

"Thanks. But I don't need your permission to make my own decisions about my father or anything else."

But the look on her face was something close to haunted, and if he were a man prone to guilt, he might feel it now. They landed not long after, and his truck was there, still where he'd left it.

When they paused in front of it, she gave it a withering stare. "This thing is quite the performance."

It was a pretty beat-up truck. But it was genuinely his.

"It's mine," he said.

"From when?"

"Well, I got it when I was about…eighteen. So going on fifteen years ago."

"I don't even know how old you are. I mean, I do now, because I can do math. But really, I don't know anything about you, Holden."

"Well, I'll be happy to give you the rundown after we meet with your father."

"Well, looking forward to all that."

She was still wearing her dress from last night. He had found a replacement shirt in the hotel shop before they'd left, and it was too tight on his shoulders and not snug enough in the waist. When they arrived at the winery and entered the family's estate together, he could only imagine the picture they made.

Him in part of a tux, and her in last night's gown.

"Is my father in his study yet?" she questioned one of the first members of the household staff who walked by.

"Yes," the woman said, looking between Emerson and him. "Shall I see if he's receiving visitors?"

"He doesn't really have a choice," Holden said. "He'll make time to see us."

He took Emerson's hand and led her through the house, their footsteps loud on the marble floors. And he realized as they approached the office, what a pretentious show this whole place was.

James Maxfield wasn't that different from Holden. A man from humble beginnings hell-bent on forging a different path. But the difference between James and Holden was that Holden hadn't forgotten where he'd come from. He hadn't forgotten what it was to be powerless, and he would never make anyone else feel that kind of desperation.

James seemed to enjoy his position and all the power that came with it.

You don't enjoy it? Is that why you're standing here getting ready to walk through that door with his daughter and make him squirm? Is that why you forced Emerson to marry you?

He pushed those thoughts aside. And walked into the office without knocking, still holding tightly to Emerson.

Her father looked up, looked at him and then at Emerson. "What the hell is this?" he asked.

"I…"

"A hostile takeover," Holden said. "You ruined my sister's life. And now I'm here to make yours very, very difficult. And only by your daughter's good grace am I leaving you with anything other than a smoldering pile of wreckage. Believe me when I say it's not for your sake. But for the innocent people in your family who don't deserve to lose everything just because of your sins."

"Which sins are those?"

"My sister. Soraya Jane."

The silence in the room was palpable. Finally, James spoke.

"What is it you intend to do?"

"You need to guard your office better. I know you think this house isn't a corporation so you don't need high security, but you're such a damned narcissist you didn't realize you'd hired someone who was after the secrets you keep in your home. And now I have them. And thanks to Emerson, I now have a stake in this winery too. You can contest the marriage and my ownership, but it won't end well for you. It might not be my first choice now, but I'm still willing to detonate everything if it suits me."

James Maxfield's expression remained neutral, and his focus turned to his daughter.

"Emerson," her father said, "you agreed to this? You are allowing him to blackmail us?"

"What choice did I have?" she asked, a thread of desperation in her voice. "I trust you, Dad. I do. But he planned to destroy us. Whether his accusations are true or not, that was his intent. He gave me no time, and he didn't give me a lot of options. This marriage was the only way I could salvage what we've built, because he was ready to wage a campaign against you, against our family, at any cost. He was going to come at us personally and professionally. I couldn't take any chances. I couldn't. I did what I had to do. I did what you would have done, I'm sure. I did what needed doing."

"You were supposed to marry Donovan," James said, his tone icy.

"I know," Emerson said. "But what was I supposed to do when the situation changed? This man…"

"Have you slept with him?"

Emerson drew back, clearly shocked that her father had asked her that question. "I don't understand what that has to do with anything."

"It certainly compromises the purity of your claims," James returned. "You say you've been blackmailed into this arrangement, but if you're in a relationship with him…"

"Did you sleep with his sister?" she asked. "All those… All those other women in the files. Did you… Did you cheat on Mom?"

"Emerson, there are things you don't need to know about, and things you don't understand. My relationship with your mother works, even if it's not traditional."

"You *did*." She lowered her voice to a near whisper. "His sister. She's younger than me."

"Emerson…"

Holden took a step toward James's desk. "Men like you always think it won't come back on you. You think you can take advantage of women who are young, who are desperate, and no one will come for you. But I am here for you. This empire of yours? It serves me now. Your daughter? She's mine too. And if you push me, I swear I will see it all ruined and everyone will know what you are. How many people do you think will come here for a wedding, or parties, then? What of the brand worldwide? Who wants to think about sexual harassment, coercion and the destruction of a woman young enough to be your daughter when they have a sip of your merlot?"

Silence fell, tense and hard between them.

"The brand is everything," James said finally. "I've done everything I can to foster that family brand, as has your mother. What we do in private is between us."

"And the gag order you had my sister sign, and all those other women? Soraya has been institutionalized because of all of this. Because of the fallout. And she might have signed papers, but I did not. And now I don't need to tell the world about your transgressions to have control over what you've built. And believe me, in the years to come, I will make your life hell." Holden leaned forward, placing his palms on the desk. "Emerson was your pawn. You were going to use her as a wife to the man you wanted as part of this empire. But Emerson is with me now. She's no longer yours."

"*Emerson* is right here," Emerson said, her voice vibrating with emotion. "And frankly, I'm disgusted by the both of you. I don't belong to either of you. Dad, I did what I had to do to save the vineyard. I did it because I trusted you. I trusted that Holden's accusations were false. But you did all of this, didn't you?"

"It was an affair," James said. "It looks to me like you are having one of your own, so it's a bit rich for you to stand in judgment of me."

"I hadn't made vows to Donovan. And I never claimed to love him. He also knows..."

"Your mother knows," James said. "The terms of a marriage are not things you discuss with your children. You clearly have the same view of relationships that I do, and here you are lecturing me."

"It's not the same," she said. "And as for you," she said, turning to Holden. "I married you because it was the lesser of two evils. But that doesn't make me yours. You lied to me. You made me believe you were someone you weren't. You're no different from him."

Emerson stormed out of the room, and left Holden standing there with James.

"She makes your victory ring hollow," James said.

"Even if she divorces me, part of the winery is still mine. We didn't have a prenuptial agreement drafted between us, something I'm sure you were intending to take care of when she married that soft boy from the East Coast."

"What exactly are you going to do now?"

"I haven't decided yet. And the beauty of this is I have time. You can consider me the sword of Damocles hanging over your head. And one day, you know the thread will break. The question is when."

"And what do you intend to do to Emerson?"

"I've done it already. She's married to me. She's mine."

Those words burned with conviction, no matter her protests before storming out. And he didn't know why he felt the truth of those words deeper than anything else.

He had married her. It was done as far as he was concerned.

He went out of the office, and saw Emerson standing there, her hands planted firmly on the balustrade, overlooking the entry below.

"Let's talk," he said.

She turned to face him. "I don't want to talk. You

should go talk with my father some more. The two of you seemed to be enjoying that dialogue."

"*Enjoy* is a strong word."

"You betrayed me," she said.

"I don't know you, Emerson. You don't know me. We hadn't ever made promises to each other. I didn't betray you. Your *father* betrayed you."

She looked stricken by that, and she said nothing.

"I want you to come live with me."

"Why would I do that?"

"Because we're married. Because it's not fake."

"Does that mean you love me?" she asked, her tone scathing.

"No. But there's a lot of mileage between love and fake. And you know it."

"I live here. I work here. I can't leave."

"Handily, I have bought a property on the adjacent mountain. You won't have to leave. I do have another ranch in Jackson Creek, and I'd like to visit there from time to time. I do a bit of traveling. But there's no reason we can't be based here, in Gold Valley."

"You'll have to forgive me. I'm not understanding the part of your maniacal plan where we try to pretend we're a happy family."

"The vineyard is more yours now than it was before. I have no issue deferring to you on a great many things."

"You're not just going to…let it get run into the ground?"

"If I wanted to do that, I wouldn't have to own a piece. I own part of your father's legacy. And that appeases me.

"So," he concluded, "shall we go?"

Chapter 12

Emerson looked around the marble halls of the Maxfield estate, and for the very first time in all her life, she didn't feel like she was home.

The man in the office behind her was a stranger.

The man in front of her was her husband, whether or not he was a stranger.

And his words kept echoing in her head.

I didn't betray you. Your father betrayed you.

"Let's go," she said. Before she could think the words through.

She found herself bundled back up into his truck, still wearing the dress she had been wearing at yesterday's party. His house was a quick drive away from the estate, a modern feat of design built into the hillside, all windows to make the most of the view.

"Tell me about your sister," she said, standing in the

drive with him, feeling decidedly flat and more than a bit defeated.

"She's my half sister," Holden said, taking long strides toward the front entry. He entered a code, opened the door and ushered her into a fully furnished living area.

"I had everything taken care of already," he said. "It's ready for us."

Ready for us.

She didn't know why she found that comforting. She shouldn't. She was unaccountably wounded by his betrayal, had been forced into this marriage. And yet, she wanted him. She couldn't explain it.

And her old life didn't feel right anymore, because it was even more of a lie than this one.

"My mother never had much luck with love," Holden said, his voice rough. "I had to take care of her. Because the men she was with didn't. They would either abuse her outright or manipulate her, and she wasn't very strong. Soraya came along when I was eight. About the cutest thing I'd ever seen. And a hell of a lot of trouble. I had to get her ready, had to make sure her hair was brushed for school. All of that. But I did it. I worked, and I took care of them, and once I got money, I made sure they had whatever they wanted." He looked away from her, a muscle jumping in his jaw. "It was after Soraya had money that she met your father. I don't think it takes a genius to realize she's got daddy issues. And he played each and every one of them. She got pregnant. He tried to get her to terminate. She wouldn't. She lost the baby anyway. And she lost her mind right along with it."

Hearing those words again, now knowing that they were true...they hit her differently.

She sat down on the couch, her stomach cramping with horror.

"You must love her a lot," she said. "To do all of this for her."

She thought about her father, and how she had been willing to marry a stranger for him. And then how she had married Holden to protect the winery, to protect her family, her father. And now she wasn't entirely convinced she shouldn't have just let Holden do what he wanted.

He frowned. "I did what had to be done. Like I always do. I take care of them."

"Because you love them," she said.

"Because no one else takes care of them." He shook his head. "My family wasn't loving. They still aren't. My mother is one of the most cantankerous people on the face of the planet, but you do what you do. You keep people going. When they're your responsibility, there's no other choice."

"Oh," she said. She took a deep, shuddering breath. "You see, I love my father. I love my mother. That's why her disapproval hurts. That's why his betrayal… I didn't know that he was like this. That he could have done those things to someone like your sister. It hurts me to know it. You're right. He is the one who betrayed me. And I will never be able to go into the estate again and look at it, at him, the same way. I'll never be able to look at him the same. It's just all broken, and I don't think it can ever be put back together."

"We'll see," he said. "I never came here to put anything back together. Because I knew it was all broken beyond the fixing of it. I came here to break *him*, because he broke Soraya. And I don't think she's going to be fixed either." He came to stand in front of Emerson, his hands shoved into his pockets, his expression grim. "And I'm sorry that you're caught up in the middle of this, because I don't have any stake in breaking you. But here's what I know about broken things. They can't be put back together exactly as they were. I think you can make something new out of them, though."

"Are you giving me life advice? Really? The man who blackmailed me into marriage?" He was still so absurdly beautiful, so ridiculously gorgeous and compelling to her. It was wrong. But she didn't know how to fix it. How to change it. Like anything else in her life. And really, right at the moment, it was only one of the deeply messed up things in her reality.

That she felt bonded to him even as the bonds that connected her to her family were shattered.

"You can take it or not," he said. "That doesn't change the fact that it's true. Whether or not I exposed him, your father is a predator. This is who he is. You could have lived your life without knowing the truth, but I don't see how that's comforting."

It wasn't. It made a shiver race down her spine, made her feel cold all over. "I just… I trusted him. I trusted him so much that I was willing to marry a man he chose for me. I would have done anything he asked me to do. He built a life for me, and he gave me a wonderful childhood, and he made me the woman that I am. For better or for worse. He did a whole host of wonderful things for me, and I don't know how to reconcile that with what else I now know about him."

"All *I* know is your father is a fool. Because the way you believe in him… I've never believed in anyone that way. Anyone or anything. And the way my sister believed in him... He didn't deserve that, from either of you. And if just one person believed in me the way that either of you believed in him, the way that I think your mother believes in him, your sisters... I wouldn't have done anything to mess that up."

Something quiet and sad bloomed inside of her. And she realized that the sadness wasn't for losing her faith in her father. Not even a little.

"I did," she said.

"What?"

"I did. Believe in you like that. Holden Brown. That ranch hand I met not so long ago. I don't know what you think about me, or women like me. But it mattered to me that I slept with you. That I let you into my body. I've only been with two other men. For me, sex is an intimate thing. And I've never shared it with someone outside of a relationship. But there was something about you. I trusted you. I believed what you told me about who you were. And I believed in what my body told me about what was between us. And now what we shared has kind of turned into this weird and awful thing, and I just... I don't think I'll ever trust myself again. Between my father and you..."

"I didn't lie to you." His voice was almost furious in its harshness. "Not about wanting you. Nothing that happened between you and me in bed was a lie. Not last night, and not the first night. I swear to you, I did not seduce you to get revenge on your father. Quite the opposite. I told myself when I came here that I would never touch you. You were forbidden to me, Emerson, because I didn't want to do the same thing your father had done. Because I didn't want to lie to you or take advantage of you in any way. When I first met you in that vineyard, I told myself I was disgusted by you. Because you had his blood in your veins. But no matter how much I told myself that, I couldn't make it true. You're not your father. And that's how I feel. This thing between us is separate, and real."

"But the marriage is for revenge."

"Yes. But I wouldn't have taken the wedding *night* if I didn't want you."

"Can I believe in you?"

She didn't know where that question came from, all vulnerable and sad, and she wasn't entirely sure that she liked the fact that she'd asked it. But she needed to grab on to something. In this world where nothing made sense, in this moment when she felt rootless, because not even her father was who she thought he was, and she didn't know how she was going to face having that conversation with Wren, or with Cricket. Didn't know what she was going to say to her mother, because no matter how difficult their own relationship was, this gave Emerson intense sympathy for her mother.

Not to mention her sympathy for the young woman her father had harmed. And the other women who were like her. How many had there been just like Soraya? It made Emerson hurt to wonder.

She had no solid ground to stand on, and she was desperate to find purchase.

If Holden was telling the truth, if the chemistry between them was as real to him as it was to her, then she could believe in that if nothing else. And she needed to believe in it. Desperately.

"If I… If I go all in on this marriage, Holden, on this thing between us, if we work together to make the vineyard…ours—Wren and Cricket included—promise me that you'll be honest with me. That you will be faithful to me. Because right now, I'll pledge myself to you, because I don't know what the hell else to believe in. I'm angry with you, but if you're telling me the truth about wanting me, and you also told me the truth about my father, then you are the most real and honest thing in my life right now, and I will… I'll bet on that. But only if you promise me right now that you won't lie to me."

"I promise," he said, his eyes like two chips of obsidian, dark and fathomless. Hard.

And in her world that had proven to be built on a shifting sand foundation, his hardness was something steady. Something real.

She needed something real.

She stood up from her position on the couch, her legs wobbling when she closed the distance between them. "Then take me to bed. Because the only thing that feels good right now is you and me."

"I notice you didn't say it's the only thing that makes sense," he said, his voice rough. He cupped her cheek, rubbing his thumb over her cheekbone.

"Because it doesn't make sense. I should hate you. But I can't. Maybe it's just because I don't have the energy right now. Because I'm too sad. But this…whatever we have, it feels *real*. And I'm not sure what else is."

"This *is* real," he said, taking her hand and putting it on his chest. His heart was raging out of control, and she felt a surge of power roll through her.

It was real. Whatever else wasn't, the attraction between them couldn't be denied.

He carried her to the bed, and they said vows to each other's bodies. And somehow, it felt right. Somehow, in the midst of all that she had lost, her desire for Holden felt like the one right thing she had done.

Marrying him. Making this real.

Tonight, there were no restraints, no verbal demands. Just their bodies. Unspoken promises that she was going to hold in her heart forever.

And as the hours passed, a feeling welled up in her chest that terrified her more than anything else.

It wasn't hate. Not even close.

But she refused to give it a name. Not yet. Not now.

She would have a whole lot of time to sort out what she felt for this man.

She'd have the rest of her life.

Chapter 13

The day he put Maxfield Vineyards as one of the assets on his corporate holdings was sadistically satisfying. He was going to make a special new label of wine as well. Soraya deserved to be indelibly part of the Maxfield legacy.

Because James Maxfield was indelibly part of Soraya's. And Holden's entire philosophy on the situation was that James didn't deserve to walk away from her without being marked by the experience.

Holden was now a man in possession of a very powerful method through which to dole out if not traditional revenge, then a steady dose of justice.

He was also a man in possession of a wife.

That was very strange indeed. But he counted his marriage to Emerson among the benefits of this arrangement.

Her words kept coming back to him. Echoing inside of him. All day, and every night when he reached for her.

Can I believe in you?

He found that he wanted her to believe in him, and he couldn't quite figure out why. Why should it matter that he not sweep Emerson into a web of destruction?

Why had he decided to go about marrying her in the first place when he could have simply wiped James Maxfield off the map?

But no. He didn't want to question himself.

Marrying her was a more sophisticated power play. And at the end of the day, he liked it better.

He had possession of the man's daughter. He had a stake in the man's company.

The sword of Damocles.

After all, ruination could be accomplished only once, but this was a method of torture that could continue on for a very long time.

His sense of satisfaction wasn't just because of Emerson.

He wasn't so soft that he would change direction because of a woman he'd slept with a few times.

Though, every night that he had her, he felt more and more connected to her.

He had taken great pleasure a few days ago when she broke the news to her fiancé.

The other man had been upset, but not about Emerson being with another man, rather about the fact that he was losing his stake in the Maxfield dynasty. In Holden's estimation that meant the man didn't deserve Emerson at all. Of course, he didn't care what anyone deserved, not in this scenario. *He* didn't deserve Emerson either, but he wanted her. That was all that mattered to him.

It was more than her ex-fiancé felt for her.

There was one person he had yet to call, though. Soraya. She deserved to know everything that had happened.

He was one of her very few approved contacts. She was allowed to speak to him over the phone.

They had done some very careful and clever things to protect Soraya from contact with the outside world. He, his mother and Soraya's therapists were careful not to cut her off completely, but her social media use was monitored.

They had learned that with people like her, who had built an empire and a web of connections in the digital world, they had to be very careful about cutting them off entirely, or they felt like they had been cast into darkness.

But then, a good amount of their depression often came from that public world.

It was a balance. She was actually on her accounts less now than she had been when she'd first been hospitalized.

He called, and it didn't take long for someone to answer.

"This is Holden McCall. I'm calling for Soraya."

"Your sister is just finishing an art class. She should be with you in a moment."

In art class. He would have never picked something like that for her, but then, her sense of fashion was art in and of itself, he supposed. The way she framed her life and the scenes she found herself in. It was why she was so popular online. That she made her life into art.

It pleased him to know she had found another way to express that. One that was maybe about her more than it was about the broader world.

"Holden?" Her voice sounded less frantic, more relaxed than he was used to.

"Yes," he said. "It's me."

"I haven't heard from you in a while." She sounded a bit petulant, childlike and accusing. Which, frankly, was the closest to her old self he'd heard her sound in quite some time.

"I know. I'm sorry. I've been busy. But I have something to tell you. And I hope this won't upset you. I think it might make you happy."

"What is happy?" She said it a bit sharply, and he wondered if she was being funny. It was almost impossible to tell with her anymore.

He ignored that question, and the way it landed inside of him. The way that it hollowed him out.

"I got married," he said.

"Holden," she said, sounding genuinely pleased. "I'm so glad. Did you fall in love? Love is wonderful. When it isn't terrible."

He swallowed hard. "No. I've married James Maxfield's daughter."

She gasped, the sound sharp in his ear, stabbing him with regret. "Why?"

"Well, that's the interesting part," he said. "I now own some of Maxfield Vineyards. And, Soraya, I'm going to make a wine and name it after you. Because he shouldn't be able to forget you, or what he did to you."

There was silence. For a long moment. "And I'm the one that's locked up because I'm crazy."

"What?"

"Did you hear yourself? You sound… You married somebody you don't love."

"It's not about love. It's about justice. He didn't deserve to get away with what he did to you."

"But he has," she said. "He has because he doesn't care."

"And I've made him care. His daughter knows what kind of man he is now. He's lost a controlling share in his own winery. He's also lost an alliance that he was hoping to build by marrying Emerson off to someone else."

"And the cost of those victories is your happiness. Because you aren't with a woman you love."

"I was never going to fall in love," he said. "It's not in me."

"Yeah, that's what I said too. Money was the only thing I loved. Until it wasn't." There was another long stretch of silence.

"I thought you would be happy. I'm getting a piece of this for you."

"I don't… I don't want it."

"You don't…"

"You have to do what you have to do," she said.

"I guess so." He didn't know what to say to that, and for the first time since he'd set out on this course, he questioned himself.

"Holden, where is my baby? They won't answer me."

Rage and grief seized up in his chest. She had sounded better, but she wasn't. "Sweetheart," he said. "You lost the baby. Remember?"

The silence was shattering. "I guess I did. I'm sorry. That's silly. It doesn't seem real. I don't seem real sometimes."

And he knew then, that no matter what she said, whether or not she accepted this gift he'd won for her, he didn't regret it. Didn't regret doing this for his sister, who slid in and out of terrible grief so often, and then had to relive her loss over and over again. At least this time she had accepted his response without having a breakdown. But talking about Maxfield cut her every time, he knew.

"Take care of yourself," he said.

"I will," she said.

And he was just thankful that there was someone there to take care of her, because whatever she said, he worried she wouldn't do it for herself.

And he was resolved then that what he'd done was right.

It had nothing to do with Emerson, or his feelings for her.

James deserved everything that he got and more.

Holden refused to feel guilt about any of it.

Very little had been said between herself and Wren about her elopement. And Emerson knew she needed to talk to her sister. Both of her sisters. But it was difficult to work up the courage to do it.

Because explaining it to them required sharing secrets about their father, secrets she knew would devastate them. She also knew devastating them would further her husband's goals.

Because she and Holden currently had the majority ownership in the vineyard. And with her sisters, they could take absolute control, which she knew was what Holden wanted ultimately.

Frankly, it all made her very anxious.

But anxious or not, talking with her sisters was why she had invited them to have lunch with her down in Gold Valley.

She walked into Bellissima, and the hostess greeted her, recognizing her instantly, and offering her the usual table.

There wasn't much in the way of incredibly fancy dining in Gold Valley, but her family had a good relationship with the restaurants, since they often supplied wine to them, and while they weren't places that required reservations or anything like that, a Maxfield could always count on having the best table in the house.

She sat at her table with a view, morosely perusing the menu while her mouth felt like it was full of sawdust. That was when Cricket and Wren arrived.

"You're actually taking a lunch break," Wren said. "Something must be wrong."

"We need to talk," Emerson said. "I thought it might be best to do it over a basket of bread."

She pushed the basket to the center of the table, like a very tasty peace offering.

Wren eyeballed it. "Things must be terrible if you're suggesting we eat carbs in the middle of the day."

"I eat carbs whenever I want," Cricket said, sitting down first, Wren following her younger sister's lead.

"I haven't really talked to you guys since—"

"Since you defied father and eloped with some guy that none of us even know?" Wren asked.

"Yeah, since that."

"Is he the guy?" Wren asked.

"*What* guy?" Cricket asked.

"She cheated on Donovan, had a one-night stand with some guy that I now assume is the guy she married. And the reason she disappeared from my party the other night."

"You did *what*?" Cricket asked.

"I'm sorry, now you're going to be more shocked about my one-night stand and about my random marriage?"

Cricket blinked. "Well. Yes."

"Yes. It is the same guy."

"Wow," Wren said. "I didn't take you for a romantic, Emerson. But I guess I was wrong."

"No," Emerson said. "I'm not a romantic."

But somehow, the words seemed wrong. Especially with the way her feelings were jumbled up inside of her.

"Then what happened?"

"That's what I need to talk to you about," she said. "It is not a good story. And I didn't want to talk to either of you about it at the winery. But I'm not sure bringing you into a public space to discuss it was the best choice either."

"You do have your own house now," Cricket pointed out.

"Yes. And Holden is there. And… Anyway. It'll all become clear in a second."

Before the waitress could even bring menus to her sisters, Emerson spilled out everything. About their father. About Holden's sister. And about the ultimatum that had led to her marriage.

"You just went along with it?" Wren asked.

"There was no *just* about it," Emerson responded. "I didn't know what he would do to the winery if I didn't comply. And I wasn't sure about Dad's piece in it until… until I talked to him. Holden and I. Dad didn't deny any of it. He says that him and Mom have an understanding, and of course it's something he wouldn't talk about with any of us. But I don't even know if that's true. And my only option is going to Mom and potentially hurting her if I want to find out that truth. So here's what I know so far. That Dad hurt someone. Someone younger than me, someone my new husband loves very much."

"But he's only your husband because he wants to get revenge," Cricket pointed out.

"I… I think that's complicated too. I hope it is."

"You're not in love with him, are you?" Wren asked.

She decided to dodge that question and continue on with the discussion. "I love Dad. And I don't want to believe any of this, but I have to because…it's true."

Cricket looked down. "I wish that I could say I'm surprised. But it's different, being me. I mean, I feel like I see the outside of things. You're both so deep on the inside. Dad loves you, and he pays all kinds of attention to you. I'm kind of forgotten. Along with Mom. And when you're looking at him from a greater distance, I think the cracks show a lot more clearly."

"*I'm* shocked," Wren said sadly. "I've thrown my whole life into this vineyard. Into supporting him. And I… I can't believe that the man who encouraged me, treated me the way he did, could do that to someone else. To many women, it sounds like."

"People and feelings are very complicated," Emerson said slowly. "Nothing has shown me that more than my relationship with Holden."

"You do love him," Wren said.

Did she? Did she love a man who wanted to ruin her family?

"I don't know," Emerson said. "I feel something for him. Because you know what, you're right. I would never have just let him blackmail me into marriage if on some level I didn't… I… It's a real marriage." She felt her face getting hot, which was silly, because she didn't have any hang-ups about that sort of thing normally. "But I'm a little afraid that I'm confusing…well, that part of our relationship being good with actual love."

"I am not the person to consult about that kind of thing," Cricket said, taking a piece of bread out of the basket at the center of the table and biting into it fiercely.

"Don't look at me," Wren said. "We've already had the discussion about my own shameful issues."

Cricket looked at Wren questioningly, but didn't say anything.

"Well, the entire point of this lunch wasn't just to talk about me. Or my feelings. Or Dad. It's to discuss what we are going to do. Because the three of us can band together, and we can make all the controlling decisions for the winery. We supersede my husband even. We can protect the label, keep his actions in check and make our own mark. You're right, Cricket," Emerson said. "You have been on the outside looking in for too long. And you deserve better."

"I don't actually want to do anything at the winery," Cricket said. "I got a job."

"You did?"

"Yes. At Sugar Cup."

"Making coffee?"

"Yes," Cricket said proudly. "I want to do something different. Different from the whole Maxfield thing. But I'm with you, in terms of banding together for decision-making. I'll be a silent partner, and I'll support you."

"I'm in," Wren said. "Although, you realize that your husband has the ace up his sleeve. He could just decide to ruin us anyway."

"Yes, he could," Emerson said. "But now he owns a piece of the winery, and I think ownership means more to him than that."

"And he has you," Wren pointed out.

"I know," Emerson said. "But what can I do about it?"

"You do love him," Cricket said, her eyes getting wide. "I never thought you were sentimental enough."

"To fall in love? I have a heart, Cricket."

"Yes, but you were going to marry when you didn't love your fiancé. It's so patently obvious that you don't have any feelings for Donovan at all, and you were just going to marry him anyway. So, I assumed it didn't matter to you. Not really, and now you've gone and fallen in love with this guy… Someone who puts in danger the very thing you care about most. The thing you were willing to marry that bowl of oatmeal for."

"He wasn't a bowl of oatmeal," Emerson said.

"You're right," Wren said. "He wasn't. Because at least a person might want to eat a bowl of oatmeal, even if it's plain. You'd never want to eat him."

"Oh, for God's sake."

"Well," Wren said. "It's true."

"What matters is that the three of us are on the same page. No matter what happens. We are stronger together."

"Right," Wren and Cricket agreed.

"I felt like the rug was pulled out from under me when I found out about Dad. The winery didn't feel like it would ever seem like home again. I felt rootless, drifting. But we are a team. *We* are the Maxfield label. We are the Maxfield name. Just as much as he is."

"Agreed," Wren said.

"Agreed," said Cricket.

And their agreement made Emerson feel some sense of affirmation. Some sense of who she was.

She didn't have the relationship with her father she'd thought she had. She didn't have the father she'd thought she had.

Her relationship with Holden was...

Well, she was still trying to figure it out. But her relationship with Wren and Cricket was real. And it was strong. Strong enough to weather this, any of it.

And eventually she would have to talk to her mother. And maybe she would find something there that surprised her too. Because if there was one thing she was learning, it was that it didn't matter how things appeared. What mattered was the truth.

Really, as the person who controlled the brand of an entire label using pictures on the internet, she should have known better from the start. But somehow, she had thought that because she was so good at manipulating those images, that she might be immune to falling for them.

Right at this moment she believed in two things: her sisters, and the sexual heat between herself and Holden. Those seemed to be the only things that made any sense. The only things that had any kind of authenticity to them.

And maybe how you feel about him.

Well. Maybe.

But the problem was she couldn't be sure if he felt the same. And just at the moment she was too afraid to take a chance at being hurt. Because she was already raw and wounded, and she didn't know if she could stand anything more.

But she had her sisters. And she would rest in that for now.

Chapter 14

The weeks that followed were strange. They were serene in some ways, which Emerson really hadn't expected. Her life had changed, and she was surprised how positive she found the change.

Oh, losing her respect for her father wasn't overly positive. But working more closely with her sisters was. She and Wren had always been close, but both of them had always found it a bit of a challenge to connect with Cricket, but it seemed easier now.

The three of them were a team. It wasn't Wren and Emerson on Team Maxfield, with Cricket hanging out on the sidelines.

It was a feat to launch a new sort of wine on the heels of the select label, which they had only just released. But the only demand Holden had made of the company so far was that they release a line of wines under his sister's name.

Actually, Emerson thought it was brilliant. Soraya had such a presence online—even if she wasn't in the public at the moment—and her image was synonymous with youth. Soraya's reputation gave Emerson several ideas for how to market wines geared toward the youthful jet-set crowd who loved to post photographs of their every move.

One of the first things Emerson had done was consult a graphic designer about making labels that were eminently postable, along with coming up with a few snappy names for the unique blends they would use. And of course, they would need for the price point to be right. They would start with three—Tempranillo Tantrum, Chardonyay and No Way Rosé.

Cricket rolled her eyes at the whole thing, feeling out of step with other people her age, as she had no desire to post on any kind of social media site, and found those puns ridiculous. Wren, while not a big enthusiast herself, at least understood the branding campaign. Emerson was ridiculously pleased. And together the three of them had enjoyed doing the work.

Cricket, true to her word, had not overly involved herself, given that she was in training down at the coffee shop. Emerson couldn't quite understand why her sister wanted to work there, but she could understand why Cricket felt the need to gain some independence.

Being a Maxfield was difficult.

But it was also interesting, building something that wasn't for her father's approval. Sure, Holden's approval was involved on some level, but…this was different from any other work she'd done.

She was doing this as much for herself as for him,

and he trusted that she would do a good job. She knew she would.

It felt…good.

The prototype labels, along with the charms she had chosen to drape elegantly over the narrow neck of each bottle, came back from production relatively quickly, and she was so excited to show Holden she could hardly contain herself.

She wasn't sure why she was so excited to show him, only that she was.

It wasn't as if she wanted his approval, the way she had with her father. It was more that she wanted to share what she had created. The way she felt she needed to please him. This was more of an excitement sort of feeling.

She wanted to please Holden in a totally different way. Wanted to make him… Happy.

She wondered what would make a man like him happy. If he *could* be happy.

And suddenly, she was beset by the burning desire to try.

He was a strange man, her husband, filled with dark intensity, but she knew that part of that intensity was an intense capacity to love.

The things that he had done for his sister…

All of her life, really. And for his mother.

It wasn't just this, though it was a large gesture, but everything.

He had protected his mother from her endless array of boyfriends. He had made sure Soraya had gotten off to school okay every day. He had bought his mother and sister houses the moment he had begun making money.

She had done research on him, somewhat covertly,

in the past weeks. And she had seen that he had donated large amounts of money, homes, to a great many people in need.

He hid all of that generosity underneath a gruff, hard exterior. Knowing what she knew now, she continually came back to that moment when he had refused to say his plan for revenge was born out of love for his sister. As if admitting to something like love would be disastrous for him.

She saw the top of his cowboy hat through the window of the tasting room, where she was waiting with the Soraya-branded wines.

He walked in, and her heart squeezed tight.

"I have three complete products to show you. And I hope you're going to like them."

She held up the first bottle—the Tempranillo Tantrum—with a little silver porcupine charm dangling from the top. "Because porcupines are grumpy," she said.

"Are they?"

"Well, do you want to hassle one and find out how grumpy they are? Because I don't."

"Very nice," he said, brushing his fingers over the gold foil on the label.

"People will want to take pictures of it. Even if they don't buy it, they're going to post and share it."

He looked at the others, one with a rose-gold unicorn charm, the next with a platinum fox. And above each of the names was *Soraya*.

"She'll love this," he said, his voice suddenly soft.

"How is she doing?"

"Last I spoke to her? I don't know. A little bit better. She didn't seem as confused."

"Do they know why she misremembers sometimes?" He had told her about how his sister often didn't remember she'd had a fairly late-term miscarriage. That sometimes she would call him scared, looking for a baby that she didn't have.

It broke Emerson's heart. Knowing everything Soraya had gone through. And she supposed there were plenty of young women who could have gone through something like that and not ended up in such a difficult position, but Soraya wasn't one of them. And the fact that Emerson's father had chosen someone so vulnerable, and upon learning how vulnerable she was, had ignored the distress she was in…

If Emerson had been on the fence about whether or not her father was redeemable…the more she knew about the state Holden's sister had been left in, the less she thought so.

"Her brain is protecting her from the trauma. Though, it's doing a pretty bad job," he said. "Every time she has to hear the truth again…it hurts her all over."

"Well, I hope this makes her happy," she said, gesturing to the wine. "And that it makes her feel like… she is part of this. Because she's part of the family now. Because of you. My sisters and I… We care about what happens to her. People do care."

"You've done an amazing job with this," he said, the sincerity in his voice shocking her. "I could never have figured out how to make this wine something she specifically would like so much, but this… She's going to love it." He touched one of the little charms. "She'll think those are just perfect."

"I'm glad. I'd like to meet her. Someday. When she is feeling well enough for something like that."

"I'm sure we can arrange it."

After that encounter, she kept turning her feelings over and over inside of her.

She was changing. What she wanted was changing.

She was beginning to like her life with Holden. More than like it. There was no denying the chemistry they shared. That what happened between them at night was singular. Like nothing else she had ever experienced. But it was moments like that one—the little moments that happened during the day—that surprised her.

She liked him.

And if she were really honest with herself, she more than liked him.

She needed…

She needed to somehow show him that she wanted more.

Of course, she didn't know what more there was, considering the fact that they were already married.

She was still thinking about what she wanted, what she could do, when she saw Wren later that day.

"Have you ever been in love?"

Wren looked at her, jerking her head abruptly to the side. "No," she said. "Don't you think you would have known if I'd ever been in love?"

"I don't know. We don't really talk about that kind of stuff. We talk about work. You don't know if I've ever been in love."

"Well, other than Holden? You haven't been. You've had boyfriends, but you haven't been in love."

"I didn't tell you I was in love with Holden."

"But you are," Wren said. "Which is why I assume you're asking me about love now."

"Yes," Emerson said. "Okay. I am. I'm in love with

Holden, and I need to figure out a way to tell him. Because how do you tell a man that you want more than marriage?"

"You tell him that you love him."

"It doesn't feel like enough. Anyone can say anything anytime they want. That doesn't make it real. But I want him to see that the way I feel has changed."

"Well, I don't know. Except… Men don't really use words so much as…"

"Sex. Well, our sex life has been good. Very good."

"Glad to hear it," Wren said. "But what might be missing from that?"

Emerson thought about that. "Our wedding night was a bit unconventional." Tearing tuxedos and getting tied up with leather belts might not be everyone's idea of a honeymoon. Though, Emerson didn't really have any complaints.

There had been anger between them that night. Anger that had burned into passion. And since then, they'd had sex in all manner of different ways, because she couldn't be bored when she shared a bed with someone she was so compatible with, and for whatever reason she felt no inhibition when she was with him. But they hadn't had a real wedding night.

Not really.

One where they gave themselves to each other after saying their vows.

That was it. She needed to make a vow to him. With her body, and then with her words.

"I might need to make a trip to town," she said.

"For?"

"Very bridal lingerie."

"I would be happy to knock off work early and help you in your pursuit."

"We really do make a great team."

When she and Wren returned that evening, Emerson was triumphant in her purchases, and more than ready to greet her husband.

Now she just had to hope he would understand what she was saying to him.

And she had to hope he would want the same thing she did.

When Holden got back to the house that night, it was dark.

That was strange, because Emerson usually got home before he did. He was discovering his new work at the winery to be fulfilling, but he also spent a good amount of time dealing with work for his own company, and that made for long days.

He looked down at the floor, and saw a few crimson spots, and for a moment, he knew panic. His throat tightened.

Except… It wasn't blood. It was rose petals.

There was a trail of them, leading from the living room to the stairwell, and up the stairs. He followed the path, down the dimly lit hall, and into the master bedroom that he shared with Emerson.

The rose petals led up to the bed, and there, perched on the mattress, was his wife.

His throat went dry, all the blood in his body rushing south. She was wearing… It was like a bridal gown, but made entirely of see-through lace that gave peeks at her glorious body underneath. The straps were thin, the neckline plunging down between her breasts, which were spilling out over the top of the diaphanous fabric.

She looked like temptation in the most glorious form he'd ever seen.

"What's all this?"

"I... I went to town for a few things today."

"I see that."

"It's kind of a belated wedding gift," she said. "A belated wedding night."

"We had a wedding night. I remember it very clearly."

"Not like this. Not..." She reached next to her, and pulled out a large velvet box. "And we're missing something."

She opened it up, and inside was a thick band of metal next to a slimmer one.

"They're wedding bands," she said. "One for you and one for me."

"What brought this on?"

He didn't really know what to say. He didn't know what to think about this at all.

The past few weeks had been good between the two of them, that couldn't be denied. But he felt like she was proposing to him, and that was an idea he could barely wrap his mind around.

"I want to wear your ring," she said. "And I guess... I bought the rings. But this ring is mine," she said, pulling out the man's ring. "And I want you to wear it. This ring is yours. I want to wear it." She took out the slim band and placed it on her finger, and then held the thicker one out for him.

"I've never been one for jewelry."

"You've never been one for marriage either, but here

we are. I know we had a strange start, but this has… It's been a good partnership so far, hasn't it?"

The work she had done on his sister's wine had been incredible, it was true. The care she had put into it had surprised him. It hadn't simply been a generic nod to Soraya. Emerson had made something that somehow managed to capture his sister's whole personality, and he knew Emerson well enough to know that she had done it by researching who Soraya was. And when Emerson asked him about his sister, he knew that she cared. Their own mother didn't even care that much.

But she seemed to bleed with her caring, with her regret that Soraya had been hurt. And now Emerson wanted rings. Wanted to join herself to him in a serious way.

And why not? She's your wife. She should be wearing your ring.

"Thanks," he said, taking the ring and putting it on quickly.

Her shoulders sagged a little, and he wondered if she had wanted this to go differently, but he was wearing the ring, so it must be okay. She let out a shaking breath. "Holden, with this ring, I take you as my husband. To have and to hold. For better or for worse. For richer or poorer. Until death separates us."

Those vows sent a shiver down his spine.

"We took those vows already."

"I took those vows with you because I had to. Because I felt like I didn't have another choice. I'm saying them now because I choose to. Because I want to. And because I mean them. If all of this, the winery, everything, goes away, I still want to be partners with you. In our lives. Not just in business. I want this to be about more than my father, more than your sister. I want it to be about us. And so that's my promise to you with my words. And I want to make that official with my body."

There were little ties at the center of the dress she was wearing, and she began to undo the first one, the fabric parting between her breasts. Then she undid the next one, and the next, until it opened, revealing the tiny pair of panties she had on underneath. She slipped the dress from her shoulders and then she began to undress him.

It was slow, unhurried. She'd torn the clothes from his body before. She had allowed him to tie her hands. She had surrendered herself to him in challenging and intense ways that had twisted the idea of submission on its head, because when her hands were tied, he was the one that was powerless.

But this was different. And he felt...

Owned.

By that soft, sweet touch, by the brush of her fingertips against him as she pushed his shirt up over his head. By the way her nimble fingers attacked his belt buckle, removing his jeans.

And somehow, *he* was the naked one then, and she was still wearing those panties. There was something generous about what she was doing now. And he didn't know why that word came to the front of his mind.

But she was giving.

Giving from a deep place inside of her that was more than just a physical gift. Without asking for anything in return. She lay back on the bed, lifting her hips slightly and pushing her panties down, revealing that tempting triangle at the apex of her thighs, revealing her whole body to him.

He growled, covering her, covering her mouth with his own, kissing her deep and hard.

And she opened to him. Pliant and willing.

Giving.

Had anyone ever given to him before?

He'd had nothing like this ever. That was the truth.

Everyone in his life had taken from him from the very beginning. But not her. And she had no reason to give to him. And if this were the same as all their other sexual encounters, he could have put it off to chemistry.

Because everybody was a little bit wild when there was sexual attraction involved, but this was more.

Sex didn't require vows.

It didn't require rings.

And it didn't feel like this.

This was more.

It touched him deeper, in so many places deep inside, all the way to his soul.

And he didn't know what to say, or feel, so he just kissed her. Because he knew how to do that. Knew how to touch her and make her wet. Knew how to make her come.

He knew how to find his pleasure in her.

But he didn't know how to find the bottom of this deep, aching need that existed inside of him.

He settled himself between her thighs, thrust into her, and she cried out against his mouth. Then her gaze met his, and she touched him, her fingertips skimming over his cheekbone.

"I love you." The words were like an arrow straight through his chest.

"Emerson…"

She clung to him, grasping his face, her legs wrapped

around his. "I love you," she said, rocking up into him, taking him deeper.

And he would have pulled away, done something to escape the clawing panic, but his desire for her was too intense.

Love.

Had anyone ever said those words to him? He didn't think so. He should let go of her, he should stop. But he was powerless against the driving need to stay joined to her. It wasn't even about release. It was about something else, something he couldn't name or define.

Can't you?

He ignored that voice. He ignored that burning sensation in his chest, and he tried to block out the words she'd said. But she said them over and over again, and something in him was so hungry for them, he didn't know how to deny himself.

He looked down, and his eyes met hers, and he was sure she could see straight inside of him, and that what she saw there would be woefully empty compared to what he saw in hers.

He growled, lowering his head and chasing the pleasure building inside of him, thrusting harder, faster, trying to build up a pace that would make him forget.

Who he was.

What she'd said.

What he wanted.

What he couldn't have.

But when her pleasure crested, his own followed close behind, and he made the mistake of looking at her again. Of watching as pleasure overtook her.

He had wanted her from the beginning.

It had never mattered what he could get by marrying her.

It had always been about her. Always.

Because he had seen her, and he could not have her, from the very first.

He had told himself he should hate her because she had Maxfield blood in her veins. Then he had told himself that he needed her, and that was why it had to be marriage.

But he was selfish, down to his core.

And he had manipulated, used and blackmailed her. He was no different than her father, and now here she was, professing her love. And he was a man who didn't even know what that was.

All this giving. All this generosity from her. And he didn't deserve it. Couldn't begin to.

And he deserved it from her least of all.

Because he had nothing to give back.

He shuddered, his release taking him, stealing his thoughts, making it impossible for him to feel anything but pleasure. No regrets. No guilt. Just the bliss of being joined to her. And when it was over, she looked at him, and she whispered one more time, "I love you."

And that was when he pulled away.

Chapter 15

She had known it was a mistake, but she hadn't been able to hold it back. The declaration of love. Because she did love him. It was true. With all of herself. And while she had been determined to show him, with her body, with the vows she had made and with the rings she had bought, it wasn't enough.

She had thought the words by themselves wouldn't be enough, but the actions without the words didn't mean anything either. Not to her. Not when there was this big shift inside her, as real and deep as anything ever had been. She had wanted for so long to do enough that she would be worthy. And she felt like some things had crystallized inside of her. Because all of those things she craved, that approval, it was surface. It was like a brand. The way that her father saw brand. That as long as the outside looked good, as long as all the external things were getting done, that was all that mattered.

But it wasn't.

Because what she felt, who she was in her deepest parts, those were the things that mattered. And she didn't have to perform or be good to be loved. She, as a person, was enough all on her own. And that was what Holden had become to her. And that was what she wanted. For her life, for her marriage. Not something as shallow as approval for a performance. A brand was meaningless if there was no substance behind it. A beautiful bottle of wine didn't matter if what was inside was nothing more than grape juice.

A marriage was useless if love and commitment weren't at the center.

It was those deep things, those deep connections, and she hadn't had them, not in all her life. Not really. She was beginning to forge them with her sisters, and she needed them from Holden.

And if that meant risking disapproval, risking everything, then she would. She had. And she could see that her declaration definitely hadn't been the most welcome.

Since she'd told him she loved him, everything about him was shut down, shut off. She knew him well enough to recognize that.

"I don't know what you expect me to say."

"Traditionally, people like to hear 'I love you too.' But I'm suspecting I'm not going to get that. So, here's the deal. You don't have to say anything. I just... I wanted you to know how I felt. How serious I am. How much my feelings have changed since I first met you."

"Why?"

"Because," she said. "Because you...you came into my life and you turned it upside down. You uncovered so many things that were hidden in the dark for so long. And yes, some of that uncovering has been painful. But more than that, you made me realize what I really wanted from life. I thought that as long as everything looked okay, it would be okay. But you destroyed that. You destroyed the illusions all around me, including the ones I had built for myself. Meeting you, feeling that attraction for you, it cut through all this…bullshit. I thought I could marry a man I didn't even feel a temptation to sleep with. And then I met you. I felt more for you in those few minutes in the vineyard that night we met than I had felt for Donovan in the two years we'd been together. I couldn't imagine not being with you. It was like an obsession, and then we were together, and you made me want things, made me do things that I never would have thought I would do. But *those* were all the real parts of me. All that I am.

"I thought that if I put enough makeup on, and smiled wide enough, and put enough filters on the pictures, that I could be the person I needed to be, but it's not who I am. Who I am is the woman I am when I'm with you. In your arms. In your bed. The things you make me feel, the things you make me want. That's real. And it's amazing, because none of this is about optics, it's not about pleasing anyone, it's just about me and you. It's so wonderful. To have found this. To have found you."

"You didn't find me, honey. I found you. I came here to get revenge on your father. This isn't fate. It was calculated through and through."

"It started that way," she said. "I know it did. And I would never call it fate. Because I don't believe that it was divine design that your sister was injured the way that she was. But what I do believe is that there has to be a way to make something good out of something broken, because if there isn't, then I don't know what future you and I could possibly have."

"There are things that make sense in this world," he said. "Emotion isn't one of them. Money is. What we can do with the vineyard, that makes sense. We can build that together. We don't need any of the other stuff."

"The other stuff," she said, "is only everything. It's only love. It took me until right now to realize that. It's the missing piece. It's what I've been looking for all this time. It really is. And I... I love you. I love you down to my bones. It's real. It's not about a hashtag or a brand. It's about what I feel. And how it goes beyond rational and reasonable. How it goes beyond what should be possible. I love you. I love you and it's changed the way that I see myself."

"Are you sure you're not just looking for approval from somewhere else? You lost the relationship with your father, and now..."

"You're not my father. And I'm not confused. Don't try to tell me that I am."

"I don't do love," he said, his voice hard as stone.

"Somehow I knew you would say that. You're so desperate to make me believe that, aren't you? Mostly because I think you're so desperate to make yourself believe it. You won't even admit that you did all of this because you love your sister."

"Because you are thinking about happy families, and you're thinking about people who share their lives. That's never been what I've had with my mother and sister. I take care of them. And when I say that, I'm telling you the truth. It's not... It's not give-and-take."

"You loving them," she said, "and them being selfish with that love has nothing to do with who you are. Or what you're capable of. Why can't we have something other than that? Something other than me trying to earn approval and you trying to rescue? Can't we love each other? Give to each other? That's what I want. I think our bodies knew what was right all along. I know why you were here, and what you weren't supposed to want. And I know what I was supposed to do. But I think we were always supposed to be with each other. I do. From the deepest part of my body. I believe that."

"Bodies don't know anything," he said. "They just know they want sex. That's not love. And it's not anything worth tearing yourself apart over."

"But I… I don't have another choice. I'm torn apart by this. By us. By what we could be."

"There isn't an us. There is you and me. And we're married, and I'm willing to make that work. But you have to be realistic about what that means to a man like me."

"No," Emerson said. "I refuse to be realistic. Nothing in my life has ever been better because I was realistic. The things that have been good happened because I stepped out of my comfort zone. I don't want to be trapped in a one-sided relationship. To always be trying to earn my place. I've done that. I've lived it. I don't want to do it anymore."

"Fair enough," he said. "Then we don't have to do this."

"No," she said. "I want our marriage. I want…"

"You want me to love you, and I can't. I'm sorry. But I can't, I won't. And I…" He reached out, his callused fingertips skimming her cheek. "Honey, I appreciate you saying I'm not like your father, but it's pretty clear that I am. I'm not going to make you sign a nondisclosure agreement or anything like that. I'm going to ask one thing of you. Keep the Soraya wine going for my sister. But otherwise, my share of the winery goes to you."

"What?"

"I'm giving it back. I'm giving it to you. Because it's yours, it's not mine."

"You would rather…do all of that than try to love me?"

"I never meant to hurt you," he said. "That was never my goal, whether you believe it or not. I don't have strong enough feelings about you to want to hurt you."

And those words were like an arrow through her heart, piercing deeper than any other cruelty that could have come out of his mouth.

It would've been better, in fact, if he had said that he hated her. If he had threatened to destroy the winery again. If her ultimatum had made him fly into a rage. But it didn't. Instead, he was cold, closed off and utterly impassive. Instead, he looked like a man who truly didn't care, and she would've taken hatred over that any day, because it would have meant that at least he felt something. But she didn't get that. Instead, she got a blank wall of nothing.

She couldn't fight this. Couldn't push back against nothing. If he didn't want to fight, then there was nothing for her to do.

"So that's it," she said. "You came in here like a thunderstorm, ready to destroy everything in your path, and now you're just…letting me go?"

"Your father is handled. The control of the winery

is with you and your sisters. I don't have any reason to destroy you."

"I don't think that you're being chivalrous. I think you're being a coward."

"Cowards don't change their lives, don't make something of themselves the way I did. Cowards don't go out seeking justice for their sisters."

"Cowards *do* run when someone demands something that scares them, though. And that's what you're doing. Make no mistake. You can pretend you're a man without fear. You're hard in some ways, and I know it. But all that hardness is just to protect yourself. I wish I knew why. I wish I knew what I could do."

"It won't last," he said. "Whatever you think you want to give me, it won't last."

"Why do you think that?"

"I've never actually seen anyone want to do something that wasn't ultimately about serving themselves. Why would you be any different?"

"It's not me that's different. It's the feelings."

"But you have to be able to put your trust in feelings in order to believe in something like that, and I don't. I believe in the things you can see, in the things you can buy."

"I believe in us," she said, pressing her hand against her chest.

"You believe wrong, darlin'."

Pain welled up inside of her. "You're not the Big Bad Wolf after all," she said. "At least he had the courage to eat Red Riding Hood all up. You don't even have the courage to do that."

"You should be grateful."

"You don't get to break my heart and tell me I should

be grateful because you didn't do it a certain way. The end result is the same. And I hope that someday you realize you broke your own heart too. I hope that some-day you look back on this and realize we had love, and you were afraid to take it. And I hope you ask yourself why it was so much easier for you to cross a state be-cause of rage than it was for you to cross a room and tell someone you love them."

She started to collect her clothes, doing her very best to move with dignity, to keep her shoulders from shak-ing, to keep herself from dissolving. And she waited. As she collected her clothes. Waited for her big, gruff cowboy to sweep her up in his arms and stop her from leaving. But he didn't. He let her gather her clothes. And he let her walk out the bedroom door. Let her walk out of the house. Let her walk out of his life. And as Emer-son stood out in front of the place she had called home with a man she had come to love, she found herself yet again unsure of what her life was.

Except... Unlike when the revelations about her fa-ther had upended everything, this time she had a clear idea of who *she* was.

Holden had changed her. Had made her realize the depth of her capacity for pleasure. For desire. For love. Had given her an appreciation of depth.

An understanding of what she could feel if she dug deep, instead of clinging to the perfection of the surface.

And whatever happened, she would walk away from this experience changed. Would walk away from this wanting more, wanting better.

He wouldn't, though.

And of all the things that broke her heart in this moment, that truth was the one that cut deepest.

* * *

Emerson knew she couldn't avoid having a conversation with her mother any longer. There were several reasons for that. The first being that she'd had to move back home. The second being that she had an offer to make her father. But she needed to talk to her mom about it first.

Emerson took a deep breath, and walked into the sitting room, where she knew she would find her mother at this time of day.

She always took tea in the sitting room with a book in the afternoon.

"Hi," she said. "Can we talk?"

"Of course," her mom said, straightening and setting her book down. "I didn't expect to see you here today."

"Well. I'm kind of…back here. Because I hit a rough patch in my marriage. You know, by which I mean my husband doesn't want to be married to me anymore."

"That is a surprise."

"Is it? I married him quickly, and really not for the best reasons."

"It seemed like you cared for him quite a bit."

"I did. But the feeling wasn't mutual. So there's not much I can do about that in any case."

"We all make choices. Although, I thought you had finally found your spine with this one."

Emerson frowned. "My spine?"

"Emerson, you have to understand, the reason I've always resisted your involvement in the winery is because I didn't want your father to own you."

"What are you talking about?"

"I know you know. The way that he is. It's not a surprise to me, I've known it for years. He's never been faithful to me. But that's beside the point. The real issue is the way that he uses people."

"You've known. All along?"

"Yes. And when I had you girls the biggest issue was that if I left, he would make sure that I never saw you again. That wasn't a risk I could take. And I won't lie to you, I feared poverty more than I should have. I didn't want to go back to it. And so I made some decisions that I regret now. Especially as I watched you grow up. And I watched the way he was able to find closeness with you and with Wren. When I wasn't able to."

"I just… No matter what I did, you never seemed like you thought I did enough. Or like I had done it right."

"And I'm sorry about that. I made mistakes. In pushing you, I pushed you away, and I think I pushed you toward your father. Which I didn't mean to do. I was afraid, always, and I wanted you to be able to stand on your own feet because I had ended up hobbling myself. I was dependent on his money. I didn't know how to do anything separate from this place, separate from him that could keep me from sinking back into the poverty that I was raised in. I was trapped in many ways by my own greed. I gave up so much for this. For him." Her eyes clouded over. "That's another part of the problem. When I chose your father over… When I chose your father, it was such a deep, controversial thing, it caused so much pain, to myself included, in many ways, and I'm too stubborn and stiff-necked to take back that kind of thing."

"I don't understand."

She ran a hand over her lined brow, pushing her dark hair off her face. "I was in love with someone else. There was a misunderstanding between us, and we broke up. Then your father began to show an inter-est, because of a rivalry he had with my former beau. I figured that I would use that. And it all went too far. This is the life I made for myself. And what I really wanted, to try and atone for my sins, was to make sure you girls had it different. But then he was pushing you to marry... So when you came back from Las Vegas married to Holden, what I hoped was that you had found something more."

Emerson was silent for a long moment, trying to pro-cess all this information. And suddenly, she saw every-thing so clearly through her mother's eyes. Her fears, the reason she had pushed Emerson the way she had. The way she had disapproved of Emerson pouring ev-erything into the winery.

"I do love Holden," Emerson said. "But he...he says he doesn't love me."

"That's what happened with the man I loved. And I got angry, and I went off on my own. Then I went to someone else. I've always regretted it. Because I've never loved your father the way that I loved him. Then it was too late. I held on to pride, I didn't want to lower myself to beg him to be with me, but now I wish I had. I wish I had exhausted everything in the name of love. Rather than giving so much to stubbornness and spite. To financial security. Without love, these sorts of places just feel like a mausoleum. A crypt for dead dreams." She smiled sadly, looking around the vast, beautiful room that seemed suddenly so much darker. "I have you girls. And I've never regretted that. I have regretted our lack of closeness, Emerson, and I know that it's my fault."

"It's mine too," Emerson said. "We've never really talked before, not like this."

"There wasn't much I could tell you. Not with the way you felt about your father. And… You have to understand, while I wanted to protect you, I also didn't want to shatter your love for him. Because no matter what else he has done, he does love his daughters. He's a flawed man, make no mistake. But what he feels for you is real."

"I don't know that I'm in a place where that can matter much to me."

"No, I don't suppose you are. And I don't blame you."

"I want to buy Dad out of the winery," Emerson said. "When Holden left, he returned his stake to me. I want to buy Dad out. I want to run the winery with Wren and Cricket. And there will be a place here for you, Mom. But not for him."

"He's never going to agree to that."

"If he doesn't, I'll expose him myself. Because I won't sit by and allow the abuse of women and of his power to continue. He has two choices. He can leave of his own accord, or I'll burn this place to the ground around me, but I won't let injustice go on."

"I didn't have to worry about you after all," her mother said. "You have more of a spine than I've ever had."

"Well, now I do. For this. But when it comes to Holden…"

"Your pride won't keep you warm at night. And you can't trade one man for another, believe me, I've tried. If you don't put it all on the line, you'll regret it. You'll have to sit by while he marries someone else, has children with her. And everything will fester inside of you until it turns into something dark and ugly. Don't let that be you. Don't make the mistakes that I did."

"Mom… Who…"

"It doesn't matter now. It's been so long. He probably doesn't remember me anyway."

"I doubt that."

"All right, he remembers me," she said. "But not fondly."

"I love him," Emerson said. "I love him, and I don't know what I'm going to do without him. Which is silly, because I've lived twenty-nine years without him. You would think that I would be just fine."

"When you fall in love like that, you give away a piece of yourself," her mom said. "And that person always has it. It doesn't matter how long you had them for. When it's real, that's how it is."

"Well, I don't know what I'm supposed to do."

"Hope that he gave you a piece of him. Hope that whatever he says, he loves you just the way you love him. And then do more than hope. You're strong enough to come in here and stand up to your father. To do what's right for other people. Do what's right for you too."

Emerson nodded slowly. "Okay." She looked around, and suddenly laughter bubbled up inside of her.

"What?"

"It's just… A few weeks ago, at the launch for the select label, I was thinking how bored I was. Looking forward to my boring future. My boring marriage. I would almost pay to be bored again, because at least I wasn't heartbroken."

"Oh, trust me," her mom said. "As painful as it is, love is what gets you through the years. Even if you don't have it anymore. You once did. Your heart remembers that it exists in the world, and then suddenly the world looks a whole lot more hopeful. Because when you can believe that two people from completely different places can come together and find something that goes beyond explanation, something that goes beyond what you can see with your eyes…that's the thing that gives you hope in your darkest hour. Whatever happens with him…"

"Yeah," Emerson said softly. "I know."

She did. Because he was the reason she was standing here connecting with her mother now. He was the reason she was deciding to take this action against her father.

And she wouldn't be the reason they didn't end up together. She wouldn't give up too soon.

She didn't care how it looked. She would go down swinging.

Optics be damned.

Chapter 16

Holden wasn't a man given to questioning himself. He acted with decisiveness, and he did what had to be done. But his last conversation with Emerson kept replaying itself in his head over and over again. And worse, it echoed in his chest, made a terrible, painful tearing sensation around his heart every time he tried to breathe. It felt like... He didn't the hell know. Because he had never felt anything like it before. He felt like he had cut off an essential part of himself and left it behind and it had nothing to do with revenge.

He was at the facility where his sister lived, visiting her today, because it seemed like an important thing to do. He owed her an apology.

He walked through the manicured grounds and up to the front desk. "I'm here to see Soraya Jane."

The facility was more like high-end apartments, and

his sister had her rooms on the second floor, overlooking the ocean. When he walked in, she was sitting there on the end of the bed, her hair loose.

"Good to see you," he said.

"Holden."

She smiled, but she didn't hug him.

They weren't like that.

"I came to see you because I owe you an apology."

"An apology? That doesn't sound like you."

"I know. It doesn't."

"What happened?"

"I did some thinking and I realized that what I did might have hurt you more than it helped you. And I'm sorry."

"You've never hurt me," she said. "Everything you do is just trying to take care of me. And nobody else does that."

He looked at his sister, so brittle and raw, and he realized that her issues went back further than James Maxfield. She was wounded in a thousand ways, by a life that had been more hard knocks than not. And she was right. No one had taken care of her but him. And he had been the oldest, so no one had taken care of him at all.

And the one time that Soraya had tried to reach out, the one time she had tried to love, she had been punished for it.

No wonder it had broken her the way it had.

"I abandoned my revenge plot. Emerson and I are going to divorce."

"You don't look happy," she said.

"I'm not," he said. "I hurt someone I didn't mean to hurt."

"Are you talking about me or her?"

He was quiet for a moment. "I didn't mean to hurt either of you."

"Did you really just marry her to get back at her father?"

"No. Not only that. I mean, that's not why I married her."

"You look miserable."

"I am, but I'm not sure what that has to do with anything."

"It has to do with love. This is how love is. It's miserable. It makes you crazy. And I can say that."

"You're not crazy," he said, fiercely. "Don't say that about yourself, don't think it."

"Look where I am."

"It's not a failure. And it doesn't… Soraya, there's no shame in having a problem. There's no shame in getting help."

"Fine. Well, what's your excuse then? I got help and you ruined your life."

"I'm not in love."

"You're not? Because you have that horrible look about you. You know, like someone who just had their heart utterly ripped out of their chest."

He was quiet for a moment, and he took a breath. He listened to his heart beat steadily in his ears. "My heart is still there," he said.

"Sure. But not your *heart* heart. The one that feels things. Do you love her?"

"I don't know how to love people. How would we know what real, healthy love looks like? I believe that you loved James Maxfield, but look where it got you. Weird… We are busted up and broken from the past, how are we supposed to figure out what's real?"

"If it feels real, it is real. I don't think there's anything all that difficult to understand about love. When you feel like everything good about you lives inside another person, and they're wandering around with the best of you in their chest, you just want to be with them all the time. And you're so afraid of losing them, because if you do, you're going to lose everything interesting and bright about you too."

He thought of Emerson, of the way she looked at him. And he didn't know if what Soraya said was true. If he felt like the best of him was anywhere at all. But what he knew for sure was that Emerson made him want to be better. She made him want something other than money or success. Something deep and indefinable that he couldn't quite grasp.

"She said she loved me," he said, his voice scraped raw, the admission unexpected.

"And you left her?"

"I forced her to marry me. I couldn't…"

"She loves you. She's obviously not being forced into anything."

"I took advantage…"

"You know, if you're going to go worrying about taking advantage of women, it might be helpful if you believe them when they tell you what they want. You deciding that you know better than she does what's in her heart is not enlightened. It's just more of some man telling a woman what she ought to be. And what's acceptable for her to like and want."

"I…" He hadn't quite expected that from his sister.

"She loves you. If she loves you, why won't you be with her?"

"I…"

He thought about what Emerson had said. When she called him a coward.

"Because I'm afraid I don't know how to be in love," he said finally.

It was the one true thing he'd said on the matter. He hadn't meant to lie, he hadn't known that he had. But it was clear as day to him now.

"Look at how we were raised. I don't know a damn thing about love."

"You're the only one who ever did," Soraya said. "Look what you've done for me. Look at where I am. It's not because of me."

"No," he said. "It's because of me. I got you started on all the modeling stuff, and you went to the party where you met James…"

"That's not what I meant. I meant the reason that I'm taken care of now, the reason that I've always been taken care of, is because of you. The reason Mom has been taken care of… That's you. All those families you gave money to, houses to. And I know I've been selfish. Being here, I've had a lot of time to think. And I know that sometimes I'm not…lucid. But sometimes I am, and when I am, I think a lot about how much you gave. And no one gave it back to you. And I don't think it's that you don't know how to love, Holden. I think it's that you don't know what it's like when someone loves you back. And you don't know what to do with it."

He just sat and stared, because he had never thought of himself the way that his sister seemed to. But she made him sound…well, kind of like not a bad guy. Maybe even like someone who cared quite a bit.

"I don't blame you for protecting yourself. But this isn't protecting yourself. It's hurting yourself."

"You might be right," he said, his voice rough. "You know, you might be right."

"Do you love her?"

He thought about the way Emerson had looked in the moments before he had rejected her. Beautiful and bare. His wife in every way.

"Yes," he said, his voice rough. "I do."

"Then none of it matters. Not who her father is, not being afraid. Just that you love her."

"Look what it did to you to be in love," he said. "Don't you think I'm right to be afraid of it?"

"Oh," she said. "You're definitely right to be afraid of it. It's terrifying. And it has the power to destroy everything in its path. But the alternative is this. This kind of gray existence. The one that I'm in. The one that you're in. So maybe it won't work out. But what if it did?"

And suddenly, he was filled with a sense of determination. With a sense of absolute certainty. There was no what-if. Because he could make it turn out with his actions. He was a man who had—as Emerson had pointed out—crossed the state for revenge.

He could sure as hell do the work required to make love last. It was a risk. A damn sight bigger risk than being angry.

But he was willing to take it.

"Thank you," he said to his sister.

"Thank you too," she said. "For everything. Even the revenge."

"Emerson is making a wine label for you," he said. "It's pretty brilliant."

Soraya smiled. "She is?"

"Yes."

"Well, I can't wait until I can come and celebrate with the both of you."

"Neither can I."

And now all that was left was for him to go and make sure he had Emerson, so the two of them could be together for the launch of the wine label, and for the rest of forever.

Emerson was standing on the balcony to her bedroom, looking out over the vineyard.

It was hers now, she supposed. Hers and Wren's and Cricket's. The deal with her father had been struck, and her mother had made the decision to stay there at the winery, and let James go off into retirement. The move would cause waves; there was no avoiding it. Her parents' separation, and her father removing himself from the label.

But Emerson had been the public face of Maxfield for so long that it would be a smooth enough transition.

The moonlight was casting a glow across the great fields, and Emerson sighed, taking in the simple beauty of it.

Everything still hurt, the loss of Holden still hurt. But she could already see that her mother was right. Love was miraculous, and believing in the miraculous, having experienced it, enhanced the beauty in the world, even as it hurt.

And then, out in the rows, she was sure that she saw movement.

She held her breath, and there in the moonlight she saw the silhouette of a cowboy.

Not just a cowboy. *Her* cowboy.

For a moment, she thought about not going down.

She thought about staying up in her room. But she couldn't. She had to go to him.

Even if it was foolish.

She stole out and padded down the stairs, out the front door of the estate and straight out to the vines.

"What are you doing here?"

"I know I'm not on the guest list," he said.

"No," she said. "You're not. In fact, you were supposed to have ridden off into the sunset."

"Sorry about that. But the sun has set."

"Holden…"

"I was wondering if you needed a ranch hand."

"What?"

"The winery is yours. I want it to stay yours. Yours and your sisters'. I certainly don't deserve a piece of it. And I just thought… The one time I had it right with you was when I worked here. When it was you and me, and not all this manipulation. So I thought maybe I would just offer me."

"Just you?"

"Yeah," he said. "Just me."

"I mean, you still have your property development money, I assume."

"Yeah," he said. "But… I also love you. And I was sort of hoping that you still love me."

She blinked hard, her heart about to race out of her chest. "Yes," she said. "I love you still. I do. And all I need is you. Not anything else."

"I feel the same way," he said. "You. Just the way you are. It quit being about revenge, and when it quit being about revenge, I didn't have an excuse to stay anymore, and it scared the hell out of me. Because I never thought that I would be the kind of man that wanted forever. And wanting it scared me. And I don't like being scared."

"None of us do. But I'm so glad that you came here, though," she said. "Because if you hadn't… I thought as long as everything looked good, then it was close enough to being good. I had no idea that it could be like this."

"And if I had never met you, then I would never have had anything but money and anger. And believe me, compared to this, compared to you, that's nothing."

"You showed me my heart," she said. "You showed me what I really wanted."

"And you showed me mine. I was wrong," he said. "When I said things couldn't be fixed. They can be. When I told my sister that I came here to get revenge, she wasn't happy. It's not what she needed from me. She needed love. Support. Revenge just destroys, love is what builds. I want to love you and build a life with you. Forever."

"So do I." She threw herself into his arms, wrapped her own around his neck and kissed him. "So do I."

Emerson Maxfield knew without a shadow of a doubt, as her strong, handsome husband held her in his arms, that she was never going to be bored with her life again.

Because she knew now that it wasn't a party, a launch, a successful campaign that was going to bring happiness or decide who she was.

No, that came from inside of her.

And it was enough.

Who she was loved Holden McCall. And whatever came their way, it didn't scare her. Because they would face it together.

She remembered that feeling she'd had, adrift, like she had nowhere to go, like her whole life had been untethered.

But she had found who she was, she had found her heart, in him.

And she knew that she would never have to question where she belonged again. Because it was wherever he was.

Forever.

* * * * *